From The Personal Library
Of
David Teruel

Kantovan Vault
The Spiral Wars, Book 3

Joel Shepherd

Copyright © 2017 Joel Shepherd

All rights reserved.

ISBN: 1548361933
ISBN-13: 978-1548361938

The Spiral Wars:

Renegade

Drysine Legacy

Kantovan Vault

Defiance
(October 2017)

CHAPTER 1

Captain Erik Debogande strained his neck against the thundering pressure of reentry, and blinked upon the tactical icon within his field of vision. It showed his ship, the combat shuttle PH-1, accompanied by its sister ship PH-4 and two tavalai shuttles, spread in wide entry formation through Stoya III's stratosphere. In his ear he could hear the terse chatter between pilots, expressing displeasure with something else following their reentry track.

"Yeah I see it." That was Lieutenant Hausler, pilot of PH-1 and senior pilot of the *UFS Phoenix* contingent. *"That's too damn close, keep an eye on them."*

"Tav'rai stupid?" complained an alien growl from the second *Phoenix* shuttle.

"No Tif," said Hausler. *"Tavalai not stupid, tavalai just damn pain in the ass."*

"Lieutenant Hausler, this is the Captain," said Erik as the Gs began to ease, and PH-1 settled into a shuddering, rocking descent. "Is there a problem?"

"Sir," said Hausler, *"those two shuttles off Tokigala just paralleled us through reentry at about half the standard safe range. It's reckless and if I had any idea who to send it to, I'd file a complaint."*

"How about a missile lock?" Hausler's co-pilot Ensign Yun suggested from the front seat.

Tokigala was a tavalai foreign affairs and diplomacy vessel from one of the largest tavalai government departments. Humans called it the 'State Department', because that harked back to lost things from human history, and the actual tavalai name required an acronym too long for humans to bother with. The State Department was an ancient beast of tavalai bureaucracy, formed directly after the fall of the Chah'nas Empire nearly eight thousand years ago. It ran all tavalai external affairs, and was held partly responsible by most humans for the belligerence that led to the Triumvirate War, and all its hundreds of millions of casualties.

Phoenix had entered tavalai space nearly a month ago, though only two weeks had passed on *Phoenix*'s clocks, thanks to time-dilation through multiple hyperspace jumps.   If not for the protection of *Makimakala*, *Phoenix* would have been attacked and destroyed immediately.   But the Dobruta vessel had its own reasons for granting *Phoenix* safe passage through tavalai space, and once granted, not even the State Department could countermand it.

The Dobruta couldn't make them like it, however, and the State Department vessels had shadowed both *Phoenix* and *Makimakala* from Alidance System, five jumps ago.   Upon arrival here at Stoya System, they had been greeted by another two State Department vessels and five tavalai main fleet warships.   The State Department ships had challenged *Makimakala*, in conversations *Phoenix* had been unable to overhear, while the fleet warships had looked on.   *Makimakala* had ignored them, and the State Department ships had had no choice but to allow Dobruta and humans to progress to the surface of Stoya III, as the fleet ships appeared to have no interest in stopping them.   State Department vessels, Erik had been pleased to have confirmed, were always unarmed.   They had plenty of shuttles, however, and these two were making a nuisance of themselves.

"*Signal from the surface,*" came Ensign Yun.   "*Doma Strana base gives us an approach trajectory, all looks good.   Kulid-One, do you copy?*"

"*Kulid-One copies,*" came the translator-metallic reply of *Makimakala*'s lead shuttle.   "*Good signal, we land.*"

Without thrust, PH-1 was nearly weightless as she fell rocking through the atmosphere.   A spacer long accustomed to weightlessness, Erik was not at all certain he liked this kind.   This was the first gravity-well he'd entered since Homeworld, and the death of Captain Pantillo.   He remembered that last descent, exhausted from preparations for the great parade and sleeping through much of reentry.   Back then, he'd thought he only had to worry about the marching, and the family reunion to follow.   He could not escape the feeling that now, like then, he was falling into a trap… only this time, he went knowingly.

His link to external visual showed the surface hidden beneath an expanse of white cloud. PH-1 and escort plunged into it, and all vision blanked, then came abruptly clear on a stunning view of mountains. Altitude was perhaps fifteen thousand metres, yet already Hausler was engaging thrust to pull them from the dive as the tallest peaks came up just below. Huge valleys plummeted into ice-cold rivers, water gleaming silver beneath the white overcast. High forests made patches of green on the lower slopes amongst black rock and white snow. And here ahead, Nav was fixing on the end-point of their inbound course.

"Wow," said Hausler, as the camera got a close-up for the first time. *"Would you look at this thing."*

Their destination was a mountain, at least eight thousand metres high. One entire section of west-facing slope had been cut away, to make an enormous, artificial feature. The feature crawled up the mountainside in several parts, some vertical, others angled, and from the machine-smoothed stone emerged the carved facades of imitation building-fronts. Like the facades of city buildings, straight lines amidst the rugged peaks.

"Nav says the feature is a touch over three kilometres high," said Ensign Lee from PH-4. *"It just climbs all the way up. Tunnels everywhere inside."*

Erik switched to full-screen view on his glasses — unnecessary, but he was further from human space than most serving Fleet officers ever got to travel. If he was going to come all this way, he might as well enjoy the view. Hausler swung past one looming mountain, the shuttle bumping through windshear and slowing as the unnatural cliff face approached. It faced a smaller, lower mountain, and as PH-1 curled around on the side-angle, the huge, deep cleft between the two vertical surfaces became visible for the first time. Down at the base of the cleft were unnatural caverns and surface vehicles, small dots far below. The main temple cliff had many levels, with landing platforms and open walkways protruding from its surface. Great pillars seemed to thrust from the rock, a carved facade in the old style of parren temple. An entire mountain, dedicated to worship, nearly twenty thousand years old.

PH-1 approached a mid-level platform, itself nearly two kilometres above the ground. Only as they approached, thrusters roaring, did Erik get a true sense of the scale, as all four shuttles lined up for landing upon the same platform with much room to spare. A touch, and they were down, and the roaring vibration stopped. Down the back, Lieutenant Zhi shouted for Echo Platoon to dismount, and Erik remained at the front command post until they were done.

"Captain, platform is secure," came Major Thakur's voice on coms. *"You are free to dismount."*

Erik unharnessed, performed a final check of his light armour, sidearm and com gear, then edged between rows of vacated armour racks and harnesses to the open rear ramp. Chill air stung his face and he resisted the urge to grab a hydraulic arm for balance as the mountain vista opened up before him. PH-1 was parked literally upon the brink of a precipice, plunging two thousand metres straight down. From this angle he could see the face of the opposing, smaller cliff for the first time. The carvings made the shape of a face — heavy-browed and alien, hewn into rock and at least two hundred metres tall. The weathered features looked as old and solemn as the mountain, with wide, staring eyes. Snowflakes blew on a flurry of wind across its dark, impassive stare.

An earsplitting roar made Erik look up. Two tavalai shuttles were passing overhead — too low to be accidental. They flew on, headed for an adjacent and slightly higher platform up the cliff face.

Erik walked past Echo Platoon marines in defensive position, beneath the shuttle's starboard weapons pod as the huge ceramic-plated beast pinged and cooled, radiating heat like an iron just removed from the fire. Ahead he saw Trace and Command Squad, waiting before PH-4, and walked to her. Beyond her was a cavernous chamber, sheltered behind floor-to-ceiling glass, behind which various alien figures milled.

"Stupid bastards from the State Department," Trace said conversationally as he arrived. "That flyby was intentional."

"It's almost as though they don't want us here," said Erik, staring upward. The sky above the cliff was cold and grey. "Fancy that."

He glanced left as footsteps approached. It was Commander Nalben off *Makimakala*, lightly armoured as was Erik, and likewise accompanied by lumbering armoured karasai — tavalai marines. Expressions were difficult for humans to read on wide, amphibious tavalai faces, but Erik got the distinct impression that Nalben was cold, and unhappy about it.

"Captain," said Nalben in his perfect English, as his karasai stopped in guard formation behind. "Are you pleased to be back on a planet after so long?"

"More pleased than you, I think," Erik replied.   "This is a little cold for tavalai, yes?"

"Human understatement," said Nalben, shoulders hunched, repressing a shiver. He looked longingly toward the enclosed glass, and warmth.   "They will be out soon.   They are arranging protocols."

He was connected to the temple occupants through coms, Erik knew. This whole complex, this whole world and solar system, were tavalai.   But the temple itself was parren, built in the latter half of the Parren Empire that followed the fall of the machines. Tavalai being tavalai, they called it still by its original parren name — Doma Strana, 'strana' meaning 'temple' in the relevant, old parren tongue.

Stoya III was a large world and had many cities in more temperate zones than this.   But the tavalai love of ancient things had compelled them to settle and occupy this old temple, and make modern use of it.   Now it was occupied by the Pelligavani — a financial department, of all things.   Erik thought it the oddest and most extravagant use of public space by a bunch of accountants. But it was so typically tavalai, to fill every last outpost with bureaucracy.

"You're sure he's here?" Erik asked Commander Nalben, eyeing the odd civilian costumes behind the glass.   Mostly tavalai, he thought, in those loose-fitting, baggy garments that passed for middle-ranking formality.

"Quite sure," said Nalben, with a trace of irritation. Tavalai could usually be relied upon to keep their promises. Human doubts were impolite. "We do not go to this much trouble for everyone. This is a most controversial figure."

"So I hear," Erik replied, with a glance up at the higher platform where the two State Department shuttles had landed. "But it wouldn't be a *Phoenix* mission if we weren't upsetting everyone."

"No," Nalben agreed. "A *Makimakala* mission neither."

Tavalai civilians emerged from sliding glass doors, and walked to the waiting crews with that familiar rolling gait. They were bundled against the cold, and carried various ribbons and flowers. Lilies, Erik identified. Tavalai preferred life in temperate places where water met the land, and had a special love for the plants and flowers that flourished on both as tavalai did.

These tavalai introduced themselves to Commander Nalben, who introduced them in turn to Erik. They were the Pelligavani, he said, and Doma Strana was their facility. That meant formalities. Erik nodded, unsurprised. One did not venture into tavalai space without expecting formalities.

It was actually kind of interesting, he thought. The tavalai bureaucrats seemed pleased to meet them, which was surprising, given the recent hundred and sixty one years of war, and so many millions dead. Perhaps it was that they knew of *Phoenix*'s split with human Fleet Command, or perhaps it was the simple prestige of a visit from such a famous name... but either way, there were smiles and bows, and the granting of ribbons and flowers. There were stamps too, of the ink variety, to be pressed into old leather-bound books on the appropriate pages. The books were astonishing. They looked many centuries old, worn to the point of falling apart, the pages smothered with older, overlapping stamps to which Erik contributed new ones.

Tavalai society was not primarily divided by race, class, caste or religion, but by institution. Tavalai accumulated institutions as some birds collected shiny objects. Erik gathered from translated conversation with Nalben that the Pelligavani had roots going back to the Parren Empire, twenty thousand years ago. Perhaps *that* was why they liked to occupy this old temple, Erik thought — both it and the Pelligavani were about the same age. The Pelligavani had produced competent economic and government administrators for various empires across the millennia, and these tavalai were as proud of their grand institution as any Fleet officer was of his own.

Most of what the tavalai called 'government' sprang from the contest of such institutions, large and small, scattered across tavalai space. Humans elected individuals to represent regions. Tavalai voted only within their institutions, and let those institutions battle it out at the higher levels to determine tavalai government policy. The Pelligavani, Erik was sure, would have internal elections in which all members voted. Humans thought tavalai undemocratic because individual tavalai had no say in who ran the entire race. Tavalai thought humans undemocratic because most humans worked in institutions without any say in who ran them. Given how most humans spent their days working under bosses they could not replace, while human government remained so distant from most daily lives, Erik thought the tavalai might have a point.

When the last formalities were observed, and the heavily armed Command Squad had been reduced to carrying lilies and wearing ribbons, all were invited inside. Trace signalled back to PH-4, and from the rear of the shuttle Lisbeth came running, with little Skah's hand grasped firmly in hers. That brought new fascination from the tavalai, at Skah in particular. Several got down on one knee to speak to the little boy at eye-level, and pat his shoulder. In his heavy parka and hood, Skah could barely be identified as kuhsi, but that tawny-furred face, big gold eyes and sharp teeth were clearly not human. Kuhsi were a species unfamiliar to tavalai, and these tavalai seemed to think meeting one was an event.

"Herro," Skah said politely, more interested in staring around at the huge cliff on which they were perched. Tavalai, he'd seen before. And said to Lisbeth, as they were finally walking inside, "Nahny cun too?"

"Skah, your Mummy has to wait with the shuttle for now," Lisbeth said patiently, also staring around at the cliffs. "Pilots have to keep the shuttle ready in case we have to leave quickly. Here, wave to your Mummy, she can see you."

She pointed back to the narrow, front-and-back seating of PH-4's business end, above the massive lower-side cannon mount and surrounded by atmospheric intakes and loaded missile pods. Behind the heavily armoured glass in the rear seat, Tif could be seen faintly, waving. Skah waved back enthusiastically. Lisbeth's eyes strayed to the looming alien face on the cliff behind. "Wow," she breathed, then turned to follow her brother, Commander Nalben and Command Squad inside.

"You brought your sister," Nalben said to Erik with bemusement. They passed through the big glass doors, and the warmth enfolded them.

"She's been off-world for four months," Erik explained. "Skah too, they were desperate to see a planet again. This one looks safe enough." He'd slowly come to accept that his options in protecting Lisbeth from danger were limited. Being on *Phoenix* was dangerous, for everyone. Excluding her from away-teams could just make her sullen and resentful, and all spacers knew that poor morale only made dangers worse.

"The little boy's mother trusts you enormously," Nalben observed.

"Kuhsi operate in clans," Erik explained. "*Phoenix* is Tif's clan now, like family. Raising the children is a clan responsibility, she knows we'll protect Skah like he's our own."

This part of the temple was all new and modern, with loading vehicles and wide branching corridors — a docking port for cargo. The modernity only lasted until the next corridor, where the modern wall fittings were replaced with luminescent cables. Yet the exposed stone walls and floors were not rough from some pre-technology era. The Doma Strana had been constructed during the height of the Parren Empire, when the parren had replaced the hacksaws as dominant species in the Spiral. The floors here were so smooth that if properly polished, Erik was sure they'd be slippery.

The elevator at the hallway's end was similarly new, and large enough to fit twenty with ease. It took them up, while holographic walls gave them a view of the mountains outside, as though millions of tonnes of rock became abruptly transparent. After a long climb, gravity eased, then restored as the car arrived. One of the Pelligavani guides spoke to Nalben in rapid Togiri, who replied in kind.

"He is here," Nalben translated to Erik. And paused to talk to the Pelligavani again, displeased by what he heard. "Apparently he will see only *Phoenix* commanders, you and Major Thakur."

Erik could sympathise with Nalben's displeasure — if it weren't for *Makimakala* and the Dobruta, this meeting would never have happened. "Don't worry Commander," he said, "if he won't allow open coms, we'll record the whole conversation whether he wants it or not. You'll get your copy."

"Thank you," said Nalben, somewhat mollified. They walked the smooth, gleaming corridor, Command Squad's armour echoing loudly between walls. "Parren leaders can be difficult. This one has that reputation."

At a new, narrower corridor, the guides stopped. Trace deactivated her armour, knelt, then cracked the upper torso and wriggled out with practised speed. She wore standard marine fatigues beneath — black pants and jacket — and grabbed a sidearm from suit storage before following, tugging a cap over her brow.

"You," she said, pointing at Lisbeth. "Furball supervision duty."

"I know!" said Lisbeth, with mock indignation.

"Furbaw!" Skah said with loud delight.

"You lot," Trace added, pointing at the rest of Command Squad, "Lisbeth supervision duty." Lisbeth gaped at her as the marines grinned. Trace winked, and nodded thanks to the Pelligavani guide before advancing into the corridor, with Erik behind.

The corridor lights made a dim luminescence on dark stone. A short flight of stairs took them down, then out to a wide room. Erik and Trace gazed about. The room was black obsidian or marble, lit by a wide rectangle of window that overlooked the mountains outside. The white overcast made sharp contrast with polished black stone, ridged mountain rock and snow against minimalist perfection. There were shapes and lines in the floor and walls, all straight, no curves. In a central, irregular rectangle in the floor, a reflecting pool, its surface as still as the surrounding stone.

At first, Erik could not see the alien they'd come all this way to meet. He looked at Trace in puzzlement, and saw her gazing dead level at one end of the reflecting pool. A closer look revealed a black cloaked figure, nearly invisible in its camouflage. The figure sat cross-legged by the pool, hood drawn up, a long pole of some kind laid upon the floor by his feet. Unmoving like the stone, and the water.

Erik heard, or rather felt, Trace take a long, slow breath. So still was this place, he could hear the air passing her lips. This was a place of meditation and calm. As Kulina, and one who waged her own life-long battle to attain inner peace, Trace would feel the resonance of a place like this in her soul.

She gestured to Erik, and walked silently across the polished floor. Erik followed, trying to make as little sound as possible. Every squeak of his shoes echoed like a sacrilege, and disturbed the tranquility.

Trace walked to the edge of the reflecting pool, a quarter-circumference around from the cloaked figure, and sat cross-legged. Erik joined her, tugging his knees into place and wishing he had her grace in that position. For a long moment, no one spoke. Light snow fell past the window, its glass perfectly clear and thick, admitting neither noise nor cold. The mountains were harshly beautiful. Erik wanted to ask Trace if they reminded her of her native Sugauli, but did not wish to spoil the silence.

Finally the figure spoke, and his words were soft, alien and unfamiliar. From somewhere within his robes, a translator voice projected louder English. *"There is a prophecy among my people,"* it said. *"One day the parren race shall be destroyed, by a great and terrible power from the edge of the galaxy. Some have thought this species is yet to be discovered. Some say it shall be the great machines, returned from the dead to wreak their vengeance. I have always thought it more likely to be the humans. And now, you have come to me."*

He pulled back his hood so that the rim sat upon his brow, showing a little of his face without removing the hood completely. Wide indigo eyes, flared cheekbones and slitted nostrils. The mouth and jaw remained hidden behind black fabric, covering the lower face. The indigo eyes remained fixed on the water.

"We come to seek knowledge of Drakhil," said Erik. "We are told that of all the parren experts on Drakhil, your knowledge is greatest."

The parren remained still. *"Why do you seek knowledge of Drakhil?"*

Erik glanced at Trace. Trace glanced back, reluctantly. And nodded. "Because we seek something very old," said Erik. "Something that Drakhil may have left behind, hidden, for twenty five thousand years. We seek it for its importance to the galaxy. And we will share it, with those who claim the heritage of Drakhil."

Still the parren did not move. But somehow, in that silence, Erik was sure they had him.

The parren might have smiled, invisible behind the veil. *"Phoenix. The galaxy has heard of you. You seek and you find, and you make trouble and enemies in all your seeking and finding. Why should I help you seek this thing?"*

"Because I heard that you are the heir to Drakhil's legacy. Perhaps I heard wrong."

The eyes narrowed. Definitely a smile. *"I am of House Harmony. I claim the leadership, though most of that House dispute it. They say that I represent an old and evil time in parren history. I say that it is our truest nature, that we have only forgotten, or chosen to forget."* His eyes flicked up, and met Erik's. An indigo stare, of depth and power. *"Drakhil is a man hated and feared by parren today. I say he was the greatest man, and so they hate me as well. To recover a great artefact of Drakhil, from the end of the Age of Machines, will invite the wrath of all my people. Are you, Phoenix, prepared to face all that will follow as a consequence?"*

"If we were not," Erik said evenly, "we would not have come to you."

CHAPTER 2

Ensign Jokono stood by a wall in Engineering Bay 17C, and tried not to get in the way. The bay was too hot even for *Phoenix*'s ventilation, suction whistling a breeze from the ceiling to pull out the heat as bulky replicators whirred and throbbed, melting steel into alloys, then shaping it within pressurised containment shells. Some further units generated raw materials for new-gen electronics, little more than containment cores bolted into the bay walls. Within them were processes far too advanced for even most *Phoenix* senior techs to understand. Engineering first-shift crew monitored the machines, and had loud conversations, and sweated.

"And why do you think Aristan is lying?" Jokono pressed the cause of all this commotion.

"Elevated vocal stress," said Styx, on uplink audio in Jokono's ear to be sure she was heard above the noise. *"I am familiar with parren vocal patterns."*

Styx's nano-tank now resided here in Bay 17C, the big hacksaw queen's head firmly secured in a liquid swarming with microscopic machines. That liquid was quarantined, for fear its contents could get out, and spread. Styx had begun reprogramming human nanos from the first moment she'd achieved consciousness over a month ago. Those nanos had built new nanos, which had built new nanos, a rapidly evolving family of micro-machines, like ten million years of organic evolution copied, synthesised, and compressed into days.

What was going on in that tank now, god only knew. Lieutenant Rooke tried to monitor it, but couldn't trust anything the tank monitors told him, so adept was Styx at controlling any system in her proximity, and edgy about her privacy. What they *did* know was that the hole Major Thakur had blasted through Styx's head four months ago was now nearly gone, just a small opening left in Styx's big, single eye for nano ingress and egress. Within that alloy head, Styx's brain was almost entirely repaired. What exactly that meant, for her and for *Phoenix*, was a matter of constant debate amongst all *Phoenix* crew, from the highest ranked to the lowest.

Some of the ship's best computer techs had run numbers based upon the observed speed with which Styx performed certain finite, predictable functions. They'd concluded that Styx's processing power was several thousand times beyond what the most advanced human simulations predicted was possible within a space the size of Styx's skull. They argued over those numbers now, in language anyone without multiple doctorates in advanced mathematics could not possibly comprehend. Jokono simply stuck to one of his prime commandments when dealing with difficult interview subjects — be wary of what you do not know. With Styx, that was nearly everything.

"What do you suspect he's lying about?" Jokono pressed.

"Organic motivations are not my speciality. We must combine analytical strengths. I will inform you when I detect an anomaly, you will calculate the related implications. For that purpose, humans possess organic hardware that I lack."

Stanislav Romki entered, looking harried and busy, as usual. "Oh, hello Jokono," he said. "Discussing Mr Aristan, are we?"

Jokono nodded. "You listened to the interview?" Rumour was, the Captain and the Major had made the copy primarily for *Makimakala*, who were pissed at not being invited to the meeting. But they had plenty of smart folk on *Phoenix* who'd wanted to hear it too.

"Yes," said Romki, "and I maintain my position that that man is trouble. He's a narcissistic demagogue who claims authority over all House Harmony, and most of his own house-aligned resent it. To say nothing of the House of Houses — the central parren leadership, who'd all like to see him killed."

"I would appreciate further analysis," said Styx. *"From the human perspective. Yours, Professor Romki."*

Romki blinked, clearly pleased. "Well... I'll consult my databases. But I reiterate — the psychological differences between human and parren are vast. Parren can change psychologies entirely, by choice, by phase of life, or by long established practice in one of their great Houses.   The Houses are the most prominent institution in parren society because they dictate the very psychology of all its members, right down to the bio-chemical level.   Humans possess nothing like this psychological variability, and certainly not the means to control it en masse, so my analysis will be lacking that insight."

"Human religion does not qualify as mass thought-control?" Styx wondered.

Romki smiled, standing aside for some techs while grasping a support by the door.   "Perhaps, but human religion has rarely specified mood.   As an irreligious man, I would argue that all human religious fanatics are suffering approximately similar psychosis. The great parren Houses dictate a multiplicity of psychoses, one for each."

"Interesting," said Styx.

Jokono wondered if Romki truly understood how obviously Styx played to his ego.   For all her claims not to understand organic minds, she was a master manipulator of some, at least.   So far she hadn't tried it with *him*, however.   Perhaps she knew he was onto her.

"Listening to the interview," said Jokono, "I'm becoming concerned that Aristan might guess at Styx's existence simply by our commanders' questions.   They are skilled, but they are not trained interviewers."

"I'd think we might be more worried that the State Department would talk to someone on *Makimakala* for that," said Romki.   "Dobruta crew are loyal, but tavalai are argumentative."

"Disruptive," said Styx, distastefully.   *"Uncoordinated. Troublesome."*   She'd made clear her dislike for the tavalai on numerous occasions.   It clearly displeased her to be travelling through their space, relying on the secrecy of Dobruta to stay hidden. *"Trusting any tavalai is unwise."*

"Well we won't get access to tavalai space without Dobruta protection," Jokono reminded her.   Doubtless she already knew that. Sometimes, Jokono thought, she pushed an idea just to see the human reaction, and learn from it.   There was no off-button on the genius of a hacksaw queen.   Everything was calculation.   "This Aristan has devoted his life to House Harmony's greatest historical figure, Drakhil.   He thinks Drakhil is a great hero of parren history, however he is reviled by most parren today.   Styx, do you think that Aristan's idea of Drakhil has any relation to the actual man?"

"Organic history is an unsettled mix of narrative mythology and invention," said Styx.   *"Aristan knows nothing of Drakhil, he merely wishes to use the idea of Drakhil to manipulate the minds of his followers."*

"Yes, exactly!" said Romki, nodding like a teacher pleased with a very bright student.   "Exactly right."   Jokono nearly smiled.

"Drakhil was the leader of House Harmony in the last great wars of the Machine Age.   He sided his faction, the Tahrae, with the drysines against the deepynines, and fought against his own people and all other organics for the continued supremacy of the machines. For this, parren history has never forgiven him, nor his House.   He is the ultimate traitor to the opposing parren Houses and denominations.   And Aristan is the ultimate traitor today, for lauding such a man.   Professor Romki, do you agree?"

"Yes, absolutely," said Romki.   "What they all forget is that the parren were a largely insignificant species before the alliance with the drysines at their height in the Machine Age.   Drysines made the parren strong, and if not for the Drysine Empire, the Parren Age could never have ruled the Spiral for eight thousand years to follow." And he laughed.   "But listen to me.   Lecturing one who was actually *there*."

"Perhaps," said Styx.   *"But I was young then, in Drakhil's time.   Constructed specifically to command in the last phases of the great war, I saw little enough action."*

Insane to contemplate it.   Styx had given up insisting that the entity currently known as Styx had *not* actually been around at the time.   It was her usual shtick about how synthetic identity shifted across the centuries, and how experiences from other entities, recorded digitally, could be experienced by herself as intensely as though she'd been there herself.

Humans didn't want to hear it. Humans just wanted to know that the sentience they were speaking to had actually *been* there, twenty five thousand years ago. Had fought in those ancient wars, and known those ancient people. To Aristan and the parren, the great and terrible Drakhil was just a legend, an ancient myth from the far distant past. To Styx, he'd been a man.

"Ensign Jokono," said Styx. *"You asked if Aristan's notion of Drakhil had any basis in truth. Aristan believes that Drakhil was a great warrior. A man who believed in true strength, and the advancement of the parren race through alliance with the strong.*

"The Drakhil I knew was a scholarly man, not unlike our Professor Romki here." Romki beamed. *"He was a most reluctant warrior who saw two paths before his people, and liked neither. Drakhil believed that his people owed the drysines a debt, and he disliked and distrusted aliens more than he disliked the drysines. We know that Drakhil was granted the drysine data-core that we seek by the last drysine command, twenty five thousand years ago, before the last fall of the Drysine Empire. The last command believed he could hide it well. We know that he put it somewhere. Drakhil was an intensely clever man, with a long-view of time and history rare among organics. I dislike that we must use this Aristan's knowledge of his House's history to find it once more. But for a prize of this value, we must risk everything to gain all."*

"Ensign Jokono," came Coms Officer Shilu's voice in Jokono's ear as he departed Engineering Bay 17C.

"Go ahead Lieutenant Shilu."

"I thought you might like to know," said Shilu. *"But while you were having your little conversation with Styx there? She was having another two conversations elsewhere on the ship, of equal complexity and sentiment to that one. One of those conversations was with me, so I can vouch for that personally."*

"Yes I know," Jokono said grimly, dodging traffic in the corridor and squeezing onto a ladder to main level. "She's become a wonderful conversationalist, but the tavalai said it best.   Bird whistles."

Like an ornithologist in a forest, Captain Pram of *Makimakala* had said.   Imitating the calls of birds to bring them near enough to study.   Or perhaps, if one had other intentions, to catch and eat.   The bird thought it heard another bird, and came rushing to mate, or defend its territory.   Like the bird, the human mind insisted on perceiving accurate communication as proof of similarity.   Like the bird, it struggled to conceive that the one making all of those convincing sounds truly understood and empathised with none of it, and was only making calculated noises for tactical effect.

"She's sure got Romki sucked in, doesn't she?" said Shilu.

"Yes she does," said Jokono, sliding down a ladder as spacers did — a recently acquired skill.   "Lieutenant Rooke too.   Don't worry, I've got an eye on it."

"We've got a mass-murdering synthetic super-intelligence aboard, and it's using us to find its personal long-lost treasure while Rooke's commandeered an engineering bay to help build it a new body.   Why should I worry?"

The cave was vast.   Water ran through it, gathered in pools, and one large lake.   Smooth stone made islands amid surrounding forests of crystal.   The crystals were white fading to pink, and brilliant in the dim light.   They grew at perfect angles, crossing like swords, ninety degrees every time.   Trace wondered why.

She should really have come down here armoured, but the Pelligavani insisted that there was only one way in, and that was from the quarters currently occupied by *Phoenix* marines.   It was a meditation chamber, the bureaucrats said.   A natural feature in the mountain, left mostly untouched, treasured by the parren who'd built the temple, and the tavalai who'd come later.   Trace could see why. Light spilled from somewhere distant, conducting optics feeding the cold sunlight from outside.   It made patterns as it washed across the fields of crystals, around bends and up slopes of undulating stone.

Pink and white sparkled up the walls, and reflected in the still waters. Distantly, water dripped. Aristan's meditating chamber had been a beautiful construction, but this was natural, and wondrous. Trace would not spoil this place with heavy armoured footsteps.

A shadow moved across the crystal fields, approaching from the single entrance. Tavalai, Trace thought, in formal robes. The rolling gait of its walk was less pronounced than she was accustomed to. Most of the tavalai Trace had seen were warriors, physically augmented and heavily muscled. This one's tread was light. A civilian, then. Like the Pelligavani, but the robes were different. Heavier, multi-layered with a big collar, suggesting a greater importance.

"Major Thakur," called the tavalai, and Trace repressed a twinge of irritation. Loud speech, in this world of calm. The echoes were tactless, like garbage thrown on the pristine stone floor. "I was told that I would find you here. A place of wonder, is it not?"

Perfect English, Trace noted. None of the Pelligavani spoke English. Tavalai were famously multi-lingual, but mostly with their own tongues. The only tavalai who stooped to learning the barbarian human tongue were those whose work specifically involved aliens. That meant tavalai Fleet, or bureaucrats concerned with alien affairs. Like the State Department.

"It is a place of wonder," Trace agreed as the tavalai came closer, rounding a still pool of water. "There are many caves on my native homeworld, but none like this."

"Sugauli," said the tavalai, stopping before her. This one had a lighter pattern to the mottled skin, and was small in stature. That, plus the smoother voice, suggested a female. The big, triple-lidded eyes swivelled inward, a wide binocular vision. "You Kulina know mountains, and mining. These tunnels must seem almost familiar to you."

Trace could not disagree. Were she not on duty, she'd have loved to sit here for a few hours in the peace, and meditate. Tranquility, so rare in her life, was a precious thing to waste.

"You are Tropagali Andarachi Mandarinava?" she asked.

The tavalai's lips pressed thin — a tavalai smile. "You may call it the State Department. I know that Togiri names are difficult for humans."

"Not difficult," said Trace. "Just boring."

The tavalai's smile hardened, but did not fade. "Please," she said, gesturing with a hand to the smooth rock about them. "We should sit. In the parren custom, in a place of worship."

"It's my custom too," said Trace, and gave an easy wave to Staff Sergeant Kono, trailing the tavalai bureaucrat to see everything was well. He'd searched her, of course, and knew that his Major had little to fear from a tavalai bureaucrat anyhow. They sat, cross-legged on the rock, and Trace found the posture more simple than the tavalai. "Were those your shuttles following us through de-orbit?"

"Yes," said the tavalai. She was calm, conversational and unworried. Intensely certain of herself, in the way of high-ranking tavalai. That she was prepared to come in here alone, with no protection, to talk to one of human Fleet's most notorious warriors from the Triumvirate War, suggested that she had a point to prove. "My name is Jelidanatagani. I am from the Department of Administrative Affairs of the State Department, as you call it. Human Wing."

"Pleased to meet you Jeli," said Trace. Jeli did not protest the abbreviation. "Please observe safety protocols around *Phoenix* vessels in future. I would hate to see a miscommunication."

"You are in tavalai space," said Jeli with confidence. "If there are miscommunications, the penalty shall be yours."

Trace considered her for a moment. 'Never play chicken with tavalai,' Captain Pantillo used to say. 'They'll die before they flinch.' The State Department had made it plain they did not want *Phoenix* here. Until now they'd been making that displeasure known mostly to *Makimakala*, their Dobruta host. Now they came to Trace directly. Trace wondered why her, and not Erik.

"You meet with the one called Aristan," said Jeli. "This is most unwise."

"I was not aware that the State Department speak for the parren," Trace said calmly. "Parren are an independent species, and can speak for themselves."

Jeli's eyes swivelled further inward, a tavalai frown. "Major. Humans have no direct experience of parren. Tavalai have known the parren since before the end of the Machine Age. We have thousands of years of established relations and diplomatic practice. We speak each other's tongues, we know each other's minds."

"You've fought wars against each other," Trace interrupted. "You've killed each other by the million. Yet you make it sound so wonderful."

Jeli's frown deepened. She gestured with one lightly webbed hand at the fields of crystals. "Do you know *why* the parren preserve these beautiful spaces? Why they value the calm and quiet? Why they spent such enormous sums on a great temple complex such as the Doma Strana in the first place?

"The parren are ruled by Houses. Each House rules a particular parren psychology. Parren psychologies *change*, Major. Some change voluntarily, others by exposure to trauma or to major life events, others with age or phase of life. But parren can almost change entire personalities, apparently at random. This biological oddity has dominated their politics, and created an obsession amongst the parren with the question of 'how to live'. For humans or tavalai, the question is philosophical. For parren, it is... how do you say? Bread and butter? It is fundamental to their daily lives, and they've fought wars over states-of-mind as humans have fought wars over political ideology.

"Today the dominant House is House Fortitude. House Enquiry rules second, then House Harmony. In the Age of the Machines, House Harmony was dominant. It was the philosophy of harmony that led the great Harmony leaders of the day to seek harmonious relations with the dominant AI-factions. The machines were not always interested, but the drysine faction was. They created the drysine-parren alliance, and drysine and parren fought side by side in the Great Machine War against the deepynines.

"When the final victory came, a parren named Drakhil was the leader of House Harmony. The other parren houses were persuaded by other species, particularly the chah'nas and the tavalai, to turn on their drysine masters following their terrible casualties against the deepynines. All turned, save for one faction of House Harmony — that faction led by Drakhil. The Tahrae, they were called — the 'chosen people'. Drakhil fought with the drysines against all the other parren, and the tavalai, and the chah'nas and others. He helped the machines to inflict some catastrophic losses upon his fellow parren. Today, Drakhil's name among parren is mud. He is a tyrant, a monster, a mass-murderer and traitor of the highest order.

"But your new friend Aristan worships him. Aristan is House Harmony, but he is of the Domesh denomination, and considers himself the heir to Drakhil and the Tahrae. The Domesh insist that Drakhil was strong, as parren today are not. They say that the parren could once again become the dominant species in the Spiral, if only they were to follow the teachings of Drakhil once more. Not only do all the parren Houses consider Aristan their enemy, the current leaders of House Harmony, Aristan's own house, also consider him an enemy. Only parren etiquette and laws prevent them from killing him directly. That, and the fear of Aristan's followers. He has billions, and they are fanatical.

"And now, the infamous *UFS Phoenix* invites this unstable and dangerous man to Stoya III, to meet and talk with him on matters that could destabilise not only tavalai-parren relations, but parren inter-House relations also. So forgive me if the State Department is a little blunt in our displeasure, but we wish to know what this is all about, before *Phoenix* leaves yet another trail of destruction in her wake."

Trace knew that she could discuss no such thing. The Dobruta were not the only tavalai institution utterly committed to keeping hacksaw technology under control. There were far more old AI bases and remnants from the Machine Age still out there, in under-explored regions of space, than most beings cared to admit. If tavalai and human leadership could agree on one thing, it was that lifting the restrictions on that old tech would start an arms race amongst the competing species of the Spiral, leading to an inevitable reemergence of sentient-level AI. Previous Spiral history showed that was a terrible idea, to be prevented at all costs.

The Dobruta drew their authority from the core legal institutions at the heart of tavalai society. Those law-bodies, taken collectively, constituted most of what humans would call a legislature. If they found out that *Phoenix* was attempting to acquire an old drysine data-core, they'd have *Phoenix* destroyed at once, whatever *Phoenix*'s pleading of a deadly new threat from alo space. Arguing with individual tavalai was like arguing with a rock. Arguing with entire tavalai legal institutions was like arguing with mountains.

Phoenix was on a mission to track down and find the data-core, under the tavalai's noses, without letting them know what it was they were searching for. As if that weren't hard enough, they also had to do it without letting the parren know — Aristan included. From all that she'd heard and read, Trace had no doubt that Jeli's assessment of Aristan was correct. The data-core, falling into his hands, would be a disaster.

"*Phoenix* is in tavalai space on the invitation of the Dobruta," Trace said calmly. "*Makimakala* knows our business, and can vouch for our peaceful intentions."

Jeli looked deeply displeased. Trace might have expected her to argue further. Instead she gazed about, at the fields of crystal.

"When this place was built," she said, "the tavalai were just a small species on a handful of worlds, struggling to survive in the Age of Machines. Humanity was pre-technological on Earth, just beginning to experiment with farming. The parren became a great species by collaborating with the machines. This temple was built with the technology from that collaboration. It would be hard to build it today. In many ways, the technology of the machines was superior to what we have today."

Trace refrained from nodding. Styx was adamant on that point.

"There are always those prepared to sacrifice civilised principles for personal gain," Jeli continued, with a hard stare. "And it is the job of civilised peoples and institutions to stop them. We will find out what you're up to, *Phoenix*. You and *Makimakala*, the Dobruta are not nearly so pleased with *Makimakala*'s actions as they've led you to believe, do not be fooled. Captain Pramodenium is not as authoritative as he's led you to believe, and we have means of forcing him to talk. Do not spend too long looking at the pretty crystals. Your time here is limited."

After dinner, the *Phoenix* officers gathered in the quarters prepared for them. Erik thought the silky black minimalism halfway between wonderful and creepy. The floors and walls were smooth black stone, and everything gleamed in the soft light. Low black bunks, thin mattresses, and black sheets, naturally. Only the outlines of doorways glowed soft white. He'd wanted more colour and vibrancy, after so long on ship. But Doma Strana seemed designed for sensory deprivation.

"Tomorrow, they say," said Erik. He'd been talking to Aristan's representatives, black cloaked and impassive like their master. "Aristan's meditating. Perhaps the morning."

"He's checking us out," said Trace. "Like we are him." She sat cross-legged on her bunk, calm and confident, almost serene. Erik could see that she loved it here. Sitting with them on the bunks were Lieutenant Chester Zhi of Echo Platoon, Lieutenant Wei Shilu of first-shift, and Second Lieutenant Kendal Abacha of second-shift. More had wanted to come, but places were limited. Shilu was present because he was *Phoenix*'s senior coms officer, and his legal training could be useful amongst the litigious tavalai. Abacha came because he'd drawn a lucky short straw.

"And what's with the robes?" Zhi asked. He was about Trace's age, and would probably have risen faster through the ranks had he been on any other ship than *Phoenix*. There, his abilities might have been conspicuous. But all the Phoenix Company officers were agreed that they'd rather be average players on a champion team than superstars on a team that never made the playoffs. "Most parren don't dress like that."

"Aristan is Domesh," Trace explained. "There's five big Houses, and each House has many denominations. Like how the Christian Church isn't just Christians, it's Catholics, Protestants, Orthodox, etc. The Domesh are one of those. They say they're returning to the old ways of House Harmony, the way things were done in Drakhil's day. To find true harmony, you must be at peace with yourself, which means rejecting pleasures, emotions, extraneous thought."

"So you gotta wear a sack?" Abacha wondered.

"Appearance matters to parren," said Erik. "To most parren, anyway. They care about how they look. But the Domesh don't care, they reject all that stuff. Concealing themselves means refusing to care about appearance, divorcing themselves from vanity, attraction."

"Utterly ridiculous," Shilu sniffed. The Coms Officer had been a dancer in his younger years, and was always elegant, in or out of uniform.

"It's not ridiculous," said Trace. "It's something I've wrestled with myself. Robes just take it a bit far."

"And they'd be a bugger to wear in armour," said Zhi.

"Or no," Trace corrected herself. "They don't take it too far, they miss the point. To find true peace you have to solve the problem, not hide it."

"I'm glad you don't wear them, Major," Erik said innocently. "I'd miss your pleasant scowl." Trace gave him a sly sideways look, as the others chortled. And surprised Erik by allowing him to have the final word.

A door hummed open, and Hiro passed through the doorway light. Hiro was present because he was a spy, and if there was ever a time and place for a spy, this was it. "Right," he said without preamble, tucking up his sleeves to sit comfortably at Trace's side. Erik noted that choice with a faint smile. "The good news is that I don't think anyone's positioning to kill us just yet, though my reach is limited."

"How limited?" asked Zhi, still damp from his shower after a long period in full armour. While the officers had gone to dinner, he'd been guarding hallways. The Pelligavani had politely not remarked on such suspicion, and provided all soldiers with meals in their quarters.

"Well," said Hiro, and flipped his glasses down to his eyes. The others copied, and holographic images appeared upon the lenses, filling the space between them. It was the Doma Strana, or a good portion of it, at least. The scale was incredible, with hundreds of levels all joined by long, vertical elevator shafts. "We're here." A portion of the graphic glowed, a series of levels illuminating. "As near as I can make out, Aristan's contingent and all their House Harmony people are here." Another series of rooms lit up, very close and a little lower.

"And you know this how?" Erik asked.

"I'll get to that. All the rest here is Pelligavani," and most of the rooms and levels glowed. "Lots of activity, lots of vehicular travel, mostly to Troiham for administrative purposes, a few cargo lifts. Definitely the potential for security issues there.

"We and the House Harmony folks aren't the only guests. Most of it's regular Pelligavani business, I'm trying to run down those records now, but the guests look legitimate so far. I'd say there could be a few hundred... including our State Department friends."

"So the bugs work then?" Zhi asked.

Hiro smiled, reached to a pocket and produced something very small, with wings. It crawled upon his hand — an insect, barely the size of his fingernail. Its wings buzzed, and it hovered a moment, then settled. "Pretty cute huh?" Hiro suggested, with a glance at Trace. "I'm calling this one Trevor."

Erik recalled the security briefing he'd only half-attended, relying on others' expertise to keep everyone safe off-ship, and being preoccupied with other things. Bugs. Bugs? He blinked. "That's not... is that synthetic? Did Styx make that?"

"I've got about six of them flying through the corridors," Hiro affirmed. "They compile data back to my network, which of course rides on the marines' network. They only need a little sunlight to recharge, and that's being beamed into the temple via outside optics."

"Aren't the security features here pretty well equipped to handle micro-machines?" Second Lieutenant Abacha queried. "When I was on staff at Aiken Station HQ I remember they had zappers in the corridors to fry things like that."

"Sure, they can recognise any *known* micro-infiltration tech," Hiro affirmed. "This stuff is hacksaw. These little guys fly straight through multi-phase defensive grids, I've seen it. They may as well be invisible, our tech can't recognise it."

"That's because they hack into defensive systems and blind them from the inside," said Trace. "They're assassin bugs. Hacksaws made them during the Machine Age to kill organics as much as spy on them. They'd arm them with nerve agents, probably stuff developed in research labs like we saw at TK55 a month ago. You can't defend against it if you can't see it coming. A few of them could wipe out a base, or cripple a ship."

"Much cheaper than a firefight," Shilu supposed.

And now we're using them, thought Erik. He'd been in Bay 17C, had seen the new machines working there. Most of those machines had been made by other machines, and were now engaged in making more machines. Styx couldn't make what she wanted with current manufacturing tech on *Phoenix*. Ideally she'd have liked an entire city's-worth of tech, but that wasn't possible. Instead she'd laid out to Engineering Commander Lieutenant Rooke a multi-phase plan, where she'd make the machines that would make the machines that could finally achieve what she wanted.

Phoenix would get out of it a whole shopping list of new technology. New coms, weapons, sensor gear. Reactive armour, she'd promised — sensor-embedded and nearly living. And new capabilities in hundreds of small components that had techs from all of *Phoenix*'s engineering and systems divisions salivating at the prospect.

What Styx would get out of it, eventually, was a body. She'd be more useful, she insisted — a capable and able-bodied addition to the crew.   Where the hell they'd keep a full-bodied hacksaw aboard *Phoenix*, Erik had no idea.   Engineering's issue — Engineering's problem.   The thought of having one of those flesh-tearing mechanical spiders roaming aboard *Phoenix* filled him with dread.   Probably more dread than was wise, he knew.   Styx was deadly enough now, in her ability to manipulate the lower-tech that surrounded.   To be frightened of a scary silhouette was stupid.   It wasn't Styx's limbs that would kill — it was her brain.

"And what happens if the tavalai discover us using one of those," Erik asked, pointing to the little thing on Hiro's palm, "and trace it back to us?"

"Well they've got this real nifty self-destruct," said Hiro. "Very high temperature, they just melt, there's nearly nothing left. Styx says it's nearly foolproof."

Styx says.   Erik knew he wasn't the only person on *Phoenix* becoming increasingly sick of hearing of the things that 'Styx says'. She was so much more advanced than them.   At what point did the less advanced creatures become so dependent upon the more advanced creature's technology that she took over completely, whether the less advanced creatures were aware of it or not?

"I was talking to some of the Pelligavani's top lawyers at dinner," Shilu volunteered.   "They were asking some very pointed questions about *Makimakala*.   I got the impression *Makimakala* wasn't telling them much, so they were hoping to get more out of me."

"Any clues as to how long we've got?" Erik asked his Coms Officer sombrely.

Shilu shook his head.   "No.   But I asked into it some more. It's pretty much what Captain Pram told us — the Dobruta get their authority from the Godavadi, which is probably the oldest tavalai legal body.   Everyone agreed that all tavalai institutions get their seniority through age, so being the oldest gives the Godavadi constitutional powers the others lack.   And yes, the Godavadi are completely outside the military chain of command, and actually lay down many of the rules followed by State Department, so neither the tavalai Fleet nor the State Department can touch the Dobruta."

"Thus Fleet and State Department all gathered over our heads," Abacha muttered. "Ready to drop legal bombs on us."

"But," Shilu continued, holding up a finger, "everyone agrees that what *Makimakala* has done in declaring this joint mission with *Phoenix* is very irregular. Word has certainly reached the Godavadi by now, and their deliberations will be coming back. Everyone I spoke to at dinner thought *Makimakala* would be called back to explain herself. At which point we'll be on our own."

"Captain Pram insists that even if that happens, we'll still be under Dobruta protection," said Erik. "He says his independent authority as Dobruta Captain gives him the power to declare superior objectives. They might be able to summons *Makimakala*, but they can't overrule his decision to grant us protection."

"Sir," said Shilu with a firm stare, "you want my honest legal opinion?" Erik nodded. "This tavalai law is all fucked up." Erik smiled reluctantly. "You know what I spent most of my time at dinner talking about? The origins of the Godavadi's legal authority. You know how many legal authorities there are in the tavalai power structure? Thirty-nine. That's just the *lawyers*. All their powers overlap, and most of their energies seem to be expended just figuring how who has what powers over whom.

"One of my dinner partners tried to explain to me the procedures for challenging legal rulings. Sir, it's like listening to a physicist trying to explain quantum particles. It takes *years*. Yet after I suggested how complicated and difficult it all seemed, to which she agreed, I then suggested that maybe most of these legal institutions could be disbanded, or rolled into several big ones. And she was *scandalised*. They don't even have courts or judges as we understand them, nothing decisive, no final authority. Just endless debates.

"The short point of it is this — Captain Pram may *say* that he has the legal authority to protect us from his fellow tavalai. But in my opinion, he might as well be claiming he's going to win a lottery.

Maybe he will, maybe he won't — either way he's got no control over it, and neither do we."

"Sounds to me," said Lieutenant Zhi, "that there's not much difference between too much law, and total anarchy."

"Exactly," said Shilu, clicking his fingers at the marine. "Tavalai think all this law makes them civilised. To me it looks like the jungle."

CHAPTER 3

Lisbeth woke.   It took a while to recall where she was, amidst PH-4's tangle of marine armour berths, on a medical gurney with some detachable padding laid down for a mattress.   It was all velcro and straps, and even through her sleeping bag something pressed, and made her hip sore, and her arm half-asleep.

It still amazed her that she'd learned to sleep in such places at all.   It was all a far cry from home, with her big comfy bed, a smattering of stuffed toys and reading cushions, and a billionaire's view across the hills to Shiwon and the ocean beyond.   But it turned out that if you were tired enough, you could sleep anywhere.   On *Phoenix* she'd discovered the true meaning of 'tired', and it was a very different thing to the 'tired' she knew from home — the 'stayed out too late' tired, or 'pulled an all-nighter to finish an assignment' tired didn't really compare to the 'two days straight studying hacksaw tech so advanced it makes your brain bleed' tired, to say nothing of 'post-combat and near-death experience' tired.

Outside the combat shuttle's hull, she could hear the wind howling.   When she'd gone to sleep, the rear ramp had been open for access by the on-duty marine guards, and the temperature in the shuttle well below freezing.   Now she peered over the lip of her bag, and tugged the heavy cap up her forehead to see, and found the air frigid, but the wind and sound distant.   One of the marines had closed the ramp, then.   Opposite her, Tif was bundled in a similar arrangement, and somewhere in her sleeping bag was Skah, mother and cub wrapped together for warmth.

Lisbeth needed the bathroom.   It was a conundrum — outside the sleeping bag was cold.   Did she *really* need to go?   She suffered through two minutes of indecision before concluding that surely someone who'd survived being shot at, hunted by hacksaw drones, and flattened at 10-Gs in ferocious space combat, could handle a cold trip to the toilet.   She reached for jacket and gloves where she'd laid them earlier — inside the bag it got too hot while wearing them.   If spacer kit did one thing almost too well, it was insulation.

Once bundled, she picked and ducked her way through the armour berths and up the starboard-side hold toward the cockpit. The toilet was behind the cockpit and near the marine-commander's post.   It was a tiny thing whose very design informed the user that he or she was a wimp for needing it, and should have shown some endurance and waited.   Shuttles were not designed for lengthy stays. It made a howling vacuum racket while flushing, too, despite sensing full-gravity.   Lisbeth thought that if she missed anything from her previous life, it was elegance.   Beds that didn't bite, toilets that didn't screech, indoor air that didn't cause hypothermia.   Colours other than steel-grey or matte-black.   Gravity that could be trusted. At least she had that here, for a short while.

She squeezed from the closet-toilet, from freezing air into frigid, and took a moment to peer into the cockpit.   The door seal was open, and in one of the two off-set observer chairs lay Ensign Dave Lee — Tif's co-pilot.   Slowly Lisbeth was getting to know *Phoenix* people as people, not just ranks and surnames.   With shuttle crew it was easy — she was an okay front-seater herself, and with *Phoenix* short of shuttle crew, Dave Lee and the others had given her many tips and simulator lessons over the past four months.   Tif had offered to sleep in the observer chair tonight — *Phoenix* regs insisted that one of the two pilots had to remain in the cockpit at all times on grounded ops in uncertain security — but Dave had insisted that mum and kid should snuggle together, which was only possible down back.   The blanket over Dave's sleeping bag was slipping, and Lisbeth settled it gently back over him.

Outside of PH-4's narrow armoured canopy, it was snowing. The snow blew in sideways, lit in a glare of floodlights that the auto-tint mostly blocked.   Out in the snow, *Phoenix* marines stood guard. They wouldn't be cold in their suits, Lisbeth knew, just very, very bored.   One of them stood close to a tavalai armour-suit, the karasai gesturing as they talked.   Not all of *Phoenix*'s crew wanted anything to do with their Dobruta allies, but some had softened, and a few had even struck up friendships.   Lisbeth wondered if any of those friendships would last, once this was all over, and everyone got to go home. How would marines and karasai keep in touch? Across a heavily armed border that restricted communications? Twice-yearly recorded messages? Hi, how's things? Let me introduce you to the wives and communal spawn?

Lisbeth shivered her way back to her makeshift bunk. At least it was nice to be warm in bed, while the freezing snow blew outside. It made her realise that discomforts aside, being within *Phoenix* security perimeters made her feel safe. *Phoenix was* safety to her now, despite her ongoing association threatening daily to get her killed.

Approaching her bunk, she noticed something on the steel-grid deck for the first time. A lily, like the ones the Pelligavani had given upon their arrival. Lisbeth frowned, and squatted to examine it. It hadn't been there when she'd gone to bed, she was certain. Someone must have put it there while she slept... and certainly it had been 'put' there, its placement was too symmetrical alongside her bunk for it to have been dropped.

Surely a marine was playing a small prank, she thought, picking up the lily. Giving her flowers while she slept, the promise of a secret admirer. Then she noticed the ribbon, and the attached plastic case containing a data-chip. Or she thought it was a data-chip, the design was unfamiliar. Alien, no doubt. Out here, everything was. But which aliens?

She thought about it for a moment, freezing cold and wanting to get back into bed... but now feeling a slow prickling at the back of her neck. Marines pranked each other constantly, but never on anything approaching active duty, which this surely was despite the lack of gunfire. And prank the Captain's *sister*? On *Phoenix*, there were macho marines known to hit on anything female, two-legged or four, human or not, on any port of call, yet gave Lisbeth nothing more forward than a wink. Not only was she the Captain's sister, but she shared quarters with Major Thakur... and even were a marine fearless enough to defy the Captain, *none* were dumb enough to try the Major.

Lisbeth uplinked to local networks, and found the guards' channel fast enough. On duty, they were most active by proximity. *"Um... hello? Sergeant Kunoz?"* Silently formulating to avoid waking Tif or Skah.

"Hello Lisbeth," came back Sergeant Kunoz's voice in her ear. He was commander of Echo Platoon, Second Squad, and had been stuck with landing-pad guard duty tonight. *"What's up?"*

"Well, um... someone left me a lily. By my bunk. I was wondering if it was one of you guys."

"In PH-4?"

"Yes." She could hear the frown in Kunoz's voice, formulated or not. *"It's got what appears to be a data-chip attached. Looks alien."*

A click as Kunoz flipped to what was presumably a command channel, to quiz his marines. Probably he'd use more profanity than he wanted her to hear. After a moment, another click.

"It wasn't my guys. Maybe one of the tavalai. They like lilies."

"A tavalai crept onto PH-4 to give me a lily?" It wasn't hard to inject skepticism into her formulation. Another click, as Kunoz checked on something else. Probably realising how silly it sounded, when she said it.

Click back. *"Lisbeth, all our cameras and scans confirm nothing's been aboard PH-4 while you've been sleeping, except marines. It wasn't Tif or Furball?"*

"Sergeant, Tif sleeps through weapons drill, Skah too. And Ensign Lee's not exactly romantic." The prickle up her neck began to spread down her spine. If it wasn't human, or other *Phoenix* crew, or tavalai...

"Yeah," said Kunoz, warily. *"I think we'd better take a look at that data-chip."*

"It's definitely a parren data format," came Petty Officer Kadi's voice from somewhere in orbit. *"It's pretty obscure though, it could take a little while to reformat it."*

"How long?" asked Erik. He sat at the table with a mug of hot coffee, having brought his own supply, knowing better than to trust tavalai concoctions. He sat with *Phoenix* crew in this accommodation level's dining room, with wide windows looking past floodlit landing pads onto further mountains. Dawn made a thin blue line above the jagged horizon. Four human months since any of them had seen a dawn.

"Um... well, we'll need to scan through Phoenix databases to find the data format, and then..."

"Let me try," came a new voice. Styx. Erik, Trace and Shilu looked at each other. Nearby, Lisbeth watched above the rim of her own coffee cup, while Hiro sat further away, dark glasses on and processing advanced security protocols to keep both this coms line, and the room, secure for talking.

"Captain, this is Rooke," came the Engineering Chief before Erik could respond. *"I'd recommend we let her — it could take us a full rotation to decode the contents otherwise, and if it's time-critical information..."*

"Do it," Erik agreed. Shilu looked unhappy. Trace, unreadable as always. But of all the senior crew, she'd been the least opposed to Styx's reactivation, despite having been the one who shot her in the first place.

"Aye sir." And there followed some brief chatter between Kadi and Rooke, technical stuff, transferring data. Then some awed murmurs. And finally, from Rooke, a stifled laugh.

"Lieutenant Rooke?" Erik asked. "What's going on?"

"Um... sir, she just reformatted an entirely new operating protocol in three seconds, from a blind start. It would have taken us..."

"A day, I know," said Erik, sipping coffee. Around Styx, such things were predictable. "Styx? What is it?"

"The contents are images. They appear to be photo-realistic copies of old paper book pages. I recognise the text, but I cannot read its contents."

"Why not? What language is it?"

"It is Klyran. It is an obscure text used by parren during my last contact with them, but the study of obscure languages was never a priority for my people."

Also predictably, the coms crackled as someone else broke into the transmission. *"Klyran!"* gasped Stan Romki, as though startled out of whatever else he'd been doing. No doubt he'd been listening in, having clearance to do that on anything old and alien-related. *"Good gods... Styx, can you transfer it to my... damn it, where are my glasses..."*

"Transferring, Professor. Do you know Klyran?"

"God no, it's been dead for twenty thousand years. It's... it's an old religious tongue, it was used by the Tahrae before they were all wiped out in the wars that followed the fall of the drysines... wow!" No doubt gasping at what Styx showed him, projected on the lenses of his AR glasses. *"Now if I... what if..."*

In the dining room, Erik, Trace and Shilu all looked at each other. Shilu rolled his eyes. Erik knew that if he let the big brains on the ship handle things, he'd still be sitting here an hour later listening to them gasp in delight. "Professor Romki," Erik prompted, "it strikes me that if Styx is so smart, she ought to be able to figure the whole language if you could provide her with clues."

"Um... well yes. Actually, that's not a bad... Styx?"

"Ready when you are, Professor."

It took ten minutes. Romki knew a few of the symbols, and Styx was very familiar with some extremely old parren language construction. From those certain points, Styx simply ran the billions of probabilities until things started to fit, and the ordering of vowels, consonants, nouns and verbs fell into place. After several key discoveries, the rest unravelled rather quickly, to new gasps of astonishment from Rooke and Kadi.

"And that could have taken a decade," Kadi informed them all.

"Hacksaw queens sure are useful time savers," Rooke agreed.

"You think Aristan's people speak Klyran?" Shilu asked Erik, off coms.

"Why give it to us to decode if they can?" Erik replied. "These are their parren ancestors, they'd have much more chance than us. This tongue's so old, even Aristan's forgotten." He glanced at Lisbeth. She looked a little rattled. No one had seen any comings or goings from PH-4, no explanation of who'd brought the lily. But if it had been one of Aristan's people... then he'd gotten right to her bedside, through *Phoenix*'s heavily armed security, and stood over her while she'd slept.

"Then aren't we running a risk by decoding it?" Shilu persisted. "What else could decode that so fast? What if we're effectively letting Aristan know exactly what we have on board *Phoenix*? Who other than a drysine queen could do that?"

Erik nodded slowly. "Then we'll have to be very careful how much we tell him. Or any of his people."

"These are coordinates," Styx decided. *"There are many coordinates, but I recognise some as describing topographical features that match the mountain range surrounding Doma Strana. There is a large middle section describing Doma Strana itself, quite precisely. From the volume of data, and its presentation, I would venture that these are the original planning blueprints for the Doma Strana complex, though coded to make them only accessible to those with knowledge of Klyran. The first entry of Doma Strana in Drysine Empire records predates Drakhil by more than a thousand human years. Those are documents of planning and intention to build."*

"From the Tahrae?" Romki breathed.

"Yes. The Tahrae were the dominant faction in House Harmony, and House Harmony was the dominant house among parren. This was a thousand years before Drakhil. Stoya III was a central world in the Empire. My people ascertained no harm in allowing the construction of parren temples here, for the political ascendency of the Tahrae among the parren."

"Wait," said Erik. "The Doma Strana was built during the Parren Empire. *After* the Machine Age had ended."

"That is what the outside world is told. The actual temple dates to perhaps a thousand years before the end of the Machine Age. No organic today wishes to admit that the Machine Age did organics any good." Erik and Shilu exchanged glances. Surely that wasn't *irony* in her voice? *"Curiously, these documents reveal a number of construction sites, although Doma Strana is today the only Tahrae temple known in the region."*

"They built *more*?" Erik asked. "Without the drysines knowing?"

"My people's empire was spacefaring, with little interest in planets. If the Tahrae intended to build more than the Doma Strana, they did not tell the Empire. This is not particularly suspicious. Tahrae at the time were drysine allies. Their activities did not threaten us even in space, much less on planets."

"It could have been a safety feature," Romki added. *"If the Drysine Empire fell, or if a faction broke off in a new AI civil war... I mean, these things happened all across the Machine Age, yes? If you wanted to safeguard the location of something for tens of thousands of years, better that the primary record keepers of the age remain ignorant, yes?"*

"Quite true, Professor," Styx agreed. *"As Professor Romki states, these coordinates appear to indicate the location of alternative construction sites in the original Tahrae documents, if that is indeed what these are. Whether anything was actually built there, none of us can know."*

"Aristan might know," said Trace. Looking at Erik, with her usual calm intensity. "But asking him would tell him just how good at decoding those documents we are."

"Thus risking that he'll guess Styx exists," Erik finished. He gazed out the windows for a moment, at the brightening glow above the rugged horizon. A cruiser hummed by, regular traffic around Doma Strana.

"What happens if he guesses that?" Lisbeth wondered.

"Well," said Erik, "this is a guy who worships a guy who was the Drysine Empire's best organic friend. I don't want that worship transferring to Styx, or to us."

"Sure," Lisbeth said drily. "Wouldn't want to make a friend for once."

"If making that friend is followed by all his enemies who fear him then trying their best to kill us?" Erik replied. "Then yes — this friend we can do without."

"Company," Hiro announced. Trace looked at him, tense and alert... but Hiro remained calm, gazing into space but seeing all on his glasses. Trace relaxed. "Down the hall. No trouble, he's approaching Corporal Haynes in three, two, one..."

"Hello Major, Captain," came Lance Corporal Haynes' voice on coms. *"I have a single parren, black robed, walking calmly. Seems unarmed."*

Trace flipped down her glasses, to take a look at the Lance Corporal's helmet-cam. "Search him and send him in," she told Haynes.

"Aye Major."

Thirty seconds later, the door to the dining room opened, and a black robed parren appeared, cowled and masked as Aristan had been. Private Krishnan followed him in, full armour looming behind the dark, silent figure.

The parren spoke, and a translator speaker spoke louder, somewhere within the robes. *"Phoenix officers are invited to attend,"* it intoned, without preamble. *"In the fourteenth taka, the upper cargo level. It is secure. The leader shall accompany."*

A short nod, and the parren turned, and swept from the room once more. The *Phoenix* crew blinked at each other. "Polite, isn't he?" said Shilu.

"The leader," said Trace. "Presumably that's Aristan. Fourteenth taka, that's..."

"Nearly an hour," said Erik. Tavalai measured time in taka, making conversions a nightmare. With the Dobruta, Erik had been getting a lot of practise. "So they drop this data chip on us, and now invite us to meet Aristan again?"

"It's almost like he wanted us to decode it for him," said Shilu. "And knew that we could, and how long it would take."

"Well," said Erik "we won't admit anything. We can't. But it would be nice to find out some more about Doma Strana's original construction plans."

"Aristan might have no idea what was on that chip," Trace cautioned. "If we go in there asking him about construction plans, he might guess *exactly* what was on the chip, in addition to guessing that Styx exists. Too many cards in his hand, and too much leverage over us."

Erik made a face, sipping coffee as he gazed at the view. On the cliff face opposite, the enormous parren face gazed back at him through the snow flurries, fearsome and impassive.

"If he does admit it was him who gave us the chip," Lisbeth complained, "then ask him how the hell. Because it's freaking me out."

CHAPTER 4

It was a long ride up the central shaft elevator to the top cargo level. They shared part of the journey with some tavalai Pelligavani, civilians about their business, both curious and polite in the presence of heavily armed humans, where other species might be terrified. Partly, Erik thought, it was just that tavalai did everything by the book. *Phoenix* was in tavalai space on invitation of *Makimakala*, and that being the case, ordinary tavalai could not conceive of possible treachery.

The car contained only humans when it arrived at the very top, and let out Erik, Trace, and the first two squads of Echo Platoon, led by Lieutenant Zhi himself. Person-sized corridors soon opened onto larger halls, where robot cargo sleds hummed by, loaded with containers. Everyone wore full armour save Erik, who was no more qualified for marine armour than the marines were to fly spaceships.

The hall opened into a wide storage room, filled with racks and walls of stacked containers, and aisles of mobile robot loaders. Freezing wind swirled, beyond the capacity of Doma Strana's heaters to warm. Erik followed Trace between aisles, as marines split left and right to secure the room. Beyond the cargo walls were landing platforms, five in total. Three held empty cargo sleds, jet-lift cruisers for freight, small and low-powered. The bigger cargo haulers must have arrived at another platform, Erik thought — probably lower down the mountain, to avoid the difficulties of elevators. Those cargo rooms would be for the long-term haulage. This room was for short-term perishables. One advantage to it being so cold up here, he thought, folding his arms against the chill — there was no need for refrigeration.

"No sign of parren," came Sergeant Kunoz's report. *"They're late."*

"Recommend we not hang about," said Lieutenant Zhi at Erik's side. "If they're not punctual, that's their problem."

"Major," came Hiro on coms, *"I'm getting a strange reading from the local coms network..."*

And his voice blanked to static. "That's coms," said Trace, checking her uplinks. Her voice was hard in a way that Erik knew from long experience meant trouble. His heart might have missed a beat, but in truth, he was getting used to it. Surely this time it couldn't be as bad as previous times? "Full withdrawal, back to the elevator, go go!"

They'd barely moved when the seal doors crashed into place about the cargo room, sealing them in. *"Fuck,"* someone announced, succinctly. *That* wasn't supposed to be possible, Jokono had assured them it wasn't.

"Blow it!" Zhi commanded. "Everyone cover! Watch your blast radius!" Erik ran with Zhi, not needing to be told, and took cover behind some cargo with hands over his ears. Then marines were letting off backrack missiles nearby, a hiss-and-boom! of headsplitting proportions, filling the room with smoke and flying shrapnel.

Without a fully enclosed helmet, Erik missed the next coms traffic from the noise, until Zhi whacked him on the shoulder armour. "That was Hausler! We have incoming marks, PH-1 and PH-4 are scrambling!" And back on coms, *"More fire on the near door! Breach this one first, don't spread your shots!"*

"Captain this is Phoenix*!"* It was Lieutenant Lassa in orbit. Speaking through orbital relays, she'd be several seconds behind developments. *"Atmospheric drone is reading you have incoming marks, five kilometres and closing fast!"*

"This is PH-1!" Hausler overrode. *"Incoming missiles, I'm reading ten! Shuttles are full evasive — Tif, break and run!"*

"Break and run," Tif agreed.

"Those missiles will be coming in here!" Trace shouted, crashing across to Erik. *"We're not getting through those doors in time, we gotta go!"*

Erik saw her coming, and realised in shock what she was saying. "Hell no! We're not leaving them here to die!"

And Trace simply grabbed him by the arm and hauled — an impossible force to resist in powered armour. *"Those missiles are after* you*! You leave, you'll save them!"*

That got him moving, running for one of the cargo sleds and scrambling into the pilot's seat. *"Krishnan!"* Trace was yelling. *"Just you, we're too heavy for more!"*

"Captain, twenty seconds!" came Hausler, tracking those missiles. *"I can't get to you, we don't have the counter measures for that spread!"*

As Erik fumbled with various controls, trying with increasing desperation to figure how to get this contraption started. "I don't know how to start it, it's all parren!" Multiple explosions as Lieutenant Zhi's marines expended all remaining ammunition on the one door.

"Captain this is Styx. Activate all coms functions on the vessel. Major, full suit coms open, give me everything." The coms panel was fairly self-explanatory, and Erik hit buttons in what seemed a logical sequence...

...and suddenly the engines were whining and howling, cockpit lights springing to life. Erik took the controls and throttles, recalling that this was a thrust VTOL vehicle and he'd need to balance it on a column of air at four thousand metres altitude...

"Two passengers," Trace told him from the rear. *"We're secure."*

"Five seconds!"

And Erik hauled them backward, judging thrust and altitude by eye as he skidded them back toward the open doors and simply fell sideways into empty space... and lost ground-effect, going with gravity as they fell from the sky like a rock, plunging down the towering cliff. Something big exploded behind them, then another, and he figured there was a good chance the later-arriving missiles were chasing them. Having no way to see them coming without his familiar sensors, he simply slammed on thrust to lurch them sideways as they fell, then again the other way. Sure enough, something fast flashed by them, then streaked up around in a long arc, suggesting it was going to try and reacquire. But the arc was long and wide — this wasn't some fancy, fast-turning aerial missile, more a mid-range strategic weapon, big on range but lower on mobility.

His eyes were picking up the control displays and Head Up Display, just from seeing what moved when he flew... or fell. And now the valley floor was racing up, a carpet of trees below rocky walls, and he powered on the thrusters once more. The sled recovered slowly — much more slowly than he'd hoped, and he gritted his teeth as the trees came up real close and racing. Movement caught his eye ahead, then an assault shuttle flashed by — not human, it was mottled brown and green, camouflage painting. Not as big as the *Phoenix* shuttles either, but clearly armed and not the kind of thing he wanted to tangle with in a cargo sled.

"We can't go back!" he shouted at his passengers, and at any *Phoenix* crew still listening above the jamming. "We just lost air superiority, our shuttles can't stand up to this many! They'll have to run and hide until we can regroup, and if we try to land in this thing, we'll be shot down!"

"Run south!" Trace told him. *"Due 170 if you can manage it! I've got an idea!"*

"Gonna be hard in these mountains, but I'll try." He kept them low, engaging more lateral thrust as he figured finally how those worked. The sled was primitive, but it was light and relatively well-powered for its low mass. The valley lifted ahead of him and he turned within the canyon walls, following the line of a small, frothing river amidst the trees. It would have been spectacular if he'd had time to appreciate it.

But now he was flying blind, and in the mountains that was never wise. Most valleys had an entry-point, but many had no exit, and then you had to hope your vehicle could climb well enough to get over and out. The sled could hover, so he wouldn't be flying headlong into any dead-ends, but if one of those enemy combat flyers decided to chase them this way...

"Guys I'm completely blind up here," he told the marines in the back. "I've got no idea how the navigation works on this thing, it's not showing me the valleys on automatic, and it sure as hell isn't showing me any enemy marks. I need you two to be my door gunners. Keep an eye out for any pursuit, and if you see it, shoot it down."

Because marine armour suits were powerful enough to do that, if enemy pilots were careless enough to expose themselves. *"We copy,"* said Trace. *"Private Krishnan, you good?"*

"I'm good!" said the Private. He didn't sound good. Erik had long ago learned not to make fun of marines who got queasy during hard flying. The ride was always far worse down back, even for experienced pilots. Erik took a quick glance back, and caught a glimpse of the cargo hold behind his seats. The sled was flying doors open, Trace hanging out one side, Krishnan the other. That extra drag was costing him speed, but pretty much anything had a speed advantage over a cargo sled, particularly at this altitude. If they were attacked, speed and mobility wouldn't save them, but marine firepower might.

Erik tried coms channels as he flew several tight turns past jagged cliffs, then a wide, sweeping bend past an enormous scree slope where nothing grew. Nothing was answering — not *Phoenix*, not Doma Strana. They'd put an aerial drone at twenty kilometres altitude before descending for surveillance cover, and now probably that was dead too. *Phoenix* was possibly manoeuvring to get back over their heads once more, but the mechanics of near-orbital velocity made that difficult, and she was currently near the far side of the planet. Coms had been routed through yet another orbital drone, this one in high geo-stationary — *Phoenix* had dozens, and they weren't hard to manufacture if one was lost. But the incomplete jamming back at Doma Strana had now become complete jamming, and there was nothing even Styx could do about that.

It occurred to Erik briefly that until now, he hadn't spared even a single thought about who was trying to kill them. And realised just as fast that it truly didn't matter, and refocused on the task at hand.

"I'm getting active tracking!" Krishnan announced. *"Something's tracking us!"*

"I second that," Trace affirmed.

"Well track him back! And I want lots of shooting even if you can't hit him! Our best defence is fear!"

Marine suits' scanning systems weren't ideal for aerial combat, but for now they were all he had. He skimmed them closer to the river around a bend, having no real idea what he'd do if someone was chasing them. The smart thing would be to land, because then they couldn't be shot down, while two marine suits could certainly do that to the enemy. Flyers shooting at grounded marines would be smarter to stay well clear and fire from range, but here in the valleys that wasn't always an option.

"I have a lock!" said Krishnan. *"Firing!"* Missile fire whooshed from the back, but Erik had no way to see if it hit anything.

"Return incoming!" said Trace. *"He's beyond visual... no wait, there it is, closing!"* At which point Erik knew there was nothing he could do beyond stay as low as possible, and hope. The missile hit a cliff wall on the left. *"I had countermeasures running, don't know if it did anything."*

"More likely we're beyond range," Erik replied through gritted teeth, swinging them through another tight gap as the valley climbed ever higher. "He's staying back so he doesn't get shot down, but the missile needs more target visuals than it's getting."

As he'd feared, the forested valley sloped up sharply ahead of him, trees thinning onto a slope of rock and scree. "Major, your door side, you're about to get a shot!" As he slammed on full power and climbed the mountainside in a blur of rock that abruptly gave way to snow and ice. He threw in a sideways slide as they neared the top, just where he figured their pursuer should be coming into visual behind... a whoosh as Trace's missile rack fired, then a thunder of rifle fire that Erik could actually feel through the controls, and god knew how marines learned to fight the recoil in a weapon that size...

Heavy gunfire kicked up snow and ice beside and ahead from a burst that would have torn them to pieces had it hit, then Erik shoved the nose down and they were negative-Gs for several seconds coming over the crest between huge mountain peaks. He recovered to streak down the face of a high knife-edge ridge, more thunder behind as Krishnan fired, both marines far too preoccupied to report on results.

More fire hit the mountain wall on his right, and Erik slammed the thrust pivot down, hearing the gasp from the marines as the sled leapt. It kicked them momentarily out of their pursuer's line of fire, but at the cost of speed, and now the enemy flyer was closing — perhaps suddenly much closer than he'd wanted.

Fire from Krishnan, then, *"Got him! He's breaking off!"* As Erik dove down the mountainside toward this new valley floor. *"How you like the Koshaim, asshole?"*

Erik levelled off above the trees of a new valley, and another, wider river. *"No, he's coming back!"* Trace corrected. *"I get no missile lock, he's got good countermeasures!"* There was a little more room in this valley, Erik saw. That was bad. There was a mountain shoulder just ahead, and he angled them for it as low and fast as he dared.

"Fire and put him off or we're dead!"

Something flashed behind, and Erik winced for the inevitable missile that blew them all to bits. *"He blew up!"* Krishnan yelled instead. *"Holy shit, he just…"*

Erik streaked over the mountain shoulder, relief dying fast as he saw another flyer ahead, a small dot but streaking fast straight at them. And saw the hypersonic contrail from the upper edge of his vision, tearing a great, white line through the sky until it reached the valley, and tore the flyer from the air in a flash of tumbling debris.

"Phoenix!" Erik yelled in triumph, just before something hit them with a huge bang, and made the sled jump. He fought frantically with the controls, full power and struggling for altitude and vertical thrust control, smelling smoke and fearing the worst. Right rear thrust was out, he could feel it without needing to read flashing parren control panels, and he had no hope of landing them vertically, nor staying in the air in any controlled manner beyond a few hundred metres. It didn't leave many options.

Then he saw the lake, long and narrow ahead, a thin slice of flatness in an unforgiving landscape. "There's a lake!" he yelled. "We're gonna crash, hold on!"

He clipped the last trees, and then the water was under him, and would end real soon if he didn't put it down right now. He wanted more time, needed to calculate, to think, to reconsider... but there was none, so he pulled the nose up and cut thrust, and hit with a force that defied description...

Phoenix bridge thundered in a hard recovery burn, as Commander Suli Shahaim roared engines at full power while skimming Stoya atmosphere, far closer and harder to the exosphere than any starship captain wanted.

"Looks like they timed it so we'd be on the far side of the planet," Lieutenant Commander Draper formulated from Shahaim's usual post — Helm, to the right of the Captain's chair and slightly behind, mostly invisible behind a tangle of displays and heavy-G supports.

This was why Suli, like most warship pilots, hated low orbit — down this low you were jammed against the planet with limited options, and unable to even maintain direct communications, let alone support options, to a ground team. Geo-stationary orbit kept you in line-of-sight, but at a distant altitude from which fire or air support would take forever to reach the surface. And while a carrier's engines were comfortably powerful enough to create a 'hover', standing a ship on its tail at 1-G thrust and no lateral velocity at all, loss of control in that position meant certain loss-of-vessel, and in Fleet came with a near-automatic court-martial.

"Incoming from Tokigala," called Lieutenant Lassa from Coms — second-shift backup now in the main seat with Lieutenant Shilu on the surface. *"It's in English, no translator."*

"UFS Phoenix, this is State Department ambassadorial vessel Tokigala. You will cease this reckless manoeuvre at once, or you will be fired upon. Please confirm your receipt of this message immediately."

"Ignore," Suli gasped beneath the hard Gs crushing the air from her chest. Everyone in high or low orbit about Stoya III could hear what was happening at Doma Strana, and knew exactly why *Phoenix* was powering at full thrust to reacquire an oversight position, and why she'd fired Anti-Atmospheric rounds immediately when the signal had reached them, in the hope of intercepting some of those attacking flyers.   That *Tokigala* was choosing to interpret this manoeuvre as hostile indicated a high probability that *Tokigala* was behind the attack in the first place.   Suli flipped coms to her own channel, direct to *Makimakala*.   *"Hello Captain Pram, this is Phoenix.   Please tell Tokigala to stay off our backs or I promise I will destroy her."*

"Phoenix I copy," came Captain Pram's reply.   *"We are manoeuvring hard to acquire position ourselves, we have our own people down there too.   Our coms are talking to Tokigala, we will try to dissuade them.   Please remain calm and patient, if tavalai Fleet chooses to engage you on Tokigala's command, even Phoenix will not survive."*

"I am aware of that, Makimakala," Suli replied.   *"But I promise we will destroy Tokigala first.   Make sure they know."*

She disconnected.   *"Won't make much difference, with froggies,"* said Draper.   Tavalai didn't change their minds just because you threatened to kill them.   Head representatives of the largest tavalai government departments in particular.

"I know," Suli replied.   The tactical picture upon her visor lenses moved, increment by increment — *Phoenix* low and fast, *Makimakala* on an intersecting trajectory also low and fast, *Tokigala* much higher above, and various tavalai Fleet vessels beyond that, including several at geostationary.   If they fired from up there, with *Phoenix* pressed against the atmosphere, there'd be no escape.

Suli flipped channels again.   *"Hello Ops, we will be flipping for braking manoeuvre in seventy-two seconds.   Ninety-eight seconds after that, we will be weightless once more and PH-3 will load and launch, do you copy?"*

"Operations copies," came the Ops manager's terse reply.

"Commander this is Jersey, I'm forty seconds out."

"This is Dufresne, I am eighty seconds out."   Because Lieutenant Dufresne was in quarters near the bridge, while

Lieutenant Jersey was quartered down by Midships, with the rest of the shuttle crews. PH-3 was Jersey's, and Dufresne their only qualified back-seater, with even Lisbeth down on Stoya's surface. *Phoenix* had one more shuttle, the civilian AT-7, but AT-7 had no weapons, and at present *Phoenix* had no pilots aboard who could fly her anyway. What good one more shuttle would do, in the face of what appeared to be coordinated treachery on the surface, Suli had no idea. But PH-3 was all they had to send, and so they'd send her, along with any more orbital ordnance that was requested.

"This is Lieutenant Dale," came the gruff, familiar voice of Major Thakur's number two marine. *"Alpha will take a bit more than four minutes, awaiting the end of burn."*

Alpha Platoon's armour suits were pre-positioned in PH-3, in case of just such an emergency. Marines practised getting into armour against the clock. Now everyone would see just how fast Alpha's marines really were. Missing the departure window by a minute would throw them three hundred kilometres downrange, and twenty minutes late coming back. It was in moments like this that Suli was glad to serve on *Phoenix*, where the odds of someone messing up were low. Now, lives depended on it.

Skah was scared. He'd been headed to breakfast with Lisbeth at the temple kitchen at this level, but then lots of people had started yelling and running, and Lisbeth had grabbed his arm and run with him back the way they'd come. But by the time they'd reached the landing platform, both shuttles were gone, taking Mummy with them, and Crazy Hausler, and Steve Lee, and Julie Yun who'd shown him how to play a fun game with dice before bed last night, sitting in PH-4's hold amidst the armour berths.

Echo Platoon marines had shouted at them to get inside, and Skah knew these marines outside their armour, when they smiled and gave him high-fives. But now they were fierce and scary, all thundering armour and massive guns, taking up cover positions in corridors as he and Lisbeth had run with tavalai workers to deeper rooms.   Then missiles had started hitting outside, with big thumps! that hurt his ears, and the sound of things breaking, as Lisbeth had sheltered with him behind some desks in a big office space, with strange stone pictures on the walls from when the temple had been a real temple, and not an office.

Now he kept his head down as his heart hammered, and just hoped that it wasn't going to be like the last time on the station a month ago, when he and Lisbeth had hid behind a bench with Jace, while a hacksaw drone had come into the room with them.   At least there was no one hurt yet, like Jace had been.   Jace Reddin was up on *Phoenix*, having recently been allowed back on light duties, his bullet wound healing well.   He was one of Skah's best friends, along with all Jace's friends in Operations, who knew that Skah had helped to save him, and now got him extra treats from the kitchen, and invited him to play games with them in zero-G, and showed him vids of their families.   It was nice to make such good friends, but Skah was sure he'd much rather Jace hadn't been shot in the first place. Being shot was bad, and so much more scary than in movies.   Jace had been in pain for so long.   Skah hoped no one would get shot now, especially Lisbeth, and grasped her arm tightly.

There were more explosions down the hall, then a tavalai marine came stomping in and talked with a human marine.   The tavalai marine would be from *Makimakala*, Skah knew. *Makimakala* had been friends with *Phoenix* now for a month.   Skah knew that a lot of his human friends still didn't like tavalai much, but they were coming to trust *Makimakala*.   When he'd been sleeping on PH-4 with Mommy and Lisbeth, some tavalai marines had come to talk, and look at him and Mommy curiously, and shake their hands.   Very few tavalai had ever seen a kuhsi, Lisbeth had said. But Skah was used to that.   Once long ago, he could recall being surrounded by other kuhsi.   Mommy said it had not been very long since they'd left Chogoth, and that he only thought it was a long time because he was very young.   But to Skah, it felt as though he'd been an alien amongst aliens for most of his life.   And given that kuhsi had murdered Skah's Daddy, and kidnapped him and Mommy and handed them to the chah'nas, Skah thought that he much preferred the company of humans anyway. Especially *Phoenix* humans.

There were more explosions, then some shooting somewhere not too far away. A marine guarding the doorway shouted something to the office room of cowering tavalai civilians, plus Lisbeth and Skah.

"There's enemy flyers landing on the upper platforms Skah," Lisbeth told him, and Skah had to concentrate very hard to understand her. Normally his English was very good, and getting better every day. But when he was scared and people were shooting, it got harder.

"Who's landing?" he asked Lisbeth. "Who's attacking us?"

"I don't know Skah." Her voice was low and cautious, but she didn't sound particularly scared. Skah found that reassuring. "There's a lot of marines here, and karasai too. It's going to take a lot more than a few flyers of enemy soldiers to get in here."

Several karasai came lumbering through the room, heading for a far door, then out past the marine guarding that side. Skah looked at tavalai civilians hiding behind desks nearby. One of them made an expression that Skah had come to know as a tavalai smile — as much an inward swivel of the eyes as a thinning of the lips. The tavalai reached to pat Skah's arm, reassuringly. Skah decided that it was sad that humans and tavalai had fought a war. Tavalai weren't so bad.

Then something exploded nearby, and the lights went out. Thunder in the doorways, as marines and karasai fired at things only they could see. Something crashed over tables, and Skah scrambled beneath a table himself, seeing the entire room lit with brilliant flashes, big marine rifles in an enclosed space. Some holes were blasted in a wall, then relative silence, as Skah's ears rang, and marines crashed into the room amongst the desks, shouting tersely at each other as their big guns panned back and forth across the tables.

Something was in here, Skah thought, and the fur prickled on his back and neck, the stub-ends of his trimmed claws catching on the carpet. The marines were wondering where it went. A flash of movement beyond the tables, dark and vanishing as fast as it appeared, but the marines didn't shoot.   They hadn't seen it, Skah realised.   Human eyesight wasn't as good as kuhsi, Mommy had said.   Nor their hearing.   Only their smell was better, and that wouldn't help them here.

He thought perhaps he should say something.   But he'd been warned so many times on *Phoenix*, 'don't get in the way of marines with armour and loaded weapons'.   Especially here, he thought, when they were jumpy and ready to shoot at surprises.   Skah kept his mouth shut, and crept slowly to one table support, and a better view up an aisle.

Then the lights came back on, and the marines were stomping back and forth between tables, looking for whatever had been here.   Whatever it was, they couldn't find it.   Skah supposed that meant it had left.   It was hard to imagine anyone could stay hidden from marines for long once the lights came back on.   Skah crept back to Lisbeth, to take her arm.

But Lisbeth wasn't there.   Skah looked around, expecting that she'd just crawled to another table as he had, to take a better look.   But he couldn't see her.   He stood up, then jumped on a table to see, startling marines who swung weapons his way, then swore.

"Goddammit Furball.   Stay down, it isn't safe yet. Understand?"

"Risbeth!" Skah called, ignoring them.   "Risbeth?"   No reply.   He spun on the marines, panicked, his heart suddenly racing in much worse fear than even when the shooting was happening. "Where's Risbeth?   She was here!   Where is she?"

CHAPTER 5

Erik woke with a vague memory of having woken before. In that memory, he'd been in water, freezing cold and fighting to breathe. So logically he'd died, drowned in the cold mountain lake, and this was... well, an odd way to discover oneself dead, cold and wet and lying on stones.

The white glare above hurt his eyes. His neck hurt worse, and his knee. But his shoulder hurt worst of all, a throbbing pain like sticking your fingers into ice water for minutes on end. And growing worse still as his head cleared.

Voices above him, about him, hands pulling him this way and that. They were removing his clothes, he realised. Then a blaze of pain from his shoulder, as though someone had stuck a knife through it, and he yelled. More voices then, and hands feeling his shoulder.

"Captain!" Trace's voice, demanding his attention. Again. Goddamn relentless woman, always demanding. "Captain! Erik! Erik, listen to me. Come on, wake up." A slap on his cheek, not hard. Erik figured he'd better wake up, or she'd start punching him next. He struggled to focus, and found her over him, bleeding profusely from a gash on her forehead. That concerned him, and he woke further. "Erik, you've dislocated your shoulder. Does anything else hurt?"

"Your head," he murmured, unable to feel his lips properly.

"I'm fine, pay attention. Does anything else hurt?"

"Knee," he murmured. "Neck."

"Can you move your fingers and toes?" He wiggled them, but it was silly, because she'd not be able to see his toes with his boots on. "Good, that looks fine. I think you got whiplashed real good, but spacers have serious G-augments, I bet that protected your spine. Now I'm going to..."

"Where's Krishnan? Is Krishnan..."

"Private Krishnan's fine, stop interrupting and pay attention. I'm going to put your shoulder back in. It's going to hurt. A lot. Bite on this."

As something pressed against his lips. "I don't want to bite on..."

"Bite on this!" she commanded, and he bit. He could feel her hands on his arm, one under the elbow, the other on his wrist. "Now get ready, on the count of three..."

But she didn't count to three, she pulled hard and fast, and Erik was glad for the thing to bite on after all. And spat it out, eyes watering as he somehow levered himself up on his good arm, fully awake for the first time as his head throbbed and swam, and his shoulder blazed like fire.

"Oh you bitch," he muttered.

"Yes," she agreed, quickly turning the belt he'd been biting on into a sling for his arm. "I'll get some painkiller in a moment. You're going to get into Krishnan's armour suit for a few minutes, it'll warm you up, you were in the water for maybe a minute, and that's enough to make you hypothermic."

Erik realised he was mostly naked, with only briefs to save his modesty. The thought of being naked around any woman he was not currently sleeping with might have bothered him, but with Trace it hardly seemed to matter. He looked about as he half-sat, propped on an elbow as Trace put the belt around his neck and hung his forearm in it, with the expertise of a marine who'd seen much worse.

They were on the shore of the lake, pale and still in the grey light. The lake was long, but its far bank was barely forty metres away. More a widening of the river than a lake, really. Along the lake front were tall green trees, conifers. One spread directly overhead, giving them cover from more aerial vehicles. About, on all sides, were huge, majestic mountains. It would have been a beautiful scene, Erik thought, if he hadn't just crashed his aircraft into that lake, and wasn't currently injured and freezing to death.

"Come on, up," Trace urged, and Erik knew better than to think she might mean 'soon'. He struggled up, accepting her assistance on his good arm. The blood on her face was all down her chin, and dripping onto the front of her jacket.

"Seriously," he told her, "your head..."

"Yes in a minute," she said firmly, leading him across the gravel lakeside. Now fully woken by the pain, Erik realised he was trembling so badly from cold that he could barely stand. Ahead lay an armour suit, on its back beneath trees. Alongside it, Private Krishnan was collecting gear from a supply pouch.

Krishnan looked up at their approach, anxiously. "He okay?" Erik wanted to retort, but couldn't get his jaw to cooperate.

"I think so," said Trace. Both she and Krishnan seemed relatively dry, Erik noted. "Captain, you need to get in the suit. It's still working, environmentals will warm you up."

He got in without protest, a bit like climbing into a coffin. He'd been in one before, sometime a long, long time ago in the Academy, familiarising himself with the crazy marines he'd have to serve with. This one fastened itself automatically to his different measurements, then sealed up with a hiss and crash. Trace put the helmet on, and then he was hearing only his own breathing... save that his toes and fingers began to tingle painfully, and then to burn as the bloodflow resumed. Despite the pain, the warmth was wonderful, and he spent several minutes regathering his memories and thoughts.

That he'd nearly just died — again — he tried not to think about. Maybe he was getting used to it. Certainly it didn't bother him as much as previous close calls had. Perhaps that had something to do with Trace. Despite her ruthless practicality, Trace believed in karma. She seemed to think that she was on some kind of karmic quest, with this mission. Given the number of times he'd found himself miraculously still alive in her presence, when by all rights they should both be dead, he had to think that perhaps she was right.

When Trace popped the suit again, he was no longer shivering. But as he hauled himself one-handed from the armour, he felt utterly drained. Trace gave him back his clothes, and they were hot and moderately dry — from the suit powercell exhaust, he realised, and gratefully pulled them on, very careful of his shoulder. Trace, he saw, had some new, fast staples on her forehead cut, which she was now putting plaster on, then tugging a cap over the lot.

"What happened after we hit?" Erik asked the marines as he dressed.

"Water's not that deep," said Krishnan, adding more equipment to the pack he'd assembled.   Ropes, flares, rations, bottles, visuals, aid kit.   Krishnan was a big guy, much bigger than Erik, who was no lightweight himself.   He had a tight beard and a lean face.   Only young, Erik thought, despite his physical presence. "The Major's suit got kinda wrecked, she got it to the shallows before dropping it, it's still there.   I got out, water was just over my head, I pulled you from the cockpit and kinda walked back here holding you over my head."

"Thanks Private."

Krishnan smiled shakily as he worked.   "Don't mention it, sir.   Thanks for getting us down in one piece."

"My pleasure," said Erik, wincing as he pulled the jacket over his shoulder.

"Those were orbital AAs that killed the flyers?" Trace asked.

Erik nodded.   *Phoenix* must have fired them immediately, sent them looking for something to kill."   There wasn't much ordnance that could get halfway around a planet in ten minutes, then pinpoint a moving target on-site, but a modern Anti-Atmospheric could.   Equipped with crazy thrust, they burned outside the atmosphere at 20Gs, entered the atmosphere white-hot before losing the outer-shell over the target area, leaving the hypersonic warhead at thirty kilometres up and looking for targets.   The original technology was alo, of course, and still a little beyond what humans could make unassisted.

"Amazing they knew which targets to hit," said Krishnan. "With all that jamming, no one could talk to them."

"But we had two marine suits shooting out the back of our sled," Erik reminded him.   "They must have seen it and concluded we were friendly.   It's pretty thin targeting parameters for usual missions, Lieutenant Karle must have reset them to emergency parameters or they'd normally not have engaged."

"Well then sir, please buy Lieutenant Karle a drink for me at the next port of call."

"You know Private," Erik panted, "after something like this, I think we could ditch protocol for a night so you could buy him a drink yourself."

"How long do you think we have before they come looking for us?" Trace asked.

Erik grimaced, trying to get thoughts clear in his spinning head.   She was right to ask him — he was the pilot, this was his expertise more than theirs.   He had to function, for all their sakes. "Hard to tell given we don't know who they were.   I reckon at least ten of them, we saw two killed... good thing with jamming is it goes both ways, they won't know their two flyers are dead, nor where they came down.   They'll search, but..." he nodded at the lake. Water flowed, a strong, eddying current, hiding all sign of their crashed sled.   "They'll see their own wrecks, but they won't see ours here as well until they search harder."

"It won't hold them that long," Trace disagreed, glancing at the overcast sky as she arranged her gear.   It dawned on Erik that with only one suit working, and both marines packing for a hike, they were going to be unarmoured from here.   Even working, marine armour as configured on *Phoenix* had limited range, especially in this terrain.   "The lake's shallow, they'll spot the wreck in a flyby.   We have to put in some distance first, and hope this overcast doesn't break anytime soon."

"Orbital sensors can't penetrate that?" Krishnan asked, also glancing up.

"Not likely," Erik replied.   "It's pretty thick.   Major, what's the plan?"   They were grounded now.   Erik outranked Trace by a full two degrees in the Fleet ranking system, yet with dirt beneath their boots, authority returned to the highest-ranking marine.   Erik could decide objectives and broad approaches, yet in deciding how to achieve them, Trace's word was final.

Trace pulled AR glasses from her pocket, put them on and tapped them a few times, gazing at the mountains up and down the valley.   Evidently the glasses were still working, and showing her navigational cues as she turned her head.   "I got some more information from Styx before we went to see Aristan," she said.   "I asked for her best guess on temple coordinates, for secret stuff the Tahrae didn't want anyone to know about. She knew the Tahrae pretty well, I figured even hacksaws can make guesses. Styx gave me two, and since we came south like I said, we're now pretty close to one of them."

"You want to go there?" Erik asked in disbelief. Not that he thought it was a bad idea. It was just the way she managed to turn this close shave with death into a stroll in the mountains to see an archaeological curiosity.

"Sure," she said, shouldering into her own, smaller pack. "Why not? Aristan chose this planet and this mountain range to meet us. The Dobruta contacted him and he told us to meet him here, of all the places we could have gone. Then he gives us this chip, which turns out to be an old map his people probably couldn't translate. He's looking for this place too, I reckon he thought we could find it for him."

"And… these people who're trying to kill us…" Krishnan said slowly as he caught on.

Trace nodded. "Don't want us finding it. My guess is State Department, but it could be Aristan's parren enemies too, possibly even his own house. Whatever, it doesn't matter now. What matters is we have an old temple to find, and if we weren't attacked, we might never have gotten permission to come and see it, and certainly couldn't do it without others watching. This way, we do. Lucky break."

That last was purely for his and Krishnan's confidence, Erik was sure. Trace was many things, but rarely cocky. She glanced at Erik's bare feet. "Come on, you're going to need a hand getting your boots on."

Their first hike was up the valley, a comfortable walk alongside the river, keeping beneath the trees for cover. They'd left armour and most unnecessarily heavy things behind, in thick undergrowth with extra branches on top — it wouldn't fool anyone who found the submerged cargo sled, but there was no point in making it easy for them either. For Erik, leaving heavy things behind meant body armour, assault rifle and ammunition. His shoulder also made it impossible to carry a pack, which left him feeling unhappily useless on this marine expedition. What he did carry was combat webbing and whatever useful things could be stuffed into its pockets, including his service pistol.

Trace led, with short rifle and pack, looking warily about beneath cap brim and AR glasses. Private Krishnan took the rear, the big man lugging the largest pack, making Erik feel extra guilty for not bearing his share. Soon Trace was leading right and uphill, followed by them meeting the snowline. The snow was thin at first, then got steadily thicker as they gained altitude. Soon it was ankle-deep, and Erik followed carefully in Trace's footsteps as she picked her way up the steepening incline.

Erik saw a few birds, and once they startled something four-legged and goat-like crashing through the undergrowth. But mostly the cold and altitude made for sparse wildlife. This part of Stoya III was only in early autumn too, he reflected. The Neremal Range was enormous, and often cold in summer. A few months later and this way would have been impassible with snow. In mid-winter nothing moved.

As they got higher Erik was surprised how good he felt. The painkiller in his shoulder had worked, and his bruised knee was loosening with the exercise, though there'd be hell to pay after he'd slept and stiffened. He even managed to marvel at the view through occasional gaps in the trees. He'd wanted more colour and beauty from his first downworld visit in four months, and well, here it was, if a little pale and white and cold. It was certainly nothing like you got on a ship or a station, and though the air was nearly painfully cold, it tasted fresh and clean in a way that no synthetically filtered air could ever taste, and smelt of pine and snow.

Trace's path found its way skilfully into a cleft in the valley-side — following the valley up from the base would have been impossible, rocky, sheer and treacherous. But climbing this wooded slope first allowed a hiker to wind her way into the new, smaller valley from higher up, and on a more gentle angle. It was the kind of thing that someone who'd grown up in mountains would know, and seeing her climb like a mountain goat ahead of him, Erik felt some comfort to know that Trace was in her element.

Behind him, Krishnan was steady and powerful, and showing no sign of tiring. He looked slightly bewildered, and almost eager, to find himself on this particular adventure. Erik supposed it was a big deal for a marine private, to be on a two-man operation with Major Thakur herself. Plus the *Phoenix* Captain, of course, but Erik had no illusions about which of the two officers Krishnan was more excited to spend time with up-close. Erik settled into as comfortable a rhythm as he could manage, and concentrated only on putting one foot before and above the other, and climbing.

Slugging their way up the new, high valley, the snow increased to knee-deep, and the trees became smaller, and stunted. Even Trace took a breath, more from sympathy for her struggling Captain, Erik thought as he sat in a roughly-dug snow seat beside her, than from any personal need. They ate rations, drank water that was not quite beginning to freeze, and took in the view for a few minutes longer.

Krishnan heard it first, and looked at Trace. The distant, echoing whine of an approaching flyer. Sitting amidst stunted pines, they weren't likely to get better cover. The sound grew, and then a military flyer howled by, heading for Doma Strana. Echoes from multiple mountains made it sound like three flyers, then one again.

"Different model from what attacked us," said Erik. "I think that's a local, maybe from Troiham. The response time is about right — it's nearly two hours away by flyer." Though fast-response jets could have gotten there sooner. He didn't know if sleepy Stoya III security forces had any of those.

"Could be friendly then?" Krishnan said hopefully.

Trace shook her head. "We don't know what's friendly. We don't know the situation at Doma Strana, if it's still under attack, if it's been occupied. We don't know if local Stoya security are acting in concert with State Department, and my bet is State Department planned the whole thing."

"Dobruta are on our side," Erik panted. "Tavalai don't fight tavalai. State Department might have orchestrated an attack on us, but they'll have made a real effort not to get Dobruta or Pelligavani in the crossfire. My bet is those were parren trying to kill us. Better parren shoot at Dobruta allies than other tavalai."

Trace nodded. "Makes sense. State Department has more leverage outside tavalai space than inside it, they're the foreign affairs division." She raised small binoculars to peer back down the way they'd come. In the distance, the flyer was now circling, the engine wail not fading.

"Sounds like they found the wrecks," Krishnan observed. "If the jamming's stopped, I bet *Phoenix* will be here soon. Even on silent coms, Styx could break in and listen to what these guys are saying."

"And if State Department are still listening in," said Trace, "the moment we call for help they could lob a missile on our coms location and there'd be nothing *Phoenix* could do about it." She glanced back over her shoulder to the peaks above. "Nice thing about this temple, if it exists, is that it should give protection from artillery, and could be defensible."

"With three people?" Erik asked.

"*Could* be," Trace repeated. "Better than a valley floor, anyway."

"You think First Squad are okay?" Krishnan wondered.

"Depends how many of those missiles followed us instead of going into the cargo room." Trace retrained her binoculars on the slopes below. "They didn't have the biggest charge, so in full armour everyone might still be okay even if a few went in. Can't do anything about it here." Krishnan nodded slowly. Evidently he knew better than to expect more concern from his Commander here. All of her marines knew that she cared for them. They also knew that she didn't waste time worrying about things she couldn't help while the mission was still on, no matter how upsetting the possibilities.

"See, here we go." Trace pointed down the mountain. "We're being followed." Krishnan frowned, squinting. Trace handed him the binoculars, still pointing. "That lower ridge, by the big brown rock. We left single-file tracks there. They were still single file ten minutes ago. Now they're double."

"Oh yeah," Krishnan said grimly as he peered. "Not great fieldcraft."

"No. Not unless they want us to know they're after us." Trace took a final swig of her water bottle, preparing to leave.

Krishnan offered the binoculars to Erik. "I'll take your word for it," Erik told him. "Why would they want us to know they're after us?"

"Make us make a mistake," said Krishnan, heaving himself, his heavy pack and rifle from the snow. "Maybe panic us into calling for help, draw an arty strike on our heads, like the Major says."

"Hang on," said Erik as he struggled up after them, ignoring Krishnan's offered hand. "If these guys were with those guys in the flyers," and he pointed with his good hand toward the sound of the circling flyer down the valley. It now sounded as though it might be landing. "Wouldn't they just call an airstrike on us themselves? Or get a lift up the mountain, instead of hiking up?"

"Yep," said Trace. "I'm guessing parren again, like the ones who tried to kill us. Working with State Department, but not aligned with local security. Probably came after us by ground skimmer, we wouldn't have heard it from up here. State Department probably helped them to Stoya quietly, under local security's nose. Kill us, remove State Department's problem without tavalai having to get their hands dirty."

It made sense, Erik thought. Tavalai considered themselves civilised and peaceful. When they wanted things done that were neither civilised nor peaceful, they turned to alien allies with less fragile sensibilities.

Trace resumed walking, straight uphill, slogging through the snow. "So at least these guys won't have air support any longer," Erik surmised. "If the ones who attacked us had to run before local security got them.   Local security would be protecting the Pelligavani at all costs."

"Sure, but we can't bet that local security doesn't have State Department moles as well," Trace cautioned.   "I want to find this damn temple.   Styx's map says we're real close, but it might be pretty high."

And deliberately hidden for over twenty five thousand years, Erik could have added, had the spare breath in his lungs not disappeared with the resumption of climbing.   If no one had seen it since then, how the hell were three spaceship crew going to do it with no specialised equipment?

Trace turned them left off the valley, and Erik realised with dismay that she was taking them up a sheer wall of broken rock ahead.   Trace saw the look on his face.   "It's worse every other way," she told him, adjusting the rifle strap around her neck, pulling it close and tight across her chest, muzzle up and butt down so it couldn't knock her out cold in a fall.   "Trust me.   How's your arm?"

Erik flexed it.   It hurt, but the shoulder was still numb with painkiller.   "I think it's okay.   It's the third time I've dislocated it, it gets function back faster if you've done it before."

"I know," said Trace.   "I saw in your medical records."

"Checking up on me?" Erik panted.

"It's my job," said Trace, eyeing the rugged slope.   It was short of vertical by perhaps ten degrees, with lots of rough rock-face and ledges for footing.   "Just try not to extend too much."

And she astonished Erik utterly by pressing both hands together before her lips, nodding her head and murmuring something beneath her breath.   Erik looked at Krishnan, and found him equally bewildered.

"Is that a prayer?" Erik asked when she'd finished.

"My people believe there's karmic fortune in mountains," said Trace.   "Every rock-face tells a story, every valley hides a secret.   You can see time itself shaped in these rocks, if you look. Come on."

The rocks were too steep for snow to accumulate, and Trace climbed quickly, hands and feet finding no difficulty on holds as simple for her as a ladder. Erik followed less certainly, trying to use his right hand as little as possible, and avoid long reaches over his head. Soon he was high, and getting higher, as Trace stopped above him, and calmly advised on where to put his hand and feet.

The cold had become very cold, and the wind stung Erik's cheeks above the thick, high collar of his jacket. Thank god for spacer insulation, he thought. None of them were truly dressed for this kind of cold, but with such well-insulated clothes, and constant activity, they'd stay warm for a while yet.

By the time he reached the top, he was exhausted, dizzy and in pain. He dropped beside Trace, gasping and fumbling for a bottle, as Krishnan pulled himself up next. When Erik looked up, he could see they'd barely made the top of the foothills that skirted a truly huge peak. It disappeared into cloud above, a thick mist that swirled and blew, as the mountain made its own weather. It had to be nearly midday, but suddenly everything looked dark. From their current position, there was a route along the ridge, Erik saw, with sheer drops on either side. Then a massive rock face, too steep for snow, disappearing into cloud.

"That's Mount Kosik," said Trace, looking instead down below for signs of pursuit. "Styx says the Tahrae worshipped it."

"How would Styx know what worship looks like?" Erik muttered past his drink bottle. He handed it to Trace, who swigged it.

"Don't know," she said, handing it back. "But it seems to me that if you were going to put a sacred meditation temple anywhere, it'd be on that thing."

"Major," volunteered Krishnan, "begging your pardon, but if we have to climb that, we're screwed."

"It goes up to thirteen thousand metres, Private," Trace admonished him. "You'd need a spacesuit on the summit. But Styx's coordinates say about a kilometre up this ridge. And I'm no engineer, but I reckon that little shoulder there looks just perfect."

Erik looked. Sure enough, about a kilometre along and above, the ridge was interrupted by a vertical rock face, before resuming. Inside that vertical rock face, he thought... if you hollowed it out? Yeah, heck of a view. And the flat top could have made for a decent landing pad, if you accounted for the ridiculous windshear off the mountain behind when the weather turned bad. As it seemed to be turning now.

"I don't think I can climb that last bit," said Erik. "That's vertical."

"That's why god invented rope," Trace quipped. "Come on, you good?"

"Major!" said Krishnan, pointing down behind. She and Erik looked. Even without binoculars, Erik could see small, dark figures making their way toward the foot of the rocks they'd just climbed. "Worth a shot?" Krishnan suggested, fingering his rifle strap.

"Five hundred metres," said Trace, with a critical eye. "Wind's picking up. The rifle's only certain to about three hundred and fifty when it's still and flat. If we sat here for five minutes and expended ammunition we might hit one or two, but the weather's turning. Let's go."

Erik did not enjoy the next bit at all. The ridge was more up than straight, and mostly on a knife-edge wide enough only for one person. On either side, an increasingly sheer and alarming drop, and now the wind was beginning to really blow, forcing even Trace to occasionally pause and crouch. Erik took his arm from the sling for balance, ignoring his shoulder's painful protests. On any ledge large enough for his boot, snow had accumulated, though the wind now whipped it away, and Trace's preceding boot cleared some more on purpose.

It seemed to take an age, but finally they reached the foot of the rocky shoulder. It was as vertical as Erik had feared — not shale or loose stone with many grips, but granite with only slim ledges and grooves for possible finger and toe holds. One look and Erik could not deny it any longer — the prospect of climbing this, in the wind that was building, frightened him more than combat.

"Well," said Trace, voice raised against the wind, "not getting up there in boots." There was more space here at the base, and she sat, and pulled at the straps. "Got some spray-on?" she asked

Krishnan, who knelt to rummage in his pack, then produced a can of spray. Trace pulled off her socks, stuffed them into her pockets, and applied the spray to her feet and toes. It formed a thin, almost plastic film — an adhesive and insulator, marines and spacers both used it to protect from cold and frostbite. Then Trace did the same to her hands and fingers.

"I'll take your boots," said Krishnan, doing that.

"Rope," said Trace, and he gave her that, the two marines all business in preparation.

"Major," Erik attempted. Wanting to call her Trace, but unable in the presence of a private. "Are you sure? Is it worth it?"

"This world used to be parren," said Trace as she worked. "They never occupied it much, never really explored, just built some temples and a few cities on the lowlands. Same when the tavalai got here — tavalai don't like the cold. They've got a lot of worlds, they never bothered much with this one. If there was a place you could hide mountain temples in for that long, it would be here."

"What if Styx was wrong?" Erik persisted.

Trace studied him. Probably she saw the fear there. Erik was beyond caring. She'd seen nearly everything else by now, why not this as well? "If she's wrong," said Trace, "or if I don't make it down, then use coms and call *Phoenix*. You might even get assistance before a missile, I'd reckon you're a fifty-fifty chance. But I've got a feeling about this one, I grew up in mountains and something about this place has just felt since I got here..." she looked about, at treacherous drops and stunning views, with an affection that Erik would never understand, "...like coming home."

Erik was seized by the strong urge to embrace her. But that was something he could *certainly* never do before a private. And it was a revelation to him, just how much of his current fear was not just being perched on a precarious ledge in strong wind and one functioning arm, with pursuers likely trying to kill them. Much of this fear was not for himself at all. It was for her.

And then she was gone, with that damnable refusal of hers to contemplate an emotional moment where it might interfere with an ongoing job, scampering up the apparently sheer rock wall like some hook-clawed climbing insect.   All Kulina learned to climb, Erik knew, but he'd never seen it quite like this.   This was the expertise of someone who'd been scaling sheer cliffs since childhood.   And it was a skill once learned, apparently not forgotten.

"Sergeant Kunoz says she scares the shit out of the officers," Krishnan muttered, apparently not thrilled with this himself.   And not caring to call him 'Captain', in this particular moment.   "None of them want to be the one with her at the moment she does something crazy and gets herself killed."

Erik knew he should have reprimanded the younger man.   It was no way to speak of your commanding officer, particularly with your ship's captain.   But right then they were all feeling very small, frail and human… or he and Krishnan were.   And he knew exactly what the Private was talking about.

"She'll be fine," he said, as much to calm himself as the other man.   Already above him, Trace was ten metres up and moving fast. "She's done this a thousand times."

Erik had thought it might take twenty minutes' careful climbing to scale the wall, but Trace did it in five.   Showed what he knew about climbing, Erik thought, as Krishnan took prone position behind some covering rock, and sighted his rifle down the ridge they'd climbed.   He had a sight on the rifle, so Erik took the binoculars and stared.   And after many long, freezing minutes, finally saw a dark figure clambering up the ridge.

"Can't see what species for sure," Erik muttered.

"Sure as hell not tavalai," Krishnan replied, adjusting his sight for a long-range shot.   "Parren look pretty much like humans from range."

Erik threw a glance back up the cliff Trace had scaled. She'd taken a rope, and said she'd find a way to use it to get them up.   Where the hell was she?

Something smacked loudly off the rock behind him, simultaneous to the shweet! of a bullet, and he ducked, swearing. "Stay down Captain!" said Krishnan.   "Just our luck, the fuckers have longer range rifles than we do.   Where is that bastard?"

Another shot, this one further away. "I see him," Krishnan announced, unflinching. "He's out of range too, 'specially in these crosswinds." He fired, a single shot, then pulled back as another shot hit nearby rocks. "I'm not going to hit much, but I can slow them down."

"What odds they've got grenade launchers?" Erik asked, keeping low. His service pistol would be even less use than Krishnan's rifle at these ranges.

"Probably much worse than that, sir." Another shot. "Otherwise they wouldn't be coming on — as soon as they get close enough, I can just pick them off on this ridge. I reckon they're just getting close enough to use their heavier stuff."

Which would clear out the base of this cliff pretty quickly, Erik thought. He cast a desperate glance back up the cliff. Where was Trace's rope? Where was Trace?

He was still wondering ten minutes later, as Krishnan reported two hits for uncertain results, but the attackers kept coming, scrambling fast from cover to limited cover. Then a voice spoke behind them, muffled. "Boys! This way, move!"

Erik spun, and saw only blank rock in the darkening gloom. Blank rock, and a small, dark opening at the base of the rock that hadn't been there before. He blinked in astonishment, then whacked Krishnan on the shoulder. "Private! Let's go!"

Erik got his feet into the opening and slid… his boots found empty air, and he pushed through on raw trust… and gasped as boots hit a hard floor. The surrounding rock was dark, lit only by a single green glow-stick. The stick was clipped neatly to Trace's collar, gleaming reflection in the lenses of her AR glasses beneath her cap brim. About her, about *them*, was a corridor, carved in rock.

Krishnan came sliding through, more awkwardly than Erik with his pack and weapon, as Erik steadied him one-handed. Trace touched a small panel on a wall, and the opening vanished, plunging them back into green-lit darkness. Erik stared at Trace in relief and incredulity.

Trace grinned at him, looking suddenly like a mischievous little girl who'd discovered a secret way to sneak somewhere she wasn't allowed.   "Can you believe it?" she asked incredulously, nearly giggling.   "This place is *amazing!*"

Erik laughed, and this time he *did* hug her.   She surprised him by hugging him back, and showing no sign of minding.   "Come on!" she gushed, with a couple of hearty whacks on the delighted Krishnan's shoulder.   "I only rushed through on my way back down, but there's a chamber here that looks *really* promising!   This way!"

CHAPTER 6

Barely twenty minutes after release, following a gut wrenching, high-G descent, *Phoenix* combat shuttle PH-3 came down hard on the mid-level landing pad on Doma Strana's main face that Echo Platoon were now insisting was best.

Alpha Platoon poured out the back, unracking in rows, local tacnet unfolding on visors as Squad Sergeants told them where to go. As soon as Lieutenant Dale was out, Lieutenant Jersey lifted PH-3 in a roar of thrusters that would have been dangerous at this proximity for unarmoured humans, but was no trouble for Dale in his armour. He thumped through the waves of hot exhaust, observing *Phoenix* and *Makimakala* guards on higher and lower platforms up and down the cliff face, watching the leaden skies.

Inside the doorway was Lieutenant Hausler — PH-1 was down on the same pad, the current policy being two airborne and one landed for fast extraction. Hausler looked stiff and uncomfortable, a marked change from his usual languid cool, his flightsuit collar high against the chill through the door.

"Lieutenant Hausler," said Dale with respect, popping his visor. A spacer lieutenant technically outranked a marine lieutenant, but grounded on a planet, command rested with the highest-ranked marine. Amongst *Phoenix* marines, in the Major's absence, that always meant Dale.

"Lieutenant Dale," Hausler said tightly. "Shuttle sitrep, we are two up and one down, as you've seen. Lieutenant Zhi deems the higher and lower pads unsecure at this time, so we're sticking to this one and the two adjoining. We've positively IDed the enemy shuttles as parren-class, they have no human designation we're aware of, perhaps slightly below our own in capability.

"Upon first contact I ordered PH-4 into a tactical retreat with PH-1, where we evaded enemy contact in the mountains. I considered the risk to *Phoenix* assets unreasonable in the circumstances — we could have destroyed several enemy vehicles but at the almost certain loss of at least one of our own given the numbers against us.   *Phoenix* only has three combat shuttles remaining, given our broader circumstances I judged that we could not afford to lose another for little strategic gain, as Lieutenant Zhi held a good cover position in Doma Strana from which he would prove difficult to dislodge."

Dale smiled grimly and held up a forestalling hand. "Lieutenant, you did the right thing.   We're short on shuttles as it is, and Zhi didn't need you."

Hausler didn't look any happier.   It was, of course, why he was uncomfortable — he felt he'd flown off and left his marines in danger.   Which he had.   But sometimes there was no other choice. "Echo marines destroyed one enemy vehicle on a landing pad, but the rest got away before the local security arrived.   We think there were about fourteen of them, all told.   We've got six local security also now airborne, as you've also seen.   We don't trust them and we're keeping an eye on them, but Kulid-One and Two have talked to them and say they seem okay.   Both the tavalai shuttles also evaded as we did, we couldn't talk to them because of all the jamming.   We still can't."

Dale nodded grimly, as several Echo marines came running in, then waited nearby — a briefing from Lieutenant Zhi, Dale thought.   "Yeah what's with that jamming?" he asked.   "Lieutenant Jersey was saying on the way down that she couldn't talk to anyone."

"We're not sure," Hausler confirmed.   "But the jamming's still going on.   It's an unusual type, we're not having much luck tracking it.   So much of the tech out this far from human space is strange to us, but even *Makimakala*'s people can't pinpoint it. We're still searching."

"And still no sign of where the Captain and the Major went?"

"Nothing yet.   The local security say they've got vehicles out looking for them, but with the jamming we can't talk to them. The Captain's a damn good pilot in anything.   If I were him I'd have put it down somewhere and hid.   PH-3 is searching for them now…"

"We saw her coming in," Dale confirmed. "Jersey's gone to join her."

"Lots of good hiding places in the mountains," said Hausler, "and jamming works both ways — an enemy vehicle that found them couldn't call for help. Plus the Major and Private Krishnan were fully armoured, and in the mountains even combat shuttles can't just engage that from range. They'd have to get in close, and marines can shoot shuttles down real easy when that happens."

Dale wasn't sure about the 'real easy' bit, but then shuttle pilots always felt their vulnerability more acutely when engaging well armed and grounded targets. Hopefully whoever was chasing the Captain and the Major would feel the same. "Good," he told Hausler. Which meant 'awful', and not good at all. "Stay in your ship, Lieutenant, I'm sure you'll be needed soon."

"Look, Ty," said Hausler. "We've got two *Makimakala* shuttles and six local security doing overhead orbits, that's plenty of local security, I should get out there and help look for the Captain and…"

"We can't trust local security," Dale said firmly. "We're only just starting to trust *Makimakala*, and they've got people down here too. We need at least one of our own shuttles on immediate standby in case we need mobility fast, and with the jamming, we can't talk to Tif or Jersey if we need them back here."

Hausler looked displeased. He nodded, tucked up his collar against the cold, and went back out to his ship. Dale nodded to the Echo marine and his partner who'd come down to meet him, and they walked together up an adjoining, black stone hallway.

"The LT's okay and no casualties in Echo," said Lance-Corporal Koch. Koch was leader of Second Section in Zhi's First Squad. It was the Major's policy that briefings and catch-ups should be left to lower-ranked marines, leaving officers to their commands instead of playing errand boy. "We were heading to the upper cargo level, a scheduled meeting with Aristan. Then the attack happened, we got shut in, we had incoming missiles on scan, the Major got the Captain out on a cargo runner… you saw all that from *Phoenix*?"

"Yes, but continue."

"Yessir... well the missiles seemed to chase the cargo runner, the Major must have figured the Captain was the target. We took a couple of hits in the cargo room but nothing direct, we've got some damaged armour but nothing more. Finally managed to blow through those fucking reinforced doors, you wouldn't believe how heavy they are... and then the enemy flyers were coming down on the higher pads.

"We had some firefights in the corridors, nothing conclusive, they didn't seem to get anywhere and we killed six of them that we saw."

"What were they?" Dale asked.

"Parren. Lighter armour, pretty advanced but... well, you pick on Koshaims with light armour, you get fucked up. Then they left and ran. The LT's got no idea what they were after, I mean if they were after the Captain, well he left, so why did they then come and land here?" Dale nodded grimly, thinking. "The froggies lost a guy, none of the civvies were hurt..."

"*Makimakala* lost a karasai?" Dale pressed.

"Yes sir."

"Send our condolences." The young Corporal blinked at him. "I mean it. We're allies, we've fought battles together. We show respect." It wasn't Dale's instinct at all, but it was what the Major would have done. With her missing, Dale felt there was nothing more important than to run Phoenix Company as she would, and let everyone see it.

"Yes sir," said Koch. "Sir... Lisbeth's missing."

Dale stopped, and rounded on Koch. "She's *what*?"

"Missing, sir. She was taking cover with the Furball and some of the froggie civs, Leech and Rakowski were there, they say someone cut the power and something got into the room, but they didn't get a clear look. When the power came back on, Lisbeth was gone. We're searching now, the Furball's pretty upset."

Dale advanced a step on the Corporal. "And you didn't think to tell me this *first*?"

"I was… I was going to…" Koch swallowed. "Sorry sir, I thought tacticals first, then…"

"Shit," said Dale, with feeling. "No blood or sign of struggle?"

"No sir. Looks like an abduction."

"*Shit!*" With more feeling this time. "I *knew* we shouldn't have let her come down here… what's coms like in here?"

"Um… actually better inside the rock than outside, I think that's Ensign Uno's work, he's got us patched into the local coms systems in Doma Strana. But as soon as we go outside, static. We've got word to the local security and *Makimakala* shuttles, told them not to let anyone leave. As far as I know, no one has."

"God damn it," Dale snarled, resuming his armoured stride. "When we get the Captain back, he's going to kill us."

"Major," Krishnan said, voice low in the echoing stone passage as they walked. "Would you like your boots back?"

"Yeah in a minute, Kel." It was his nickname, Erik vaguely recalled — Kelvin Krishnan, a bit tame by marine standards. But Krishnan had only been in the service for a year, and on *Phoenix* for less than that, so likely he'd acquire a more colourful one before long.

"How did you get in?" Erik wondered. "Can't those guys after us just get in the same way?"

"No chance," said Trace with certainty. "Look, I don't know what's going on, but when I started using these glasses up the top, an icon appeared and led me to a hidden hatch… I think the hatch was using holographic projection to camouflage itself, like the one you came through, but it's damn tough and will take a lot of explosive. So I figure that buys us some time.

"The glasses started transmitting… I know, they interact with local networks, but this was different. They're still doing it. I think whatever Styx loaded onto them when she sent me the coordinates are working as some kind of code, talking to these local systems, opening doors."

"Well she's drysine," said Erik. "The temple is Tahrae, they worshipped the drysines."

"Used drysine technology to build it," Trace added meaningfully. "So of course Styx can talk to it."

"Think she uploaded that onto your glasses on purpose?" Erik asked. "Without telling you?"

"Wouldn't care if she did," Trace admitted. "In fact I'll give her a fucking kiss when I get back."

Private Krishnan stifled a laugh. "I'm sure she'll love that, Major."

The corridor was much like the ones in Doma Strana — black and smooth, but without any functioning light, and no side doorways that Erik could see. "You think there's some kind of central computer system?" Erik wondered. "Still functioning after all this time?"

"It's not impossible," Trace admitted. "But the door functions could be just isolated. Doma Strana piped sunlight in from outside, the power requirements aren't big, if they used solar recharge they'd keep running indefinitely."

"Definitely some kinda breeze in here," Krishnan observed, smelling the air. "I guess it's so windy, they could just have small openings, like ventilation. Wouldn't take any power."

"Sure as hell no heating," said Erik, flexing his aching shoulder. It was a relief to be out of the wind, but still the temperature was below freezing, their breath pluming before them. "So we're thinking this place is... twenty six thousand years old?"

"Built about the same time as Doma Strana," Trace agreed, leading them left up an oddly-shaped, but perfectly regular, spiralling staircase. "Not hard to build without anyone noticing you're building it, using drysine cutting tools and taking centuries to do it. Whatever plan was behind this place, it was long-term."

"A plan for what?" Krishnan murmured, looking nervous that the Major was leading up the staircase with her weapon still slung. Trace seemed certain this temple was deserted.

"My guess?" said Trace. "Secrets."

They emerged into a high-ceilinged room, lit by a single beam of white light from a small, high window. That beam of cold sunlight made a diagonal white stripe across the smooth black stone. It added to other white, diagonal stripes within the stone itself — white marble of some kind, Erik thought. The natural striations within the mountain, polished and incorporated into this chamber's design, like white stripes on a black tiger. The effect was surreal, and austerely beautiful.

"Here," said Trace, stepping on silent, bare feet into the middle of the chamber, pulling off the cap and stowing it in a pocket to clear her vision completely. "The glasses are showing me icons. There's low intensity communication happening between them and the chamber... over here it's showing me a planet." She pointed at one featureless wall. "And over here another planet." Pointing another way. "There's some kind of script... it doesn't look like the main parren stuff, it could be Klyran, I don't recognise it."

The ceiling above made a high dome. Erik thought it looked like photographs he'd seen of very old Christian churches from Earth.

"Were there any other passages the way you came down?" Erik asked, searching for any sign of a door. "Or other icons on your glasses, showing other ways to go? I mean it has to be larger than just this room and some vertical levels and stairways, doesn't it?"

"Yeah," said Trace, looking around in wonderment. Their voices echoed beneath the cold, silent stone. "Unless we're missing something right here. Private, hand me my boots."

Krishnan did that, and she prepared one for her foot while wandering to a new wall... and something hissed. Then a section of wall began to move. "Cover!" Trace demanded, moving back to another wall and unslinging her rifle fast, while Krishnan did the same against the opposite wall, and Erik pulled his service pistol.

There followed a hush of stale-smelling air, not quite a breeze, just a movement, a breath upon the skin. The panel turned aside, on bearings that shuddered only a little with the wear of millennia. Then stopped, with a soft, final thud. Krishnan pulled small night-vision goggles from his pocket, but paused as faint lighting flickered down a passageway beyond, as though beckoning them in.

"Oh no *way*," he breathed.

"Does it look clear to you?" Trace asked quietly, unable to see the whole way down from her position.

"Clear from here," Krishnan replied.

"Same here," Erik echoed. And Trace put her rifle carefully on the floor, and resumed pulling her boots on. "We're going in?"

"You bet your ass we're going in," said Trace, with something approaching excitement.

Erik grinned, somehow finding her enthusiasm infectious. "Major, just a thought… I don't know if you've played VR games at all?"

"Only training sims, you know that."

"Well, in any of the games I used to play, back in another life when I had time for fun and games? We go in there, we'll get attacked by ancient robots, booby traps and zombies before we've gone ten yards."

"Well, you should be an expert then," said Trace.

"Does that mean I get to take point?"

"Hell no," Trace replied, finishing her other boot and taking up her rifle. "This one's for the marines. You stay between us and back three steps. Private, left and right, real slow and careful."

"Major," Krishnan agreed, moving cautiously forward with rifle ready, peering down the corridor. Trace came up on his right, glancing back at Erik to judge his spacing, then nodding when Erik moved to the correct spot. Erik switched the pistol to his left hand, grimacing at a flash of pain in his shoulder.

"I'm serious about those booby traps," Erik murmured, trying not to make an echo down the corridor. "These systems are still working after twenty six thousand years. That means they're built not to age. They could have put anything into these walls."

"They wouldn't have opened the doors," Trace said confidently. "They'd have locked us out, and booby trapped the waiting room. Too risky to booby trap the corridors. Things stop working after so much time, a wall or a locked door is the best defence, no moving parts to fail." She gestured them forward.

"Maybe it just wants us inside to trap us here for the next twenty six thousand years," Krishnan murmured, walking carefully, his rifle ready. "Maybe *that's* the trap."

"Could be," Trace agreed. "But Styx has this location now, and our enemies do too. This place has officially been discovered. We have to take advantage of being the first inside."

The corridor ended in a stairway, not far from the entrance, but invisible in the blackness until they were close. Trace and Krishnan climbed on either side, rifles ready, while Erik remained several steps behind and toward Trace's side of the hallway.

Atop the stairs, the black stone opened into a tall, circular chamber, and Trace pocketed her glow-stick in favour of a wide-beam flashlight which she clipped to the side of her rifle. Krishnan did similar, panning wide to reveal inlaid patterns on the stone walls, and crumpled cloth about the perimeter of a circle on the floor.

Erik stared at the circle, creeping forward as the two marines made a circuit of the walls. The floor circle was inlaid with gold, and contained a seven-pointed star and scrawling, alien script. At each point of the star lay crumpled cloth, black and folded, and appearing to contain... something. As he came closer, crouching to peer in the poor light, he saw that the contents of the cloth were bones, and the cloths themselves were dark parren cloaks of the kind worn by Aristan and his acolytes.

"Seven bodies," he told the others quietly, and his voice echoed in that ancient hush. So many millennia since words had been spoken in this place. Before each of the bodies lay a staff, also like Aristan had held. Erik reached and tried to pull one of them apart — traditional parren pole-arms were one-third blade beneath the deceptive sheath. But the sheath would not budge. "They've got their koren with them. They're ceremonial weapons, so these guys would be acolytes of some kind. Tahrae, I imagine."

"Ceremonial deaths," Trace replied, sweeping her flashlight over them from a wall. "I don't know what the seven-pointed star is.   But there's seven of them, and they're entombed in here, so maybe a ritual suicide."

"Guardians," Krishnan murmured.   "Sealed in to guard whatever's here, forever.   Maybe they just sat here meditating until they starved."

"Quite possibly," said Trace.   "Sounds like the kind of thing Tahrae would do."

Krishnan frowned, still circling.   "This part of the wall here looks like a curtain."   As his light illuminated it properly for the first time.   He crept toward it.

"Careful with those bodies," Trace told Erik.   "Plenty of cultures don't like people interfering with the dead.   If they'll booby trap anything, it could be corpses."

"I hear you," said Erik.   He gave up trying to remove a pole-arm sheath.   Rusted tight, he thought.   There was so little moisture in this air, yet still the blades had rusted, a fractional degree every thousand years.   After so many thousands of years, there'd be nothing left.   The lacquered wood shafts fared better, treated against moisture and bacteria, but even they looked dried and stale.   Erik prodded gently at the inside of a paper-thin remnant of cloak sleeve, and a bone powdered at his touch, crumbling on the floor like sand.

"Whoa!" shouted Krishnan, leaping back from the curtain-section of wall he'd opened, as Erik fell flat and Trace braced herself for shooting.   In the glare of flashlights, the swinging curtain revealed a familiar, single red eye, fronting a big, armoured, spider-like body.

For a long, heart-pounding moment, the three humans stayed dead-still, braced for shooting as Krishnan's echo faded from the walls.   A while later, no one had died, and Erik's heart began to recover.   "Drysine drone," he said, levering himself carefully off the floor with his good arm.   His right shoulder throbbed once more, jarred in the fall to the floor.   "Looks dead."

Trace crept forward around the wall, then peered past the curtain at close range.   "I don't know if they're capable of playing possum," she murmured.   "Drones aren't that subtle."

"It's drysine," Erik disagreed, pistol still pointed at the drone's single eye. For whatever good it would do. "If any hacksaws could be subtle, drysines could."

"Usually they make some kind of noise, just running," Trace added, listening closely. "Even drysine powerplants aren't advanced enough to be quiet. This one's dead silent. I think he's gone."

"Could have gone into some kind of shutdown mode," Krishnan disagreed. His voice was shaky, suggesting he'd received the worst fright. Abruptly face-to-face with a drysine drone, unarmoured, was a death sentence if it was live and hostile. "And that signal from your glasses could be about to wake it up, Major."

"That's possible too," Trace admitted. "I just don't know how even one of these things could still be alive that long. There might be a power recharge here somewhere, but there's no powerplant, only very light solar, far too weak to power this monster. The ones in Argitori were in good condition because they'd never gone into shutdown, they'd constantly repaired themselves. And the ones in the Tartarus were in total vacuum — no rust, no bacteria, no decay. This one's been sealed into an atmosphere with at least a little moisture in it for twenty thousand years with no power. The steel's too advanced to rust, but I'd say his insides are dead and rotting."

It sounded obvious when put like that, with Trace's usual calm logic. Krishnan took a deep breath, and lowered his rifle. "So why's the drone here then?" He looked at the seven ancient bodies about the star on the floor, then back to the drone. "Guarding them? Making sure none of them changed their mind about suicide, tried to get out?"

"Maybe," said Trace, moving past the curtain and into the small alcove with the dead machine, peering closely about at the walls. "Unless we find some kind of record, I'm not sure there's any way to know."

Erik peered more closely at something amidst the robes, and the powdered white bone of a collapsed skull. It looked like a blob of black rubber, withered with age, but when he touched it, it fell apart in microscopic strands, and faded to dust.

"This is cybernetic," said Erik. "They had some kind of cybernetic uplink implants, hard to tell what they were, they're so old. I'm no augment specialist, but it looks completely different from what we have."

"The Tahrae worked hand in glove with the machines," said Trace. "Makes sense they'd take augments from them too."

"No way they'd trust just any parren with advanced network augments," Erik murmured. "The drysines' network technology was the biggest edge they had on organics. They'd only share with the most trustworthy. These guys were the elite, the ones the machines trusted." He stared at the drone, crouched and thinking. "I think they ran here. They were losing the war, the Machine Age was ending, the drysines and Tahrae were both being slaughtered. Their own people had turned against them. Everything they'd known was about to become extinct."

Trace nodded slowly, peering at a small hole in a wall. "Here's something," she said. "Looks like a lens." She took off her AR glasses, and held them before the hole where the tiny projector could be directly in line. "Come on Styx, do your thing."

Something flashed on her glasses, then a series of thin lasers beamed from the surrounding walls. Caught in their midst, Erik stared, then stood and moved back to a wall as the holography resolved into a humanoid figure. Resolution was limited, the holograph little more than a moving line drawing, in glowing blue light. It resolved even now into a parren face, rotating even now to face them... or to face Trace, Erik thought, as she occupied the location that had activated the hologram. The eyes were indigo, like most parren, wide and haunting. The hairless scalp was covered with a tight skullcap, and his collar was wide. Erik wondered how it was possible to read significance into clothing, given how many times fashions could change in twenty five thousand years.

The humans stared... and Erik realised that if there was sound, they were going to need translation. He fumbled for his pocket unit, a constant habit for a commander amongst aliens, and flipped it on just in time.

The parren began speaking, in strong alien vowels that echoed within the stone. But the translator gave only static. "Dammit, it doesn't understand the tongue!" Erik exclaimed.

"Must be Klyran," said Trace, putting her glasses back on and blinking on icons. "Come on Styx, don't tell me you forgot to load a translator function…" And she nearly grinned in amazement, as Erik's translator began speaking English. Erik spared an incredulous glance, and Trace nodded affirmation — Styx had indeed loaded a Klyran translator to the glasses, having only just figured out that language herself, and perhaps anticipating an encounter like this. Romki insisted that 'genius' was a completely inadequate term to describe what Styx was, and again, he seemed correct.

"…I do not know how to do more than doubt," the translator intoned, without emotion. The parren's voice held far more feeling than that. The alien words seemed tired, almost drained. *"We stare at the abyss, and I see blackness. Blackness everywhere. I knew only to follow the path of hope and harmony. I never sought this conflict. I never sought this slaughter. I know that history will not know this of me. That my enemies will seek to erase all knowledge of who I am. Who I was."*

"Drakhil!" Erik breathed. "It's Drakhil, it has to be!"

"To any who may find this, know only that I followed the path. I have many regrets, but no apologies. What I did, I did for the greater harmony. The harmony that lies beyond one's people. Beyond one's faith. Beyond one's self. I was on the path, and together, the machines and I, we would have reached it. Perhaps in some distant time, far from now. But the path was laid, and it would have lain completed, in time. Given time." A deep, holographic sigh. *"But time was not granted. The coming of the great harmony has been delayed, perhaps forever. Or perhaps you, whomever you are who reach this, and hear this, can restore the path. It takes only a will. Unbending. Unbreaking. Forever."*

Those wide, alien eyes seemed to stare through stone.   Erik took a quick glance at Trace, emerged from the alcove beside him, and found her mesmerised.   *"Such a heaven shall not be in my time. Nor shall the first stone on its path be laid by me.   But perhaps, I think, by others.   In time.   The machines tell me that we have barely days until the end.   Our bases fall, our fleets shrink.   Our losses long ago became unsustainable.   They will chase us until the ends of the universe.   No one will hide us.   Nowhere is safe.   Everything that we are, that we were, is fated to die.*

"But there is harmony in hope.   There is harmony in continuations.   In seeds, that planted deep, will one day grow in the rain.   Know that I have planted seeds.   Most cannot be found.   Will not be found.   The galaxy is vast, and the summer rains wash away all trails.   This information cannot be granted to just anyone.   Only the worthy can know.

"If you are listening to this message, then you, dear listener, are worthy.   Follow the trail, as you have followed this one.   For I have written a diary.   Five copies I have made."   Drakhil raised five fingers, in case there was any doubt.   *"Their locations can be found in the data that follows.   Be patient.   Once found, the diaries reveal much else.   Secrets, beyond imagining.   Secrets to things that must now be destroyed, and fall to ruin, least they come into the hands of unworthy enemies.   Resurrect them, you can.   In the right hands, they could restore harmony to the Spiral, and set us all on the path to peace."*

Drakhil's lips moved, in a faint, bloodless smile.   *"To be harmony is to accept one's fate, and not complain.   One's fate is not one's to choose.   Know this, and across all this expanse of time and space, we shall be brothers, you and I."*

CHAPTER 7

Commander Nalben was waiting for Dale at the broad, transparent entrance to the high landing platform. He was flanked by several of his karasai, arms folded and unbothered by the approach of the Alpha Platoon marines.

"Lieutenant," said Nalben, with what Dale had learned to recognise as a tavalai frown. "Are you sure it comes from here?"

"Very sure," Dale growled.

"I must insist against *any* violent action," said Nalben. "Believe me I understand the urge. State Department have long been enemies of Dobruta, and this action has killed one of our karasai. My thanks for the official condolences, by the way."

"Your warrior died in a good cause," said Dale. "*Phoenix* honours him." Nalben considered that cautiously, half-surprised, but suspecting some kind of trick. "I need a close look, Commander. Our analyst on *Phoenix* requires a very close look. We have marines on neighbouring platforms, coms reception configured precisely. Our analyst needs to be certain."

Nalben's eyes widened slightly, as he understood. "The analyst is sure?"

"The analyst is nearly sure. This will confirm it."

Nalben held a commanding finger at Dale. "No violent action, Lieutenant. Tavalai Fleet has its issues with State Department also, but they will not stand to see a State Department vessel or State Department personnel assaulted while under their protection. They will retaliate, *Phoenix* will be destroyed, and there is nothing *Makimakala* can do to stop it."

This tavalai, Dale realised, was expecting the humans to do something reckless and emotional. It was tavalai prejudice, of course. Humans thought tavalai cold, legalistic and unfeeling. Tavalai thought humans violent, unreasonable and unstable. Neither prejudice was particularly accurate, but like most prejudices, they were grown large from small grains of truth.

"There will be no violence," Dale said coolly. "Protecting *Phoenix* is my first and primary concern at all times."

Nalben looked most uncertain at that. Then he forced himself to nod — a human gesture. "Very well. Proceed, with caution."

"Commander," said Dale, and moved past toward the big, heavy-glass door. The rest of First Squad — Forest, Tong and Reddy — came with him.

On the cold, windswept landing pad outside sat a tavalai civilian shuttle. It loomed larger than a *Phoenix* combat shuttle, with an outline not nearly as ferocious. Standing before its open rear ramp were several well-bundled tavalai civilians, and some armed guards. The guards were civvies as well — VIP protection, with rifles, light body armour and other gear. Against marine armour at this range, they might as well have been unarmed.

A single tavalai civilian strode to meet him — a smaller, slimmer stature than the broader tavalai men. Tavalai women were rare in the military, but Dale had heard they dominated some of the powerful bureaucracies.

"This is the secure landing space of the Tropagali Andarachi Mandarinava," the woman told him with firm hostility, and perfect English. "By whose authority do you venture here?"

"Commander Nalbenaranda of the *Makimakala*," Dale informed her. And dialled up his coms reception to the preset coordinates Styx had laid in. Behind him, his section did the same. "Your shuttle emits a command frequency. It is transmitting to multiple small drones at various altitudes about Doma Strana. The effect is a multi-phase jamming signal, military grade. This attack on Doma Strana is yours, and were you in human space, you would all be dead by now."

The woman blinked at him, the translucent third eyelid flicking back and forth upon her big, wide-set eyes. Jelidanatagani, the Major had said her name was. Surely it was the same woman. The description matched, and Dale was sure he'd seen enough tavalai by now that they no longer looked entirely the same.

"We are *not* in human space," the State Department ambassador said coldly. "Any aggressive act toward *Tokigala* or her associated vessels, or her crew, will see *Phoenix* destroyed. I can assure you of *that*, Lieutenant."

"A little longer, Lieutenant," came Styx's voice in his ear. *"I am processing now, my signal is good. Keep her talking."* Hiro had reconfigured the signal back to *Phoenix* through Doma Strana's main communications uplink, a beast of a thing that even this jamming apparently could not block. It had allowed Styx into all associated Doma Strana functions. Dale had little doubt the entire temple could belong to her in seconds if she chose. From there, access to every temple sensor, and every marine sensor, had told her there was something very suspicious about the command signal coming from this *Tokigala* shuttle.

"One of our crew is missing," said Dale. "Lisbeth Debogande, the Captain's sister. We hold you responsible for her safety."

"You have no grounds for such accusations here," the bureaucrat snorted. "Even your own species has disowned you, and your firepower here in tavalai space is utterly outmatched. You are surrounded, and you have no friends save for one lonely Dobruta vessel whose captain shall surely in turn be called to answer for his protocol breach in inviting you here against all established rules of the Dobruta themselves. Soon you will lose even this protection, and then you shall be utterly defenceless, in tavalai and human space alike. Let us see who is throwing accusations about then."

Something flickered on Dale's scans... and suddenly the visor readout of his coms reception flickered. Coms abruptly came clear, the static vanished, and with it, a full reestablishment of marine tacnet outside the Doma Strana. Now he could see the friendly blue dots of the marines alongside him, and the hostile red dots of the tavalai before him... and here, to one side of his graphic, blinked an incoming feed via relay from *Phoenix*, with one hundred percent clarity.

One of Jelidanatagani's guards came to whisper something in her ear, and she frowned, appearing unfocused for a moment as she checked her uplinks.   And then retreated out of immediate hearing distance, to the shadow of her shuttle, discussing with handwaving alarm with those security, and two more civilians who emerged in haste from the shuttle's ramp.

"Phoenix this is Dale," said Dale, no longer needing to go through Doma Strana's big dish.   *"The jamming seems to have disappeared.   Was that Styx?"*

"Yes Lieutenant," came Styx's reply.   Pleased as he was to have the jamming gone, Dale didn't like that.   When he talked to *Phoenix,* he wanted *Phoenix* to reply, not the alien machine intelligence they'd once been sworn to destroy.   *"Their command codes are primitive, I have infiltrated the signal and disabled each transmission node.   In fact, one of their aerial drones has now become a minor hazard, and should impact the mountains two point four kilometres north of Doma Strana in approximately eighty seconds.   That was careless of me, I am out of practice."*

Jelidanatagani's hand waving ended, and she strode back to Dale with a look of accusation.   "What did you do?" she demanded.

The sheer nerve of tavalai still sometimes took Dale's breath away.   To a military officer, jamming coms was as much an act of war as shooting bullets, but here a State Department bureaucrat was horrified that *Phoenix* should defend itself against unmanned jamming drones, as though the humans weren't playing fair.

"Lisbeth Debogande," Dale replied, having no intention of discussing how they'd done it.   "Where is she?"

"No human technology can infiltrate and disable our secure networks so easily," the bureaucrat retorted with deep suspicion. She shot Commander Nalben a dark look, back by the access doors. "Higher powers forbid that the Dobruta have shared high-level secrets with you."

"No need," said Dale, turning to go, with a signal to his marines.   "We've been dealing with cheap tavalai junk like you for decades."

A loud boom rattled the ceiling, and rained dust in fine clouds. Erik squinted to avoid getting any in his eyes, and tested the weight of his pistol in his left hand. Further up the hall, Private Krishnan emerged from cover against one wall and peered up at the opening in the ceiling.

"Didn't get through!" he called. "I think they're testing the amount of explosive they'll need, too much and they'll bring the roof down and won't get a clean breach."

"Wouldn't want that," Erik muttered. There were running footsteps behind, and Erik glanced, but obviously it was Trace, running up from the stairwell.

"Okay, I've hidden the glasses in a small alcove by one of the airvents," she said, unhitching her rifle and pressing several grenades into Erik's hands. "We're not getting any reception, this rock is too thick for transmission, but it's better than nothing."

"Be a pity to have downloaded the whole of Drakhil's message just to have these assholes steal it," Erik suggested.

"Wouldn't it?" Trace agreed. "I've set up the lower fallback position, it's just spare ammo with the excess gear, we need to move lighter up here in first defence. Now, when the shooting starts, you're to stay behind me at all times, and lob a grenade only when I say so. How's your throwing?"

"Oh, right-handed? Great. Left-handed, not so much." He glanced at the ceiling, as Trace rearranged her remaining gear with purpose. "How long until they breach, do you think?"

"Real soon." Trace reconsidered the grenades. "Only throw when we're falling back past you, or when there's only one of us in front of you. Got it?"

"Yeah, because otherwise I'll throw short and blow one of you up instead."

"Which would be annoying," said Trace, getting ammo into the correct webbing pouch, then sighting her rifle. "You did throw a grenade in training, right?"

"Training grenade, sure. They don't trust spacers with dangerous things."

"Just warships that can kill planets."

"Hey, I'm qualified to kill planets. Just not people." Trace made a face at him, as though restraining a laugh. The kind of face you made at someone you thought was kind of funny, without wanting to encourage them too much. It was almost a goofy face, and it intrigued Erik because he'd seen it a few times before. No one else in the galaxy could have imagined Major Trace Thakur, holder of the Liberty Star, being goofy. But he was discovering that Trace had layers, and only very good friends of equal or superior rank, or outside her chain of command entirely, got to glimpse the inner-most layer. He wondered what or who she'd have been if she'd never discovered the Kulina, or become a marine in the war. Probably some nice, smart girl, he thought, who was very good at her job, liked a laugh, and was a bit of a nerd.

The thought made him smile, in spite of everything. Trace Thakur, marine nerd. Her personality type was always going to be obsessively good at something. If she'd attached herself to computers, she'd have been like Lieutenant Rooke, a tech-nerd with obsessive focus and a head full of numbers. But instead she'd attached herself to the Kulina, and by extension the marines, with equivalent results.

She saw him smiling. "What?"

"You," he said. "It's been fun serving with you, Major. And I'm amazed we made it this far."

Trace's smile was faintly incredulous. "Yeah, well I'm not done yet. I think there were only about ten chasing us up the mountain, Krishnan says he hit two with you back on the ledge, and getting in here through these narrow spaces is going to cost them. You stay behind me and don't blow yourself up, we'll get out of here yet."

"Yes ma'am." And Trace gave him a full 'what's got into you' look, but not displeased. It wasn't that Erik wasn't scared. It was more that he'd become accustomed to being scared, and Trace's reassuring presence was the best cure he knew. And if he was about to die, then damned if he'd miss one final chance to needle her, and get her back for all the times she'd aggravated him, while he still could.

"Shit, I haven't been called 'ma'am' since my last school visit." And she took position ahead of Erik, and called up to Krishnan, "Private, what can you hear?"

"I hear them working!" Krishnan replied, fifteen metres further up. He was placing grenades, and setting a timer. "Two charges, left and right! They should survive the entry blast, then catch them at best cover when we get them under fire."

"Don't hang around or they'll bring the ceiling down on your head!"

"You did school visits?" Erik asked her. "Before or after the Liberty Star?"

"Oh before," said Trace, sighting down her rifle, braced in a crouch. Erik flattened himself to the wall directly behind. "That fucking medal made it nearly impossible for me to go out in public. One more reason I hate it."

It surprised Erik. She'd never talked about it so openly with him before. "That medal inspired a lot of people," he told her.

"I don't care," said Trace. "Public inspiration is a job for pop stars, politicians, and other frauds and con artists. To find that overnight I've been put into that company, in the minds of billions, is depressing."

"Inspiration got us through the war," Erik countered.

"Firepower got us through the war," Trace retorted. "If people want inspiration they should search for some in a mirror. And if they don't find any, well it's not my job to give it to them."

Erik snorted derisively. "Well shit," he teased her. "Aren't you awesome."

"Yeah I know, right?" she said, and Erik could hear the grin in her voice. "Some of it's even rubbing off on you, I see."

A big explosion rocked the hallway, and Erik ducked as a cloud of dust and bits of rock came down from cracks in the marble ceiling. Trace barely flinched. Then Krishnan threw himself back as a second explosion blasted dust and rock. Erik pulled his pistol, squinting into the dust and aiming left-handed, not liking his chances of hitting much and hoping that Krishnan kept well out of the way.

After several seconds, the follow-up assault had not come. Krishnan began working his way back along the wall, aiming at the cloud of dust... and then they heard the shrill howl of engines. "That's one of ours!" Erik declared with delight. "That's one of..."

Something dark and cloaked dropped through the opening, and both Trace and Krishnan fired. It hit the floor with an unmoving thud, as a second followed, ducked sideways off the ground as Trace and Krishnan adjusted aim... Trace fired once, and he dropped as well.

"Nice shot Major," Krishnan said tersely. "Beat me to it."

Heavy cannon roared outside, with an echoing shudder they could hear through the mountain, high velocity rounds designed to kill small spaceships, pulverising any parren still left atop the mountain ridge above. The engine-whine came no closer, the flyer at hold-off range, far enough to not expose itself to groundfire, yet close enough to make devastating short work of infantry.

Suddenly Erik's iris-icon was blinking at him, and he focused on it. A link opened. *"Hello Captain!"* came an anxious, familiar voice on the other end. *"This is Ensign Lee on PH-4, are you there?"*

"Hello Ensign Lee," said Erik with utter relief. "Hello Tif. We're in a temple in the mountain, the entrance is right where you were just firing, and we're right below it."

"Yeah, we just blasted some guys, they were fixing us with a missile-tracker, we didn't wait around to see where the missile would come from. A couple of them escaped into that hole, are you guys okay?"

"Yes we're fine, Major Thakur and Private Krishnan just shot those two who jumped in, all three of us are okay."

"Are there any more up there?" Trace prompted him.

"Are there any more hostiles above us?" Erik relayed.

"Negative Captain, we blew a couple off, and the others kinda jumped, there's not much room." Erik shook his head at Trace, who signalled Krishnan. Krishnan moved carefully forward to examine the bodies, rifle levelled. *"Look, we can get in and pluck you off that ledge if you can get out that way? Tif's telling me*

the crosswind's getting a bit hairy, so one at a time and nothing fancy."

"I copy that PH-4, if you could hold in proximity for ten minutes, we have some important stuff we have to recover first. In fact, if you could drop us a holograph scanner, that would be a real help."

"I'll... we'll check, should have one on board somewhere." As Krishnan signalled to Trace — both bodies were dead. *"Did you find something down there, sir?"*

"You could say that." Trace looked at him with a relieved smile, and gave his good shoulder a whack. "I want to make sure we recover all of it — better get Styx on uplink to see if we're about to miss something."

"Yes sir."

"How's everyone else? What's the status on Doma Strana?"

"The attack's been dispersed, Doma Strana appears relatively secure and there are no Phoenix casualties." A nervous pause. *"Um, sir? There's something else, about your sister."*

Erik's smile faded, and Trace's smile with it, to see the look on his face. "Lisbeth? What's happened to Lisbeth?"

Lisbeth awoke. It was a strange kind of awakening, uncertain of where she was or why she'd been sleeping. Or who she was, or what her name was.

Her hands were bound, and she lay in total darkness, feeling loose canvas about her. Surely she'd suffocate... but there was an air mask of some sort over her face, feeding her cool, synthetic air. It smelled too clean, as all pressurised air did, devoid of other flavours. Probably, it occurred to her, it was feeding her some kind of anaesthetic, too. That would explain why her thoughts seemed to drift, and why the sure knowledge that she'd been kidnapped did not reduce her to a sobbing panic.

The ground seemed to shake, a low rumbling. She had a memory, sleeping on the maglev from Shiwon to Dadri, on

Homeworld. She'd been just a young girl, and had been travelling on her own for the first time, zooming through the night in her sleeper bed, comfortable in the knowledge of the forests and mountains rushing by outside. Well, just her, and a half-dozen well armed security. She'd been going to stay with cousins, and see the sights, and do some shopping. She doubted they'd have shopping where she was going now.

The bump of an airpocket... definitely she was flying. An atmospheric flight, as anything heading to orbit would have flattened her with heavy-Gs by now. She wondered vaguely who, and why, and where she'd end up. And if she'd ever live to see Erik or her other family again, or even to see another day. Perhaps, she thought. Or perhaps not. It felt odd, to be so unbothered, while still so lucid. Odd, and greatly relieving. She was tired of being scared.

CHAPTER 8

Two of *Makimakala*'s shuttles gave PH-4 a close escort back up to *Phoenix*. There followed a brief, hard burn to put *Phoenix* back on intercept orbit over Doma Strana in another ninety minutes, Erik having decided that continual high-G push-orbits, as such manoeuvres were known, might eventually aggravate a tavalai ship into shooting at them. Another ninety minutes until PH-4 could make a return descent, this time with Ensign Jokono and some Engineering techs who could assist with basic forensics. All while Lisbeth was... wherever she was.

Trace escorted Erik to Medbay personally, through the zero-G hub to the crew cylinder, then down to main deck, while Private Krishnan found some spare armour in Assembly and prepared to head straight back down to his platoon in Doma Strana on PH-4. Erik's painkillers were wearing off as he walked gingerly down Main-A corridor, his arm around Trace's shoulders for balance as his head spun, and passing spacers gave him looks of mixed relief, concern and sympathy. Everyone had heard about Lisbeth. Many probably now wondered at the wisdom of having had Lisbeth on the ship in the first place, given the emotional vulnerabilities it created for their Captain, and thus for them all. Well dammit, it hadn't been his idea to have her on board. He felt sick, and hoped he wouldn't throw up in front of everyone.

'Doc' Suelo saw him immediately, in a medbay unusually free of patients for this, *Phoenix*'s most recent voyage. Suelo helped Trace get his jacket and shirt off, and set about a mobile ultrasound scan of his shoulder.

"Close the curtains," Erik ordered hoarsely, and Trace did that, enfolding them in a little privacy. And then it was a struggle to keep the tears at bay, and his breathing calm. Suelo worked without comment, and Trace sat with him and held his good hand, as she'd sat with so many of her marines before in this medbay, saying nothing, just letting them know that they weren't alone. Suelo would say nothing to others, Erik knew. And despite their hardass reputations, marines were less judgemental of emotional pain than most. They knew it better than most, and upon seeing it in others, knew 'there but for the grace of god go I'.

"Erik, they *took* her," Trace said firmly. "Understand what that means. Killing her would have been easy, but they chose the much harder option and took her. That means they want her alive. Having her alive gives them leverage, over you. I think we'll be hearing from whoever has her shortly. And then we'll see what we can do about it, culminating with us putting a bunch of bullets in a bunch of heads. Got it?"

She sounded upset herself, Erik thought. Lisbeth had been her bunkmate for the past four months. Trace hadn't had a bunkmate for a long time, commanding officers typically bunking solo. Everyone had gotten the impression she'd been enjoying it.

Erik nodded. "Yeah. I just need a moment. Go take your AR glasses to Styx and Romki, I'll be down real soon."

Trace nodded, got up and left with a kiss on his forehead. She did that with her wounded marines too, Erik knew, both male and female. There was nothing more to it than that. But it surprised him how good it felt.

Jokono was still uncomfortable in the *Phoenix* spacer blues. For most of his life, his uniform had been a civilian suit, its weight and folds as familiar to him as his own skin. But now in the Doma Strana, the uniform saved a lot of trouble, as tavalai military and civilians alike understood that those colours meant *Phoenix*, and authority with the humans who mattered.

"No identification," said a *Makimakala* crewman via his belt translator, set for English. The tavalai crouched by the bodies of two dead parren, lightly armoured and lightly armed. *Makimakala* karasai had killed these two, at the cost of one of their own. One parren's head was missing. Or not missing, but rather redistributed about the corridor walls and floor. The other had a hole in his chest big enough to put a fist through. Human marines weren't the only

ones to pack very big guns. *"Standard light armour, parren design, made for stealth, yes?"*

The crewman looked up at an armoured karasai nearby — a middle-rank, Jokono thought. The tavalai equivalent of a sergeant, perhaps. The karasai grunted. *"They don't fight heavy,"* he said. *"Light force, move fast. That's how they kidnap human crew."*

There was a touch of contempt in the karasai's voice, even through the translator. Jokono ignored it, looking over the corpses in the hope they'd tell him something more. "What do you think they were after?" he asked both tavalai. In the smooth, black hallway, more tavalai and human ship crew were moving. Marines and karasai stood guard, and tavalai civilians watched on with big, anxious eyes.

"Maybe your Captain's sister was the target," the big karasai suggested.

"Or your Captain himself," the crewman added. *"They did try to kill him."*

"But continued their attack on Doma Strana even as he was escaping," said Jokono, stroking his chin. "And I'm not so sure they *did* kidnap the Captain's sister."

Both tavalai frowned at him. Jokono beckoned them to follow, and walked the short distance to the office doorway. Inside, a former temple room had been converted into modern office space with transparent com screens and display partitions. Some were now broken, some desks askew and large bullet holes in the walls where *Phoenix* marines had sprayed fire at something they couldn't see. Jokono walked to where one of *Phoenix*'s techs had found a dislodged ceiling panel, an interlocking piece of ceiling, now missing and exposing a dark hole within.

He pointed. "That's an old temple access. We're not sure if it's ventilation or designed for some other purpose, possibly a multi-purpose conduit built just in case."

"More likely a murder hole," the tavalai crewman said grimly, walking around to peer up at it from a different angle. *"Big parren temples are full of intrigue. Murders, assassinations. They build it into the architecture, sometimes."*

Jokono nodded, having read similar, disquieting things. Once upon a time, such things had been just tales to most humans, lost amongst the countless stories from the many species who lived far beyond human space, and had no interest explaining themselves to human ears. But now, all those distant tales were coming to life, very close and personal. "So which parren know this temple best? And could already be in place to surprise our marines, and snatch our personnel?"

The tavalai looked at each other.

"Captain," came Jokono's voice from down on the surface, as Erik sat on the bridge and sipped coffee. *"Hiro's quite sure it was Aristan's people."*

Erik nodded slowly, thinking a thousand thoughts at once. Most of them involved blasting parren heads, and parren ships. Focus, he told himself. You can't let your emotions fly the ship, Captain Pantillo had said. There's no place for rage in the captain's chair.

He took a deep breath. "How is he so sure?"

"Hiro is missing one of his surveillance units." Erik recalled the little synthetic wasp, buzzing above Hiro's palm. Styx's technology. *"He's not receiving a signal from it now, it lacks long range coms and is programmed to be stealthy. But Hiro says it was tracking Lisbeth when she vanished, on his instruction. He says he'd know if it had been destroyed, and it would never just disappear without a trace. He's certain it stowed away with Lisbeth, possibly in her pocket. The final signal it sent, and the final known location of one of Aristan's teams, were identical."*

"You mean we have a bug actually *on* her?" His heart started thumping, with sudden, ferocious hope.

"Hiro thinks so, yes. He'd told it to keep an eye on her specifically."

Thank god for Hiro, Erik thought. If that bit of foresight ended up saving Lisbeth's life... "When will we hear from it, if it has attached itself to her?"

"At the earliest opportunity, he says. But it will wait, it can't give itself away. Styx will know more."

"Styx?" Erik asked to the air.

"The tracker has limited communications functions of its own," Styx said, as calm as ever. *"If it needs to talk, it will infiltrate local networks and use them to communicate instead. If it sends a coded signal, I will process it. May I have full access to Phoenix communications sensors in case of encoded incoming signals?"*

Erik signalled at Shilu, who was looking at him from Coms. Shilu nodded, and did that. Of course, Styx probably didn't need permission, but so long as she was being polite, they'd play along.

"Ensign Jokono, do you think Aristan helped to set up the ambush on us? Is he in on it, with the State Department and whoever these parren are?"

"Well... to know that for certain would probably take a far longer period of investigation than we have available, Captain," said Jokono. *"But from discussing matters with Lieutenants Zhi and Dale, and now with what Hiro shows me of encrypted network activity within Doma Strana leading up to the attack, I'm actually inclined to believe that Aristan was the* target *of the attack. Perhaps even more than us."*

To his right, and his front-left, Erik could feel Commander Shahaim and Lieutenant Kaspowitz's stares boring into him. "So it was one of his many parren enemies? Working with the State Department?"

"It's only a guess at this point, Captain. But it's my best guess."

"State Department has good reason to want Aristan dead," Kaspowitz added. "He's destabilising the current parren regime. If they got rid of both him and you, Captain, at the same time, they'd consider that a good day's work."

"Using aliens to do their dirty work again," Shahaim muttered. "Typical tavalai, never get their own hands dirty."

"So if Aristan did take Lisbeth," said Erik. "Why?"

"Captain, the smart money's on leverage. Over you."

"Leverage for what?"

"I suppose we'll find out."

A full rotation, and a flurry of activity between *Phoenix* and *Makimakala* later, all the senior crew plus Commander Nalben were crammed into *Phoenix*'s briefing room, in a circle of chairs about a central holographic space. Plus two more of *Makimakala*'s senior crew, it was eighteen people in total, in a room designed to hold no more than twelve.

Before all this assembled military authority, it was the civilian, Stan Romki, who held court. "So we've seen the recording now," he told them all, seated in a front row, AR glasses high on his bald head, a slate of notes on his lap. "Styx confirms that it is certainly Drakhil himself, and that it appears to have been recorded in the final months before the fall of the Drysine Empire. The encryption built into the temple is a very high class of very old drysine code. Styx says it's nearly unbreakable for non-drysines, and would have erased itself if anyone had gained entry by forcible means. We can only guess how many of these hidden places remain elsewhere in the Spiral — the message gives no clue, only to say that there are others, but most will never be found. Given the scale of the space over which they've been dispersed, over the scale of time since the end of the Drysine Empire, I think that's probably true.

"Now in the recording, Drakhil mentions a diary, apparently written by him. Five copies, in five locations, he says. And sure enough, there follows a lot of very old drysine code that even Styx struggles to make sense of. She suspects Drakhil was using encryption patterns that even she has lost — perhaps Drakhil was suspecting that it would be parren who recovered this recording, with drysine assistance, and certainly not humans with drysine assistance. If Styx has a failing, it is that neither she nor her people made a particular study of their parren allies, and so her knowledge of their language, mathematics and codes is incomplete. But one of the five entries did reveal itself to her immediately, as it is based on

102

the Klyran tongue, which she has just recently come to understand. And here I shall pass over to Commander Nalben."

Everyone looked at the tavalai commander.   Odd, Erik thought, that until quite recently, it would have seemed sacrilegious to have a senior quasi-military tavalai on board.   Now it was almost normal.   Erik had to fight his own utter disinterest in the topic at hand, his brain clamouring instead for news and clues of Lisbeth, and ways of tracking her, and getting her back.   But if Aristan's people *had* kidnapped her, then the odds were that it was somehow tied up with the data from the small temple he and Trace had found. And it was almost certainly Aristan's people who had laid that flower by Lisbeth's bunk in PH-4, with the data chip that had led Trace to the temple in the first place.   Unravel this mystery, and perhaps the other, more alarming mystery would become more clear.

"Thank you Mr Romki," said Nalben, in that thick, throaty tavalai voice.   "My experts and I have searched our records on the data given to us by Mr Romki and your... helpful drysine friend." There were some ironic smiles around the group.   "The location of the one diary provided to us was a bit obscure.   The name given is Chon Il, which was unknown to us.   Yet some long arguments among our experts about the translations between old parren and old tavalai tongues — the details of which I shall spare you — have convinced us beyond doubt that the location revealed to us is the Tonchalda System."

He activated the room holographics, and the central space within the circle of chairs came to life — a star chart, a blizzard of inhabited systems, linked by the glowing lines of established space lanes.   The image zoomed inward, centring upon one system in particular, labelled in tavalai script.

"As you can see, Tonchalda is today a parren system.   Like Stoya, it has a history of Tahrae habitation, and today has a large parren population whose settlement origins go back to the early days of the Parren/Drysine Alliance.   In those days, Harmony House ruled, and the Tahrae ruled Harmony House.   Tonchalda was a regional centre of government, and played an important role in both the Tahrae's rise in the Drysine Empire, and then in the Parren Empire that followed the end of the Machine Age.

"But Tonchalda was not always a parren system. For a period of several hundred years, Tonchalda was captured by chah'nas forces during the fall of the Parren Empire and the rise of the chah'nas. Chah'nas won the military victory, but naturally, administering the system fell to their trusted bureaucrats, the tavalai.

"The Dobruta maintain extensive records of all such old historical events, given our interest in old hacksaw artefacts. And so we scanned our records for any sign that tavalai forces may have encountered such an artefact as Drakhil's diary. Sure enough, hidden amongst several centuries of ship traffic, logs and details, we found this little gem — a priority message from a local surveyor in the Vedavan, who were a branch of a very early branch of old Parren Empire era administration. A tavalai administrative division, with no legislative power of course, as the chah'nas held all that for themselves. But a department of managerial expertise, to handle new conquests in the ongoing wars following the collapse of the Parren Empire.

"I will spare you the technical protocols and their significance for now — I shall have a fully detailed copy of our reasoning available for you after, for your further reading. For now, it is enough to say that this local surveyor found something at Torea, the local Tonchalda temple complex. His priority message is garbled with out-of-date encryption we can no longer penetrate, but it brought an analysis team running from various major institutions.

"This analysis team included a tavalai named Cheliratanga. Now Cheliratanga is a name still familiar to all Dobruta. We learn about her in our tertiary education, because she pioneered a new field of hacksaw encryption and machine language. Her breakthroughs are legendary, and many have speculated how they came about. Now… the first of her technical papers on this subject, as it happens, was published three years after her assignment to the analysis team on Tonchalda. From there, those papers flowed in a steady stream."

"You think she found something?" Erik asked.

"Yes," said Nalben. Erik thought he sounded a little excited. As though this line of enquiry might be about to shed light on mysteries the Dobruta had puzzled over for thousands of years. "Records show that following a year spent on Tonchalda, she retreated to a research facility at Dovadara and was based there for the majority of the rest of her life, slowly building herself into a legend of tavalai academia. Clearly she found *something*. Many have speculated what, as the records are classified. Perhaps now we know."

"But how can you tell if it's Drakhil's diary?" Lieutenant Kaspowitz asked. "There are a lot of old objects in the Spiral. She could have found anything."

"Appropriation orders," said Nalben, with something approaching triumph. Blank stares from the humans. "Apologies, this will seem needlessly complicated to humans. You have my two assistants to thank for it — Ensign Tov and I believe the equivalent rank is Petty Officer Ben." He indicated the two other seated tavalai, names abbreviated for human convenience. "Together we have had no sleep the past cycle, as we've followed this trail through the tavalai bureaucracy for nearly twenty thousand years.

"Whenever an old, important artefact is moved from one tavalai department to another, an appropriation order must be filed. The process is long and complicated in direct proportion to the importance of the object being appropriated. For one particular object within Cheliratanga's possessions at the time of her death, there was placed an appropriations order the scale of which I've rarely seen.

"It is a twenty-five stamp job," added Petty Officer Ben from his seat beside Kaspowitz, in much more heavily-accented English than Nalben used. "Most jobs require no more than five stamps. A ten stamp job is a very large and complicated order. Fifteen stamps is nearly unheard of. This one had twenty-five stamps. It is the kind of thing that becomes a bureaucratic legend, only this one appears to have been kept very quiet."

"Twenty-five stamps, wow," deadpanned Lieutenant Rooke. "Exciting."

"To a tavalai bureaucrat, thrilling beyond words," Nalben assured him. "Yet as Ben says, there is no mention of it elsewhere in the records. So very big, and very secret — this record could only be accessed by Captain Pram himself, even my security clearance was not high enough.

"Anyhow, this object was then moved multiple times over thousands of years, as you might imagine — it is called a different thing on each occasion, it was a nightmare to find it in the records, but again, the scale of bureaucracy required on each occasion gives it away to the persistent. From age to age it has been moved, always in the deepest secrecy, always to and from the most secure facilities. And today, we think we have found it... though it will take further quiet research to be certain."

"I don't get it," Commander Shahaim volunteered. Suli Shahaim was always the first to admit that, if it was the case. Erik thought everyone could learn from her example. "How can you know that this object is Drakhil's diary? It was found at the right location and is very important, but anything beyond that is speculation."

"Because," said Commander Nalben with a twinkle that Erik had never seen in a tavalai before, "we have access to the current personnel records of the base in question. And please be aware, before I show these to you, that in doing so I am breaching such a huge number of security rules that the authorities will not have enough bullets with which to shoot me."

He activated the hololink once more, and tavalai faces appeared. Rows of them, with accompanying text. Formal identifications, such as might be used in a secure facility. "Now none of you humans here read Togiri save for Mr Romki, so allow me to translate for you."

He pointed to the first name. "Sidasani Masansarai. Professor of Parren Studies, Podi University, currently on state assignment to the facility in question. Her academic speciality? The life of Drakhil, and the end of the Drysine Empire.

"This next one here," and he pointed to the next, "is Jonarata Jeritali. Also a Professor of Parren Studies, but his speciality is linguistics.   His special project has been an attempt to reconstruct the Klyran language... no doubt he would now love to meet Mr Romki and your drysine guest, and would doubtless be both thrilled and angry to find that you've translated that lost tongue before him.

"The next one is Agital Periti.   An advanced systems technician from Copibal, specialisation in theoretical drysine systems, parren-alliance age.   And the next one, whose name is so long I shall spare you, a drysine-age encryption specialist whose last major project was to construct a working model of drysine thought-patterns in an attempt to create a drysine code-breaker.   Evidently they are struggling, and from personal experience, I'd guess they have been struggling for many thousands of years."

He looked about at them all, and found only silence, and wide stares.   Erik thought Nalben looked a little smug.   For a tavalai, that was a more familiar expression.   "Nearly all of the historians have some special interest in Drakhil," Nalben summarised.   "The rest are code-breakers.   We cannot access personnel records back more than a few years, but in what we can access, the pattern repeats.   Clearly the object found all that time ago was Drakhil's diary, one of the five copies he mentioned.   And by appearances, it's in some kind of encrypted, electronic form, and they've been trying all this time to break it.   Apparently without success."

Erik glanced at Romki.   The professor was literally gnawing on his finger, as though to restrain himself.   "Styx?" Erik said loudly to the air.   "I'm sure you're listening.   Does any of this sound plausible to you?"

"Hello Captain," came Styx's mild, feminine voice over room speakers.   *"All of this sounds plausible to me.   Highly plausible.   Given some time to examine the Commander's data, I could come to a more exact analysis."*

"And do you think it's likely that the tavalai authorities have not been able to break Drakhil's encryption for all these millennia?"

"Yes Captain.   Breaking drysine encryption is not simply a question of mathematical persistence.   Drysine psychology is fundamentally different from organic psychology.   We possess two

very different types of sentience. Organics do not perceive many things that to the highest AI minds seem obvious. That being the case, endless amounts of time are of little benefit to those attempting to break this particular code."

"She's right," Romki added. "To pick a lock, you need a key. There are complications built into drysine thought that organics do not possess. You can try to pick a lock with your bare fingers for as long as you like — without the key, or any tool approximating one, time will not help you."

"An excellent analogy Professor," said Styx. "Drakhil will have used the highest drysine encryption to encode his diary, making it impossible for any undesirables to read its contents. Probably this was achieved by the last drysine queen to see him alive. And no, in case you were wondering, that was not me."

The organics looked at each other. They had been wondering. "But you could decode it yourself?" Erik pressed. "If we could recover it?"

"Certainly," said Styx.

"Wait a moment," Kaspowitz interrupted, suspiciously. He looked at Nalben. *"Which* tavalai department now has the diary?"

"The Tropagali Andarachi Mandarinava," said Nalben. "Which you call the State Department." Groans and rolling eyes around the group.

"Of course they do," Lieutenant Shilu muttered.

Erik took a deep breath, and looked at Trace. She looked deep in thought, and in no hurry to take over this very spacer discussion. "And what do you think our odds are of finding another of Drakhil's five copies?" Erik asked Nalben.

"I think your Styx had better answer that," Nalben replied.

"Captain, as Professor Romki says, knowledge of parren society is not my strength. If Drakhil was using such references to influence his coding, then I will be as helpless at decoding it as tavalai are at decoding his diary. I have good human assistance on hand, but no parren assistance, and even today's most academic parren have little accurate knowledge of Drakhil's time. Perhaps progress could be made, but it could take years."

"We don't have years," Trace said with certainty. A silence followed, as everyone considered that. Trace looked at Nalben. "Can you get the diary back?"

"From the State Department?" Nalben nearly laughed. "Not without a war, no." Tavalai rarely if ever fought wars, at least amongst each other.

"So," said Trace, deliberately. "Can we steal it?"

CHAPTER 9

"Maybe he didn't do it." Trace floated by Berth Three in Midships, zero-G in light armour as the regs dictated, with potentially hostile visitors coming aboard. About her, secured to the cargo net walls in case of shooting, the full Third Section of Bravo Platoon, similarly armed and armoured with weapons ready.

Erik said nothing, floating in armour with just his holstered pistol, watching the Operations crew as they worked the airlock, and the parren shuttle docked at the far side. Aristan's personal ship was now in geo-stationary orbit parallel to *Phoenix*, barely two hundred kilometres away. The ship's approach had been by Aristan's own request, as was this meeting. The berth crashed and hummed as outer airlocks opened, and a crewwoman signalled that someone was coming up.

"Because it would seem a little reckless to come aboard *Phoenix* immediately after kidnapping Lisbeth," Trace added. Watching Erik carefully, for any sign of response. Erik stared at the airlock. Trace was concerned at the pistol in his holster, he knew. She needn't have been, he wasn't about to shoot the one person whose safety was likely most directly linked to Lisbeth's.

The nearside outer airlock hummed, then a pressurising hiss. The inner doors slid, and immediately a marine moved to intercept the black cloaked figure that emerged, while two more angled for killing shots if he tried anything. The first marine frisked the parren, while an Operations crewman indicated that the airlock scanners had found nothing on his person. The frisking marine indicated the same, and their Sergeant indicated for them to move.

It left Aristan himself, cloak and hood billowing in zero-G, held in place by design with no more than velcro tabs. The indigo eyes were wide and unblinking, shifting first from Erik to Trace, then back again. He held to the airlock's single control rail, designed for that purpose. Erik judged by the way he floated that spacetravel was not strange to him.

Aristan activated his belt translator. When he spoke, English followed. *"We have your sister. But I think you know."*

Erik could have happily drawn and shot him, right between the eyes. But he could not. "Why?"

"Options. She will be treated magnificently. Far more closely to that which she is accustomed, than aboard this vessel." He looked up and about at the high cargo nets, the storage bays, the grey steel and furled acceleration slings. Then the wide, alien eyes came back to Erik. *"You found the lost temple. My people are now negotiating with the tavalai of this world for rights of access."*

"What rights of access do you have on this tavalai world?" Trace asked coolly. She had the hard-eyed look that she got when figuring her way through a dangerous situation, accumulating information.

"House Harmony has negotiated rights of access to Doma Strana, as you have seen. All of this was once parren space, in recent antiquity. We visit when we want. The tavalai respect antiquity. What the parren have built, the parren may claim, for all purposes but ownership." The indigo eyes came back to Erik. *"We will be granted access to the lost temple in time. What did you see there?"*

"Is that why you kidnapped my sister?" Erik asked darkly.

Beneath his veil, Aristan may have smiled. *"Drastic. Considering we shall know the temple ourselves soon enough. No, Phoenix. You are on the trail of Drakhil's legacy. I am Drakhil's legacy, as are my people. You will not keep these findings to yourself. You will share. Yet you have your own interests, as I have mine. Your people and mine barely know each other. Some persuasion, I decided, was in order. Without it, I have little leverage to bear."*

"What 'Drakhil's legacy'?" Erik retorted. "What are you talking about?"

"There are tales. Legends of the Tahrae, long lost yet still whispered. Tales of Drakhil's last words, kept deep in tavalai vaults. Last words containing the greatest secrets of the old Drysine Empire,

when the Tahrae were vast and powerful, and House Harmony ruled the Spiral at the Drysine hand."

"And you want them back," said Trace.

"Of course.   It is my destiny.   Have you found their location?   With your Dobruta allies, I would not think it too much trouble to search ancient tavalai records and find what I seek.   The tavalai are meticulous."

Erik gave Trace a wary look.   Aristan knew entirely too much already.   Someone must have told him, he decided.   Probably the Dobruta, given that the Dobruta had been the ones to invite Aristan here, to meet with these strange, renegade humans who sought things that no humans had ever before been inclined to seek. Erik had that dark and recently familiar feeling of vast forces moving behind the scenes, arranging things where none aboard this ship could see them.   Arranging things for their own purposes alone. If Erik had come to appreciate any single thing since Captain Pantillo's death, it was just how ignorant most humans remained of the older and most ancient powers in the galaxy.   A naive and inexperienced human, in a very powerful warship, could stroll into such things unawares, all brimming with false confidence that he knew what was going on and could handle anything that came his way.   If he had ever felt anything like that at first, since leaving human space, the feeling was by now long gone.

"So you seek what we seek," said Erik.   "You only wish to ensure that you get your share, at the end of the search."

Aristan inclined his cowled head, a graceful bow. *"Precisely."*

"And we get Lisbeth back… when?"

"When I am confident that there is nothing more to learn."

"When *Phoenix* has expended her usefulness to you, you mean."

"I have learned a human word.   Honour."   He spoke it slowly, with his own lips, and the translator-speaker remained silent. *"I have researched this word enough to be convinced — the concept is the same, between your people and mine.   The parren have honour.   We value it highly.   Upon my honour, your sister is safe.*

So long as Phoenix does not seek to deny that which is rightfully mine."

"Will you help?" Trace asked.   Erik did not like that at all, but Trace was not looking his way.   "You seem to know a lot about this.   Will you help us to reclaim what you want?   Are you useful for anything, besides abducting harmless civilians and threatening their siblings?"

Aristan regarded her for a longer moment.   Perhaps the pause meant that he was displeased by her words.   *"We will do anything to reclaim Drakhil's legacy.   Anything.   Should you discover its location and require of my people to spend their lives like coin to acquire it, we shall do so."*

"We'll let you know," said Erik.   "You're dismissed."

"You have capabilities aboard," Aristan pressed.   *"The data chip I gave you was in Klyran, a tongue long lost to my people.   I do not see how you could have found the lost temple without first knowing Klyran.   How did you learn it?"*

"Maybe if you kidnapped another ten of us we'd tell you," Erik growled at him.   "Only next time, I don't think you'd survive the attempt."

"They have been trying to end the line of Drakhil for more than twenty thousand of your years," said Aristan.   *"It is not ordained that they shall succeed."*

The Gs pressed Lisbeth into her acceleration chair, wrists bound to the chair arms and sucking in the air in tight, gasping breaths as time aboard *Phoenix* had taught her.   There had been a landing, then a transfer to a shuttle, a bag over her head and unable to see or smell anything.   Then a hard climb to orbit, a sensation she knew from her co-piloting, and now an outbound run at 3-G, heading for jump.

She was still in the shuttle, clamped to the outside of some larger ship as *Phoenix*'s shuttles ran attached to the outer hull.   It could have been owned by whoever had taken her, or it could even be a neutral freighter, taking a paying passenger where it wanted to go and asking no questions. She'd heard nothing of her abductor's voices, yet she was fairly certain they were parren. Their silence alone indicated as much. Parren were disciplined, and conscious of appearances, while sard cared not at all what other species thought of them, and tavalai could not be kept quiet under wet cement.

There were other, lesser species in tavalai-sphere space, but few of them would want to stick their noses into sensitive tavalai business, to say nothing of parren business. Tavalai dealt with transgressions firmly, but were capable of mercy in the face of contrition. Parren, according to everything Lisbeth had heard and read, were not. Moreover, parren space today was vastly smaller than it had been when they'd ruled the Spiral in the eight thousand years between the fall of the machines, and the rise of the Chah'nas Empire, but still it remained enormous. Romki had told her that in his opinion, the parren remained the fourth-most-powerful species in the Spiral, after humans, tavalai and — following recent alarming discoveries — the alo. One did not take parren lightly, nor meddle in their affairs and expect not to get burnt.

The fearlessness of her earlier wakening was gone, along with the airmask that had no doubt provided it. Now Lisbeth was properly terrified, and almost thankful for the heavy Gs that gave her heart its excuse to thump and pound within her chest. Almost as bad as the personal terror was the fear of what use her predicament would be put to. Leverage against *Phoenix*? Against her family? By whom, and for what purpose?

Worst of all, she'd just begun to think of herself as a contributing member of the crew. Not nearly as skilled and disciplined as most, yet useful, in her own small way. It had been such a battle to get Erik to agree to let her go down to the surface on Stoya III. And now this, proving all of Erik's protective fears correct. He'd been right to protest, because after all she'd been through, she was just a helpless little girl after all.

Tears leaked from the corners of her eyes, squeezed shut as she fought for breath, the familiar reflex of augmented circulation, bloodstream micros shuffling the blood along at double-time, irrespective of her pulse and breathing.

Something buzzed by her ear.   At first she thought it was some piece of com equipment malfunctioning, but there was no headset on her ears, under or over the bag on her head.   Then she felt the tiny, sharp feet of something crawling on her neck.   Another wave of panic struck her — some awful insect had gotten aboard and was inside her hood, where she was powerless to swat it with her wrists tied to the chair arms.   If she cried out, no one could come to help her — 3-Gs for a duration was immobilising for even augmented spacers, and in the roar of thrust shaking the hull and rattling everything within, no one would hear her anyway.

She felt the insect walk up to her jaw, and tried to shake her head, hoping it would fly away.   It buzzed again, an odd, repetitive pattern.   Then she realised.   Doma Strana had been very high altitude, over four thousand metres, and was very cold.   Most flying insects, like the kinds that buzzed, used sunlight and heat for much of their energy.   Thin air, cold, wind and snow were not their friends, and the insides of the temple itself had been pristine, and no place for bugs.   Plus, even small insects would have better sense under 3-G thrust than to walk up vertical surfaces.

This was one of Hiro's synthetic recon bugs, then.   Lisbeth gasped upon her next exhaled breath, this time with relief.   It must have been monitoring her, and stowed away in her clothes when it saw her in trouble.   She feebly supposed that it was a bit odd to respond to a hacksaw-tech assassin bug, crawling on your neck, with relief.   But this one, Hiro had insisted, had reliable objectives.

"Can you speak to me?" Lisbeth managed a whispered hiss. The bug buzzed, alternating short and long.   "Right.   No coms. Well stick with me.   Where we're going, I might need some help."

The first jump pulse hit her, as the ship's hyperspace engines powered up for departure.

"There goes another one," said Second Lieutenant Geish on Scan.   "That's four in the last hour."   The icon on Erik's display was moving, trajectory lines rearranging as steady thrust pushed it into orbital escape.   The icon's ID tag showed that it was a tavalai freighter, departing Stoya III's second main orbital station.

"If they wanted to move Lisbeth," Shahaim added, "they'd hub-dock the shuttle at one of the stations, then direct transfer to the ship on the station rim.   Avoids station security, plus we can't track it."

At Scan Two, Second Lieutenant Jiri nodded.   "Yeah, I've been tracking that since Lisbeth vanished, not a single shuttle up from Stoya III has made direct dock with a ship.   If they're moving Lisbeth, they're doing it via station hub."

"Hiding what they've done so we can't run the fuckers down and gut them before they leave system," Kaspowitz muttered.

Because *Phoenix* could, of course.   Erik watched all the outbound icons — four in the last hour, as Geish had said, another thirteen in the three hours before that.   Adding up the timelines, and how long it would have taken a vehicle leaving Doma Strana under cover of jamming to reach a nearby spaceport, then an orbital shuttle up to a station… there had been about forty of those in that time period, within reasonable flying range of Doma Strana.   Any of them could have been carrying Lisbeth, and now any of these departing ships could be carrying her too, and like the baffled victim of a master shell-game player, *Phoenix* had no idea under which cup their desired thing was hidden.

Erik itched to give the command to run them all down, and board each in turn before they could run for jump.   Even then, he'd never get them all in time.   And the tavalai Fleet would have something unpleasant to say about a human vessel in tavalai space, running down local traffic and boarding them under arms.   He dreamed an impossible dream.   All of this firepower at his disposal, and he'd never felt so helpless.

"We'll get her back, Captain," said Shahaim.   "*Phoenix* never leaves crew behind."   There were growls of agreement across the bridge.

Erik took a deep breath.   The whole thing was so intensely personal, but there was no privacy for him here, not on this.   In this matter, there was far more than just Lisbeth's life at stake.

"Okay," he said, "we have to talk about this. Us command crew. Lisbeth is crew now, but she's also my sister. That's against Fleet regs, for reasons that are even more obvious now than usual, but then I seem to recall it wasn't my idea to bring her aboard."

They were all listening. Strapped into their posts, eyes on screens and fingers working where required, but listening.

"First of all, it's a conundrum. Lisbeth is one person, and all of you are my brothers and sisters too. Her life is no more important than that of any of us, and we can't risk everything just for her." He took another deep breath. His voice had nearly cracked on that last sentence. Saying it, and meaning it, was one of the hardest things he'd done, sitting in this chair. "On the other hand, as the Commander says, Lisbeth is also *Phoenix* crew. And *Phoenix* does not leave crew behind."

It wasn't even technically true. Ships left crew behind all the time — marines on station, engineers stuck outside fixing things when a new threat emerged on scan. But those were unavoidable, and as soon as the opportunity presented, ships would return and search. In the war, there were always smaller ships, recon runners, who would return to the scene of battle and sweep for survivors. Sometimes those ships had encountered tavalai runners doing the same, and each had ignored the other by mutual, civilised agreement, and sometimes even tagged enemy survivors for the others' benefit. Now there were no friendly runners, no one else to go searching for Lisbeth's location. Out here, it was just *Phoenix*, and *Phoenix* had to look after its own.

"Captain?" said Second Lieutenant Karle from Arms. "This State Department vault, where *Makimakala* thinks Drakhil's diary is hidden. Can we get in there? Can we steal it?" Erik glanced at him — the Arms One post further right, largely hidden behind Erik's command displays, as everything was largely hidden, on a cluttered, intensely engineered warship bridge. "Because it seems to me that that's what Aristan wants, and that's what we want... so maybe Lisbeth's not in much danger after all. Because we and Aristan seem to be going in the same direction. She's just his insurance policy, in case we screw him over."

Erik nodded slowly. And glanced around the bridge, inviting others to have their say. "How do we get in there?" Kaspowitz asked. As one of the three *Phoenix* bridge veterans, besides Shahaim and Geish, he usually felt it fell to him to ask hard questions. "*Makimakala* haven't said where it is, but it's bound to be somewhere in the heart of tavalai space. What excuse would we have to go there?"

"And then once we get there," added the frequently gloomy Second Lieutenant Stefan Geish, "how do we break into what's certain to be one of the most heavily secured facilities in the known galaxy, steal something that's been one of the State Department's most highly prized secrets for the past fifteen thousand years at least, and then get away alive?"

"Captain," interrupted Lieutenant Shilu at Coms One, "I have *Makimakala* incoming. It's Captain Pram."

Erik blinked on his screen icon, flashing as Shilu put it there. "Hello Captain, this is Debogande."

"Captain Debogande," came Pram's familiar, throaty voice. *"I'm afraid we have been summonsed to Tivorotnam Station. Both of us, effective immediately. It seems that recent events will require a full briefing to the authorities."*

Erik frowned. "Which authorities, Captain? Who has summonsed us?"

"Tavalai Fleet, Captain Debogande. And they seem no happier with me than they are with you."

It took a full three hours for *Phoenix* to reach Tivorotnam Station under insystem traffic rules, a trajectory *Phoenix* could otherwise have achieved in minutes. And that, Erik thought grimly, was probably a large part of the problem — State Department had warned them against violent manoeuvres in Stoya III orbit, and *Phoenix* had not only ignored them, but threatened to fire on them. He'd been warned by Captain Pram in the strongest terms, prior to entering tavalai space, that tavalai took their rules and regulations very seriously.   Breaking them, even under emergency circumstances, was not something to be done lightly, least of all by renegade human vessels only allowed in tavalai space upon the very irregular authority of the Dobruta.

Several large tavalai warships shadowed them all the way in, none quite as devastating as *Makimakala* or *Phoenix*, but making clear their very official displeasure by positioning themselves to create a crossfire of both vessels between them.   Cruising up to a big tavalai commercial station filled with watchful civilians, Erik had the image of a naughty schoolboy being escorted to the headmaster's office by several very stern teachers.

Both *Phoenix* and *Makimakala* were directed to take hub berths, then were permitted to take shuttles direct to the rim, bypassing internal station protocols.   Erik supposed that marching a bunch of military humans through the middle of a busy station would create more commotion than tavalai Fleet desired.   Tavalai media were reputedly even more noisy and troublesome than the human kind, and prone to asking their superiors difficult questions of the type that many human media had learned to reluctantly decline. In human space, reporters had been given strict guidelines as to what was and was not allowable during the war.   But in tavalai space, telling tavalai to stop arguing was like telling them to stop breathing, and about as productive.

Erik took PH-1, which docked at an upper rim berth.   No armour or weapons were allowed, and so he strode at Trace's side with only Staff Sergeant Kono and Private Kumar for an escort. The rim berth was isolated from the rest of station, reserved solely for tavalai Fleet, as apparently were these entire few levels of the rim.

They were greeted at the airlock by fully armoured karasai with big guns, then escorted down bland station halls where the only other tavalai were Fleet.   Erik yawned and popped his ears repeatedly in the higher tavalai air pressure, sweat already prickling on his brow from the crazy humidity.   If this was what tavalai found 'normal', no wonder they brought their own water bottles aboard whenever they came to *Phoenix* — they feared dehydration in the dry human air. Passing Fleet tavalai looked at them, then studiously looked elsewhere and hurried on, as though they'd been specifically instructed not to stare. Through open doorways, Erik glimpsed offices, not unlike a human Fleet HQ. He tried to imagine what it must have been like during the war, for HQs like this, dealing with the mess created by warships like the one currently docked at the station hub, crewed by people like Trace and himself.

At an intersection corridor he met Captain Pram and his senior karasai — Djojana Naki, who was Trace's equivalent on *Makimakala*, plus two more karasai guards — having docked at a shuttle berth on the opposite side of the station rim. The *Makimakala* crew were just as unarmed and unarmoured as the humans, but they were free of armed station escort — that precaution was reserved for humans. Pram nodded to Erik, and they turned to walk the next length of hallway together.

Erik tried an uplink com for silent conversation with his counterpart, but received no icon. Perhaps Pram did not trust the local station networks. Or perhaps he did not wish to demonstrate to local Fleet just how closely he and the humans were now working — that the captains would share uplink protocols for secure, direct communications. No doubt *that* would raise a few eyebrows... or produce a few one-eyed squints, as was the tavalai equivalent expression. Or perhaps they just were simply in that much trouble, and talking, even silent talking, was simply not allowed.

The hallway descended some steps, then passed some big seal doors into a wide office. The far wall was mostly windows, a heavily-reinforced view of rotating stars and passing ship traffic, with the occasional glimpse of the turning Stoya III horizon. A central indentation in the floor before the windows made the ubiquitous tavalai bowl-chairs, a hollow space about a central table. Standing before it were four tavalai of varying colours, from mottled tan-brown to mottled grey-black. All four wore the uniforms of spacers — three captains and one admiral... or tvorata and ebono, as the tavalai called them.

The Admiral, whose skin was almost reddy-brown, said something in untranslated Togiri, at which the armoured karasai nodded, and clumped back to wait at the door. Pram indicated that his two unarmoured karasai should join them.

"Go," Trace said to Kono, in a low voice. "It looks official, we'll be fine."

"Will there be refreshments?" Kumar wondered. Another officer might have been unimpressed — the situation looked serious, Kumar was only a private amongst captains and admirals, and now he was being a smart ass.

But Trace smiled. "You wouldn't like it Bird, tavalai don't like sugar."

"Figures," Kumar complained, and went with his Staff Sergeant to the doorway. The doors hummed shut, and the command crew of *Phoenix* and *Makimakala* stood grimly opposite the line of stern-faced tavalai commanders. Erik waited for the lectures and threats to begin.

Instead, Captain Pram walked to the Admiral and grasped him by the shoulders. The Admiral did the same back, and they both broke into chortling, snorting laughter. Erik stared, then looked incredulously at Trace. Even more amazing, Trace gave him a similar look, so astonished that her usual discipline faded. It occurred to Erik that he'd never heard a tavalai laugh. Given the circumstances in which they'd usually met, he doubted Trace had either. But now, watching Pram laugh and clap his comrade on the arms, Erik found that suddenly sad.

Pram repeated the greetings with the other captains, although with more restraint, and introduced Djojana Naki to each. And then, with both standing aside, he switched to English.

"Gentlemen," he said, "this is Captain Debogande of the *UFS Phoenix*, and his marine commander, Major Thakur. Captain, Major, this is Admiral Janikanarada, Captain Delrodaprodium, Captain Toladini and Captain Panditatama. For human convenience, you may call them Admiral Janik, Captain Del, Captain Tol and Captain Pandi."

"Captain," said Admiral Janik, and swaggered to Erik with that familiar tavalai gait, his hand extended. "I am sorry for the great display on the way in. We had to make it look convincing."

"Ah," said Erik, shaking the Admiral's hand, as Trace did in turn. "You are maintaining appearances. For the State Department?"

"Always," said the Admiral, soberly. "Please, we will sit. Would you have a drink? No alcohol, of course."

They went to the bowl table, which was designed for perhaps twelve and fit the eight of them comfortably. A uniformed staffer emerged with drinks, which sure enough were dry and bitter, without a hint of sweetness. But they were cool, and welcome in the oppressive humidity. Erik wished he could loosen his collar, but as an officer amongst alien officers he could not contemplate the impropriety.

"Captain," Admiral Janik said to Erik, "my sympathies about your sister. I am sorry that we cannot help you track her, for Fleet are restricted in our ability to monitor tavalai civilian traffic, by tavalai domestic law. Those who abducted her will surely be using tavalai freighters, probably docking an external shuttle so as not to trouble with freighter manifests or pass inspections — on their way out of tavalai space the inspections are light, customs agents are mostly concerned with what enters our space, not with what leaves."

"Thank you," said Erik. He was quite certain that if he allowed it, the tavalai would sit and talk over drinks for a long time before coming to the point. Given the events of the day, he had no patience for it. "If you'll forgive me Admiral, my ship has many pressing concerns at this moment that I'd like to address. What is this about?"

Admiral Janik blinked. "Hmm," he said. "So." Whether he was offended at the rushed pleasantries, or just wondering how to begin, Erik did not know or care. "I understand from my friend Captain Pram that you have recently come into some information about an item you would like to recover. An item that currently resides in a top secret State Department vault."

Erik and Trace both shot Captain Pram alarmed looks. "I should have explained," said Pram, "but there was no time. Admiral Janik and I go back a long way. We both have similar feelings about the State Department. These feelings are shared by a large portion of the tavalai Fleet."

"I was under the impression that the Dobruta are not popular amongst your Fleet either," Erik replied.

"The two are not exclusive," said Pram. "You must understand. Under this State Department, we have had many small wars, and just recently have lost a very large one. Many in Fleet are not impressed at how the war began in the first place, nor how it's been prosecuted since. We have lost so many lives, Captain. As humans have."

"More," said one of the other tavalai captains, grimly. "Many, many more." His tone was resentful. Erik spared him a glance, watchfully.

"And now there is the matter with the sard," said Admiral Janik. "All policies dictated by State Department, as you call them. Before that, as you'll know, it was the krim."

"We know," said Erik, with another glance at the resentful captain. That captain looked aside... perhaps an acknowledgement that his species weren't the only ones with cause for resentment.

"For thousands of years, the State Department in its many varieties has managed these affairs," Janik pressed. "Many in Fleet do not feel they have managed it well. I cannot tell you exactly what we want to do about this — that decision is far above my rank. But I can tell you that State Department is most obscure in their ways, when they have in the past promised to be transparent. Some of those secrets, they hide in a vault."

Erik opened his mouth to say 'ah'... and stopped it. He looked at Trace. Trace's look was wary. It didn't take a very suspicious person, at this point, to smell an enormous set-up. "Let me guess," said Erik. "You, too, know of things hidden in a very secret State Department vault that you would like to see for yourself."

"You guess correctly," said Janik.

"And you can't get access officially, because getting anything from State Department bureaucracy is like trying to get blood from a stone."

"Interesting analogy," said Janik, unblinkingly serious. "And also correct."

"And so in typical tavalai style, you need someone else to take all your risks for you, so that if we get caught, you can deny all knowledge and blame it on the crazy renegade humans."

Janik might have smiled, that inward swivel of wide-set eyes. "You're very good at this guessing business, Captain Debogande. You might like to try a casino, I believe they're called in English?"

"Wait," said Trace, interjecting with her finger point-down on the table. "Let's be clear about this. You want to help us to rob the State Department's most secure vault?"

"A crazy notion that I will deny to my dying breath should I be accused of it," Janik answered. "But yes."

"And why should we trust you?"

"Because firstly," said Janik, "if you wish to recover the item in question, I believe you have no other choice. Those are quite rare, they don't exactly grow on riverbanks. And secondly, the worst that could happen to *Phoenix* in this venture is that you could all die, and your ship be destroyed. Believe me, in tavalai space, there are far more simple ways for me to arrange that. If I wanted you harmed, I'd choose a method far less potentially incriminating to myself, don't you think?"

"You want to help?" said Erik. "You could start by telling us where this vault is."

"And when I tell you," Admiral Janik replied with a more obvious smile, "you'll understand exactly why you so badly need my help."

CHAPTER 10

"It's in Kantovan," said Erik. The senior officer crew, assembled in the briefing room about the central holographic space, were too professional to mutter in disbelief. But Erik could see it in their eyes.

Kantovan System had been the seat of power for Spiral government for more than six thousand years — perhaps three-quarters of the time since tavalai had been the dominant species after overthrowing the chah'nas. Even human schoolchildren knew of Kantovan — the great Tsubarata parliament in orbit about the desolate but habitable world of Konik, the vacant seats for humanity in the great Chamber of Species left empty since Earth's destruction a thousand years before.

"That's one of the busiest systems in tavalai space," Kaspowitz observed. "One of the busiest systems in the Spiral."

"Yes," said Erik. He sat on the edge of his chair beside Trace, and indicated to Stan Romki, who stood. "Stan knows tavalai space better than any of us, so he'll take it from here. Stan?"

"Thank you Captain." Romki usually looked self-conscious, talking to military people whose intelligence he didn't always respect. In the past, the disrespect had often been mutual. But now he looked calmer, perhaps more confident of his place here amongst the crew, despite his ongoing lack of rank or uniform. He flashed a holographic map of Kantovan System in mid-air within the circle of chairs. "Kantovan has a single G1 Class star, and three middle-distant gas giants with some enormous industrial operations — those three between them account for two-thirds of all the system traffic, there's nearly a hundred million tavalai in those facilities alone.

"The other third of the traffic is here, at Konik." He zoomed the image, upon a yellow-brown world with white-capped poles and a scattering of temperate seas and lakes. Orbiting was a very large moon, shining white with thick cloud, and a single, very small planetoid in much closer orbit. "Konik was settled during the Parren Age — it was an unbreathable dustbowl when they started, but the terraforming kicked in a thousand years later and now it's quite pleasant. Some greenery and natural water systems about the poles, but the equatorial belt's still largely dead.

"Konik declined under the chah'nas, but came roaring back under the tavalai. There were already parren, chah'nas and other species living there in settlements thousands of years old when the tavalai took it over, so rather than boot them out, the tavalai allowed free cities, where the usual restrictions of tavalai citizenship are waived, and species from all across the Spiral can emigrate and settle if they choose. There's about thirty of them on Konik, countless smaller settlements, total population about a billion, barely a fifth of them tavalai.

"The biggest city you've probably heard of is Gamesh, right here on the temperate fringe." Another zoom, to an overhead image of a sprawling settlement across yellow-brown plains. It looked huge. "I think it's about forty million people now — the tavalai are very vague, the whole point of free cities is to keep the bureaucracy to a minimum. And it works, because there's real money there, along with some truly depressing poverty, but beings keep coming. I even met a few humans when I was last there."

"You'd think the froggies would learn that they'd do better without their bureaucracy," Shilu remarked. It had been a pet hate of his, since *Phoenix*'s first entry into tavalai space. As Coms Officer, and legally trained, Shilu was the one who got stuck with all the paperwork. "Given that when they remove it, that happens." He indicated to the huge, thriving city.

"Yes, that does happen," Romki agreed. "And so does poverty, crime and even malnutrition. By 'free cities' they really do mean free — the tavalai government doesn't provide much in the way of services, and people who go there are on their own."

"Sounds fine by me," said Lieutenant Dale, on Trace's other side. Trace smiled faintly.

"Isn't the marine corps a curious place for a libertarian?" Romki asked him condescendingly.

"Sure," said Dale. "Isn't academia a predictable place for an asshole?" Nearly everyone laughed. Erik saw Romki uncertain for a split second, and on the verge of temper, or upset.   But a glance Erik's way, and Trace's, showed them both smiling broadly, and Romki joined them.   Very slowly, he was learning what on *Phoenix* passed as basic social skills.

"Yes," Romki admitted, adjusting the AR glasses on his bald head.   "Yes, I suppose it is.   Anyhow, Gamesh is a central control and supply node for the entire system, more than any other Konik city, and operates many of the Tsubarata's security functions from the ground.

"The Tsubarata, of course, is in geo-stationary orbit directly above Gamesh."   The holographics zoomed on the small planetoid. It looked like a big rock with a pair of giant, metal bands wrapped around its girth.   "The rock itself is about eighty kilometres in diameter.   Those twin bands are habitation rims, as on any space station, but on about ten times the scale, running on magnetic rails about the rock.   Within are huge zero-G storage and manufacturing regions, but the primary business of government and all its attendant bureaucracy lives in those habitation rings.   The population is about a million permanent staff and other civilians, but on important political occasions that can as much as double.   But, if what the Captain tells me is correct, the Tsubarata is not specifically what we're interested in."

"The State Department have headquarters there," said Kaspowitz.   "The vault isn't in their Tsubarata HQ?"

"No," said Romki, with a quizzical look at Erik.   He switched the holographics again, and the image zoomed upon the large, white-clouded moon, in much further orbit about Konik. "Apparently the vault is here.   Kamala, Konik's moon."

"Kamala?" said Kaspowitz.   A disbelieving smile spread across his face.   "Kamala's a hell hole.   It's a greenhouse world, it's mostly CO_2, the surface is high-pressure and super hot.   You land a regular shuttle there, you get crushed, then incinerated."

"Exactly," said Erik.   "They use heavy descenders to get to the surface.   It's fast work, even the biggest of them can't last more than an hour or two, and every now and then they lose one."

"And the Kantovan Vault is at the bottom of *that*?" asked Shahaim, pointing at the thick blanket of high-pressure cloud.

"Hell of a hiding spot," said Erik with a nod. "If it were anywhere else, anyone could access it. On the surface of Kamala, it's nearly impossible. Heavy descenders are rare, difficult to fly, and in tavalai space even more difficult to licence. Taking one into Kantovan System will immediately raise suspicions."

"And where exactly is the vault, on the surface?" Shahaim pressed.

Erik smiled grimly. "No one knows. Descending ships must first visit one of the atmospheric floating platforms above the clouds, then wait for security clearances in a coms and navcomp blackout. The atmospheric platforms circle the moon every five or six days on high-altitude winds, and take the platforms random places — by the time clearance comes, you could be anywhere. With clearance comes descent coordinates, which the pilot flies semi-manual because the conditions are so unpredictable, but without external reference he's got no idea where he is. And upon ascent, the descender's navcomp is erased, so there's no record of where it's been. Even tavalai Fleet doesn't know where the vault is on the surface, and no orbital scanning can penetrate those clouds. Radar won't do it — the vault is underground. From orbit it looks like just more hot rock, and State Department control all orbital permission anyhow — only State Department vessels are allowed in close enough orbit to scan."

Kaspowitz extended long legs, and crossed both them and his arms, regarding Erik skeptically. "Well that sounds nearly impossible. Basically we'd need permission from State Department before we go down to rob their vault."

"It gets better," said Trace. "The vault has the highest level security on all accesses, so you can't sneak anything inside — no weapons, bombs, tools, nothing. There are armed guards too, with considerable firepower, so we'd have to deal with them as well."

"Barehanded," Dale grumbled.

Trace nodded enthusiastically. Erik found himself watching her. If he'd seen her like this before he'd gotten to know her better, he'd have suspected she was enjoying herself. Now that he did know her better, he was certain of it. "And lastly, here's one for you, Rooke."

"Yeah?" Lieutenant Rooke perked up. He'd already been listening intently, as expected of *Phoenix*'s Engineering Commander and all-round whiz-kid.

"Graviton capacitors."

Rooke's eyes went wide. "No!"

"That's impossible," Kaspowitz snorted. "There's no such thing as artificial gravity." As Navigation Officer, gravity in all its aspects was a central feature of Kaspowitz's professional life.

"What do they use them for?" Rooke pressed Trace, ignoring Kaspowitz completely.

"Defence of the inner vault," said Trace, eyes gleaming. "The actual storage vault. It's ringed with graviton capacitors to the force of one hundred Gs. Anything attempting to approach it will be crushed."

"Cool!" Rooke exclaimed. Trace nodded in agreement, and even Dale looked amused to see his Major's mood.

"They'd collapse the entire chamber," Kaspowitz snorted. "Hell, if it worked as well as all the nonsense I've heard about artificial gravity, they'd collapse the entire moon, it's nuts."

"I thought you just said it wasn't possible in the first place," Shahaim challenged him.

"And I'm pointing out the many reasons *why* it's not possible."

"Yeah," Rooke interrupted, "and there's a huge difference, Kaspo, between not possible for humans, and not possible for everyone else. There's been high-tech sentience in the Spiral for tens of millennia before humans even got into space — how would you know if something wasn't possible?"

"It's called physics," Kaspowitz said firmly. "I've got degrees in it."

"Styx?" Rooke called to the empty air. "Artificial gravity, is it possible?"

"Yes," said Styx.   Rooke gave Kaspowitz a 'so there' look. Kaspowitz scowled.

"So let's get this straight," said Shahaim, calm and methodical as always.   "If we're even going to consider this, we'll need to divide the mission into the following tasks…"

"Hold… hold on a moment," Romki interrupted, and got a hard look from Shahaim.   "With apologies, Commander, but… let's not just go tearing off on some new exciting mission before we've exhausted all the possibilities.   Firstly, I mean, it's quite obvious that this Admiral Janik character is setting us up for something.   Let's consider it — first the Dobruta invite us into tavalai space, having arranged a meeting with Aristan himself, a very controversial character in parren and tavalai space… and despite all the protestations of how unpopular the Dobruta are with tavalai Fleet, our friend Captain Pram just *happens* to have a friendly admiral here waiting for us and Aristan, who just *happens* to have an idea for breaking into this secret State Department vault?"

He looked around at the circle of chairs, in moderate disbelief.   As though thinking that *surely* he couldn't be the only person here intelligent enough to see something so obvious.

"Never occurred to us, Stan," said Erik.   Small smirks from the other officers.   Realisation dawned on Romki's face — Erik had to give the man credit, he *was* very fast to pick up things he'd overlooked.   Like the fact that all of the officers here were privy to other command meetings, where things were discussed that Romki wasn't invited to.   "But now that we have you here — what do *you* think is going on?"

"Well who can say, with the tavalai," said Romki with some exasperation.   Adjusting his glasses again, a nervous habit.   "And my studies are focused more on tavalai civilian and social structures, military matters aren't my specialty.   But I'd guess some sort of power play.   It's not surprising that elements of tavalai Fleet are unhappy with State Department, but I'd severely doubt that their stated reasons for wanting us to rob that vault are their *only* reasons. Possibly not even their primary reasons."

"But they'll never tell us," Shahaim resumed, still displeased with being interrupted, "and we've already concluded that devious help is better than no help. And so, as I was saying — we'll need to break the mission down into components.

"Component one; we need a good reason to go to Kantovan System. A good lie, like the one we spun our own Fleet at Heuron, before they suspected we'd gone renegade."

"I've got an idea," said Erik. "I'll flesh it out a bit more before I spring it on you, but I think it's promising."

"Is it as good an idea as the one we had at Heuron?" Trace asked.

A few months ago, Erik would have demurred, saying that it wasn't for him to make that judgement. "I think it might be better," he said instead. "It's certainly a lot bigger."

Trace smiled. "Can't wait."

"Second component," Shahaim continued, "we need as much intelligence on that vault as possible. We can't possibly plan a robbery if we don't know what's down there. So we need to find a way to acquire that information."

"Well our king of acquiring information is currently down on Doma Strana," said Trace. "Our two kings, actually. When Jokono and Hiro get back, we'll put them onto it."

"We're going to need a *lot* of tavalai help on that," Shilu added, sitting with his usual elegance, legs folded, lean-faced and cool. "My Togiri isn't wonderful, but Lieutenant Lassa's is excellent, and she knows tavalai society quite well... not to Stan's standard, but well enough."

Erik nodded — Lieutenant Angela Lassa sat Coms on *Phoenix*'s second-shift, and was Shilu's contemporary in all such matters. "That sounds like a team. We'll put Lieutenant Lassa in command, Ensigns Jokono and Uno, plus Stan, of course. Stan, we'll need you to help make a list of all the people who might be helpful to get us information on anything connected to the vault — anything about Gamesh, the Tsubarata, Kamala, etc. We need contacts."

Romki nodded, without enthusiasm. "I'm not certain I know anyone helpful in those fields, but I'll try."

"Third component," Shahaim continued, "we'll need a heavy descender. A good one."

"There's only one species that make those to specifications," said Kaspowitz, gnawing a thumbnail. "And we'll want the best."

"You're the Nav Officer," Erik told him, "you'd have as good an idea of where to look as any. We may have to send a party to acquire one, depending on how helpful Admiral Janik can be. My guess is he can get us cover, but can't do anything so direct as buy or lend us one himself. He'll want to cover his tracks from his enemies."

"I'll get onto it," Kaspowitz agreed. "I've heard a few things about where one might be found, maybe our tavalai friends can help us confirm if they're true."

"Fourth component," said Shahaim, ticking off another finger. "We'll need some kind of crazy plan for fooling the State Department's traffic control system to the vault from the inside. Because we sure as hell can't blast our way down there — in Kantovan System we'd be dead faster if we tried something violent than if we did it right here in Stoya. Much faster."

"Anything run by computers, we're good with," said Rooke. Erik thought he looked nearly as enthusiastic as Trace. "We've got Styx."

"We do have Styx," Erik agreed, though cautiously. "What's five, Suli?"

"Fifth component," said Shahaim, "is the attack plan on the vault itself, assuming we can pull off all the rest, and fool the traffic control system into allowing our heavy descender down there. That component will have multiple sub-components, including how to get weapons and equipment past the outer doors, how to bypass or subdue any guards as needs be, and finally how to overcome those… " she looked at Rooke again.

"Graviton capacitors," said Rooke, like a kid explaining to his mum about the latest must-have gizmo.

"Right, sure."

"I've got that one," said Trace. "Theoretically there's not much difference between a covert assault mission and an advanced robbery. It'll be interesting." Which was why she liked it so much, Erik guessed. Professionals always wanted to test themselves, if only to learn new things. But a true professional could never afford to test herself on something frivolous. This, however, was incredibly important. In combination, it made a job like this, for Trace, a thing of genuine enthusiasm.

"Might have you contemplating a career change," Erik suggested. Trace rolled her eyes.

"If I might venture," Styx suggested over room speakers, *"I may have an effective method of dealing with the graviton capacitors."*

"You do?" Rooke almost gasped.

"But if implemented, it will take some preparation. And I will need a more accurate description of the capacitors' capability than has so far been supplied."

"Right," said Erik, looking around. "Final thoughts?"

"Yes," said Dale, arms folded. "This is nuts."

"More nuts than Heuron or Tartarus?" Trace asked her second-in-command.

Dale thought about it. "No," he said finally. "No, I think this is about business-as-usual nuts. Which means, with all respect Captain, that we probably can pull it off, because we're *Phoenix* and our capabilities are pretty nuts too." Erik couldn't help smiling at that parochialism from the gruff, cynical marine. And he could not deny that it warmed his heart. "But it's a hell of a risk. And no matter how good you are, if you take enough crazy risks, one of them will bite you eventually."

Erik didn't mind Dale's observation. This was the place for such observations, if they were constructively put. And besides, Dale was right. "The Major has told me on a number of occasions that a risk is only a risk if there's a choice," said Erik. "If there's a dangerous option, and a safe option, then the dangerous option is clearly a risk. But as I see this situation, our only safe option is sitting it out and doing nothing."

"I'm not suggesting that, sir..." Dale said with an offended growl.

Erik held up his hand. "I know you're not. You least of all, Lieutenant. But if the only safe option is not actually an option, then there is no risk, because there's no choice. We're hunting a data-core that contains the sum total knowledge of the Drysine Empire. With it, we suspect, are all the detailed ways in which the drysines beat the deepynines, in the biggest war the Spiral has ever seen. The deepynines are back, in alo space, and if we're going to have to beat them again, then that data-core will be essential, because right now all humanity is in the dark against them."

He looked about at them all. Serious faces watched back. "We *must* have that data-core. It contains secrets even Styx never had access to, and has no record of today for security reasons during the Drysine Empire. And Drakhil's diary is the best lead we have on finding it. Drakhil himself practically admits that it leads to the core, and other treasures like it, on that recording the Major and I recovered with Private Krishnan."

"Drakhil also said there were four more copies," said Romki

Erik nodded. "Hello, Styx?"

"Yes Captain," came Styx's patient voice.

"No one knows the scale of the old parren civilisation better than you, and the Tahrae's power within it. You know of all the places where Drakhil might have hidden another diary. How long do you think it might take us to find another?"

"For all their failings, the tavalai are certainly the most intellectually curious of the species to have occupied this region of space. Clearly they have found one copy, as the Dobruta records indicate. If they have only found one copy, in all their millennia of searching for such artefacts, then that would appear to indicate that those diaries are extremely difficult to find. And the odds that another species has found something, that the tavalai could not, seem low."

"And what about the codes that Drakhil reveals in his recording?" Romki pressed. "With further work..."

"Professor, I am unable to decode them. You have seen my capabilities. If I cannot decode them now, then I do not think it likely that I could find additional information in coming years that could help me decode them. Perhaps it will be possible, after some years, but I feel we are mostly agreed that such a period is too long to wait, for so uncertain an outcome."

"Well I'm uncertain that's correct," Romki hurried, "and I think that…"

"Professor Romki," Styx interjected. *"We discuss matters of probability, across the great span of the galaxy. The probable chance of an intersection between two possible points. I feel that I am best equipped to calculate such things of any being on this ship. And, if you will excuse my feeble knowledge of old Earth history, I feel that to chase these other copies of Drakhil's diary may be the equivalent of setting us upon a quest for the Ark of the Covenant. Or perhaps the Holy Grail. It will not end well, if ever."*

Erik blinked, having been unaware that Styx knew *any* Earth history. Then again, *Phoenix* possessed an encyclopedic library, which probably took her seconds to read and process. Romki sighed, and rubbed his head. "Yes," he said heavily. "Yes, I see your point."

"The Ark of the what?" Rooke asked him.

"Never mind child," Romki said tiredly. "I assure you, it's nothing like as thrilling as graviton capacitors."

Having no hope of sleep, Erik headed for the gym, then detoured to Midships in search of the latest commotion there. In a cargo hold off Berth 4, not far from the hydraulic grapples holding PH-4 to *Phoenix*, Skah had gotten himself wedged into a small access where no one could reach, and was refusing to come out. Some of the Midships second-shift looked quite concerned, floating in a zero-G cluster about the access, calling to the boy, trying to coax him out.

"I don't know Captain," said Spacer Roi helplessly when he enquired. "He just squeezed in there and wouldn't come out. He looks upset, he's just ignoring everyone."

Skah was popular shipwide, but after he'd helped save the life of Spacer Reddin on Joma Station, Midships Operations in particular considered him family. Now they were enticing him with promises of games. Petty Officer Zerkis was offering a candy snack. "Wouldn't hold my breath, Petty Officer," Erik told him, gliding up alongside. "He's not a pet, his life's not all food and walks."

He peered into the access, good for storing long loads, like bundled acceleration slings. Now at the far end he spied Skah, knees up and ignoring everyone, wedged in tight.

"Skah!" he called. "Skah, it's the Captain!" A furtive upward glance from beneath big, folded ears. "Skah, it's not safe to stay unsecured in Midships. Not safe, understand? If the ship has to move quickly, you can't get to an acceleration sling, and you'll get hurt."

"Actually reckon he'd be safer in that little tube than most places," Zerkis said in a low voice.

"Yeah, until we have to make a lateral spin and he shoots right out." Erik looked about, and saw Tif approaching with her usual lithe grace, rubbing tired eyes and correcting course past crew with little touches on handholds.

"What probren?" Tif asked wearily, coming to an easy stop. Erik indicated the tube, and Tif peered in. She growled and coughed at her son, unimpressed and none too sympathetic. Skah said something back, his voice small. Tif's reply was several volumes louder, irritable.

When she received no reply, she gave Erik a look of exasperation. "Upset 'bout Risbeth. You fix. I fright crew, on duty, no tine for kid ganes." She pushed off and headed back to the core, and gravity, and bed. Several of the crew exchanged looks. Kuhsi parenting styles were not soft and cuddly. Kuhsi kids were supposed to be functional parts of society, not just ornaments for their parents' emotional pleasure. Erik thought of his mother, and figured both he and Lisbeth knew something about that.

"Skah," he called down the tube, "I'm Lisbeth's brother, and I'm a lot more upset than you are. But you don't see me hiding in some hole, do you? Now come on, you're making trouble and if we have to move suddenly, you're going to get someone else hurt or killed." And to the crew about him, "Be firm, give him orders. He's used to that and I don't think he'll take you seriously, otherwise."

And he pushed off, following his pilot's lead.

He'd barely made it to the central core when Lieutenant Dufresne called from the bridge. *"Captain, we have a priority message from station. They say that Tokigala is charging Phoenix with multiple counts of violation, including lane violations, threats to fire upon a State Department vessel... you can guess the rest."*

"I can," Erik agreed, grabbing a handline to send him flying up the core from Midships to crew cylinder. "Do we have the exact language?"

"No sir, it's just a relay from station bridge at this point."

"Request the original, please." As several spacers came whizzing back the other way, through the narrow core. The connecting spine passed, and now the core walls were rotating as the crew cylinder spun.

"Yes sir, we're doing that. Sir, there's a new message direct from a tavalai ship on the rim, name Propanpala. ID says it's a legal department vessel, one of the bigger departments... it's coming through now, would you like a relay?"

"Don't bother Lieutenant, I'm on my way up to bridge now. ETA four minutes."

"Aye Captain."

Erik grabbed a coffee from the kitchen on the way — or rather, a spacer at the head of the short queue grabbed it for him, as was ship practice when senior officers got in line. It made him a minute late, five minutes instead of four, which would have horrified him a year ago. But when one was captain, and matters were not desperate, he figured he could afford another minute for coffee.

"Captain on the bridge!" Dufresne announced as he came in.

"You have command, Lieutenant Commander," Erik told LC Draper in the command chair.

"Aye Captain," Draper echoed, "I have command." He pointed at a display, as Erik took hold at Draper's side, ducking to peer over his third-in-command's shoulder. "Here's our translation — it's all very officious Togiri. Lieutenant Lassa says it's almost another language."

"It's tavalai legalese," said Angela Lassa from Coms One. "It's a total bitch to translate, it makes English legalese look simple. But the translator tells me that it's a summons."

"A summons to where?"

"I'm not sure, sir. The literal wording here is…" and she ran her forefinger across the text carefully, "…'the highest decisional authority'. Which could be any of about five tavalai courts, depending on which one they figure has jurisdiction. But the gist is that State Department are charging us with misbehaviour, and we'll have to answer those charges."

"Just great," said Draper. "That'll tie us down for the next few months at least. They'll kill us with lawyers, Captain. We'll get buried under them, and from there we can't do shit. We'll be stuck in court indefinitely."

"Sir," added Lassa, "I don't think this has much to do with us at all. I think this is a powerplay between State Department and the Dobruta. Dobruta invited us into tavalai space, and now State Department are rescinding that invitation. They can't do it directly, as I understand it the Dobruta do have the authority to give us protection here. But if the State Department has twisted this legal authority's arm to charge us with something, they can tie us down irrespective of the Dobruta's protection. That protection is only from physical harm, not from unrelated legal proceedings once we're here."

"Probably that was a part of the State Department's stitch-up in the first place," Dufresne agreed. "Use parren factions to attack us, then charge us with disorder if we retaliate. Either way, they've got us."

"I'm getting a new transmission," Lassa added. "It's from *Makimakala*, it's also heavy legalese. It looks like they're countering." She glanced over her shoulder at him. "Captain, should I query them? Find out what the hell's going on?"

Erik thought about it, staring grimly at the screens while sipping his coffee. He'd known they were asking for trouble, coming into tavalai space with only a Dobruta captain's word for protection. If he'd only known how *much* trouble... but he shoved that thought aside as soon as it surfaced. It was childish to complain about it now, whatever had happened to Lisbeth, and whatever the crazy troubles and schemes swirling about this Kantovan Vault. It was what it was, and he'd chosen this route with his eyes open. They all had, Lisbeth included. And now they were here, and stalling indecision wasn't going to cut it. To be in command meant to make decisions. So here came the first big one of his shiny new captaincy.

"Lieutenant Lassa, open a channel for me. I want *Propanpala*."

"Aye Captain," she said with faint puzzlement. "Channel to *Propanpala*." A pause as *Phoenix* queried the tavalai vessel. "I have confirmation, channel is open. *Propanpala* indicates translators are active, go ahead Captain." State Department and Dobruta dealt with humans all the time, and had lots of English speakers. *Propanpala* was from one of the huge central legal bureaucracies, and its operatives wouldn't have a dozen English words between them.

"Hello *Propanpala*," said Erik, "this is *UFS Phoenix*, Captain Erik Debogande speaking. For most of the last one thousand human years, humanity's rightful seat in the Tsubarata Chamber of Species has been empty. In all the troubles between our two species, no human has come forward to claim this chair. Tavalai laws state that the human entity claiming the Tsubarata chair needs to be a standing member of a major human political institution, in the direct employ of the central human government.

"On behalf of all humanity, *I* now claim the Tsubarata chair, on behalf of all humanity. It is my understanding that the Tsubarata

Parliament is currently in its four thousandth, one hundred and forty first sitting. The *UFS Phoenix* claims its legal right under tavalai law to travel to the Kantovan System, and occupy humanity's offices, and address the Tsubarata Parliament on the behalf of all humans in the Spiral. It is also my claim that this legal claim takes precedence over all other, frivolous claims against us, as the Tsubarata has superior status to the frivolous agencies that make them.

"The *UFS Phoenix* will await your considered reply. Captain Debogande, ending transmission."

About the bridge was silence, save for the ever-present white noise of control systems, ventilation and cylinder rotation. Those crew who could spare their eyes for a moment were staring. A few were grinning. Erik looked at Draper, and found the expression of a teenager whose crazy friend had just aligned a skateboard trick that would either set new records for awesomeness, or result in some spectacular injury. Or both.

Erik shrugged, and sipped his coffee. "Gets us to Kantovan," he offered. "And with any luck it'll get these lawyers off our ass."

"And neck deep in a whole new sea of Tsubarata lawyers," Lassa added, awestruck. "Sir... I mean it's brilliant, but..."

"It's more than brilliant," said Draper. "It gets us nose-in to the Tsubarata itself. Right up against the main control centre for everything in Kantovan System..."

"And we've got the Spiral's best codebreaker aboard," Dufresne said slowly, light dawning in her eyes.

"Exactly," said Draper. "Styx can get right into their systems, and *that* gives us a chance at that fucking vault."

"*If* they let it happen," Lassa cautioned. "I mean, we're not even still technically Fleet and thus human government employees, they've called us renegades and tried to kill us..."

"There's no mention of that distinction anywhere in the relevant tavalai laws," Erik told her. "I had Lieutenant Shilu check it with Romki. Maybe this isn't what they intended, but tavalai are legal nitpickers and if they haven't written their own damn laws properly, that's their problem."

Lassa didn't answer, her attention back on her screens. "Sir? Coms traffic between tavalai vessels just went nuts. Not just legalese, now heavy encryption."

"Which vessels?" Draper asked.

"Um… all of them. Looks like."

Draper smiled broadly at his Captain. "Outstanding."

CHAPTER 11

Lisbeth's ill treatment lasted until arrival after first jump. Then she was brought aboard ship by cloaked and faceless parren, and given quarters on the crew cylinder rim. She'd feared a prison cell, or worse, but the chambers were comfortably ten times the size of those she'd shared with Major Thakur on *Phoenix*. Given that *Phoenix* was a spartan military vessel that wasted no mass, it wasn't saying much. And yet, the parren room was long enough to see the slight curve of the crew cylinder floor — a lengthwise rectangle with decorative wall panelling, abstract patterns of grey and blue, and even some low, fixed furniture against the rear G-wall.

Her bunk was large against one side, and again luxurious by *Phoenix* standards. The opposite wall had a small, contained bathroom, little more than a closet, but any private washroom on a spaceship indicated a first-class cabin for a high-status passenger. And there was a display screen, but it remained blank when activated, and her uplinks gave her nothing.

A worse development was that the fear, newly awoken before that last jump, now faded once more. Normally she would have welcomed that decline, and hoped that it was a sign she was becoming braver. But now she stood on the bunk to sniff the air from the ventilation grille. It did not smell much different — parren were oxy-breathers like most of the primary Spiral species, and oxygen-nitrogen mix smelled mostly all the same. But she was certain that whatever her captors had put in the air-mix of her breather mask when they'd first taken her, was now being pumped into this room as well.

That made her angry. She didn't want to be sedated, and she didn't trust that parren knowledge of human biochemistry was sufficient that they wouldn't be causing her harm. And so she stuffed sheets from the bed into the ventilation grille, which was dangerous and against all regs on any ship, because of course, that was where her breathing air came from. But it had made her feel considerably better to have some way of fighting back.

Soon enough some parren had entered, and while one had watched her, unthreateningly, another unblocked the vents. Then both left. Lisbeth promptly stuffed the vents again, and four times the game repeated. Each time she glared at them, to make her displeasure known. Now she was certain that the vents were feeding her sedative, because normally she'd have been terrified her captors would strike her, or do some other retaliation. But now, she felt nothing.

On the fifth time the parren came to unblock the vent, one of them indicated to it, and made a switching motion with his (or was it her?) hand. Then what might have been a placating gesture. Then, once again, they'd departed. It was victory of sorts, though of course she had no idea if the parren had been telling the truth. The sedative, if sedative it was, was odourless, and she could only take their word for it. She did not feel a sudden rush of fear returning, but then, it was very clear by now that these parren were infinitely patient, and had no intention of harming her. No doubt she was valuable, though to whom, and for what purpose, she could not guess.

She thought about it for a long time, as the parren ship made what she guessed was an inertial crossing of a star system, heading for jump on the far side of the gravity-well. Those usually took a few days at least, and sometimes far longer, depending on how much of the crazy velocity the ship retained from jump entry. She might be stuck in this room for a long while, with no sense of the passage of either time or distance.

The first parren to come with food also brought a hand-controller for the wall screen, evidently not game to give her uplink access. The food was reasonable too — segmented portions of small, bite-sized meals on a tray, each delicately flavoured and subtle. The light soup that accompanied it was a revelation. Lisbeth flicked on the display screen, and found some basic channels. She couldn't recognise the script that described them, but as she clicked, she was astonished to find human entertainments. All 2D and non-interactive, but some of them entirely familiar — there was tennis and football, some popular talk shows, including one from Lisbeth's native Shiwon.   Some odd sensation that was, to see the homespun mundanity of 'Live with Juniper Roberts!' being played here, on a parren ship, headed for god-knew-where in parren space.

And there were soap operas, and movies, and... she blinked, as a porn channel opened.   Parren had put *that* on her entertainment package?   Well, she supposed they had no idea what any individual human might want to watch.   Captured and frightened (or she was pretty sure she was frightened, past the sedative) she was hardly in the mood.

Mood.   Parren were all about mood.   Sedative in the air, and quite probably in the food as well.   Happy, familiar things on TV, or even raunchy ones.   Comfortable quarters.   Everything a human captive might need to make her more manageable.   Parren civilisation was dominated by the fear of changing moods.

Only that wasn't quite right, she thought as she switched channel to some horse showjumping, eating some tasty coleslaw salad.   Parren called it a 'phase', she recalled from her meagre readings.   There were five primary parren phases, and it was no accident that there were also five primary parren Houses, one for each.   Each phase was a personality, and most parren switched personalities several times in a life.   Usually it passed without drama, as an individual reached a certain point of life, or came to a new understanding of his or her place in the universe.

Switching between phases was called a *troidna*, meaning a 'flux'.   When a parren switched phases, they moved from one of the great parren Houses to another.   When common folk fluxed, it caused little concern.   When great leaders fluxed, the foundations of great institutions rattled.   And when huge numbers of parren all switched together at the same time, in response to some calamitous event... then, sometimes, entire civilisations fell, and millions died in terrible wars.

Aristan threatened such an event with what he was seeking, Lisbeth knew.   Such a great revelation about the past history of House Harmony could send billions of parren fluxing from one phase to another in a great tide.   And the tavalai's State Department, it seemed, were terrified enough at the prospect to try and kill senior *Phoenix* commanders before it could happen. Or whatever they'd been trying to achieve with the attack on Doma Strana. Fat lot *she'd* know, she thought sourly, abducted and locked in the hold of a parren ship.

It only took a day until the second jump, then another day to reach a planet. Lisbeth had no idea which planet, the screen display had not said, not even in that strange parren script she couldn't read. But she was escorted from her quarters by more hooded and cloaked parren, through the zero-G central core into Midships, and then a shuttle.

She was further surprised that there were no more bags over her head, and no restraints on her wrists or ankles. They did not consider her to be any sort of threat, she thought drily, as the shuttle clamps disconnected with a crash and lurch. And with parren it was difficult for a human to judge whether what seemed politeness was actually just formality, or scathing contempt dressed as formality. The books Lisbeth recalled reading on the subject had insisted that parren weren't big on spontaneity. Now it seemed those books had been understating things.

As with most shuttles, there was no view on the way down, and she had no uplinks or AR glasses to access external feeds. Finally the retros roared, and the shuttle came to a light thud as the landing gear touched, then the roaring ceased. Lisbeth disengaged her own restraints, as parren in the wide, otherwise unoccupied cargo hold did the same. They waited for her, polite figures in rows, faces hidden, hands clasped beneath the sleeves of long robes.

Lisbeth stared at them all, defiantly. Then the rear cargo ramp clanked and descended with a hum, and she squinted into the sudden rush of sunlight. One of the robed parren presented her with some dark glasses, for the light was bright indeed. Lisbeth put them on, and walked with her robed escort down the ramp and into the light.

The first thing she noticed was the view.   The landing pad was high, perhaps the height of a smaller tower in a large city.   It sat upon the corner of a truly huge building, like a giant square, with tall, flat walls of what looked like stone.   No, she reconsidered as she stared around — it was trapezoid, wider at the base and tapering slightly as it rose.   The landing pad was two-thirds of the way up, upon a corner-shoulder of a separate level that ran right around the circumference, like the battlement of some old castle.   The entire structure *looked* like a castle, Lisbeth thought, with yet another level rising above this, sheer walls and narrow, arched windows with balconies ending in turrets and crenellations high above.   The base of the castle was the size of many city blocks, and the entire thing, she was certain, could have held hundreds of thousands of people... depending upon the internal layout, of course.

Below was an enormous expanse of interlocking courtyards. They were flat, and made patterns like a patchwork quilt.   Some were huge and featureless, great expanses of stone and paving that must surely heat to boiling temperatures in the midday sun.   Others were smaller, intimate, and landscaped like gardens.   Carefully tended hedgerows separated them, many with artificial streams, flanked with what looked like weeping willow trees, trailing long, golden fingers in the water.   All of the courtyards were precisely square, but the size of the squares varied, creating a mathematical jumble of interlocking yet misaligned sides.   Deliberately misaligned, Lisbeth thought, to create this precisely imprecise effect.

The courtyards stretched for kilometres.   Then came the buildings, old-style spires and tile rooves in one quarter, and low glass towers in another.   Beyond those, hills covered in trees.   The air was warm and the bright sunlight slanted golden and thick. Lisbeth turned full about, staring past the shuttle and her escort, and saw in another direction wide and featureless pavings, like a desert of blank stone, ending only in another castle-like structure of at least the same size as this.   Perhaps this was a palace complex?   A temple site of some kind?   She wished she knew where she was, but was nearly embarrassed to admit to herself that even if she were told, it wouldn't have helped her.   From the distant buildings came the hum of city life, traffic and activity.

Against the building sides, large doorways slid open, blast protection from landing shuttles.   A row of robed figures emerged from each doorway, yet these were not the black and austere robes of Aristan's kind.   These were dazzling, red and gold and blue, their hems sweeping the black-scarred pad surface.   Jewellery gleamed on tanned parren arms and fingers, and indigo eyes fixed on Lisbeth beneath headdress and crests of gold and other, precious decoration. Lisbeth stared, as both brilliant rows advanced on her from opposing sides, then met precisely in the middle, and stopped.

One of Lisbeth's robed captors strode forward to meet the greeting party.   Words were exchanged, with elegant, almost lisping parren vowels.   Lisbeth stared at the contrast they made — the dark robed parren who'd captured her, and these decorative newcomers. *This* was more like the human notion of the parren, brilliant and glamorous, dressed in finery that communicated signals of rank and identity that went back thousands of years.   Aristan's Domesh insisted that *they* were the truest, oldest part of parren identity. Lisbeth wondered if it were possible that both could be true.

The dark robed parren seemed to be challenging the leader of the greeting party.   The leader seemed unimpressed, and unyielding, glancing occasionally to Lisbeth.   Finally the dark robed parren also pointed her way, and seemed to be describing her, and her situation. Lisbeth tried to draw herself up, thankful that she was at least well rested and well fed, whatever her other, recent ordeals.

Finally the Domesh stood aside, and the leader of the greeting party approached.   He looked down at her from an imperious height, and produced an ornamental staff, held crosswise before him.   Then, with a single motion, the end of the staff was pulled, and a slim, silver blade was produced.   Lisbeth's heart, recently settled, abruptly startled… but the tall parren turned the blade around in his hands, and presented her with the hilt.   Lisbeth blinked.   Perhaps she should ask what the hell was going on, but it was all done in silence, and the presentation was so perfectly visual that somehow, she thought that words would spoil it.   Did they even have translators present?   Surely none of these magnificent aliens spoke English.

"You have been transgressed upon," said the tall parren, proving her wrong.   The accent was strong, pleasant and slightly lisping. "You are offered recourse."

Lisbeth blinked again.   "Recourse?   Recourse against whom?"

The English-speaking parren gestured with a flourish to her black robed guard.   They knelt, in unison.   The one nearest removed his hood, exposing a bald, smooth head and slim neck.   His eyes remained fixed on the landing pad, expression hidden behind his fabric mask.

Again the tall parren gestured with the hilt of the sword. Demanding she take it.   "Recourse?" Lisbeth said in horror as it dawned on her.   "You mean I can kill them?"

"You were taken against your will," said the parren. "Harmony demands that a price must be paid."

"Against *all* of them?"

"Should harmony demand it."

Abruptly, Lisbeth nearly laughed.   It was all so absurd. "I'm not going to kill them!   Besides, I'm sure they were just following orders."   Upon a wild impulse, she nearly asked if she could kill the one who gave the orders.   But that would be reckless. Major Thakur approved of strength and bravery, but not recklessness.

"You show compassion," said the parren.   "Compassion is harmonious.   But a price must be paid, nonetheless."

The guards remained kneeling.   In a flash, Lisbeth recalled something else she'd read about the parren — individualism was anathema to their societies, and they regarded tavalai and human versions of democracy with horror.   For a society where individuals could swing from one psychological state to another en masse, creating the most frightening upheavals, too much individual choice could be genuinely catastrophic.   And so parren had this, a formalised, ritualised society that put as many brakes on the sudden fluxing of psychological phases as possible.   Ritual created stability, and structure.   Without it, parren could flounder, and their societies become dangerous anarchy.

Finding herself abruptly in the middle of it all, Lisbeth realised that these parren weren't going to take no for an answer. Humans had abandoned a lot of old ritual because they could. Parren could not, and it was important to them not by whim or choice, but as food and water were important.   She'd have to do *something*.

Lisbeth took a deep breath, and grasped the hilt of the blade with one hand, willing it not to shake.   She could do this, she thought.   She was one of the heirs to Family Debogande, and she was not a total stranger to formality and ritual.   It was just that none of *those* rituals had involved killing people with swords.   She held up the blade and examined it.   It was light and slim, and gleaming in the golden sunlight, looked very sharp indeed.

She pointed the blade at the first dark robed parren who knelt.   "Tell this one to extend his arm," she said.   "Sleeve back." The tall parren said something in the local tongue, and the kneeling Domesh did as she instructed.   The exposed forearm was tanned almost to reddy-brown, and slim, as all parren were slim.   The eyes remained fixed on the pad, unblinking.

Lisbeth tried to steady her hammering heart.   Several deep breaths to stop her hand from shaking, and she laid the sharp edge to the parren's arm, and slid it.   And nearly gasped, because she hadn't intended to do it hard, yet the slide of sharp steel upon skin produced an immediate flow of dark red blood.   She nearly apologised, but stopped herself in time.   Her victim never flinched.

"There," she announced, turning on the tall parren.   "The price has been paid.   I am satisfied."   She offered the parren his blade back, without quite the stylish grace with which he'd given it, but he took it, and looked content.   Words were exchanged, and the Domesh stood, and moved quietly off the pad, in flowing dark lines. "Now, I want you to answer my questions.   Where am I?   Which planet, and which system?   And why was I taken?"

The tall parren actually smiled.   It surprised Lisbeth only because she'd never actually seen a parren's mouth move before —

the only ones she'd met to date were of Aristan's kind, robed and masked with only the eyes showing. "You are on Prakasis. This place is Kunadeen. And you were taken by long tradition of the parren clans, to protect the interests of the house and family. So long as those interests are met, you will be entirely safe. If your clan acts *against* the interests of the Domesh, it shall be otherwise. But come, Lisbeth of Family Debogande. I will show you your accommodations."

Erik strapped himself into the observer chair behind AT-7's pilots' chairs, as Lieutenant Jersey and Ensign Singh completed pre-flight. Trace took Observer 2, not her usual seat on a shuttle, but on the civilian AT-7 the rear layout was different, and there was no complement of marines to lead anyway, just Kono and Rael from Command Squad, plus Lieutenant Shilu. And on this flight, unlike others, they were promised a view.

Phoenix held at geostationary orbit, nearly forty thousand kilometres above the surface of Ponnai, the single inhabited world of Tontalamai System. Tontalamai was a monster, tavalai heartland into which very few humans had ventured in the past hundred and sixty years, and few enough even before then. Even after eight thousand years of dominance, tavalai continued to value some parts of their galaxy more than others. That which they'd lost to humans were mostly less important territory, which was not to say that losing it had not hurt terribly. But Tontalamai was a different place entirely, where tavalai had sunk their civilisational roots upwards of thirty thousand years ago, while the machines were still in charge, and tavalai had needed a place to hide and find some comfort in the places hacksaws rarely went.

Erik gazed at it out the main canopy now, a big continent below, the edge of night sweeping across the blue-green globe, leaving a trail of gleaming civilisation in its wake — the lights of many cities. Twelve billion tavalai on Ponnai, it was said. Seven major stations and numerous minor ones formed great orbital rings about it, and between those and the big mining stations on the uninhabitable outer worlds, the system traffic had to be seen to be believed. Erik thought it was even busier than Homeworld, perhaps by as much as half, an endless stream of busy ships, and a new jump entry every ten minutes at least, coming from all corners of tavalai space. Some on Homeworld had thought the tavalai a beaten people in the wake of the war, their economy ruined, their confidence shattered. Captain Pantillo had warned him that the reality was nothing so drastic, a notion that Romki had seconded. Being here now, and seeing this, Erik began to see the truth of it.

Lieutenant Jersey talked to the tavalai Fleet ships that had shadowed them through jump. *Makimakala* had a shuttle marked for descent as well, but now Erik's feed from *Phoenix* Nav showed him another three projected tavalai military shuttles coming down as well. To an outsider, it would look like tavalai Fleet escorting an unfriendly vessel. But now, there was Admiral Janik's offer of assistance to consider, and his declaration of common cause against State Department. As with all things bureaucratic and political with the tavalai, Erik doubted it was that simple.

"Captain, I have the course feed now from Ponnai Central," said Ensign Singh in AT-7's front seat. Singh was the oldest of *Phoenix*'s shuttle crew, and had been baby-sitting less experienced pilots for decades. *"Looks like we get in at two hours after midnight, local time."*

That didn't bother Erik — on *Phoenix* time that would be mid-afternoon, and Lieutenant Commander Draper was working a double-shift in the big chair. But the timing was curious. "Looks like they don't want us down when anyone will make a fuss. Lieutenant Lassa, any sign of a reaction on the surface?"

"No sir," said Lassa from *Phoenix* Coms. *"If the general population knows we're here, they're keeping quiet about it."* Tavalai security censorship was less severe than the human variety, on ship movements and general conversation both. *Phoenix* had not been broadcasting itself, transponders silent in a way that was itself conspicuous in a busy system. Surely the tavalai had amateur ship-watchers who scanned the skies for interesting vessels, and tried to

figure the who, what and why from those movements.   Some such amateurs had gotten themselves in big trouble on Homeworld.   Erik recalled his Uncle Calvin talking about defending one such amateur in a pro-bono civil liberties case, who hadn't realised his pastime could land him in such hot water.   Calvin had argued hard, but as usual, Fleet had won.   Two years in prison, for an innocent hobby.

"Tavalai politics are completely different to human politics," Trace said from Observer 2.   "The big institutions control all the vote, there's no such thing as a big popular vote like we know it.   I wouldn't expect any help there."

"I'm not," said Erik, as Jersey completed her pre-flight, and cut grapples with a clang.   "But if we claim the human chair in the Tsubarata, it's going to be a huge big deal.   You have to wonder." Jersey hit thrust, a gentle push toward the planet, all that these civilised space-lanes would allow, and Erik settled in to review personnel files and reports for the next hour.

Reentry was in a four-ship formation, wide-spaced and safe, and a common sight for any of the millions of Ponnai residents below within visual of their fire-trails across the night sky.   Then came descent, through some thick cloud and turbulence that bumped them around to a degree that might have been dangerous to an airplane, but was nothing to a shuttle with no truly atmospheric control surfaces, and designed to be treated like a pinball in combat.

"You know, I always hated atmospheric turbulence when I was a cadet!" Erik yelled across to Trace as they thumped and rattled, bright flashes lighting the canopy and held to their seats only by the harness.   "Nearly failed an early airplane solo because I got nervous in cloud!"

Trace did not reply, eyes closed and distant.   She did that for control… which meant she wasn't enjoying the turbulence at all. Erik smiled, and enjoyed the stomach-lurching falls that much more, knowing that here was one thing he did far better than her.

With a final rush of cloud, they were suddenly clear, and beneath them was a city. *What* a city.   Well after midnight, yet still it glowed and sparkled with endless towers and street lights, and a profusion of civilian air vehicles, a swarm like ten thousand fireflies, streaming in lines. It looked much like a human city, and yet somehow not — the buildings were wider, and well integrated into complexes, where human buildings stood separate and competed for space like sapling trees in a rainforest, each fighting to be first to reach the light. But the complexes were spectacular, ten or fifteen buildings in cooperation, working together off a single architectural plan. Erik saw an endless cityscape of them, stretching away on all sides amidst patches of darkness where the city lights did not penetrate — public parks, perhaps. The complexes were like snowflakes beneath a microscope, he thought — a symmetrical complexity, some tall, some shorter and some both, but all ingenious.

It fully struck him for the first time exactly where he was. On an alien world, the world of an enemy he'd spent much of his life at war with. He'd been on worlds before where aliens lived, but never a heartland world like Ponnai. A world so intensively tavalai that the tavalai knew it as humans from old Earth must have known their various, lost nation states.

"Did Earth ever reach twelve billion population?" Trace wondered aloud above the engine roar — off-mike so she didn't crowd coms with chitchat. History had never been Trace's strong point, Erik reflected.

"I think it did a few times briefly," said Erik, gazing at the lights as Jersey performed a left bank, following the Central-proscribed course. "About a fifth of them Indians, toward the end. Your people."

"My people were Nepali."

"That was a cultural choice, made by the first settlers. About eighty percent of the actual first settlers on Sugauli were Indian, relatively few Nepalis."

"Don't tell me who the Sugaulis are," Trace retorted. "I was born there."

"Sure," said Erik, smiling. "Why should facts matter?"

Jersey was bringing them down toward an amazing complex of buildings, rows of interlocking towers arranged in irregular concentric circles, like a maze. Thrusters angled as the shuttle shook, and tower-tops rose slowly past the canopy. "Ensign Singh," said Erik on coms.   "How much of this complex belongs to the Pondalganam, does the nav display tell you?"

"*Yes sir,*" Singh replied.   "*It looks like all of it.*"

Wow, Erik thought.   There could have been forty large buildings in the complex — a city in its own right, on many less populated worlds.   Romki said, and Captain Pram agreed, that there were about thirty-nine major legal institutions in tavalai space, and hundreds of minor ones.   The Pondalganam were one of the oldest and largest — still only a third the size of the very biggest, but making up in pedigree what they lacked in scale.

Tavalai legal institutions acquired official responsibilities the same way that ocean ships acquired barnacles — by the sheer accumulation of time.   The Pondalganam had been heavily involved in the legal arguments that had laid out the functioning of the Tsubarata, and the laws that defined how the various species of the Spiral would interact with the tavalai's central power.   As those arguments had progressed, the Pondalganam had come to be seen as the leading authority on the new inter-species laws that ruled the tavalai Free Age, and thus their power over the Tsubarata had been enshrined.   The Pondalganam were not a body that decided who got to sit in the Tsubarata and who did not — they were the body that guarded the rules that governed the process of finding out.   The adjudicators, who conducted the debate, and ensured everyone played by the rules, like referees in a football game.   Only these referees also owned the field, and all of the equipment by which the game was played.

AT-7 dropped into a layer of surface mist, white swirls and spirals blasting about the canopy until the landing legs touched, and Jersey cut thrust.   "*We are down, all systems green and no one is shooting at us,*" she announced as the engine howl declined.   "*I count that a success.*"

"Good work guys," Erik told the pilots, unfastening the harness and removing the headset.   "What's the weather like out there?"

"Well hold your nose and equalise," Singh told him over the back of his chair, as the engines faded enough to talk without shouting. "It's a muggy hundred percent humidity in one-point-three atmospheres, so you can imagine. About thirty percent oxygen, currently thirty-five degrees celsius, forecast is rain, then more rain."

"Great," said Erik, standing and stretching as best he could in the cockpit. "Today's forecast is soup."

"Hot soup," said Jersey, peering at tavalai pad crews hurrying outside. "Just hold another minute, we've got Fleet escort coming down alongside, lots of jetwash." And she grinned to herself. "Holy shit Captain, this place is amazing. Think we could go for a stroll? Buy some souvenirs?"

"At two in the morning there won't be much open," Erik told her. "But who knows, we might be here a while. Stay on alert, if there's any trouble with locals just nod and do whatever they say, we can't stop it. I'm pretty sure we'll be fine, froggies don't mess with their guests, but even so."

The atmosphere did feel a lot like hot soup, but it smelled also of trees and moss. Erik yawned and equalised the pressure in his ears as it flooded the shuttle's rear, sweating almost immediately in thirty percent greater humidity than a human's preferred air pressure could hold.

"No wonder tavalai like this place," Trace suggested, leading the way down the ramp by habit, Staff Sergeant Kono and Corporal Rael on the flanks, with Lieutenant Shilu trying to look elegant and composed as usual. On the pad, running lights strobed the misty air, and tavalai figures moved purposely, some pad crews, others not.

Some of the latter came toward AT-7's pad, in colourful robes that Erik had never seen before. The folds and belts of those robes looked highly impractical for space stations, with ornamental loose ends, dangling beads and silver weights. These were planet-tavalai, the vast majority of the tavalai race, just as with humans... though apparently much more appreciated by their spacers than in human space. Save for those on Stoya III, Erik had only met the spacer variety before.

The tavalai stopped in a neat row, and made a gesture of both hands before their faces, webbed fingers interlocked. Erik had seen that before, but only in movies. He returned it, which he understood was the protocol, and was gestured by one to follow. The humans did, as the tavalai led the way across the steamy landing pad between the hot pings from cooling shuttles, as cool rain spattered, and lightning danced behind the surrounding towers.

About the edge of the pad was a decorative moat, filled with lilies and fish, then big glass walls about the base of one of the towers. The humans were led within, and a wall of air-conditioning hit them, with physical relief. Erik wondered if it were always on this high, or if the tavalai had turned it up especially for their guests. About was an enormous atrium, the inner ten floors of the tower were all exposed glass levels, with great copper-coloured art features suspended in the middle space between, full of decorations, and no doubt symbolism, that escaped Erik completely.

"Should have brought Romki," Trace murmured, reading his thoughts. "Lieutenant, anything?"

"No, you've got me, Major," said Shilu, mystified and intrigued. "I know some of their legal principles and social structure, but that's it." But Stan Romki was busy, and Erik was not sorry for it, not wishing to have a loose cannon on this particular trip.

Ahead the floor rose in steps — Erik knew a little of tavalai architecture, and knew that this rise, like the bowl seating they preferred, symbolised the riverbank, or the shore line, the boundary between water and land, the time-honoured meeting place of this semi-amphibious people. Arrayed upon the steps were at least thirty tavalai, in a kaleidoscope of colours. Many held lilies and ribbons, and there were more conservative, monochrome robes worn by officials carrying great, worn old books, and others with stamps. The full official welcoming party, from the heads of the Pondalganam Syndicate, some of the most high-ranking tavalai in the entire Tontalamai System.

Erik considered them as he approached, and thought that for all the tavalai's stuffy formality and exasperating stubbornness, this was truly a remarkable quality to recommend them. *UFS Phoenix* had been a name hated and feared throughout tavalai space during the war, and yet here they were, welcomed in time-honoured tavalai tradition because this was simply how tavalai did things, and all the personal grievances in the world would not change it. This was not a people that would ever be ruled by their baser instincts — by fear, rage or hate. That was the best of the tavalai. But then, neither were they a people to be driven by compassion or sentiment, either. Tavalai did things *properly*, or not at all. They were predictable, and sensible, by their own calm logic, at least. They made good friends and awful enemies, and were relentless on principle where humans so often rushed to emotion. Lately, Erik had been wondering more and more how it was that with all the truly awful species in the galaxy, humans had managed to acquire these exasperating but fundamentally civilised people as their number one enemy. Lately, indeed, it had not seemed right.

"Fleet escort's remaining outside," Staff Sergeant Kono said in a low voice, glancing behind so his superiors didn't have to. "*Makimakala* too. I don't think they have the authority to be in here. Just us."

"Then who the hell invited *them*?" Corporal Rael wondered, looking at some new entries, marching across the wide floor from adjoining doors. There were five of them, in the utilitarian business attire of tavalai bureaucrats. Some of the multi-coloured tavalai were staring at them, most unimpressed at this dull intrusion. One gave a signal to some others, who to Erik's astonishment produced small instruments — some simple steel chimes and wooden pipes, and struck up a tune.

Another robed Pondalganam strolled to intercept the five dull-clothed intruders, and an argument started. More joined it, and soon the argument was louder than the music, and considerably less harmonious. One of the intruders tried to shut down the musicians, gesturing at them to stop. The musicians ignored him, and played louder. More Pondalganam intercepted the offending intruder, followed by more shouting, in the hoarse, staccato trills and chatter of excited Togiri.

Erik and Trace exchanged glances. "Could be worse," Erik suggested. "Could be shouting at us."

"And they may yet," said Trace.

Finally a smaller intruding tavalai, who had been waving a bit of paper around, began loudly reading from it. Slowly, one by one, the bright-robed Pondalganam ceased their agitation, and their music, and listened soberly. The smaller tavalai — a woman, Erik thought — pronounced with increasing confidence and ease, as she felt the weight of the room's attention upon her. When she finally concluded, the room was silent.

The leading Pondalganam conferred, a small huddle in hushed, displeased tones. Then one came to Erik and Trace, with another smaller Pondalganam — also a woman — at his shoulder. The head Pondalganam spoke, and the woman translated, in fluent, if hoarse, English. "The Tropagali Andarachi Mandarinava have presented us with a deferral," the woman translated. Erik guessed that translating was her sole function. Surely an institution that dealt with the affairs of the Tsubarata, the great parliament of aliens, would need to speak a few less familiar tongues.

"State Department," said Trace, with no great surprise. They looked at the intruding five tavalai. The small woman, their leader, folded her paper and put it away, with a look of grim triumph. "We had the red carpet rolled out for us, and the State Department are rolling it back up."

"What is the nature of this deferral?" Erik asked the Pondalganam, via the translator. "I had thought that the Pondalganam were unchallenged in their authority over matters of the Tsubarata?"

The translator spoke quickly to her superior, then back again as he replied. "The Tsubarata is the parliament of the tavalai-sphere species. Humanity is not a tavalai-sphere species. You are a recent enemy, and our relations with you are bound by treaties at the war's conclusion. Those treaties are the legal preserve of the Tropagali Andarachi Mandarinava, the State Department, as you call them, and..."

"No no, wait wait," interrupted Lieutenant Shilu. "We've read over the documents carefully, they pertain to the claiming of representation for a species' chair in the Tsubarata. No specific mention is made of who might be claiming that chair, or whether they might be in the tavalai-sphere or not…"

"Yes yes," the translator said drily, not bothering to consult her superior.   She made a calming gesture.   "We are aware of technicalities. It will require a review."

"What kind of review?" Erik asked, attempting calm. "Taking how much time?"

"It is unknown," said the woman, with a head-weave, a tavalai shrug. "Time enough. Perhaps days."

"How many days?" Erik insisted, his voice hardening.

"At least ten."   Erik barely refrained from rolling his eyes. "Many parties must be consulted.   And then the State Department will surely launch a counter-claim."

"And how many counter-claims are they entitled to?"

"The circumstances vary. Usually five."

"Months," Shilu said bluntly. "We're talking months."

"We don't have months," Trace insisted.   She was holding a gymnastic yoga pose on the room floor, in singlet and under-shorts. Erik sat stretching in his — an entirely adequate routine, he thought, but barely the equal of Trace.   Super-fitness could actually detract from a pilot's reflexes by inducing muscle fatigue, and Trace's professionalism didn't live or die by fractions of a second as his did.

"I know," said Erik. The dawn sun was rising above a misty, humidity and cloud-drenched cityscape.   The colours were spectacular, every shade of red and orange, yellow, pink and violet. Air-traffic swarmed, a thousand zooming, blinking lights, and lightning flashed from one of the never-ending tropical storms.

The Pondalganam had offered each of the humans a separate room, but the grounded-posture of *Phoenix* crew with regard to security was Trace's job, and she preferred them in just two adjoining rooms.   Each was spacious, with huge floor-to-ceiling windows, big display-screen walls, and large beds.   The senior officers' room also had a rock-pool decoration, as apparently any space without a water feature was poor aesthetic form. Water bubbled and played over smoothly rounded stones, and combined with the view, the effect was soothing.

Erik's new coms unit had not been confiscated, and lay on the floor beside him as he stretched. Probably the tavalai knew it had some additional capabilities, but were confident in their own network systems' ability to resist intrusion. That was a miscalculation on their part, as this coms unit had been upgraded by *Phoenix*'s engineering staff, and Petty Officer Kadi in particular, who was learning new tricks from Styx's network capabilities every day. Luckily for the Pondalganam, Erik had no intention of using it to penetrate their networks, though it did allow him to block the bugs monitoring this room.

Hiro was currently using a capability even more advanced than this, on Daravani Station. He'd left *Phoenix* at Stoya, and flown into Tontalamai on Aristan's personal vessel. On Daravani Station, the plan was, Hiro would go with Aristan, disguised as an acolyte in parren robes. Aristan was adamant that he could get a human aboard in this way, tavalai security being reluctant to check identities beneath acolyte robes for fear of causing cultural offence — something that had apparently been sensitive between Aristan's people and tavalai authorities in the past. From there, Aristan insisted, there were ways of penetrating State Department information systems — for one as capable in such things as Hiro, using *Phoenix* capabilities. Again, Erik wondered just what Aristan knew about *Phoenix* capabilities. And what he'd make of Styx if he did learn of her existence, given that Styx had once been at the top of the drysine leadership, in partnership with Drakhil himself.

A coms uplink flashed in the corner of his glasses' vision, and he blinked on it. *"Sir,"* came Lieutenant Lassa's voice in his ear, *"boarding is confirmed for two hours from now exactly, the tavalai Fleet warship Lilipetilai will be sending two shuttles. They confirm that no armed crew or karasai will enter, this will be an unarmed inspection, but it will be extensively covered by recording devices."*

This, too, they'd agreed upon with Admiral Janik at Stoya. Knowledge of what tavalai Fleet was proposing to help *Phoenix* with could not be spread. Everyone had to maintain the appearance of suspicious relations, and Admiral Janik had been firm that if tavalai Fleet did not carry out a full inspection at Tontalamai, then State Department would insist upon doing it themselves. The Dobruta invitation that brought *Phoenix* legally into tavalai space meant that *Phoenix* could not be disarmed, and Fleet would not risk a boarding-in-force under those conditions, lest jumpy humans open fire. It did, however, mean that a lot of things on *Phoenix*, that not even tavalai Fleet knew the existence of, would have to be placed elsewhere, on the off-chance that Fleet decided to do an actual inspection, and not just a fake one to ease State Department suspicions.

"Very well Lieutenant," Erik told Lassa, reaching to grasp his toes. "Make the necessary preparations." He could not say more than that — his coms device would only block bugs in this room, not on the uplink to *Phoenix*.

"Yes sir. Everything okay down there?"

"Very good, yes. Except that we're now adjusting to city hours, and will be very tired shortly."

"Yes Captain, Phoenix will adjust her hours to match yours." Because in reality, the ship ran by the captain's hours, not the other way around.

"Understood *Phoenix*, Captain out."

"I hope whoever boards us has more information on Kantovan than the Admiral did," said Trace, having shifted her pose to something slightly less excruciating. "And speaks some decent English."

"Well, we have Romki on board if they don't. And Styx."

"Styx doesn't like tavalai," Trace reminded him. "She might be the most prejudiced member of the crew."

"Yeah," said Erik. "Alarming, given the power of life and death she once held over them."

"We don't actually know *what* she did during the Empire. She might not even be that old, she might just be making it all up."

Trace lowered herself, and splayed legs, head down to one knee. "She's not going to like being shifted and hidden from that boarding party, either."

"You really think she has that many opinions and emotions?"

"I'm sure of it. And I think it's safer to operate on the assumption that she could at some point make an irrational and violent move. All this pretence at machine-calm and logic runs directly against the history of the Machine Age and all its wars. It could just be another show put on to fool us, like how she butters up Romki with praise, or how she pretends to be female. She could be seething with rage and resentment, just below the surface. We'd never know."

Erik thought about it, watching the sunrise. "Why do you think she chose female?" he asked. "You think she figured she'd get an easier run with us?"

"Definitely," said Trace, switching legs. "Firstly, we were already calling her a queen, but also, there's more men on *Phoenix* than women, and men will forgive women more quickly than other men. Styx is easily smart enough to spot it. Just because she doesn't share our psychology doesn't mean she can't apply that big brain to analysing it. Like Romki does to other aliens."

"Or like an etymologist does with ants," Erik muttered. He had so many things to think about, but all he could think of was Lisbeth. Where she was now, whether she was okay, what she was doing. He lost track of time for a moment, and then the bed shifted as Trace sat beside him, and handed him an odd-looking tavalai cup — oval-shaped, to better fit webbed tavalai hands.

"We get Lisbeth out," said Trace, reading his mind once more, "by getting that diary from the Kantovan Vault. Think on that. Focus on it, and get her back." Erik supposed she didn't need great powers of mind-reading to know his thoughts. It would have been obvious to less astute observers than Trace.

"You lost your brother?" Erik knew she had. He'd never asked her about it before.

"Yes," she said quietly. "Aran. He was nineteen. I was ten. A mining accident." A pause, as lightning flashed near, and heavy rain made a dark mist of one third the view. "The difference between Lisbeth and Aran is that Lisbeth isn't dead. And it's within our power to keep it that way."

Erik took a deep breath. "I think I'd like to be Kulina. All of these attachments make focus difficult. Everything hurts."

"Still hurts as Kulina," said Trace. "But channelled."

"Did you become Kulina to escape that pain?" He looked at her. She looked troubled, but mostly for him. He wasn't supposed to ask her this, he knew. No one else did. And with them, she had the rank to refuse to answer. But he was Captain, and Trace had said many times that Captain and Marine Commander should have if not *no* secrets between them, then as few as possible. Despite their very different jobs, it was always the closest working relationship on a carrier. When a carrier captain deployed his marines on a station, the marine commander had to know that he'd move heaven and earth to get them all off again. And when a marine commander was fighting to secure a dangerous facility, the captain had to know that she'd make any sacrifice to safeguard their ship. In many ways, the wider distance between them, as marine and spacer, made the need for trust that much greater.

"In part," Trace said finally. "But I'd been interested in the Kulina for a long time before. Aran's death was clarity for me, I suppose. And I think I thought I'd join him before long. That felt right, somehow." She gazed away, out the windows. "I think the ten-year-old me still feels a bit guilty sometimes. That I'm still here, and he's not. I loved him a lot. He was the only close family I ever did."

Erik took a deep breath. "I'm sorry. I shouldn't put you on the spot. I know you don't like to talk about it."

"You don't need to apologise to me," said Trace, with a very flat stare. "For anything. Ever." Erik thought about it. And realised that for all her often brutal prodding and riding, she'd never asked him to. "I don't talk about it with the rest of the ship because I have appearances to keep up. Senior officers don't advertise inner workings and frailties. When the people beneath you start psychoanalysing your orders, you're screwed, and then they are."

"You've never tried to work on appearances with me?" Erik asked her with an edge.   She'd certainly used every bit of her Liberty Star-winning, hardass persona with him, to beat him into shape after Captain Pantillo had died.

Trace smiled slyly.   "Well it's not like I could compete on image with a *Debogande*."   And brushed at his shoulder, as though polishing.   Erik shoved her, or tried to, because she caught his arm in a half-lock, but refrained from breaking his wrist.   "Come on, you're supposed to be thinking of a way around this State Department roadblock.   You're much better at this legal stuff than me, I mean there must have been a dozen attorneys present at your birth, you're born to it.   What's your plan?"

"Take a shower," Erik told her with a smile.   "You're sweaty and you smell."   Trace laughed, and got up to do that.   Erik couldn't help notice that the muscular body he'd found off-putting a few months before was starting to grow on him.   "You'd really tell me anything if I asked?"

"What am I?" she retorted in mild exasperation.   "Some bad-tempered dog that'll bite your hand off if you look it in the eye? You're the damn Captain, you get answers when you ask."

"Are you a virgin?" Erik challenged.   Because some had wondered, and it was the kind of thing genuine friends would know of each other.

"Because I don't screw with crew?" Trace laughed, heading for the shower.   "I get station leave like any marine, I've got money to spend, and there are facilities on station that cater to horny marines.   Figure it out."

"Seriously?   You use *professionals*?"

"Hey," said Trace, pausing at the bathroom door, "if you know one thing about me, it's that I value professionalism."   Erik laughed.   "You can do better than that."

"Did you actually *enjoy* it?" Erik retorted.   "Or just get it out of the way, like how you drink those horrible vegetable smoothies because you need the hunger to go away so you can concentrate on being a hardass marine again?"

Trace hung in the bathroom doorway for a moment, studying him with dark eyes no longer quite so amused.   Not angry, just thinking about it... and perhaps considering what it meant he thought of her, that he'd asked her at all.   Then she nodded slowly, as though conceding something.   Exactly what, she didn't say. "So," she said.   "Do you even *have* a plan for State Department?"

"Sure I do," said Erik.   "It'll be fun.   You didn't answer my question."

"That wasn't a question," she said sourly, and disappeared into the bathroom.   "It was a statement with a question mark."

CHAPTER 12

Commander Suli Shahaim sat in her quarters just off the main corridor to the bridge, and sipped tea. The flavour was more agreeable to her guest, a tavalai warship captain named Konapratam. Lieutenant Kaspowitz alone of the bridge crew joined them, as Shahaim's quarters were barely large enough for more.

Out in *Phoenix*'s corridors, the 'inspection' was underway. Konapratam's people were putting on a good show of making it look serious, with cameras to record everything, but the inspection's route had been handed to *Phoenix* in advance, and hiding things they'd not wished seen had been a simple matter of avoiding those highlighted spaces. Admiral Janik at Stoya had set it all up in advance, of course. Suli thought it obvious, and increasingly suspicious, that *Phoenix* was being set up for something. Possibly something that went back to *Makimakala*, in granting them protective authority to enter tavalai space in the first place. Tavalai Fleet were locked in an internal struggle with State Department, and were limited in how far they could go themselves. In true tavalai style, they'd let the aliens do the truly disagreeable and dangerous things, and let them take the blame if it all went wrong. *Phoenix* was about to be used, then hung out to dry.

The real question was that if *Phoenix* truly wanted Drakhil's diary, did they have any choice?

"It goes back a long, long way," said Captain Konapratim, seated on the chair before Suli's small wall-table. Suli and Kaspowitz sat side by side on her bunk. "Well before the Triumvirate War. Well before the destruction of Earth, and the end of the krim. Some of it is technical, in that State Department has an active charter, meaning that it has taken every opportunity to expand its legal capabilities over the millennia. Fleet has an inactive charter, meaning that our powers are endlessly limited. We are defined by what we *cannot* do, while State Department are the opposite. We have different philosophies of governance, and had you the time and the language skills, I could point you at a thousand expert histories describing this conflict of administrative posture. You have not read these works? English translations, perhaps?"

Kaspowitz repressed a smile. "No," Suli said evenly. "In the Triumvirate War, we've been busy fighting. I'm sure there are people in Fleet Intelligence who have read those works, but human Fleet has no culture of sharing those things with line commanders."

The tavalai Captain nodded gravely. "Human Fleet keeps its captains starved of information. There is no debate for broader matters, and no culture of enquiry."

"Key point of difference between human Fleet and tavalai," Kaspowitz said with typical dryness. "We're a combat force. You're a debating club."

Konapratim's thick tavalai lips pursed in a smile. "The Spiral is full of species that won the battle only to lose the war. We shall see which approach wins in the end."

"With respect," said Kaspowitz. "What we won was no battle. It was a war."

"One hundred and sixty one of your years," said the tavalai. "An eternity for humans. A blink of an eye for tavalai." Kaspowitz might have retorted, but Suli silenced him with a warning look. Her ability to do that was a very recent thing, derived solely from her new Commander's rank. It still felt odd, to use it like this on her old friend.

"Please continue," she told Konapratim.

"Yes," said Konapratim. "With this philosophical and structural difference as its foundation, State Department and Fleet's differences have only grown wider. The alliance with the sard is one point of difference. Many in Fleet feel the sard are more trouble than they're worth, and an eventual long-term threat to us. State Department feel differently.

"The krim were another matter. Developing relations with the krim, much of Fleet were also opposed to. But State Department meddles, and expands, and thinks like great empire-builders without a thought to the unpleasant business of those who must carry out the building. It got Fleet into a war with the humans when State Department told us to impose the peace, between you and the krim. It was only a little war by tavalai standards, but many in Fleet recall it bitterly. Some even say it was our very worst moment, fighting the victims of a terrible aggression, to force them to accommodate their invaders, mostly so that State Department could save face."

Suli frowned. "You mean to tell me that tavalai Fleet *sympathised* with humanity?"

"Of course," said Konapratim.

"And yet made war on us anyway," Kaspowitz added.

"We are soldiers," said the tavalai. "As are you. We follow orders. Tavalai governance is chaotic, but its rules and structures are firm. State Department run tavalai foreign affairs, and the foreign affairs of all the Free Age. Fleet's opinion will be heard, but we have no command to dictate our own affairs.

"In truth, tavalai Fleet blame State Department in large part for making an enemy of humanity. We have never been able to entirely blame humanity for hating us. State Department had limited control of the krim, but that was itself by design — they could have restrained them, but chose not to. Krim-region space was not fully explored by us in advance of krim expansion, and so it was not especially surprising when the krim discovered a previously unknown, sentient-inhabited world in their path. And then, as many humans have noted, once humans were discovered, the State Department had a choice between two possible sentient allies — the krim, or the humans. But adopting humans as allies would have meant throwing the krim overboard, which for State Department would have meant a further loss of face. Fleet always felt this a poor choice.

"And from these compounded mistakes, you have the reemergence of the ridiculous chah'nas, and opportunity created for the conniving alo... a whole big mess." Konapratim sipped his tea, as though to calm himself. Suli thought he looked agitated when discussing it. By tavalai standards, anyhow. "Fleet considers that State Department created the Triumvirate War by their own mismanagement. Many of us feel they should be brought back down to Earth... I believe is the unfortunate human expression."

"What's in the Kantovan Vault that you want so badly?" Suli asked.

Konapratim said nothing for a long moment. Suli thought that perhaps she wasn't going to get an answer, and began readying her stern lecture on what poor form it was to expect *Phoenix* to risk itself doing tavalai Fleet's dirty work without knowing why.

But then..."Records," Konapratim said sombrely. "Many records. Things that State Department has never shared with anyone, despite so many statutes on the books requiring that they do so."

"What kind of records?" Kaspowitz pressed suspiciously.

"*Old* records," said the tavalai. "Records of decisions made within State Department. Who made them, and why, and what were the hidden details the rest of us were never allowed to hear."

Suli's eyes widened. "You mean... State Department decisions? The krim? Earth?"

"And many others of far less interest to humans," Konapratim agreed. "But of very great interest to the tavalai of the Fleet, who over the many thousands of years have died in their millions, on the horns of these consequences. For that many years, we have insisted that those millions, and their ancestors, deserve to know for what they died. Yet State Department have refused. No longer. The Triumvirate War was one stupid conflict too many... what is the human expression? The straw that broke the...?"

"The straw that broke the camel's back," said Suli. "A camel is an Earth creature, used in the old days for carrying loads."

"Yes, I see. In Togiri we say, 'a bubble too many.' For deep diving, you breathe out many bubbles to dive deeper. Too many bubbles, you go too far down, and never regain the surface."

"Why not do it yourself?" Kaspowitz asked.

"Because if we were caught, it would be turmoil. Not civil war, but as close as tavalai come. Plus, you have the opportunity, as we do not."

"Lucky us," Kaspowitz muttered.

"And much of Fleet are not agreed," Konapratim added.

"How many?" Suli asked.

"We are a trusted faction. Our interests coincide with yours. But we must act fast, for we cannot keep this secret forever."

"And if State Department find out what you've done, after the fact?"

Konapratim smiled. "If we find what we expect to find, after the fact, there may *be* no more State Department." Both Suli and Kaspowitz stared. "Thus rather solving several problems for both our peoples, all at the same time, wouldn't you say?"

Suli's coms uplink blinked, and she opened it. "Go ahead Lieutenant Lassa."

"Commander, we're receiving a huge spike in relevant communications down on the planet." Lassa sounded a little worried. *"It... sounds like the Captain has made a public statement to the entire planet."*

Suli frowned. She couldn't recall *that* having been discussed at a command meeting. "What did he say, Lieutenant?"

"That UFS Phoenix is in orbit about Ponnai, and that we're seeking the human chair at the Tsubarata." Suli and Kaspowitz looked at each other. *"You know, all the stuff we agreed not to tell anyone, and tavalai Fleet agreed to keep secret too. In case it made a fuss. Commander, my... my screens are lighting up, I'm getting... oh, about several hundred queries? It's like everyone on the planet suddenly turned their coms on us and started asking questions."* A brief pause. *"Make that several thousand."*

"He was talking to Captain Pram and *Makimakala*'s legal officer about some stuff," Kaspowitz said with eyebrows raised. "I guess this is it."

"Well," said Suli, not knowing what to think. "I suppose this is why they call it a 'Captain's call'. Captain Konapratim, we have a developing situation down on..."

"I heard," Konapratim affirmed, looking disconcerted. "I was just uplinked to my ship, they told me. Your Captain makes a bold move, to declare himself so openly. *Phoenix*'s presence in tavalai space has not been widely known until now."

"I think this is the Captain's way of saying we're all-in," Kaspowitz told him.

"All-in?" Konapratim hadn't heard that one before.

"A human gambling term," Suli explained. "When you bet all the money you have on just one hand. Big risk, big reward."

"Yes," said Konapratim, still uncomfortable. "We would have preferred a more quiet approach. This seems... reckless."

"Yes, but you see," said Kaspowitz, a finger raised warningly, "you can't play games with humans, and expect us to behave like tavalai."

Konapratim did not look very happy about it.

The convoy of cruisers arrived at midday to take Erik and Trace to the Karlabarata, the Parliament of Ponnai. They sat in the rear and watched the passing towers for several minutes, then descended upon an enormous courtyard, circular about a central fountain. Around the fountain, Erik saw as he peered down, were a giant mass of tavalai, all staring upward. Many thousands, Erik thought. Away from the courtyard, a wide, straight path climbed numerous sets of stairs between the sheer walls of a monumental building complex in grey and green stone.

"Was your idea," Trace reminded him.

"And you're the one who wanted me to be Captain," Erik retorted.

"No, I wanted you to realise that you already *were* Captain," Trace said reasonably. "And I didn't say it was a bad idea. How do I look?"

There was mild humour in it, as neither of them were dressed for grand public occasions. Erik had considered breaking out the dress uniforms, but that would have spoken of a self-importance exceeding *Phoenix*'s current circumstance. *Phoenix* was a fighting ship, not a diplomatic vessel, and he didn't mind if everyone knew it. Trace wore her usual marine blacks, neat and trim, and quite presentable with the uniform jacket to cover the harness attachments and the worst of the wear and tear. His own spacer blues were the same, save for more pockets.

"Good," he said, and meant it. "What about me?"

She looked him up and down. "Like a captain," she said with satisfaction.

The cruiser touched down, the gull door cracked upward, and hot, thick air flooded in. Erik climbed out, then Trace behind... and a roar of tavalai voices hit him like a wave. All about were rows of tavalai security, some armoured and armed, holding back the great sea of tavalai civilians. Security drones hovered overhead, scanning the crowds, and many dignitaries scampered to their places, robes aflutter. One dignitary beckoned them on, and they went, completely at the mercy of tavalai decorum, and surrounded by mobs a fair proportion of whom sounded as though they'd like to tear them limb from limb.

Erik tugged on his cap and walked, Trace at his side in her own cap and glasses, scanning the crowd for any sign of trouble. It was all a lot more chaotic than Erik had expected from tavalai. Tavalai democracy was a democracy of institutions, not people. There was no such thing as 'one person, one vote' among tavalai — tavalai worked in institutions large and small, and voted for the leaders of those institutions only. The institutions were intensely democratic, on a level unmatched anywhere in human society, and it made tavalai politics generally free from the kind of opportunist populism that made human democracy such a double-edged sword. The institutions then regulated and controlled tavalai politics, and subdued the public reaction to sudden events... like the arrival of a blood-soaked human carrier whose Captain now wished to claim humanity's long-vacant place in the Tsubarata.

But this public response felt anything but restrained. Erik saw media drones past the security versions, hovering behind the cordon lines, and more cameras watching from behind the great, multi-storey glass in the building walls to either side. The walk was a pedestrian avenue, through the grand architecture of the central world parliament of Ponnai. Erik had known that what he'd done would be enormous — a Spiral-shaking choice, at least in symbolism. Apparently it was now the leading story in all the news networks on Ponnai, and throughout the Tontalamai System. Soon it would spread to the rest of tavalai space.　　As an heir to the Debogande business empire, Erik was somewhat accustomed to the theoretical concept of fame.　　But to be confronted with it so starkly as this — the centre of attention for an entire world and all its twelve billion people, and shortly to the hundreds of billions beyond — was a different matter entirely.

As always in moments of stress, he took his cue from Trace — walking straight and cool, both calm and watchful, neither shutting anything out, nor overwhelmed by all the sights and sounds trying to clamour their way in.　　They climbed some great, wide steps, their footsteps in unison, and then the flanking crowds were ending, where civilians no longer had access within the Karlabarata Parliament.　　Atop the steps stood a particularly important-looking tavalai, in white robes with some sort of cape.　　In one webbed hand, a smooth black cane with a gold head... but he did not seem old, nor did he lean on it for balance.　　Ceremonial, perhaps, like so many tavalai adornments.

The white-clad tavalai rumbled Togiri, and his belt-translator spoke English at them.　　*"Captain, Major, I am Prodamandam, Speaker for the First Chamber. We are late, walk with me."*

He turned and walked, very brisk and businesslike for a tavalai, usually so methodical and patient.　　Erik joined on his right, Trace on his left, many security making a phalanx before and behind as they moved, even in this absence of apparent threats.　　Though the crowds were gone, the steps remained full of tavalai Erik took to be parliament staff, come out to stare, and a few to record with personal devices.

"You play a dangerous game, Phoenix," Prodamandam said as they walked, tapping the ground with his cane in rhythm.　　*"This public announcement has activated a clause in many institutional legal charters that the institutions did not know they had.　　The restoration of the full Tsubarata, with all the Spiral species represented.　　It has forced a vote in the First Chamber, where all the institutional heads of Tontalamai now gather, and this vote can overrule anything that State Department can do to block you.　　It*

seems that you have been well-advised in our laws.   Troublingly well-advised, for many."

They weren't happy with *Makimakala*, Erik knew.   And not just State Department, either.   Many tavalai didn't think it proper that the Dobruta should be giving a human vessel such free access to tavalai space, with full weapons and marine complement intact, whatever their escort.   If only they knew the full extent of it, Erik thought.

"There are things in the Tsubarata that need to be said," Erik replied.   "By a human, as humans have not spoken there since the dark times of the war against the krim."

"And what would you say, that has you headed there in such frantic haste?"

"I believe that it is my legal right to speak there," Erik replied.   "Which would make it the tavalim's legal obligation to be patient, and listen when the time comes."   It was very forward of him, given his present position — a controversial and largely unwelcome guest in tavalai space.   But tavalai were fond of blunt-speaking, which Erik thought had much to recommend it, given the dangers of the language barrier.

The Speaker smiled, as they ascended another flight of grand stairs.   *This is the human daring that we have heard so much about in the war.   You have a power play in mind, and you have been well-advised by one of our own factions.   But remember well, Phoenix — not every daring human act in the war was successful.   Many met with disasters of your own making, from which not even the miracles of alo technology could save you."*

Erik only smiled.   Of course the tavalai believed that their conservative, methodical way remained best, and that the only reason the humans had won was their 'magical' alo technology. Well, they could continue to believe that if they wished.   As uncomfortable as this thrust into the tavalai political limelight was, Erik thought that the more noisy and visible, the better.   Political institutions — and *all* tavalai institutions were political on some level, including Fleet — thought only in political dimensions.   The more focused on political plots they became, the less chance that any of them would consider the true reason why *Phoenix* was headed to Kantovan System and the Tsubarata.

Atop the next stairs ahead loomed the enormous glass wall of the Karlabarata Parliament entrance. To the left of those stairs, Erik saw with alarm, were a small group of humans, in Fleet uniforms. His heart sank. Humans did come here, in small, controlled groups. This had to be one of the inspection crews, their presence arranged by the peace treaties, to keep an eye on tavalai Fleet and levels of disarmament, and to see that the beaten party was not violating any terms.

"The crew of Albatross," said the Speaker as they climbed the final stairs. Erik thought he had not sweated so much from just a few stairs before in his life. *"They do not seem pleased to see you."*

There were ten of them, Erik counted — seven spacers and three marines. One was a captain, and all were staring daggers at Erik and Trace as they passed. "Traitors!" one of them snarled.

"Millions of humans died to keep the Tsubarata *out* of human affairs!" another said coldly. "And now you piss on all their sacrifice!"

"Your mother will be *finished* when this gets back to human space, Debogande!" a third called as they passed. "Finished, you hear me?"

Trace's hand brushed Erik's as they approached the great glass entrance. She was not looking at him, but Erik knew it had not been an accident. He took a deep breath, as the glass wall loomed above, and then they went inside.

CHAPTER 13

After a week on the austere parren ship, Tif was about ready to leave. The ship was one of Aristan's, and she, Ensign Lee, Ensign Pratik and Second Lieutenant Hale had all transferred to her at Stoya System. They'd done it through *Makimakala*, on a routine shuttle flight, so no one watching would suspect that some of *Phoenix*'s crew had left their ship. Eight rotations had taken them across two jumps to Tagray System, which Aristan's people claimed to know well.

Now they were disembarking at Ruchino Eighty-Six, an industrial station in orbit of the rocky inner world of Ruchino. The main airlock was crowded with dark parren robes, held in place only by light velcro tabs. Being kuhsi, Tif was spared the inconvenience of having to dress like one of Aristan's acolytes. Humans were very rare in tavalai space, and suspicious too, given the nature of their mission. Kuhsi were human allies, and a long way from tavalai space, yet had not directly participated in the Triumvirate War, and so were afforded certain freedoms. Kuhsi did travel, even the occasional female, though that was dangerous. Tif checked her pocket once more for the short pistol the marines had given her, with grave instructions on its use. Aliens did not alarm her so much, out here. The prospect of meeting fellow travelling kuhsi did. Nearly all of those were males, and some reacted to a free-travelling female with violent offence.

The outer airlock door cycled, and cold air rushed in. Immediately Tif wrinkled her nose — Ruchino Eighty-Six smelled unlike any station she'd ever visited. Not a bad smell, but an industrial one, thick with operating gases, industrial smoke, and the discharge of many operating machines. Most stations had filters to clean the air more thoroughly than this, but this station was old, and not designed for comfort.

She followed the lead parren out, hand-over-hand up the guide-lines from the airlock. The lead parren's name was Toumad, and he was one of Aristan's trusted operatives. Aristan had offered to help *Phoenix* on this mission, and it had been the parren who'd suggested Tagray System, and Ruchino. It had been parren who had first established industry at Ruchino, some twenty thousand years before. Ruchino Eighty-Six was far more recent than that, but despite this all now being tavalai space, parren had never lost their connection here. Toumad insisted that he had contacts here, who could provide what they needed. Tif did not trust him in the slightest, and knew the humans felt the same. But in this space, humans and kuhsi were the true aliens, and utterly reliant upon the assistance of locals.

Customs checks were a zero-G automated gate, with just a single odd-looking alien for security. 'Koromek', Remy Hale identified the species for her — with wide breathing-gills in a fan about the lower jaw, and big tusks from the mouth, looking more well suited to water even than the tavalai. Koromek were one of the tavalai-sphere species that the rest of the Spiral rarely got to see, but were quite common in these free-range regions of tavalai space, where the non-tavalai had been so well entrenched before the advent of the First Free Age that the tavalai had not bothered to burden them with tavalai-style government and bureaucracy. Free-range regions could be chaotic, Tif had been told, and occasionally lawless. The koromek saw Tif's pistol without expression, once the automated gate identified it, and waved her through. The parren-robed humans were not inspected beneath their cowls. Tif thought that an automated gate could probably identify a non-parren by biometrics... but if the guard didn't care about her gun, he probably cared as little about disguised humans. Or perhaps Aristan's acolytes had an understanding with local security.

Past the customs gate, they entered Ruchino Eighty-Six's primary core. Residential hub stations were designed as much for people as cargo, but industrial stations like Eighty-Six had ninety percent of their mass here, in the non-gravitational core. It made an enormous hollow cylinder in space, with a double-shelled hull through which large cargos, and sometimes entire small ships, could be brought through giant airlocks to the inner, pressurised station. Ruchino Eighty-Six had multiple habitat rings, spinning about the primary core to make a gravitational environment for inhabitants, but those were only small, with four rings accounting for no more than fifty thousand people each.

The primary core was a maze of gantries and structures. Much of the central space was cargo, but just as much was machine shops and fabricators — great exposed workshops where mechanics from multiple species worked on heavy gear that could not be handled on a gravitational station — or haggled for contracts with passing customers. The parren hooked on to passing handlines through the transiting personnel passages, little more than open steel frames to guide people through the giant industrial space without getting minced by large moving parts, or electrocuted by something else.

Tif stared about at the haphazard, often ramshackle working spaces as she flew, one hand hooked into the humming handline, and wondered if they could really find what they needed here. Certainly there was little tavalai government. Tavalai bureaucracy would never stand for all this mess, for one thing. And probably they'd tax everyone a lot more, and have all these small, independent operators complaining, or shifting elsewhere to avoid it. She was familiar with some of those issues from her time with Lord Kharghesh in the royal residence of Koth. Lord Kharghesh, his handsome head on her pillow, discussing tiredly with her the difficulties of governance in their increasingly complicated and modernising world. His fingers tracing gentle circles in the fur at her belly, his warm breath in her ear...

She shook the memory off, as the handline turned a corner, swinging her out wide past oncoming traffic. Her Lord had been so pleased that the women of his nation would come to live in and see a wider world than the inside of some betrothed family's kitchen. She wondered if he'd ever imagined she might see quite so much of the wider world as this.

They passed the great, rotating inner bearing of the station habitation arms, and then the leading parren took the off-line, abandoning handles for a new passage past huge haulage racks, where loader-arms the size of shuttles howled and shuddered on runners amidst the flash of warning lights.   The new passage allowed progress only by hand and foot grips, but Tif was well used to that by now, and glided gently from hold to hold with little touches as they flew by.   To the hull-side now were offices, zero-G glass fronts where more aliens worked and floated, and then some big, steel-framed workshops.

Here the parren turned off, and came to a halt at the framework personnel entry for one such workshop.   Within, a huge brace held a ground-crawler of some description.   It was cylindrical, with big, fat tires that appeared to be made more of gleaming ceramic than any kind of rubber or steel.   Workers drifted over it, and orange sparks shrilled and fountained where a new part was shaped to fit a damaged section.

"That's a heavy-duty prospector," said Ensign Remy Hale with amazement from beneath her hood and cowl.   "They must be using it on the surface of Ruchino."

Ruchino had slightly less than what humans considered 2-Gs — a touch more than that for kuhsi.   It was a big world, far bigger than Tif's native Chogoth, with a dense metal core and an even denser atmosphere.   Its plentiful minerals made it a miner's paradise, and created these huge belts of industrial stations in its orbit, but the atmosphere and gravity combined made it a difficult proposition to operate in both safely and profitably.   It was completely uninhabitable by any Spiral species, save for those that lived in pressurised habitats, and could handle a crushing 2-Gs for extended periods.   Tif knew of only one species that could.

A tavalai worker came floating to the parren, and spoke to Toumad.   Toumad then pointed at the humans, and Tif, and beckoned them on, while the remaining acolytes remained holding to the personnel entry frames.   A simple rope line provided guidance to an office segment behind a transparent shield at one side of the workshop.   Tif sprang from the framework in her turn, and a few gentle touches of the rope made sure she arrived at the office space entry frame, and caught a support.

The dark-tinted shield wall made a transparent view of the ongoing work on the heavy-duty prospector, saving more sensitive eyes from the glare of welders. Projection screens overlaid technical graphics onto parts of the shield, for engineers to come and peer at, or transfer onto personal units. A number of aliens examined those displays, or did other work at zero-G office stations, while others rummaged through an adjoining tool-storage section, assembling welders or changing out of safety gear. Perhaps half were tavalai, and the rest a mix of... four species, Tif counted.

Toumad led them drifting past wall-fixed terminals and partitions, then arrived at a rear office. There, a big, grey kaal sat comfortably braced between multiple displays, examining screens with his four eyes while eating something from a jar with stubby fingers. He fixed Toumad with a displeased stare, then unbraced his bulk from between the screens, and drifted to a near ceiling brace, which he caught with his upper hands. He growled something, a voice like large rocks grinding together underwater, a guttural rumble.

"What do you want?" Tif's belt translator spoke to her in English. She could have had it set to her native Gharkhan, but that would set up a three-way translation in her head between English, Gharkhan, and whatever tongue the kaal spoke. English alone could make Tif's head spin, and she thought she'd actually manage better if she kept Gharkhan out of the mix.

Tif knew she wasn't the first to notice the similarities between kaal and chah'nas. Each were six-limbed and four-eyed, but there the similarities ended. Kaal were huge, half the size again of even large humans, in height and girth. Their homeworld had nearly 2.5 Gs, and they'd evolved accordingly — multiple thick limbs for support, huge muscles about a strong skeletal structure, and a slow, lumbering gait when walking.

They'd been tavalai allies for as long as anyone could remember, due in large part to the difficulties of getting off the kaal homeworld. Kaal had been quite advanced when tavalai had found them, but still unable to venture into space, thanks to the punishing physics of their native gravity-well. Tavalai had given them the stars, and once there, kaal had proven themselves brilliant engineers, inspiring the tavalai to build larger and larger structures, and teaching them much of their current famous ability.   Kaal had remained unmolested for most of the Machine Age, in large part due to their planet-bound status rendering them, in the machines' eyes, an impotent threat.   But once in space, they'd become the tavalai's most reliable ally, and fought with them in nearly every conflict since.

Humans had found kaal a limited threat in the Triumvirate War, thanks to their ineffectual slowness in infantry combat, and kaal had rarely fought in that manner.   But in space combat their heavy-G bodies turned slowness into speed, as their fast, mobile ships had pulled G-stress that only the alo could match.   As a species, kaal were reputed to be as gruff and impassive as they appeared, with a frequent taste for violence and contests of strength.   But Tif had also heard that amongst each other, kaal could be quite affectionate. Certainly their species-bond to the tavalai was so fanatical, it looked to her like its own type of love.

Toumad spoke, gesturing to the humans.   *"The offer I spoke to you of,"* his translator offered.

Ensigns Pratik and Lee, and Second Lieutenant Hale, removed the veil from their faces.   The kaal's four eyes narrowed slightly, a displeased expression.   He stuck a thick finger back in his jar, and pushed some foul-looking sludge into his mouth.   Kaal had only small teeth, and ate mostly pastes, Tif recalled.   Something to do with heavy-G digestion, no doubt.   Ironic to first meet one here, floating gracefully in no gravity at all.

"Who?" the kaal growled, via his translator.

"*UFS Phoenix*," Hale replied.

The kaal snorted, and made a dismissive gesture with two unoccupied hands.   *"Don't need this nonsense. Go away."*

He'd heard of *Phoenix*, then.   By this stage, Tif guessed most of the Spiral had.   *"Rejecting this business,"* Toumad told him, *"will affect other business."*   With meaning.

The kaal stared longer, sucking on his paste-covered finger as he considered that.   *"What business?"* he said finally.

"A heavy descender," said Hale.   "And a crew.   A covert mission."

"Don't need covert business," the kaal snorted. *"Go away."*

"And enough money that you can retire for life, and live rich, if you like," Hale added.

Again the long, thinking pause from the kaal. Another long suck of a paste-covered finger. Tif could smell the paste now, and it was foul. *"What kind of money?"*

"Family Debogande money," said Hale.

That got the kaal's attention. Human families and politics got little enough attention in this part of the Spiral, but anyone hearing about the *UFS Phoenix* would also be hearing all about Family Debogande. *"Family Debogande pay for this job?"*

Hale nodded. "Yes. Kantovan System. Kamala moon."

"Kamala impossible. Moon atmosphere like tenth hell. Go away." But his enormous body language gave no indication now that he actually wished them to go away. Tif began to suspect that it was a kaal figure of speech.

"I was told that you built and modified the best heavy descenders in the Spiral," Hale said evenly. Tif knew that Remy Hale's family worked in real estate. Perhaps she'd acquired some of this negotiating prowess from them. No doubt Captain Debogande would not have sent *Phoenix*'s second-highest engineering officer if she didn't have some skills at this. "Perhaps I heard incorrectly?"

"You hear right," the kaal grunted. *"Covert business. Covert against who?"*

"Tavalai State Department."

"No take covert business against tavalai authority," the kaal snorted, and this time seemed to mean it. *"Go away."*

"This covert business is sponsored by tavalai Fleet," said Hale. "Tavalai Fleet, that fought side-by-side with kaal in the Triumvirate War, and many wars before. Fleet does not like State Department causing so many tavalai and kaal to die in stupid wars. State Department keeps secrets from tavalai Fleet. Tavalai Fleet wants those secrets. The secrets are in a secure vault, at the bottom of Kamala's atmosphere. *Phoenix* is going to retrieve them for tavalai Fleet."

If ever there was a time for a no-nonsense kaal engineer to tell the silly human to go away, it was now, confronted with the scale of what was being proposed. But the kaal just looked at Hale, eyes half-lidded, many calculations zooming through his thick but very intelligent head. Finally, he turned a ponderous glance upon Toumad, questioningly.

Toumad nodded. *"Human speaks the truth. You know it's truth. What she proposes is impossible without tavalai Fleet."*

"In Kantovan System, yes," the kaal grumbled. *"Impossible."* He turned his big head back to Hale. *"Crew take big risk. Expensive."*

"Not to Family Debogande," Hale said firmly.

"Land at Kamala vault. How?"

"We're developing a plan. Top *Phoenix* and tavalai Fleet officers." The kaal looked unimpressed. "There is an inspection station. A customs gateway, an atmospheric city, above the densest clouds of Kamala."

"I heard of this place. All inspectors State Department tavalai. No like humans, no admit humans. Inspect descender, find hidden crew."

"We'll get to the inspection point on two ships," Hale explained. "Inspection first, on your descender. Then we move hidden team inside. *After* the inspection."

"No killing," the kaal growled, with a big finger raised for emphasis. *"No kill tavalai, not even State Department. Not even for tavalai Fleet."*

"No killing," Hale agreed. Tif knew she had no way of guaranteeing that. She wondered to what extent kaal understood dishonesty. "We promise."

"Descender still have pilot crew. Will be present for inspection."

"Your crew," Hale told him. "Hire crew. Rich crew, once we're finished. And one *Phoenix* pilot, to be sure."

"No human pilot," the kaal disagreed, loudly. *"Human barely allowed in tavalai space. State Department space? No chance."*

"Not human," said Hale. "Kuhsi." She pointed at Tif.

The kaal drift-turned to consider her for the first time. The heavy head and jaw were scaly in part. Looking at him was like looking at a rock, some stone-demon from Tif's childhood tales, brought to life off a mountain side. *"Kuhsi, pilot? Experienced?"*

"Very experienced," said Hale. "But co-pilot on a descender. I hear they take a lot of practise."

"Female kuhsi?" said the kaal, with surprise as he figured it out. *"Female kuhsi no fly. Female kuhsi cook."*

Tif knew a calculated insult when she heard one. It sounded like a challenge. She flexed her hands and fingers, extending all six claws to their full extent. She doubted they'd do more than scratch a kaal's hide, but most other species had to be more careful. And she bared her teeth, ears flat, and hissed at him.

The kaal laughed, a deep, rumbling chuckle that never reached his face, but set his shoulders and chest bouncing. *"So,"* he said. *"Kuhsi co-pilot. Come, we go gravity rim. Talk this proposal some more."*

"No go away?" Hale pressed, with mischief.

"No go away," the kaal agreed with amusement. *"Or no go away* yet, *tiny human."*

Lisbeth sat curled in a comfortable chair upon her enormous balcony. The apartment behind her was also enormous, with wide, sliding doors onto the balcony, veiled by silk curtains that drifted in the warm breeze. Lisbeth read a large paper book, spread in her lap, the glasses on her face translating parren symbols into English ones as they followed the gaze of her eyes.

Occasionally her eyes left the book to look upon the vast courtyards. Even in the late morning, they were endlessly active. In the early morning they'd been full of parren in their thousands, mostly black-clad Domesh, arranged in ranks with military precision, performing calisthenics and martial arts. About them had flowed the runners, in great, snaking lines. Eventually the two would change, the runners halting in lines to begin calisthenics, while the previously-ranked would begin their run.

In the green garden corridors that divided vast swathes of paving, other activities were underway. Lisbeth glimpsed smaller groups of parren, seated, perhaps meditating. Others carried sheets of canvas, and easels. Insects shrilled in the building heat of morning, and the breeze that had been cool was now warm. The further reaches of the endless paved expanse began to shimmer, swimming with heat haze. In the blue sky above, birds circled on building thermals.

So this was the great and mysterious parren kingdom, Lisbeth thought to herself. Back on Homeworld, she would have given anything for the chance to travel and see it in person. Well, almost anything. Certainly she'd not have chosen *this* manner of travel. But now that she was here, she figured she should make the most of things.

One of Lisbeth's maids interrupted her reading to place a tray upon the low table before her. Upon it were small bowls of light foods — a little vegetable salad, a bite of a small roll, a piece of sliced meat about some rice-like grains, held in place with a small spike. Lisbeth could certainly see the appeal of being held hostage by the parren instead of the tavalai. To be sure, tavalai would never kill a hostage... nor probably even take one in the first place. But for food such as this, her stomach felt it was worth it.

"More food at mid-morning?" Lisbeth asked the maid, placing aside her book.

"It is late morning," said the maid's translator. *"This meal is Tovanah. A light course, in preparation."* In preparation for the next meal, Lisbeth thought with a smile, leaning forward to take one of the bowls. Parren ate their small snacks with fingers, then washed in the finger bowl on the tray. The maid moved an incense burner from the balcony railing to the table, filling the air with sweet scent. It kept the bugs away, Lisbeth gathered.

"What is your name?" Lisbeth asked the maid.

"Semaya," the maid replied. Like all high-class parren, Semaya was impossibly graceful. Her robes were light and silken, of subtle blues and greens, and tasteful jewellery on her wrists and ankles. Unlike the Domesh of this temple, she did not wear black, and made no attempt to cover her appearance. Slender and utterly hairless, Lisbeth thought her very beautiful, in that ethereal, alien way of her people.

"And you are Togreth?" Lisbeth pressed.

"Yes," said Semaya. That was rare. Most of her maids had not answered direct questions, in the four days she'd been here. Perhaps something had changed. Or perhaps she'd been asking the wrong ones, unable to tell who was the most senior. Perhaps that was Semaya.

"Will you sit with me?" Lisbeth asked, gesturing a chair opposite. "I have many questions." Semaya inclined her head gracefully, and folded her willowy limbs into the chair. Lisbeth smiled, uncaring that it was not a very parren thing. She doubted that any amount of imitation would encourage these people to consider her one of them. "How does one become Togreth?"

As far as Lisbeth had figured out, the Togreth were like the House Harmony civil service. Everyone else belonged to a denomination within the House, but the Togreth were neutral, and treated all denominations as equals. Or, at least, that was the theory.

"There are many trials," said Semaya. *"When one is newly phased, one can choose one's denomination. The most scholarly may apply to become Togreth."*

"Oh, so you've studied?" Lisbeth asked with enthusiasm. "I've only just completed my own studies in Engineering. Starship engineering in particular. I was nearly at the top of my class."

Semaya inclined her head. *"It is good. Togreth are drawn from all studies. My own are the great works and histories."*

"A historian!" said Lisbeth. "I should like to learn some parren history. I'm afraid my current knowledge is woefully poor."

"My knowledge of human history also," said Semaya. Lisbeth wondered how that could be true, given the last thousand years of human history had radically reshaped the Spiral. But she had more pressing things to learn, and thrust the urge to chat aside.

"This is the Domesh Temple?" Lisbeth asked. "How old is it, and the Kunadeen?"

"This version of the Kunadeen Complex is nearly nine thousand years old," said Semaya, with the cool grace of a tour guide reciting long-repeated facts for an ignorant tourist. Nine thousand parren years, Lisbeth thought… so nearly seven thousand human ones.

"This version?" she interrupted.

"The Kunadeen Complex has been destroyed three times. Once when the machines fell, and once again at the end of the Parren Age, at the hands of the Chah'nas. And a third time, in the Age of House Acquisition." Another of the parren internal House wars, Lisbeth thought as she took vegetable salad from the small bowl with her fingers. *"Following the third destruction, Kunadeen was left in ruins while a new ruling complex was constructed for House Harmony in Trasirtis System. It lasted for five thousand years, before the seat of Harmony power was returned here to Prakasis, and the Kunadeen was rebuilt anew."*

"And the Denomination Temples," said Lisbeth, pointing to the huge trapezoids that dotted the many kilometres of paving and garden partitions. "Have there always been ten?"

"There has been debate," Semaya admitted. *"Denominations come and go, while temples last far longer. The Harmony leadership is reluctant to allow more than ten temples in the Kunadeen, yet currently there are fifteen notable denominations. The mathematics are not always conducive."*

"I saw recent construction here," said Lisbeth. "On the one occasion I was allowed out for a walk." She hoped that the resentment survived through the translator. "How new is this Domesh Temple?"

"It is not yet completed," said Semaya. Aha, thought Lisbeth. She'd *thought* it looked new, whatever its ancient stylings. *"An old temple of the Tahrae stood on this very spot, but was destroyed long ago, when the Tahrae fell. These foundations have been left unbuilt since that age, yet the rise of the Domesh gave rise to this new temple, upon that very foundation."*

"That sounds… controversial," Lisbeth suggested.

Semaya's indigo eyes flicked to someone past Lisbeth's shoulder. Lisbeth looked, and saw a Domesh warrior, in black robes and veil, hovering near. Timoshene, she thought. He was her tokara, her personal guardian in this place. Exactly what that meant, she was still not clear. *"Yes,"* Semaya answered, with graceful diplomacy. *"Quite controversial. The Incefahd Denomination were quite opposed. And still are."*

The Incefahd were the ruling denomination in House Harmony. Lisbeth did not need to be a great parren scholar to sense that relations between them, and the Domesh, were extremely tense. "And the Incefahd fear that the Domesh will supplant them? Take over the rulership of House Harmony?"

"Yes," said Semaya.

"And is there trouble here?" Lisbeth pressed. "Between Domesh and Incefahd?"

"Between Domesh and many," said Semaya. *"The Domesh gain followers faster in the flux. Soon they will be dominant. Domesh interpretations of the great teachings of harmony are controversial. The other denominations suggest they are… antiquated."*

"Some people consider that a compliment," said Lisbeth, with a glance back at Timoshene. Timoshene said nothing, a watchful black sentinel.

"Indeed," said Semaya, with a graceful incline of the head. *"The human comprehends well."*

"And why was I brought *here*? I mean, I'd have thought, if you were going to kidnap someone, you'd keep them quietly, and not… I don't know… parade me around for everyone to see." She could not keep some of the frustration and contempt from her voice.

Semaya looked faintly puzzled. *"All denominational affairs are ruled by the Kunadeen. This is the seat of power for all House Harmony. One does not defy the Kunadeen."*

Which meant that kidnapping was normal, and legal, Lisbeth thought. She'd thought as much, and now had it confirmed. "You have no laws against kidnapping innocent people?   To blackmail their brothers?"

Semaya's puzzlement faded.   *"No,"* she said coolly.   *"It is within House law, for millennia.   The Domesh gain status with your presence.   To gain a hostage of status is worthy.   To gain an alien of such status as UFS Phoenix provides, is a thing indeed."*   She rose gracefully back to her feet.   *"But I must return to my duties.   Peace unto you, my lady."*

"One more question, please," said Lisbeth, and Semaya paused in the middle of a graceful gesture.   "Him."   She indicated Timoshene, standing behind.   "He is my Tokara?   What does he do, exactly?   He's barely spoken a word, and will not answer questions."

"Understand, my lady," Semaya said sweetly.   *"The Domesh Denomination has many enemies, inside and outside of House Harmony, and you will have many guards while you are here.   Most would like to see this alliance between the Domesh, and the UFS Phoenix, fail.   Your life gives leverage over Phoenix.   Your death will break it."*

Lisbeth took a deep breath, and gazed out at the shimmering courtyards.   "I thank you for telling me."

"And," said Semaya, in final parting, *"should your brother fail in his mission, or displease the Domesh in any way?   Your Tokara is charged to be the one who will end your life."*

CHAPTER 14

Erik and Trace's arrival at the Karlabarata Parliament put all planetary business on hold for much of the day. The institutional representatives who made up the parliament had rushed to form committees, and Erik and Trace were escorted from one to the other, to speak a few words, and then be ushered off while the representatives deliberated.

In between meetings there was a meal of many green and salty things, though the smoked fish was quite nice. Eventually word came through that the committees had agreed with near unanimity that *Phoenix* should be allowed to represent humanity in the Tsubarata, the precise details of which decision were explained to them at length by several very serious and slightly awestruck lawyers. Erik tried not to think too much about the scale of what he was doing. His ultimate mission was to recover an old drysine data-core, something he'd thought logically could be better achieved by stealth. This current situation was hardly stealth, but he didn't see that there was another way... and truly, if *Phoenix* was going to wander tavalai space, through civilised systems with billions of eyes watching, what else could he expect? There was no way to do it quietly, given all that had transpired between the tavalim and humanity over the past thousand years. He just hadn't thought that the opposite of 'quietly', would be this.

After the lawyers, the politicians came. Speaker Prodamandam explained that politically, there was difficulty. All the millions of tavalai deaths in the Triumvirate War required some acknowledgement. There must be a gesture, to appease even the level-headed and under-emotional tavalai public.

And so Erik and Trace found themselves on another cruiser, flown away from the Parliament and across the city. It was evening as they landed, on the wide, curving bank of a river. The slope down to the water was all parks, gardens and tall trees, before a skyline of riverview towers. Lining the riverbank, as they were led amongst armed security away from the cruisers, were a huge throng of civilians, clustered in their tens of thousands, necks craned to glimpse the humans.

At a wide patio before descending stairs, the inevitable waiting honour-guard, robed with tavalai formality. But this time, Erik saw with astonishment, it was children. They stood in rows, each with a lily, and several with garlands. Erik and Trace stopped where indicated before them, and several children came forward, nervously. Erik had only seen tavalai children a few times in person. Never had the circumstance been a pleasant one. Their heads were too large for their bodies, with big hands and feet, webbing particularly prominent between the fingers before it withdrew somewhat with age.

These kids tottered forward, following the gestures of their elders, and Erik sank to one knee to take his lilies, and accept a garland of flowers. He smiled at the kids, and they blinked with their big, froggy eyes. A few looked scared, which made him sad. But then, what else could he expect? Given what humans had actually done to so many tavalai, over recent years? This was not the childish fear of the innocent and unworldly. It was an entirely reasonable fear, born of too much experience. On this world, he was the bogeyman, and a thousand friendly smiles would not change it.

The children were ushered aside, and he and Trace were led down the wide stairs to the river. Between them at the river grew a forest of steel trees. Or they looked like trees, a twisting length of metal rising from the paving, rotating like a DNA helix. All the 'trees' were the same height, yet as the riverbank dropped lower, they rose up as the slope declined. Walking amongst them, Erik saw that their sides were engraved with hundreds of tavalai words. Thousands. Not spaced in sentences, but divided into pairs in rolling, looping Togiri script. Names.

"It's a memorial," he murmured to Trace. "A war memorial. These are the names of the dead."

Now there were stairs climbing the sides of the steel trees, in a spiral, where visitors could climb and read the names written further up.   Atop the spirals, the stairs made walkways, a second layer where visitors could walk above, and take in the view.

"Why the forest?" Trace asked quietly.   She looked quite affected, Erik saw, her long-stemmed lilies in one arm, garland around her neck and gazing about at it all.   "Why do it like this?"

It was a long way from the more subdued, minimalist tone of human memorials and cemeteries, Erik guessed her thoughts.   And then he realised.   "The earliest tavalai civilisation was tree-houses," he said, recalling that school lesson.   "There were vast swamps. Tavalai climbed trees, and made walkways between them."   He gestured about.   "Like this.   They're coming home.   All the dead. They're home."

The memorial did not stop at the river's edge.   Here the water flowed in channels between the 'trees', as the ground advanced onto the river, on raised platforms, creating the impression of a swamp — water and land mixing together, in very tavalai style. Finally the trees ended at a vast, artificial semi-circle in the river.   In the precise centre of that circle, a great sculpture rose from the deeper water, half giant tree, half burning fire.   Strands of sculpted steel bent and swirled about each other, as though the river itself were burning.   Beyond it, and just above the far bank, the yellow sun set within a pink and orange sky, the reflection of which set all the river to flame.

"How many names, do you think?" Trace asked as they gazed at the beautiful, alien scene.

Erik thought of each written name, the size of it, the number on each steel tree.   Multiplied by the number of trees.   Maths were much more a starship pilot's strongpoint than a marine's.   "A few hundred thousand, at least," said Erik.   "That's just for Tontalamai System's losses alone, I think."

"We put some of these names here," Trace said quietly.

"Undoubtedly.   And they put names on our memorials too."

Trace took a deep, humid breath.   "This was never right.   Of all the people worth killing in the galaxy... not tavalai."

"I know," Erik said tiredly.   "I think we've all known.   It's taken a huge, concerted effort, from humans and tavalai together, to deny that truth.   We *could* have been friends.   Too many other powers wanted it otherwise."

"No," Trace disagreed.   "Too many of *us*.   Humans and tavalai together.   We did this.   We should own up to it.   Particularly the ones who made it happen, and had a chance to stop it, but didn't."

"We're in," Erik told the assembled senior crew in the briefing room, barely a single rotation later.   He'd slept a little on the ground before departure, then most of the way back up, save for the most violent part of ascent.   That, plus a quick meal, a shower, and now a covered mug of coffee in his hand, were all he needed to get his brain ready for the briefing.   The planet-sized shot of adrenaline, from what they were all about to attempt, didn't hurt either.

"The Pondalganam have confirmed our berth at Tsubarata Main."   The holography displayed a large map of the famous planetoid and its encircling steel rings.   Erik pointed at a spot near the rotating rings with his laser pointer.   "We've got an inner berth, zero-G, which just means they don't want all our marines disembarking on their G-rim."

"I wouldn't either, if I were them," Trace remarked, sipping one of her famously unappetising smoothies, in a new, clean-pressed uniform.

"I'm speaking at the main Parliament roughly… twenty-four linear days from now.   For us, it's about fourteen, after our jump."

"What are you going to say?" Kaspowitz asked wryly.

Erik repressed a smile.   "I'm sure I have no idea."   He'd always been good at public speaking, and had been encouraged by his parents to pursue it.   As a Debogande, it was a useful skill to have.   He'd given his share of presentations, for family or school events, and since in Fleet, though there he'd tried to avoid the media appearances that Fleet's PR machine would try to thrust him in, not wanting special recognition from his name.   He'd never been particularly nervous before, even in front of large crowds of important people. But the idea of speaking on behalf of all humanity at the central parliament of the tavalai-sphere peoples, was daunting even for him. Particularly knowing that everyone back home would see it eventually, and would hate him for it, whatever words he actually spoke.

"Now, being docked at the Tsubarata would normally be no security concern for anyone there," Erik continued. "But we have Styx aboard, and so far we have good reason to believe that State Department remain ignorant of her presence. The only people who know are us, and *Makimakala*, and Captain Pram has sworn all his crew to secrecy. Tavalai don't break those sorts of rules lightly, and State Department would have raised holy hell if they even suspected Styx existed, so for now I think we're okay on that front.

"The next point is that *Makimakala* can't help us on this one. We knew it was coming, and sure enough they've been officially summonsed back to Dobruta HQ, which is so secret they won't say where it is, other than it will keep them occupied for a long time. So no more direct help from the Dobruta, no more translations, no more chiding on how recklessly we employ hacksaw technology. For this one, we're on our own."

Somber glances were exchanged between the crew. Erik had half-expected some rowdy remarks about how they preferred it that way, but there were none. *Makimakala* was still not exactly a friend, but in the past few months, they'd become far less than an enemy. Until this point in tavalai space, *Makimakala* had been *Phoenix*'s guarantee of safe passage, where no human warships were allowed. To lose that company now made everyone feel a lot more unhappy than they'd have believed three months ago, when the Dobruta ibranakala-class had thundered into Joma Station dock with all guns bristling.

"While the Major and I have been on Ponnai, Ensigns Uno and Jokono have been with Aristan's people on Daravani Station. Jokono, over to you."

"Yes," said Jokono, looking almost a little nervous upon the edge of his chair. Erik supposed that for all his civilian experience,

Jokono had never been involved in planning a military mission before. But beneath the nerves, with Jokono, there was always that professional calm... mixed with no little intrigue, to find himself in yet another new and challenging circumstance. It was the kind of professional confidence that Erik always found calming, like that of a wizened old cabinet maker, enthusiastic about attempting an unusual new style of table, and now considering which tools he'd need. "I won't bore you with the details of what Hiro and I got up to on Daravani Station — suffice to say that Aristan's people got us in, disguised as acolytes, and once inside, some of Hiro's new hacksaw technology made accessing some local tavalai Fleet computer systems a relatively simple matter.

"We've been piecing that data together with the data that the 'friendly' elements of tavalai Fleet have given us, and this is what we've been able to discern." He activated a holography hand-controller, fingers splayed upon icons hovering in the air before him. The big hologram zoomed out from the Tsubarata, to show the red-brown world of Konik about which it orbited, and the outer moon of Kamala. "All vessels landing at Kamala must first land at the floating facility of Chara. Its location in the upper-atmosphere of Kamala is unknown at any given time, as we've discussed. What we haven't known until now is how clearances are given and received for each vessel to progress from there, down to the surface, and the Kantovan Vault.

"We now know that vessels landing at Chara must not only undergo a full physical inspection there, but will have their orders transmitted simultaneously to the State Department Headquarters in the Tsubarata, *and* to a secure facility in the city of Gamesh, on Konik." He indicated the big, brown planet. "That secure facility is in turn located within the Gamesh command network. Confirmation of these orders from Chara must be sent electronically, and independently, within the same thirty second window, back to Chara, from both the Tsubarata HQ *and* from Gamesh. It's like a security lock demanding two keys be inserted and turned simultaneously by different people. If one of the recipients does not recognise the vehicle they're being asked to clear, or delays answering for thirty seconds or more, it's a security red flag and the ship in question will probably be boarded, and its crew detained."

"So not only will we need forged electronic orders for the ship that lands on Chara to give to the command post there," Hiro chimed in, far more relaxed and comfortable in his chair, "but we'll need to have teams in place to infiltrate both Tsubarata State Department HQ, and State Department's Gamesh facility, and simultaneously intercept and respond to those messages. Without State Department noticing."

Grim stares from the assembled officers. They were elite, but infiltration cloak-and-dagger was not their speciality. "I'm guessing tavalai Fleet will be no help there?" Shilu said.

"No," Erik agreed. "Fleet have no sway with State Department, and no agents within. Or at least, none they're prepared to use for something like this. Now Hiro thinks we can infiltrate the State Department HQ in the Tsubarata. It won't be easy, but we'll have Styx right close-by in *Phoenix*, and with her help, we can pretty much hack into anything."

"It's not a hacking job, though," Hiro added. He'd produced a nail file from somewhere, and used it calmly. "Those systems are autistic, simply not accessible from outside. Styx can help me get in. Me, and a few others, maybe. Once inside, I can be in position to intercept the incoming signal from Kamala, and confirm it as though it were approved by State Department. Konik will have to be someone else — I can't be two places at once, and Konik looks like the bigger job, more suited to marines."

"We'll want to avoid killing tavalai if at all possible," Shahaim told him. "Both the Dobruta and tavalai Fleet have been pretty clear on that from the beginning. Can you do that?"

Hiro stopped filing. "That depends."

"On what?"

"On how badly you want this thing to work," Hiro said darkly. Shahaim took a deep breath, and looked at Erik.

"We'll cross that bridge when we come to it," Erik told her. "Jokono, we're going to need our other security expert down in Gamesh. Same deal, we're going to need that facility infiltrated, so

196

that when the message comes in from Kamala, it can be intercepted and confirmed as though it were State Department doing it. The big complication is that you won't have Styx on-hand to help you do it."

Jokono nodded slowly. "Who am I with?"

"Lieutenant Dale," said Trace. "And some of Aristan's people. There are plenty of parren on Konik, and the cloaks make a good disguise for humans. We'll make a team, your discretion and Dale's — yourselves, a few of Aristan's best parren, and a *Phoenix* tech to run that side of it. We've got good data on the facility, and you'll have fifteen days to put together your plan."

Jokono glanced at Dale. Dale winked at him. "Piece of cake, Joker."

"Ensign Hale's team are due in Kantovan nearly six days before we are," Erik continued. "We'll have to get them their orders for the vault — tavalai Fleet have told us they'll do it, since our transmissions will be monitored. Tif will be co-pilot, and although State Department know we have a kuhsi pilot, we don't think it's likely they'll have biometric data on Tif herself."

"And if they do?" Kaspowitz asked. "Seems a risky assumption."

"The pilot crew of that descender will be all hired guns," Erik told him. "If something goes wrong, we've no guarantee they'll risk their necks for us. We need a *Phoenix* pilot aboard."

"And you think Tif will risk her neck for us?" Kaspowitz pressed.

"Yes," Hausler said firmly. "Absolutely."

Erik looked about, and saw little doubt on the faces of those who knew Tif best. "Once she's down on Chara, Chara will inspect the ship, then send confirmation back to the Tsubarata and Gamesh for clearance. We need our team to land on Chara in advance of Tif's arrival, and get off without detection, then get onto Tif's ship *after* the inspection, also without detection." More grim expressions from the group. "Major?"

"My team will depart for Kantovan on a separate vessel," Trace confirmed. "We'll have to make the transfer here, and quietly. Tavalai Fleet say they can get us a ride on a Fleet transport, they land

197

on Chara all the time, but don't actually descend into the atmosphere — State Department won't give even them clearance for that. Or not to the vault, at least. We get down in advance of Tif's landing, then get aboard after inspection."

"Since I know that none of the marines will ever ask this question," Kaspowitz said drily, "I'll ask it myself. Does it have to be you?" Looking at Trace.

"It doesn't *have* to be anything," Trace told him with mild amusement. "But it's going to be me, because this job will take marines, and quite likely shooting, with the armed guards in the vault, and we'll need an experienced combat officer to pull it off. I'm sure my lieutenants could pull it off as well, but it's imperative that this mission succeeds, and I'd like to think I wasn't promoted to this rank by accident."

Dale gave Kaspowitz a challenging look. Kaspowitz put up his hands, and backed out gracefully. Trace took control of the holographics herself, and a new display appeared, of what looked like an armoured bunker. "This is the vault," she said. "Or it's what Hiro's best information says is the vault. Thank you Hiro."

"Not at all, Major," said Hiro, with a smile like a knife.

"We still don't know where it is, but the coordinates are sent direct to the descender's navcomp following State Department clearance. Chara could be a fair way from those coordinates when they come through, so it could still be a long flight time to get there. On return ascent, all vehicles have their navcomps erased. Communications with the ground are non-existent, as total stealth is the only way to hide the location. The vault will verify codes on landing. Our cover story, courtesy of tavalai Fleet, is the recovery of a State Department artefact that Fleet do know for a fact exists. Different State Department divisions in different systems will requisition artefacts or secure records frequently, leading to covert vessels approaching and departing Kamala about once every five days. They're usually unmarked, often flown by hired crew who know nothing about the mission. It's State Department's way of ensuring personnel security, apparently they've had trouble in the past with attempted infiltrations kidnapping vessels and torturing crew for information. Hired crew don't know anything, and there's nothing in the descender's navcomp until *after* they've landed on Chara."

"Why not give the courier vessels more protection on the way in and out of the system?" Shilu wondered. "An armed escort?"

"There's too many of them," said Erik. "Insufficient resources, and tavalai Fleet's tired of diverting resources on State Department's whim. Plus there's distrust between Fleet and State Department, obviously, and State Department don't trust Fleet guarding them either. It's worth pointing out here, in light of this situation, that Kantovan System is the one place in tavalai space where State Department vessels are armed. They're not actually State Department, but they're registered in State Department's name — officially it's for Tsubarata security, but unofficially it's the vault."

"It's not the artefacts that need guarding in transit," Trace reminded them all. "It's the access codes and procedures for the vault itself. The really valuable stuff in there rarely leaves, and hasn't done for centuries. To access it, you go there, then return without it.

"Now when an otherwise unknown courier lands at their door, the vault takes a single container through their airlock, fetches the requested item, puts it into the container, and sends it back out. That's it. Less important items, like the one Fleet have suggested we pretend to be claiming, we can take out on loan, like a book from a library. The really important stuff, we'd have to enter the vault to observe personally... but even then, no one's allowed past the lobby."

"So we put a bomb in the container," Dale suggested. "Blows the doors halfway in."

"Thus bringing down the second security doors behind it," said Trace, "even less penetrable than the first." She indicated that spot on the hologram. "Plus the doors have sensors that will detect any technology operating within the container. So no bombs, and none of Styx's little recon bugs either. They'll be spotted, and we'll be screwed.   Life signs too, we can't just put a marine in the box and sneak in."

"So what then?"

"We put one of Aristan's people in the box," said Trace, with a glance at Erik.   They'd talked about this, with Aristan himself. Aristan was adamant.

"While giving no vital signs?" Shahaim asked.   "Life-support is technology too."

"Aristan's people can trance-hibernate.   For up to half an hour, without life support, with minimal vital signs.   The box will have a false bottom.   It should get him in.   We've got details on the doors, we're fairly sure he can get the airlock to cycle from within. And then we storm the vault."

"Hang on, *storm*?" said Shilu.   "I thought the idea was to kill as few tavalai as possible?"

Trace smiled broadly.   "The vault's not guarded by tavalai. It's guarded by sard."   She looked around, and saw dawning realisation.   And on a few, satisfaction.   Dale looked positively eager.   "Now, does anyone here have a moral objection to killing lots of sard?"

She looked pointedly at Romki, the only one of them who might.   Romki sighed, and scratched his bald head.   "Such a dilemma," he said drily.   "Being the only man on a warship with a conscience."   A few of the crew looked offended.   Trace only smiled more broadly.   "Fine, whatever.   Let's kill some sard, I suppose another fifty won't make much difference after the ten thousand or so we did last month."

"A hundred and fifty," Trace corrected.

"And how many marines are you taking?" Dale asked.

"Can't fit more than Command Squad," said Trace.

"Eight against a hundred and fifty?" Shahaim asked.

"If we surprise them, most won't be armoured in time," Trace reasoned.   "We will be.   Seems fair to me."   She had some ideas, Erik knew.   He doubted the sard would enjoy finding out.

"You'll need full armour to make those odds work," said Dale. "You're going to move fully armoured marines through Chara, without being spotted?"

"We've got good intel on Chara," Trace assured him. "It looks possible. And we'll have help, tavalai Fleet in Chara HQ who will fiddle the surveillance cameras for us. Not many people walking around outside on Chara, population's not big, and you can't breathe without a suit." Dale rubbed his square jaw, staring at the hologram. No one respected Trace more than Dale. But Dale, and most of the marine officers, believed that she was needlessly reckless of her own life in particular. "There are some more interesting defences in the vault, but nothing that a general command meeting need address. It's marine business. What we *do* need to address, is graviton capacitors."

She zoomed the hologram onto one part of the image. It was a wide hall, running deep and mostly horizontal beneath the hill behind the vault. At the end, it widened to a spherical chamber. Within the hole, yet not touching the sides, hung a spherical chamber. It did not appear to be touching the sides of the shaft in any way, but hovered, as though repelled in equal measure from the walls of the shaft.

"That could just as easily be magnetism," Kaspowitz offered, squinting skeptically at the image.

"Except that magnetism wouldn't make the vault harder to access," said Trace. "Graviton capacitors do." Kaspowitz looked unconvinced. "The intel says that's one hundred Gs in there. Short-range gravitons, only affecting a ten metre radius about the vault."

"Short-range gravitons," Kaspowitz snorted. "There's no such thing."

"Would you be happier if we just called it magic, Kaspo?" Trace asked him, still amused. "Fine, it's one hundred Gs in there, by magic."

"Armour suits couldn't withstand a hundred Gs," said Dale. "They're rated to about thirty, in manoeuvres. The servo-mechanics would crush. Then the drive chain, and the reactor…"

"Would collapse," said Lieutenant Rooke, with the impatience of someone kept waiting until he could speak about the really exciting bit. "Yes, we know. Styx has a solution."

"More magic?" asked Kaspowitz.

Rooke took a deep breath. "No. A drone." Everyone stared at him, save for Erik, Trace and Romki, who already knew.

"You're... she's going to build a hacksaw drone?" Kaspowitz asked with alarm.

Rooke nodded, with nervous excitement. "We've got a lot of parts left from Argitori. No functioning CPUs, the Major's people were thorough when they killed them the first time. But lots of body parts. With Styx's new fabricators, she says she can replace the parts we don't have, and make a new CPU, a new brain. Only drone-level, nothing like as smart as her, and completely compliant, it would follow orders and nothing more."

"You mean it would follow *her* orders," Shilu said grimly.

"And it will be armed," Trace added. "We've got plenty of their weapons, some extra firepower wouldn't go astray."

"Wonderful," Dale muttered. Of them all, Dale, Kaspowitz and Shilu were the most concerned by Styx's presence.

"How does a drone help you with the graviton capacitors?" Shahaim asked.

"Styx says a drone can handle one hundred Gs," said Trace. "Barely, and it will require some modifications. But it will be able to enter the vault without us having to deactivate the capacitors first. Which, as it turns out, we've no idea how to do. Rooke thinks they'll be so deeply dug into those walls that it would take high explosive anyway, and that much high explosive would destroy the vault in the process."

"Well," said Dale, "you'll have to leave real soon to get there ahead of us. Styx can't make a new drone in a week, can she?"

"Human inefficiencies allowing," came Styx's voice over speakers, *"the drone in question will take approximately thirty-seven hours to construct."*

"You're kidding," someone said.

"Rooke?" asked Erik.

"Well, um, she's been practising," said Rooke. "Building those new fabricators, I mean… she's nearly completed the new model, which is, well…" he gave an exasperated laugh. "It's nearly as amazing as hacksaws themselves, it's not technology that any of us have any clue how to operate, it's nearly organic in…"

"Lieutenant," Trace interrupted. "Focus." It was a running joke between them, and Rooke bit back an apology, that turned into a grin.

"Right. Sure. Thirty-seven hours… we've got all the parts, Styx thinks if we give her command control of Primary Re-Fab One she can reconfigure the main components in under ten hours. We'll have to run all the other fabs to get the secondary parts, and she's already got synthetic eco-systems of neural micros running from the reconstruction of her own brain. She thinks the new fab she's built, plus those micros, should let her make the drone's brain, which is the only bit we don't have."

"Styx, you can't just repair an existing brain?" Erik asked the empty air.

"There is not enough functioning core left for regeneration," said Styx. *"Extensive regeneration is a function primarily for higher designations like myself. Common drones can regenerate from moderate damage, but not from catastrophic damage."*

"What will the new drone's capabilities be?" Trace asked.

"At the beginning, almost nil. It will learn rapidly. A new drone can achieve full function within one hundred human hours."

"You mean we're going to have to teach it to walk?"

"It will teach itself to walk," said Styx. *"But further interactions will expand its capabilities faster, as with an organic child."* Trace looked intrigued.

"Congratulations Major," Erik told her. "You're about to become a mummy."

CHAPTER 15

Lisbeth was awoken by the sound of distant shuttles landing. They had a curfew, she thought, and were not allowed low passes even in the daytime, save for the occasional VIP transfer. Lately there had been a lot of big ones, far larger than *Phoenix*'s assault shuttles, landing several kilometres beyond the eight-kilometre wide square courtyards of Kunadeen Complex. The roar of landing retros echoed from multiple temple walls, each adding a new complexity and direction to the sound.

She stared at the ceiling, her mind swirling with bad dreams and recent facts from her readings. Parren history, parren psychology, a great, tangled mess of wars and upheavals, separating relative periods of stability. In truth, parren society was stable most of the time, which only made the upheavals that much more terrifying. The last really big one had been sixteen hundred years ago, had deposed House Acquisitive from power, replacing it with House Fortitude, and killed a hundred and seventeen million parren. Though some of her readings insisted that those figures had been distorted by the winning side, and understated the true casualties by a factor of between five and ten. In between the big upheavals were countless smaller ones, many just as scary if you were in the middle of them, but far more isolated.

Parren had five primary phases, or states of mind. House Fortitude was just what it sounded, and espoused the virtues of stoicism and displays of strength. House Enquiry were philosophical, and produced many great scientists and thinkers. House Acquisitive (her translator informed her was the closest English word) were primarily in business. House Creative were intensely introverted, their greatest denominational heroes known for locking themselves away for years while hatching grand design schemes, many of them artistic, some of them not. And then, House Harmony, those people of mellow disinterest, who sought to balance all competing interests, and to be impartial between them.

Why parren brains shifted between these mental states, even parren scientists had multiple conflicting theories. Most speculated some variation on the need to maintain social harmony in shifting circumstances, though ancient, pre-technological parren had seemed to only flux between phases in response to external circumstance. With the arrival of modernity, external circumstances could be more easily controlled or ignored, and the great parren flux had begun to lead the circumstance, rather than follow it.

Ancient parren societies had made great, mystic religions out of it, with all sorts of incredible, arcane symbolism, and a myriad of dramatic and often bloody tales, or legends, about parren whose lives were torn asunder by the flux... or once destroyed, rebuilt anew. There were tales that equated the five phases with the five parren seasons... though Lisbeth thought the obvious asymmetry of five seasons, instead of the more reasonable human four, spoke to the parren's insistent search for meaning in the great cycle, that they imposed their phases onto *everything*, whether a true parallel existed or not.

Today, modern science had laid a new layer of myth, legend and fact atop the old, but had not replaced it. To Lisbeth it seemed that the old priests had now been replaced by the psychologists, who occupied a pseudo-scientific role much like an old-fashioned priesthood — advising the top leaders, whispering in their ears, dictating events from behind the scenes and holding themselves separate from the fray. Many among the Togreth here in Kunadeen, she'd gathered, were also Shoveren — the Masters of the Phase, as all psychologists were known. Lisbeth had had several friends in university studying to be psychologists, and thought the parren would find it quite obscene just how ordinary and average that was, among humans. Here, only the very best and brightest were allowed, and those only after the most rigorous testing. Even with her very high scores, Lisbeth doubted she'd have made the grade. Erik might have, though. And Major Thakur, almost certainly... though perhaps would have proven temperamentally unsuited.

Somewhere high and distant, a new shuttle thundered toward a landing. Lisbeth glanced toward the balcony door, open in the warm night air to let in the breeze, and to allow silent passage to the Domesh guards who wandered through at all hours of the night, silent so not to wake her. She rarely ever saw them, though, so adept they were at fading from shadow to shadow in their dark cloaks. Occasionally one had given her a start, but she was coming to welcome their presence, particularly following Timoshene's warnings of the dangers.

She glimpsed a guard now, a dark shadow in the doorway against the faintly billowing silk curtain. The shadow raised a weapon at her. And jerked, with a strangled grunt, arms contorting. The pistol fired, and put a hole in the ceiling. Two more shots from across the room, and the dark figure in the doorway fell, a crumpled heap on the floor. Lisbeth stared, her heart only now hammering in panic, too late to help her if she needed to flee. Which of course she hadn't done... just sat there in her bed, half-upright on her elbows, propped in such a way to make a more perfect target.

Domesh guards converged on her, weapons drawn. One went to turn on a light, and was stopped with a hissed command by another. No lights — there could be a sniper, and the Domesh worked well in the dark. Lisbeth didn't know where a sniper could be based — the nearest temple building was two kilometres away, and none of them had precise line-of-sight on her room. Time amongst *Phoenix* marines had given her at least that much appreciation of simple ballistics.

A guard examined the body, feeling within the robes. He spoke to his fellow guards, cautiously, and a conversation started. They seemed puzzled, and wary. Lisbeth recalled her AR glasses, and leaned to the bedside table to fetch them, ignoring shaking limbs to put them on her face, and insert one earpiece. Lenses flashed icons at her, and she blinked on one — translate, it said. But the guards were not speaking any parren tongue the glasses were programmed to recognise.

Timoshene crouched by her bedside — Lisbeth recognised his eyes, even past the hood and veil in the dark. When a man was tasked with potentially killing you, you remembered his every detail. *"Erudarn says the intruder was not killed with bullets,"*

Timoshene's translator speaker announced, and Lisbeth pulled her earpiece out. *"He says the intruder was dead beforehand."*

And the Domesh named Erudarn jumped backward in startlement, eyes following something fast-moving that rose from the body. Like a man badly startled by a wasp. More words followed, fast and alarmed. Domesh guards crept across the floor, staring upward and about, searching the air. Lisbeth took deep breaths to calm herself. She thought she should get up, but doubted she would be any safer if she did. *Phoenix* marines had always preferred her to stay where she was until ordered otherwise, rather than have her rushing around on her own initiative. She doubted the Domesh would think any differently.

"You have a protector," said Timoshene. Lisbeth stared at him. Beneath the veil, she caught a flash of amazement in his indigo eyes. *"We heard stories, of the UFS Phoenix, playing with the technology of the ancient ones. All Domesh warriors have heard tales of the assassin wasps. They are the oldest tales, from Drakhil's time. And now they have returned, with you."*

Barely half-an-hour later, Lisbeth's chambers were a hive of activity. She sat at her table, beneath the muted yellow light that imitated two dozen candle flames, wrapped in her bedrobe and sipping some tea. Domesh doctors examined the assassin where he'd fallen, while dark robed guards moved silently from chambers to balcony, indicating with pointed fingers where access may have been achieved, piecing together the assassin's movements. Togreth maids stood silently in the corners, imperiously ignoring the wary glances the Domesh sent their way.

By Timoshene's words, the maids should have been the primary suspects for letting the assassin inside, yet Lisbeth doubted it was that simple. From what she'd read, the Togreth were mostly what they said they were — impartial servants of the House itself, who took no part in denominational disputes. And no doubt her Domesh guards had vetted all of these personally, for an extra level of screening.   But that was the rank-and-file… Timoshene's suspicions were of the leadership, and their political compromises. And Lisbeth thought of human Fleet, and how despite everything that had happened, most *Phoenix* crew would still trust another Fleet captain or lieutenant implicitly.   Such middle-ranking officers were below the level of politics, and so remained principled and impartial, ruled primarily by their own conscience.   It was only at the very highest level of command, tangled up in political concerns and double-speak, where the rot set in.

A new Domesh entered with several more guards, black robes sliding over the cool pavings.   The Domesh approached Lisbeth's table, with several glances at the surrounding air.   He sat opposite — another man, Lisbeth saw.   All the high-ranking Domesh were men, unlike many of the other parren denominations and houses.   A people who denied themselves everything would logically start with desire, and that was difficult where the sexes mingled, whatever robes they hid themselves beneath.   To ensure a purity beyond temptation, one of the genders had to go, from the top ranks at least.

"I am Gesul," said the man's translator as he spoke.   *"I am the second-most in charge, you would say, of the Domesh.   I am told you brought a friend with you from Stoya."*   Lisbeth said nothing, and sipped her tea.   She did not yet know what would be safe to say. The Domesh had a fascination with the drysines, that was obvious. And inevitable, given their primary fascination with Drakhil, the drysines' most loyal organic servant.

"Where is Aristan?" Lisbeth wondered.   It seemed odd that he would not have returned yet from Stoya.   Because surely, if he were here, he'd have visited a matter such as this in person.

"Occupied," said Gesul.   *"Does it think?   Do you command it?"*

There was little point in denying it, Lisbeth thought.   There was little use in fighting to keep a secret that no longer existed.   But if she went *with* it… possibilities dawned.   Possibilities like no longer feeling so damn powerless, the plaything of alien power games that aimed weapons at her brother's heart.   She pursed her lips upon the brim of her cup. "You could mistreat me yourself, and find out," she suggested.

Gesul took a deep breath, and leaned back in his chair. He gazed at her for a long moment, as though with revelation. *"We have tales of Phoenix's exploits. Out in the far rim, on the edge of sard space and barabo. A great battle, against some remnants of the ancient ones. You were there?"*

"That depends," said Lisbeth. "Most of the peoples of the Spiral have sworn not to toy with such things. I'm unfamiliar with the parren position."

"House Fortitude enforces those laws. Possession of this forbidden technology is punishable by death. Best that you do not allow this knowledge to anyone beyond the Domesh."

"That seems unlikely," Lisbeth retorted. "Given that I'm a prisoner here, with precious few guests. Besides, I have no such possessions. Only friends." She glanced back toward the assassin's body in the balcony doorway. "Whose is he?"

"Unclear as yet," said Gesul. *"We will investigate."*

"Your best guess?"

"Such guesses are needless. All fear the rise of the Domesh. We gain new followers in the flux, by a scale unknown to any other denomination. Soon we will rule all House Harmony. The other denominations all see it, and see that your brother's venture with us may hasten their demise. It does not matter 'who'. It is an unmysterious mystery." He glanced up at the surrounding air. *"Please inform your friend that we are not its enemies. We strive to protect you from harm, as it does."*

"Up to a point," Lisbeth said coolly.

Gesul's eyes regarded her seriously. Recognising a threat, however she'd intended it. *"Should your brother succeed, it will not come to that. The Domesh intend only harmony between Phoenix, Debogande, and Domesh."*

"Ah." Lisbeth smiled, humourlessly. "Harmony." It was one of those words that sounded nice, if you didn't think too much about it. Lately, with human Fleet killing its own people to achieve its own style of harmony, Lisbeth was wondering if some tavalai-style chaotic discord might not have more to recommend it.

From somewhere beneath the collar of her robe, she heard a faint buzz, a thrumming of small wings against her neck. She smiled more broadly, feeling suddenly quite bold. "I would like to get out of this room," she said. "I feel that humans and parren — or Domesh, at least — should get to know each other better. Particularly as you're about to become such a great force in parren affairs. Family Debogande would be well served to know such powerful parren, in the interest of harmonious human-parren relations, wouldn't you say?"

Gesul's eyes gleamed. *"You wish to see the power of the Domesh. I will show you."*

At dawn, Lisbeth was led out amidst the crowd of dark robed Domesh at the base of the Domesh Temple. Timoshene led the way, as chants and shouts rose from the courtyard, and grand, echoing announcements were made on loudspeakers that could surely be heard from one end of the Kunadeen Complex to the other.

Lisbeth saw a Shoveren — a psychologist, in human terms, but for the parren something closer to a holyman and master of rituals. This one was dressed in stately blue, which seemed the colour for those amongst the Domesh who did not wear the black robes, yet were unwilling to display the more traditional parren finery. The Shoveren's helpers clustered about as he moved past, clutching old books, and bearing high banners inscribed with stylised symbols that seemed to Lisbeth vaguely familiar from her recent readings. Domesh parren faded from the entourage's path, and the psychologist-priest gave Lisbeth an imperious stare.

Lisbeth wondered at this crazy contradiction of the Domesh, that they denied all colour and vibrancy in such a colourful, vibrant people. They needed the Shoveren to conduct ceremonies on the scale of what this was turning out to be, yet the Shoveren could never dress as Domesh did, nor entirely embrace their interpretation of the Harmony Phase. How then could the Domesh ever rise to rule House Harmony, when they would forever be reliant upon those who did not share their denominational beliefs?

Timoshene and company led her up stairs to the platform that separated her from the courtyard, then slid between rows of watching black robes to the front. There at the railing, Lisbeth gasped to see the scale of what confronted her.

The entire main courtyard before the Domesh Temple, stretching for half-a-kilometre before her, was full of parren. They stood in countless rows, with the morning sun rising upon the hills at their backs, and the rows divided further into phalanx blocks, like the division of regiments in some old, pre-technological army. Each phalanx was assembled beneath a variety of banners. A light breeze twirled at long streamers atop the banners, the majestic waving of a thousand, winding fingers in the golden dawn.

"It is the Isha," said Timoshene at her side, his translated words sounding this time in Lisbeth's earpiece, so as not to spoil the very parren scene. *"Fifteen times in a standard year, the newly-phased assemble, to pledge allegiance."*

Lisbeth stared across the endless crowd. Perhaps half-a-million strong, she thought, doing a rough count of ranks, then multiplying. *This* was why she'd been hearing shuttles landing all through the night. Parren from across a hundred systems had been assembling here, to pledge their new allegiance to the Domesh.

"They all come here?" she breathed. "All the newly-phased?"

"Only those that choose the Domesh denomination. There are fifteen recognised denominations within House Harmony. The Domesh currently rank fourth amongst them, in numbers. In the current flux, we shall soon be second, behind the Incefahd. Perhaps in no more than a year. From there, ultimate power within House Harmony is at hand."

"What happens when there are more Domesh in the Harmony Phase than any other?"

"There must be a count, and the count must reveal a majority, in declared denomination. A full majority is not required

— a denomination will assume the leadership of the House if it has the most declared, even should it have no more than a third of the total number. Currently, we estimate this should take no more than two standard years."

"And the Incefahd denomination will just hand you control of House Harmony?"

"No," Timoshene admitted. *"Sometimes the rules are not followed."*

"And what happens then?"

"Trouble."

Lisbeth nodded in awed silence, doing some more fast maths. Half-a-million here. Fifteen times in a full year. That made seven-and-a-half million parren in a year... but Timoshene was talking about standard *parren* years, which were three-quarters as long as a traditional human year. So ten million parren in a human year, becoming newly-phased adherents to the Domesh. But there were at least four hundred billion parren, divided almost equally into each of the five houses. So eighty billion per house, divided mostly into fifteen denominations... which made five-point-three billion per denomination, if distributed equally. And the Domesh were much larger than average — the second largest, Timoshene said. That could mean twenty or twenty-five billion followers. Which made this gathering before her...

"How many of the newly-phased come here to the Kunadeen?" Lisbeth asked. "To show their loyalty like this?"

"Less than one-in-a-hundred," said Timoshene. *"This is barely a raindrop in a downpour."* Ten million a year, thought Lisbeth. Times a hundred, was a billion, and then some. Meaning that the Domesh were adding somewhere over a billion new followers each year, and what she saw before her, in regimented, disciplined ranks, was only the tiniest fraction of the movement unfolding across parren space.

"How do they decide a denomination?" she asked. "Parren phase to one of the five Houses, one of the five states of mind. But denominations are not phased, they're chosen."

"Yes," said Timoshene, with a final pride, as though she'd answered her own question without realising it. *"The parren wish to be strong again. Like the humans, we too have lived beneath the heel of others' boots. The time has come to make the other species of the Spiral feel the weight of* our *heel for a change."*

Gamesh security stank. Dale passed the security station without incident, past bored kratik contractors, his forged ID scanned, his passbook stamped, and that was it. The arrivals hall was none too impressive either, exposed steel and bare fittings, the smell of recycled air and crowded with aliens.

He kept his head down, gloved hands folded within the wide sleeves of his robe, dark glasses firm above the facemask, not an inch of bare human skin exposed. Soon their two parren guides were through — neither of them as well-covered, to demonstrate to any watchful security that at least *some* of these dark robed figures were actually parren. But the security were *all* contractors, and Gamesh's reputation as one of the most successful free-cities in tavalai space had not been gained by prying too deeply into the backgrounds of visitors, nor on placing too many restrictions on how long they could stay, or what they got up to.

After the parren came his familiar Alpha Platoon, First Squad team — Lester 'Woody' Forrest, Cilian 'Tricky' Tong, and Peter 'Spots' Reddy. He'd had the option of sifting through Alpha Platoon for volunteers — which would have been pointless, because all hands had been raised — or of searching for those with the best qualifications. But in truth, none of them were truly qualified for this very civilian job, save perhaps for Ensign Jokono, who also accompanied them, along with Petty Officer Kadi from *Phoenix* Engineering. But now, beneath their black cowls and masks, he had only the vaguest idea who was who.

The parren led the way through the throng, eight black clad figures drawing only a few stares from passing aliens. Despite Gamesh being a free-city, a half of those passing were tavalai, most hauling luggage, or having it trail after them on carry-bots, as display boards showed the latest arrivals and departures, and speakers announced things in languages other than Togiri. They crossed an open-air walkway from the spaceport terminal to the adjoining elevated maglev, and Dale caught his first proper view of Gamesh — great, red-brown mesas looming beneath a dull yellow sky, the city washing at their feet like an ocean, teeming and untidy with noise and commotion. Overhead, a lander thundered skyward, heading for one of the many huge transit stations in geo-sync about the world of Konik.

Dale's team had come from one such station just that morning, having arrived by civilian freighter after a week-long journey from Ponnai, following a transfer there via a tavalai Fleet shuttle to avoid State Department suspicion. Security on some of the general stations was as tight as usual in tavalai space, but on those whose traffic was mostly a direct-ticket down to Konik, it was slacker than a barabo station. But slack or not, neither he nor his team had any weapons, and though there was no immediate danger in crowded, buzzing Gamesh, he felt naked without them.

Their luggage caught up with them while waiting on the platform — carry-bots whizzing and darting through the crowds, handing off bags and collecting homing tags before zooming off. Then the maglev arrived, a whooshing hum as it arrived, and disgorged another throng of people. Dale's group found standing room by a maglev window, and gazed out at the city as it whizzed by below.

Gamesh had no apparent centre, just an endless sprawl of dusty buildings in all different styles and architectures, with organic clusters of towers erupting from major traffic intersections. It did not look like one of the wealthiest cities in tavalai space. In fact, Dale thought it looked like a giant slum, every view faded and brown with wind-blown dust from the surrounding desert. So little water anywhere. Dale wondered how the tavalai in particular could bear it.

The maglev headed straight for one of those enormous mesa cliff-faces, then accelerated as it plunged into a tunnel. For a moment there was only hissing speed, and flashing tunnel lights. Then an eruption of sunlight, and they were zooming along the lower side of a far-side cliff, the maglev track built into the rock, and now flashing past buildings that had done the same, crawling up the rocky face as though attempting escape. Beyond and below stretched a new section of the same, sprawling city, only this neighbourhood looked larger, denser, more clustered together, and framed all about one side by a semi-circular stretch of red cliff.

The maglev arrived at a cliff-side station, then disembarkation took them down long elevators to the cliff base, and a crowded taxi-circle amidst the tall, wealthy buildings there. Up here, they had a view, Dale thought, gazing up at the towers as they waited for the queue ahead to claim their vehicles. The apartments in these towers looked enormous, with wide windows and balconies, while the streetscape was surprisingly green and pleasant. Finally they reached their vehicles — two groundcars, as the parren had informed them that aircars were not always secure even in Gamesh — to take them to their destination.

The cars took them through an increasingly confusing maze of roads before plunging into tunnels, which emerged startlingly into vast underground spaces. Here were new buildings, lights ablaze in the dark of permanent night, as overhead, enormous steel gantries held up the ceiling that supported the upper-city. Dale had been told that Gamesh had once been a vast underground city, but you really had to see it to appreciate what that meant. For thousands of years after first settlement, Gamesh had been uninhabitable on the surface. Terraforming took a long time, so the first settlements were built in the great underground caverns, valleys and basins that dotted this region. The first engineers had built these colossal 'rooves' over the top of those hollows, to create contained underground spaces, where air was not lethal.

When the terraforming had sufficiently changed the atmosphere, and created some large oceans and forests in the temperate zones, Gamesh and other Konik cities had begun to emerge above ground, but had never abandoned their subterranean heritage. The resulting, twenty thousand plus year evolution had created this tangle of unplanned, unregulated urbanity, which somehow got by, and made its inhabitants a lot of money, despite its often bedraggled appearance.

The groundcar took them down smaller streets, then into a tangle of narrow lanes and little shopfronts. Finally they halted, and emerged amidst the raucous glow of too many advertising signs, aliens, automated vehicles and the occasional bot pushing and sidling past this new obstruction. Food stalls, Dale identified most of the storefronts, seeing lots of aliens eating, and two nearby animatedly discussing in loud voices above drinks and smokes. Mostly tavalai food, Dale thought, as at least three-quarters of the people here were tavalai, and the food looked mostly fishy. And could that small crowd of tavalai at the next cross-corner be queuing to get into a nightclub? Or maybe a brothel? He repressed a shudder at the thought. His curiosity only went so far.

The parren took them down a narrower lane, then up tight stairs where the smell of someone's recent cigarette mingled with the smell of oily cooking from nearby. Two levels up, and the parren pressed a door intercom. A wait. Then a green flash of deactivated security. The door opened, and a broad tavalai face peered out, then grunted assent and let them in.

The apartment within was much larger than the narrow lanes and stairs had led Dale to expect. Jokono indicated to the marines, and they fanned out to inspect the place, checking bedrooms, peering out windows into lanes below, while Petty Officer Kadi carefully placed his important gearbags on a chair, and the two parren faded into the shadows of a corner, watching. When the marines were satisfied, Dale threw off his hood with relief, and began unwrapping the robe. That damned black fabric had been his prison for the past several days, and 'never again' would still be too soon. From the gasps of relief his marines gave, he knew they felt the same. The two parren gave them looks, perhaps offended.

The tavalai who'd let them in was watching them from his open kitchen, with great, refrigerated wall racks. He had a cane, Dale saw, an unglamorous, gnarled stick in an equally gnarled hand. From his stance, and the way the skin sagged about his big, wide-set eyes, Dale thought he might be very old. His expression seemed wary. Most tavalai were businesslike with introductions and meeting new people, even those they disliked. The old tavalai simply watched, and said nothing.

"You're Tooganam?" Dale asked. "Our contact? Is this place yours?"

"Yes," said Tooganam, in English. And then, with the aid of a belt-speaker, *"Fleet sent you."*

Dale nodded, then sucked up his misgivings and walked to him, hand extended. A human custom, but tavalai did something similar, sometimes. That he still felt as comfortable shaking hands with a tavalai as he did kissing a scorpion was neither here nor there — the Major had given him a job to do, and his personal feelings were irrelevant. "I'm Lieutenant Tyson Dale, Commander of Alpha Platoon, *UFS Phoenix*."

The tavalai took his hand, with equally little enthusiasm. Not rude, and not frightened. Just old, and cautious. *"Tooganam. Former Djara, Partik Regiment."*

Shit, thought Dale. Just wonderful. Djara was a rank roughly equivalent to Sergeant, and 'partik' was Togiri for the number thirty. "Karasai," said Dale, darkly. It explained the watchful look in Tooganam's eyes. Some *Phoenix* marines had adjusted to working with the karasai of *Makimakala*. Others took time. Dale had always gritted his teeth and done his job, because it was what *Phoenix* and Major Thakur required of him. She seemed to have no difficulty at all, which was not surprising, given how little of normal human trauma seemed to touch her. But for all that Dale truly believed the Major was twice the combat officer he'd ever be, she was still just a kid next to his years in the war. She'd lost dozens of friends and comrades to the tavalai, and the karasai-marines in particular. But Dale had lost hundreds. "How many years?" he asked, keeping his expression cool.

"Forty-three of mine," said Tooganam. *"Maybe... thirty-five of yours?"* Dale grunted. It sounded about right. *"Three tours. The last was ninety years ago."*

"The early war," said Dale.   Most humans thought *he* had been in active service an awfully long time, but Tooganam had beaten it by about five years.   Tavalai lived very long lives, and Tooganam looked much nearer the end of his than the beginning. Probably that would put him in his late-two hundreds.

"Why do you work with Fleet?" Tooganam asked.

Dale couldn't tell him.   "You know the mission?"

"Kamala.   The Kantovan Vault.   Some thought it might be a myth.   Fleet tells me otherwise."

"Phoenix has some common interests with your Fleet," Dale told him.   "Things in the vault that need to be seen."

It seemed enough for the old ex-karasai.   He snorted, a loud sound from wide nostrils, and waved for them all to sit, stomping in his kitchen to put some large pots on the stove.   He moved heavily, with no grace at all, but he rummaged through drawers and utensils with the ease of a man at home in his own kitchen.   *"Food,"* he said.   *"You'll probably hate my food, but you'll eat it.   You're not in human space anymore."*

"Noticed," Reddy grumbled, collapsing into a deep-cushioned sofa.

"Thanks," said Forrest, more diplomatically.   "Tell him thanks."   With a warning stare at his Lieutenant.   'Woody' Forrest had been with Dale for two years, one of those at his present rank. It was long enough that he felt licence to let his LT know when he was being an ass.   Forrest was as old as Dale, and had begun his working life with a comfortable career in banking.   Then his marriage had ended, and at what had felt like a dead end in life, and with no kids, he'd signed up.   Forrest was everything Dale was not — well educated, somewhat wealthy, an all-round nice guy who got along with military and non-military alike.   Had they met in Forrest's previous, civilian life, Dale was certain he'd have found the banker irritating as hell.   But two years of wartime service in Phoenix Company had a way of making natural enemies into inseparable friends, and he needed Forrest in Alpha Platoon the same way a body needed kidneys.

Dale snorted in reply, and stretched his left arm over his head — that shoulder had never been the same since tavalai shrapnel had smashed it twelve years ago, in the Battle of Jericho System. He'd been Forrest's rank, back then.

"I heard you," Tooganam answered Forrest, amidst clangs of pots and pans. *"No need to thank me, I'm just the operative. I may be retired, but I have many old friends in those places. They tell me to do things for the tavalim, I don't ask why."*

By the windows, some fish and odd, turtle-looking creatures swam in a circular tank. Above the tank, mounted on a wall, were tavalai ribbons and braid. Tong peered at them. Dale knew that Tong had some similar, battlefield souvenirs. Tavalai liked ribbons, used them in ceremonies, and special ones served as humans would use medals.

"Wow," said Tong. "I think these are magoridi ribbons."

"Ma-go-ridi," Tooganam corrected him gruffly from the kitchen — the same word, but utterly changed in the pronunciation.

"What'd I say?" Tong retorted. "That's a big deal. Like, maybe a Gold Starburst equivalent. One below the Liberty Star."

"And I knew a hundred tavalai who won no award nearly as big," Tooganam retorted, *"and all of them better karasai than me."* It was the kind of thing the Major would have said, Dale thought... only without the self-deprecation. *"This will take time to heat. Tea first."*

They all sat, while Tooganam brought them tea on a tray. The limp was pronounced — probably a war injury, Dale thought. It looked like a prosthetic leg — at a certain age they didn't always link perfectly with the brain, creating limps. Tavalai tea was quite passable, hot and herbal. Tooganam took a chair the humans and parren had left for him, all now seated save for Jokono, who hovered in the shadow by a window, peering into the lane while listening to the marines talk with Tooganam. No doubt he figured the marines would have more in common, and held back to listen. But it made Dale that much happier, to have that experienced, watchful presence, non-military and familiar with both civilian environments and covert operations, taking everything in.

Petty Officer Kadi sat with some particularly high-tech AR glasses on his face, making adjustments to various holographic icons that only he could see. Kadi was young, squat and brown, with lively eyes and a tech-nerd's lack of people skills. But Dale had needed a serious network-tech on this mission, and asked Lieutenant Rooke to find a volunteer. Rooke had not been surprised at Kadi's enthusiasm, and had told Dale that Kadi's older brother had been a marine on the *UFS Pursuit*. He'd been killed in action three years ago, fighting to win some big mining facilities off the sard. Rooke thought that Kadi felt he had something to prove, and had warned Dale to keep an eye on him.

"So explain this to me," Dale asked of Tooganam, relaxing into a casual drawl with the tea in one hand, hooked over a raised knee. One marine to another over a drink, he thought, might make the old tavalai more talkative, and get his Gunnery Sergeant off his back. "Fleet and State Department. Tropagali Andarachi Mandarinava. What's the deal? Because it seems like it goes back not just to the start of the Triumvirate War, but to the invasion of Earth by the krim."

Tooganam snorted laughter. *"Boy,"* he said, and Dale blinked. *"Boy, how old are you?"*

"Forty-nine"

"So you've been around for one-twentieth of the thousand years humans have been in space."

"FTL space, sure," Dale growled.

"In human years, I'm… what is it now… two hundred and seventy? Yes, two hundred and seventy. And I've still only been around for one-one hundred and fiftieth of the time the tavalai have been in space with faster-than-light travel. You need to realise the age of these issues that confront you. Tavalai Fleet have been at odds with State Department, as you call them, since the beginning of the First Free Age. Since the end of the Chah'nas Empire, do you understand that?"

"Yes, I know what the Chah'nas Empire was," Dale said sourly. "Why haven't Fleet done something about it?"

"Oh they have!" said Tooganam, eyes wide with indignation. *"Many things. Many challenges to State Department authority, many attempts to wrest back control. But always the great legal institutions fight back, they have no love of State Department, but neither do they like to see Fleet with so much authority in its hands, to make the rules for all tavalai. We tavalai do not like tyrannies. Give it enough time, and they fear tavalai Fleet could become like your Fleet."* With a pointed stare at Dale.

A year ago, Dale would have been mightily offended. Now, not only would it have been impractical, but he could not shake the unpleasant feeling that Tooganam might be right. "Humans had great, free democracies on Earth," he said instead. "They died with the krim. Since then, we haven't had the luxury of so much freedom."

"Never a luxury," Tooganam disagreed. *"Not for tavalai. No more than air and water. State Department think they know best. Fleet has warned them otherwise, with humans most recently. These mistakes have left us dead on the ground like leaves. We used to joke, in the karasai, even as far back as the early war when I was serving, that we'd rather be shooting at State Department than humans."* He took a deep breath. *"And perhaps that is our greatest failing as a people, that we did not."*

"No," said Reddy. "You get aliens to do your dirty work for you. And so here we are. Reporting for duty."

Dale looked warningly at Reddy. 'Spots' was small for a marine, an orphan with a record of petty crime who'd been headed for nothing much at all before signing up. He had a quick temper and a quicker laugh, and was one of the best pure riflemen in the entire Phoenix Company.

Tooganam looked at him too. *"Maybe so,"* he said sombrely. *"Maybe so. You will need to infiltrate the State Department facility here. I know the way."*

"And we'll need weapons," said Dale. "Good weapons."

Tooganam smiled humourlessly. *"You're in the right city for that. Unsavoury elements run deep in Gamesh. You have money?"*

"Plenty."

"Good.   Today, you rest.   Tomorrow, you get weapons. Then, we will see about displacing these State Department dry-skins from a pond or two."

CHAPTER 16

After dinner with the *Satamala*'s officers, Trace made her way back through the tavalai warship's midships to the primary berth airlock, with a greeting to the tavalai Operations crew on station there. Not that they were 'guarding' the berth containing the human marines, of course. Just watching, unarmed and unthreatening, and reporting to the *Satamala*'s bridge about every human that passed through the airlock in either direction. Automated monitors could have done it, but the tavalai seemed to have some notion that these humans had tricks up their sleeve, and weren't taking any chances.

Wiser than they probably knew, Trace thought, as she floated through the lander's main passage to the primary crew level. Tavalai Fleet had brought them this ship too, an unarmed and unremarkable cargo hauler, like tens of thousands of others through tavalai space. Latched onto the side of *Satamala*'s midships, it had many times the cargo capacity of a shuttle, but lacked the mobility. *Satamala* was making a cargo run to Kamala, primarily on the excuse of picking up something they had in storage on the Chara floating city. It was nonsense, but State Department had as little access to Fleet facilities on Chara as Fleet did for State Department's, and could not stop Fleet from visiting even if they wished to. Today, the lander's big holds held a most unlikely cargo.

Trace over-handed her way down corridors and past accommodation doors, then through a stairwell with no need of the stairs in zero-G. The cargo holds were compartmentalised, a necessary feature on any manoeuvre-capable hauler, to limit the damage if loads broke free under thrust. In the compartment below, Staff Sergeant Gideon Kono and Private Leo Terez were doing zero-G marksmanship drills in their suits. In the nearby ceiling, Private Zale had cracked his suit with an armoured fist still locked magnetically to the big, empty cargo claws, and was making adjustments to a troublesome servo.

He saw Trace, and called on coms to Kono and Terez, "Guys, the Major's here. Watch your movements." And to Trace, "How was dinner, Major?"

"Salty," said Trace, as the two manoeuvring suits in the cargo space ceased, with final jets of white thrust. "How's the suit?"

"It's fine," said Zale. And, a little embarrassed, "Actually I could use a hand on this." Because Zale was quite new, a replacement for Trace's old friend 'T-bone' Van who'd died at Heuron, and Trace always made a point with the youngsters of insisting they ask for help if they needed it. Because if his suit malfunctioned in a firefight after he'd been too proud or embarrassed to ask for help, people were going to die.

"Ask Jess," Trace told him. "She's good with suits and she's always free."

"Actually, Jess is up on *Satamala* with Bird doing their PT…"

"Jess is always free," Trace corrected him, and pushed off across the empty space.

"Major," came Kono's amplified voice from within his armour suit as she passed him, *"you sure you don't want to cut Jess some slack? Argitori was rough, and she…"*

"Jess can pull guard duty on the kid like all the rest," said Trace, catching a floor brace and swinging. "If she begs off, there's a price for that. There were a lot more in Argitori than just Jess." She regathered, and pushed off for the adjoining door in the cargo partition wall.

That door was left open for now, in case people needed to move quickly. Trace swung through. In the far compartment, the big cargo nets were deployed down the hold sides, and the claws open on the floor to take the weight of non-existent crates. Floating against the near cargo net by the door was Corporal Rael, Command Squad's Second Section commander. Trace floated to him about the edge of the cargo net, and found him with visor open, the sound of music playing in his helmet. Rael was one of the best-looking guys in Phoenix Company, if she ever noticed. Trace thought he should really be an officer, but despite serious smarts, he'd just never been able to see himself applying for officer candidature straight out of school. As Dale had drily informed her, not every working-class meat-head was so fanatically devoted to self-improvement as she'd been.

"Hey Major," he said as she approached. The music stopped.

"Leave it on," said Trace. She didn't mind a few distractions on this guard duty, with music at least. She didn't actually think the danger was that great. Yet. "Maybe the kid likes music."

The kid, disconcertingly, was playing with some light, steel objects the *Phoenix* techs had fabricated for him before they'd left Ponnai. The objects were basic geometric shapes — squares, triangles, decahedrons, with odd sides magnetised. If arranged correctly, they could be joined to make all kinds of larger, more complex structures. The kid found them endlessly fascinating, with the prolonged concentration that only a machine intelligence could manage.

"I played him a bit, on speakers," Rael admitted. "Didn't react much." Unlike the rifles on training-setting in the next hold, Rael's Koshaim-20 was fully loaded. He left it relaxed, pointed away, but for this journey, the rule was that at least one fully-loaded Koshaim should accompany the kid at all times, just in case.

"Maybe he's just got better taste than you," Trace offered. "I've got something for him, I'll stay to the right of your line of fire."

"Yeah, and why not do that from over here?" Rael muttered, readying the rifle at little.

"Coz I like making your life difficult," said Trace, and pushed off toward the near cargo claw. Within, close enough to push off the big, steel fingertips with nimble legs, the kid floated amidst his toys, tumbling them about, fixing them together, experimenting with position and contact. Learning.

Trace caught a big cargo claw and swung to a halt. "Hey kid," she said, and the drysine drone turned on her with startling speed. The direct stare of those twin, offset eyes was disconcerting. The drone was nearly twice her size unarmoured, and looked much bigger than that with all ten pairs of multi-articulated legs extended. The dexterity of those legs was incredible, even at this early stage of development. The little forward pair operated like human hands, but with many times the joints and exploratory antennae. The second, intermediate pair would join them, to create a four-handed grip on anything larger and more complex. Its body was in two main segments like an insect, a big central abdomen containing all the leg mechanisms and associated drive train, and a rear thorax for powerplant and weapon attachments. They'd brought weapon pods aboard with it, but kept them very, very separate for the time being.

Trace still recalled the shock of seeing a non-human sentient for the first time with her own eyes. There were none on Sugauli, so she'd had to wait until leaving the Kulina academy there, and arrival at one of the big Homeworld Stations, on her way down to Fleet Academy in Shiwon. On the station had been chah'nas, whom every human child had seen many times on viewscreens... but still, to see them in person had been another matter entirely, so tall, six-limbed and *alien*. And smart too, often sarcastic and dry, and a green human kid's brain had taken a while to process it all, like the shock of first encounter with zero-G, and sorting up from down where neither existed anymore.

But all of that shock of the strange and new was nothing compared to what confronted her here. This was technology *so* far beyond what any sentient organic species was capable of producing. A technology so advanced it was alive, in the most inhuman, inorganic, alarming and unpredictable way imaginable.

"Here kid," Trace said, reaching into a pocket. "I brought you something." She produced a plastic cube, segmented into squares. One of the tavalai crew said it had been left aboard by a child passenger, and now gave it to her to give to Skah, when she saw him again. She didn't think Skah would mind the newest kid on *Phoenix* borrowing it for a bit. "You see, these squares are different colours. And you turn them around like this," and she abandoned her grip to demonstrate, "to try and make all the colours line up on one side of the cube, or the other. Here, you try."

She tossed the cube to the drone, who caught it with a precise flick of one main leg. The little claws grasped, with astonishing gentleness, and transferred it quickly to the small, inner arms. The motion sent him drifting, and the kid caught one of the cargo claws with several limbs, his main attention on the toy cube before those twin drysine eyes. The eyes and head moved rapidly back and forth, calculating furiously. The little limbs tried twisting the cube. The colours rearranged. Then again. Then again.

"Isn't that cute," said Rael, in a tone that suggested otherwise. The kid twisted faster and faster, not making any appreciable progress in getting all the colours in the one place. "He does actually see colours like us, right?"

"Not like us," said Trace, watching with intrigue. "He sees a lot more than us. But he should be able to play this game." And to the kid, "Hey no, that's too fast, you'll..." with a pop, some plastic squares broke off and flew away. "Break it," Trace finished.

The drone looked about in astonishment, head darting, tracking those escaping pieces with something like alarm. It snatched at one, hitting it and sending it tumbling faster. Then it pushed off and swung, chasing that piece, and caught it just before its leg-grip on the cargo claw became too far to reach. On the way back, it collected two more pieces, and then with all four front legs working furiously, tried to put them back together.

Trace could not help thinking that it looked like childish distress — the kid who accidentally broke his toy, and now tried to fix it without knowing how. Stop it, she told herself. It's a machine. Stop anthropomorphising it to make it more familiar. And she lost her train of thought completely as the kid grasped a new cargo claw and pushed straight toward her.

"Hey, hey hey no!" Rael called from his net, raising the rifle and pointing.

"Wait Corporal!" Trace said loudly. In truth, she was less alarmed than she should have been. Thinking that she knew its intentions, just because this was what a human child would have done, was exactly the danger she was trying to ward against. The big, alien drone came straight at her, legs catching and bracing on the claw she held to, and its inner arms reached… and offered her the broken plastic cube. The big, double-eyed head swivelled and ducked, examining her, examining the cube. Reading her face for expression clues? Could hacksaw drones do that, at any age? Humans were evolved for it specifically, but machines had no need of it… especially when they'd spent the best part of their existence exterminating organic sentience and not caring a bit what their victims thought.

Trace took the cube pieces, carefully. It set her drifting, and the drone actually put a small manipulator hand to her side, steadying her. Trace thought that one, simple act was about the most astonishing thing she'd ever experienced in her life. The plastic parts looked as though they'd fit back together easily enough, so she held them up before the drone's eyes, showing him. Then placed one piece back in, and pushed, with a satisfying click. The drone reacted, a head jerk and refocus, as though… surprised? Pleased? Another piece, and a click. Then the last. She twirled the cube's rotating parts several times to be sure, then handed it back.

The kid took it, more carefully this time, and began twisting. Then pushed away from Trace once more, utterly preoccupied with its new game.

"Its limbs aren't powerful enough to kill yet anyway," Trace reminded Rael, as he lowered his rifle. The kid probably didn't know what that big metal stick did yet. But he would. "Styx says that develops later, with motor-skill maturity."

"Styx says a lot of things," said Rael. "Giddy says he wishes you'd stop sticking your head into things just to see how they work."

"This may come as a surprise to you, Corporal," Trace told him acidly. "But Staff Sergeant Kono is not my mother."

"That's definitely her," said Lieutenant Geish on Scan. He, Erik and Shahaim were gazing at the Kantovan scan feed, focused now on one particular freighter that had emerged from jump nearly two rotations ago, from twenty-nine degrees off solar-nadir. *Phoenix* did not have access to civilian shipping manifests, so they had no way of telling who was hauling what until they came within visual range. But they did have access to other civilian feeds, and one of those had just now settled upon the freighter *Ikto*, and the curiously-formed lump on its midships flank.

"Definitely looks like a heavy descender to me," Shahaim agreed. If anyone could identify a ship-type at a glance, it was Suli. "It's about twenty percent larger than it otherwise needs to be, I think most of that is shielding."

"Going to need some engines on it," said Jiri from Scan Two.

Erik opened a channel to Engineering. "Hello Lieutenant Rooke?"

"Here Captain."

"Thought you'd like to know, it turns out the freighter *Ikto* is in fact hauling a heavy descender. It looks like Second Lieutenant Hale came through, right on schedule."

"Of course she did," said Rooke. *"Now we just hope Tif can fly the damn thing."* Rooke would not be the only one hearing that message, Erik knew. Lieutenant Alomaim in particular would be very relieved. Not to mention a certain surly little boy, whose behaviour had been lately deteriorating, with one of his regular tutors with the Major's Command Squad, another kidnapped by parren, and his mother on a mission to acquire the descender.

Erik switched the scan feed to look at Kantovan once more. They were chasing the Tsubarata's orbit now, cutting within five hundred kilometres of Konik's upper-atmosphere before they headed back out to geostationary orbit. The red-brown world filled all external view to one side, the northern pole nearly visible on this orbit, and where the colour changed in a great band of blue and green in the northern summer. That was the terraforming, where the planet's water had reconsolidated into seas, islands and trees. But it was cold and frozen half the year, and many of the cities preferred the warmer, equatorial deserts, some of which were only now starting to bloom themselves into vast, grassy plains. A naturalist documentary had made interesting viewing on the way in — some imported eco-systems set up in the newly living regions, wild creatures from various worlds let loose upon the plains and in the seas, to see if they could properly bring the world to life.

Kantovan System was nowhere near as busy as Tontalamai, with its primary inhabited world catering to barely a billion people, compared to twelve billion on Ponnai. But it was busy enough, its outer-system industrial operations perhaps even bigger than Tontalamai, and its space-lanes full of insystem freighters. Scan also showed Erik fully thirty-two tavalai Fleet warships. Exactly how many of those were in on this deal he didn't know, but guessed it would be only a handful. Admiral Janik had never claimed to represent more than a small splinter of opinion within Fleet. If *Phoenix*'s plans here were discovered, or someone betrayed them, all of this tavalai firepower would no doubt settle upon *Phoenix*, with inevitable results.

Perhaps just as well Lisbeth wasn't here after all, Erik thought grimly, eyeing the feed coming in from Tsubarata itself. An honoured guest of the parren, as Aristan had described it, might make her currently the safest member of the crew.

"Captain," said Shilu at Coms, "I'm getting direct queries from the planet's surface. I think they're all civilian, possibly news networks. The authorities aren't giving them access to us on the orbital coms networks, so they're just firing them up from the ground on this pass. All very illegal, I think."

"Tavalai media don't care much about that," said Erik. "What are they asking?"

"I haven't opened a channel to find out," Shilu admitted. "Would you like to?"

"Better not," said Erik, recalling the scenes on Ponnai. "Best if we save our talking for the Tsubarata."

Arrival at the Tsubarata was nuts. Word had beaten *Phoenix* to Kantovan, and Tsubarata Central's feed was buzzing with ships, traffic, warnings and protocols, some of which had Shilu feeding terms into an advanced translator program, as the regular translator proved unhelpful.   Tavalai Fleet vessels held overwatch positions, creating clear fields of fire all about the Tsubarata, and Erik was quite certain their weapons were live.   *Phoenix*, coming here, had caused a big commotion, and there was no telling just how upset various parties might be, or what they might be prepared to do about it.

Berth was a breech-berth against the planetoid's side, necessary given the tiny but real gravitational field generated by the rocky mass.   Docking formalities that should have taken minutes, instead took hours, and Erik got the clear impression of bureaucratic chaos in the rock.   With Trace and Dale absent, Lieutenant Jalawi had command of Phoenix Company marines, and all save Erik's small personal protection were fully armoured and armed, just in case.

Finally clearance arrived, and Erik strapped into the back of PH-1, with Shahaim and Shilu for company as second-shift took over the bridge, and Lieutenant Alomaim plus three unarmed and unarmoured marines of Bravo Platoon for escort.   The flight to the rim gave him his first clear view of the Tsubarata — its huge, rocky length half-lit in the glare of sunlight, ringed twice about its mid-girth by habitation rims, rapidly revolving.   The curve-gradient on those rims had to be amongst the lowest in the Spiral, Erik thought, with an eye-popping thirty-kilometre radius.   To generate Gs at that width, they had to spin relatively fast, but still only accumulated to point-seven of a G, he'd learned.   Hausler took off after the indicated berth now as it came zooming toward them about that rocky horizon, with a hard burst of thrust that reminded all watching that *Phoenix* was a military ship, with pilots of military inclination.

Lieutenant Hausler docked with his customary precision at the lower-rim berth, grapples tight and armscomp live despite strict Tsubarata instructions to keep weapons offline.   There were small vessels everywhere, shuttles and runners with security IDs, and Erik recalled a childhood memory — a tavalai diplomatic ship, arrived at Homeworld to discuss the war, accompanied by talk of negotiated peace.   Its arrival had held all Homeworld System transfixed for days, with scenes at Fajar Station quite similar to this, crowds of ships and crowds of people, all wondering what came next.

Lieutenant Alomaim and his three First Squad marines climbed the access tube first, with Erik last for security's sake.   At lower-rim dock there were no crowds, the usually-busy space closed down for this VIP arrival.   Armed tavalai escort greeted them with little fanfare — civilian, Tsubarata guards with simple green uniforms, as the military had no official role in the running of the Parliament.

Erik, Shahaim, Shilu and the four marines were escorted into an elevator, which whisked them up to the main rim level, and opened onto an enormous floor, with a ceiling nearly a hundred metres above, at the top of the Tsubarata rim.   To either side of the steel canyon were vast walls, broken by balconies and huge stretches of window, within which conference rooms would look down upon the foyer floor below.   The walls and ceiling were decorated by pennants and holographic displays from various alien races, only a few of which Erik immediately recognised.   And the wide, polished floor was decorated with starburst patterns that Erik fancied would only make sense when viewed from those balconies and windows high above.

Upon the floor, a crowd of aliens surged for a view, held back by tavalai security.   The roar of alien voices assaulted Erik's ears, and Lieutenant Alomaim's marines interposed themselves before their ship's officers, looking about in alarm.   Tavalai officialdom hurried back and forth, and several beckoned for the humans to follow, while another tried to shake Erik's hand, only to be stopped by the marines.   Erik leaned to shake his hand anyway, as watchers yelled or trilled, and camera drones jockeyed for position.   Erik recalled Captain Pantillo's lessons in bearing, and straightened his shoulders, chin up, doing his best to look unperturbed at all the noise.

Some large doors in the great, high walls swallowed them, and here in the hall stood not the big tavalai welcome formality that Erik had expected, but a single, very alien figure.   Sulik, Erik recognised only from old school lessons, never having seen one before in person.   This sulik was a little shorter than him, and hunched with a body more horizontal than vertical, like some great, walking bird of old Earth... save that the sulik had long arms that could double as legs when speed was required.   Its neck was long, its face like a great cross, with mouth on the lower stem and eyes on the wide stem, and a tall head crest on the upper.   It wore a large breathing device over mouth and nostrils, as sulik preferred a much more oxygen-rich atmosphere than this one, and could become out-of-breath in thin non-sulik air.

"Greetings," it said via a translator speaker, past a natural voice that sounded more animal-screech than language.   Erik had not found an alien more disconcerting to meet in person since the first time he'd seen a sard, but sulik were known to be gentle, and relied entirely upon tavalai for security.   Their home space was far from here, and small, and in a galaxy such as this one, utterly vulnerable.   *"I am Tua, I am your Tsubarata liaison.   You will wish to see your accommodations.   But you are here to claim the Human Chair.   I will show you."*

Tua took them down wide halls, lined with offices, and explained how the mural decorations on the walls and high ceilings indicated which Tsubarata species each section belonged to.   This section was for the kratik, who were small with bony, reptiloid snouts and carnivorous teeth, and the decorative scenes here were of deserts, red sands and canyon walls — scenes from their homeworld, Tua said.   Many kratik were out of their offices to watch the humans with beady eyes, and Tua assured the humans that only those with security clearances were allowed in the parliament offices, unlike the main lobby.

At the next length of hallway, the decor changed to green forests and tall, trapezoid temple-looking buildings.   It was the parren quarter, and here the halls were lined with slim, indigo-eyed parren, many colourfully dressed and looking anything but the austere, black-clad version that Erik had come to know. The parren did not chatter, and many bowed serenely as Erik looked at them, to which Erik replied with polite nods. All this colour was what Aristan's acolytes were rebelling against, Erik thought. The most extreme fringe of House Harmony, discarding all this frivolous decoration in pursuit of ultimate inner-peace.

They took a corner, and were confronted with another great crowd before some sealed steel doors that blocked off the hall. All looked, and Erik saw many recording devices, and official-looking staff, recording events. And *here*, Erik saw as that crowd parted, were the tavalai with their formal ribbons and books of stamps... as though somehow, the true event were not the arrival at the lobby, but here, before some big closed doors.

"What place is this?" Shahaim asked their guide as they approached.

"Human Quarter," said Tua, waving at those still obstructing the way to move. *"Last officially opened one thousand and forty six of your human years ago. Unopened since."*

"No one's been in there for a thousand years?" Shilu asked with disbelief.

"Every local year, a Tsubarata engineering team perform a brief structural integrity examination. Life support is held at sub-optimal for habitation, temperatures cold for historical preservation. Life support has been activated for several rotations in anticipation of your arrival, but there is no lighting — lighting power has been permanently deactivated as a safety measure. Please, tavalai formalities. This way."

The tavalai did indeed have formalities, with their books, stamps and ribbons. Erik and the others performed them all with mounting nervous excitement that verged on dread. There had been talk that the tavalai had put the human section of the Tsubarata into cold storage, but no one had considered they'd done it quite this thoroughly. But of course, tavalai were the Spiral's leading students of history, and (some tavalai complained) prisoners of it. The old was worshipped, often to the disdain of the new, and now that Erik thought about it, it seemed a most obviously tavalai thing to do.

When all the pages were stamped, and the ribbons presented and pinned correctly to bunch on the human crew's lapels, a signal was given to open the doors. Voices fell to a hush, spoiled by the creaking grind as several big tavalai maintenance crew wound the emergency door mechanism by hand, turning a big, detachable handle in the wall. The air seal broke, and a gust of cold air swirled about the group, smelling old and stale. It reminded Erik of the way the air had smelled within the hidden parren temple he'd discovered with Trace and Private Krishnan. Tua said the life support had been flushed for a few days, so air would be breathable in there... but a lot of old air would remain, drifting in corners the filters had not reached.

Engineering crew gave the humans flashlights, with further ceremony, and slowly the steel doors lifted enough that all could see within. The hall continued, identical on the far side to the near, but dark. Some banners fell limp down the walls, like dead things. In the shadows, nothing moved. Erik felt as though the surrounding cluster of Tsubarata species were holding their collective breath. Many cameras filmed, their operators awed. It struck Erik once more just what enormity he was confronting here. Humans had pointedly refused to set foot in the Tsubarata for a thousand years, save for the occasional diplomatic visit by a lone ambassador and a few staff. And here was he, single-handedly reversing that solemn history with this act.

This heist had better work, he thought to himself. Because if it didn't, then likely no one would ever learn the true nature of what *Phoenix* had been attempting, and Fleet would brand them the worst kinds of traitors for as long as humans existed to remember.

Erik turned on his flashlight, and looked at Tua. *"I cannot enter,"* said Tua. *"It is forbidden. This is human territory, by old tavalai law. Tsubarata engineering staff have had an overriding allowance once-per-year, but none other. This place is yours."*

Alomaim nodded at Gunnery Sergeant Brice, who in turn indicated Private Ito, who wordlessly joined her on guard at the human side of the door. In case someone tried to lock them inside for the next thousand years, Erik thought sourly, as Alomaim took the lead without having to be told, panning his light from side to side as warily as he would a weapon, if he had one. Private Cruze walked at their rear, the three spacer bridge crew between, staring about in chill incredulity.

The limp banners on the walls were scenes of Earth. They were faded and stiff with age, but all synthetic materials aged slowly, and in environmentally-controlled environments, even moreso. Flashlights caught the shapes, glaring on indistinct images, and Erik walked closer to peer at one. It was of an old, steel tower, tapering as it climbed above an ancient cityscape, a jumble of rooves in a style no one built any longer.

"That's Paris," Shahaim breathed at his side, staring. "The main city of France, in Europe."

"I know," Erik said quietly. "They called it the City of Light."

"The krim bombed it a hundred and fifty six years after First Contact," Shilu said coldly. "In retaliation for the resistance. Several million dead, right there. The tavalai responded by trying to force the Landorf Accord onto us, at gunpoint, in the name of peace."

The next banner was of a beautiful iron-arch bridge across a harbour, above an even more beautiful building like a yacht's white sails. The next, an amazing city of clustered hundreds of old towers upon a narrow island surrounded by rivers and joined by big old bridges. And the next, an incredible, ancient white building with minarets and spires, carved with intricate inlays of the finest detail. All gone, along with most of their inhabitants of that time. Old human roots, old human origins. On so many worlds today humanity thrived, but there was nothing like this save occasional imitations, striving to remember what could never be properly recreated. All the Spiral's other species retained the living memory of who they'd once been, but humans had lost theirs forever.

Erik was totally unprepared for how upsetting it was. The loss of Earth was old history now — the defining foundational myth of human civilisation. It had occasionally seemed odd to him that everyone regretted it as much as they did, given how much they worshipped the great tales that had come as a result — the glorious wars, the heroism and sacrifice, everything that had forged this current human age in the hottest fires, and given all humans a united purpose, and a steel resolve, as they'd never had before. But these Tsubarata halls were not the faded pages of some dull history book. This was real — faded and stiff with age, but frozen in time. All the species' sections in the Tsubarata were decorated as their assigned inhabitants chose, and this was what the humans had chosen, a thousand years before, to remind them of all that was best about the place where all humans were from.

"Suli," said Erik, "Tua said this place was last fully occupied a thousand and forty six years ago. Who do you think that was, exactly?"

"Damned if I can remember," Shahaim murmured, and called the *Phoenix* bridge. "Hello *Phoenix*, I'd like a history check, please. Who was the last human ambassador in the Tsubarata?"

"Hello Commander," came Lieutenant Lassa's reply from Coms, *"we were just wondering that ourselves. His name was Guo Chun. Humans had a presence here for a hundred and forty eight years, from just after the krim invasion, right up to the First Human-Tavalai War over the Landorf Accords. When we started fighting the tavalai, the order was given to vacate the Tsubarata, Guo Chun gave one final speech in the Parliament, and made a motion that the krim should be forced to vacate human space at gunpoint. That was the... seventy-second time a similar motion had been presented, thirty times by us, thirty-five times by the chah'nas, five times by the kuhsi, and twice by the alo."*

"Yeah, our good buddies the alo," Shilu muttered, walking slowly up the hall and panning his light.

"After the krim were beaten, our next visitor was... three hundred and seventy three years after Guo Chun left. That was a multi-party delegation, all Fleet Admirals, and they were here for forty hours only. Long enough to deliver demands, and leave. Since then, another fifty-odd visits, none longer than a few rotations. All of those during the peace, none during the Triumvirate War, and

all quartered on their ships.   No humans at all, for any reason, for the last hundred and sixty three years."

"Coming here is symbolic," said Erik, remembering now to put on his AR glasses, to give *Phoenix* a visual feed of what he saw. "The real talking happens elsewhere.   No humans wanted to give this place any status.   This place made a lot of decisions that led to the loss of Earth.   Humanity speaks for humans, this place does not."

Alomaim peered into a doorway, and Erik joined him.   It was a lobby, with a secretary's desk before several large office doors. On the walls were photographs of a sporting event, great stadiums, athletes receiving medals, happy people celebrating, and people of different races embracing.   "Oh my god," Shahaim murmured, running her flashlight across the pictures.   "It's the Cairo Olympics. Some said it was the greatest Olympics ever.   Two months after it finished, the krim fleet arrived."

Erik went to the desk as the others fanned out.   The inbuilt network systems looked fine on the outside, and he opened desk doors, searching for the main processor.   On a shelf, stored out of sight, was a framed photograph, smothered in dust.   Erik pulled on gloves, took it out, and wiped a thick layer of dust from the glass cover.   The faded, cracked image was of a young man and two little girls, likely his daughters.   Typically he'd have expected a family photograph to be all smiles, but the man and his daughters looked sad.   As though they were trying to put on a brave face for the photo.

"Captain I'm running a search on those faces," came Lassa's voice, seeing what he saw.   *"Cross-referencing for known Tsubarata personnel at that time... I've got a match.   That's the husband and daughters of Michiko Tanada, she was a personal assistant to one of the ambassador ranks.   All Japanese, the Japanese were hammered in the resistance wars of..."*

"Twenty-six eleven to twenty-six fourteen, I know," Erik murmured. "The planetary occupation preferred islands, they're an easier landmass to control.   The major krim groundstations were Japan, Britain, Java, Cuba, Madagascar, Sri Lanka, Taiwan."

238

There were classic films made about the uprisings, compulsory viewing for all schoolchildren no matter how upsetting. The krim had been rocked, and the retaliations were horrible. Erik stared at the little girls' sad eyes in the photo. What had they seen?

"Records say one of those girls got off Earth before the end," Lassa continued sombrely. *"She was in Fleet, had three kids of her own, and contributed to Lifeboat. So she's a Founder. Amazing."*

Lifeboat had been the great repopulation program, where genetic material had been taken from all survivors, and mixed to create vast new populations of children. They'd been grown in artificial wombs, in far-off parts of space where the krim couldn't find them. They'd been raised Spacers, in spacer facilities, and like most of that generation had gone their entire lives without setting foot on a planet. Parentless children, raised in great communal groups, older kids looking after younger ones, all semi-military and regimented as much by organisational necessity as by the need to make more soldiers for Fleet. Lifeboat had saved humanity, and along with the hundred year space-industrialisation program that followed Earth's destruction, was one of the greatest successes to be pulled from the ashes of catastrophe. Junwadh Debogande, to the family's everlasting pride, had played a prominent role in both.

"Captain," came Lieutenant Alomaim's voice on coms from the next room, *"I suppose that means the krim's quarters are still preserved here at the Tsubarata too?"*

Erik peered up from behind his desk, to stare at Shahaim. She stared back. "Son of a bitch, I hadn't thought of that," she muttered. The old enemy, long extinct, suddenly seemed very real, and very near. Erik thought it one of the most surreal sensations he'd experienced since this whole mess had begun.

"Let's go down there and trash it," Private Cruze growled. *"Full extinction's not dead enough."*

"What *did* happen to the krim stationed at the Tsubarata?" Shilu wondered.

"They went home when they were losing badly," said Erik, peering back under the desk to give the AR glasses a good look at the processor mechanism. "There were always rumours of tavalai-

239

based krim getting away, or the tavalai hiding them so the species wouldn't die out.   Captain Pantillo said it was unlikely — krim don't travel well and they're a swarm-species, like the sard.   They have a herding instinct, they all head back to the pack when they're in trouble.   I don't trust Fleet on much, but the Captain said Fleet were pretty sure they got them all, and on this I believe them."

Alomaim came back in, flashlight on the ceiling to make light without blinding anyone.   "All clear in there, Captain.   It's a conference room, I think the ambassador's quarters are further up."

"Well," said Erik, "the AR glasses seem to think the network systems could be working.   Looks like we've found ourselves a base of operations in the Tsubarata."

Alomaim made a face.   "An unarmed base of operations. We can't get weapons past the Tsubarata guards."

"We will find a way," Erik said with determination. *"Phoenix*, are you listening?"

"Here Captain."

"I want an engineering party in here ASAP, I want portable powersources in case we can't get power back direct from Tsubarata. I also want enough marines to guard the place without weapons, plus they'll be doing a full recon on the Human Quarter — I'd rather keep spacers on *Phoenix* for now.   And I want Hiro over here, and as many ideas as anyone's got for how to get into State Department's facilities from this location."

"Aye Captain, we're on it."

CHAPTER 17

Dale stood by the parked groundcar, and waited. They were directly beneath Gamesh's steel roof that had once separated the old city from the inhospitable air outside. Now the huge gantries were wearing, many thousands of years old, but built so large it would take thousands more years until its age made for any danger of collapse. Support trusses made triangular shapes between beams that were larger than football fields. Larger, perhaps, than entire stadiums. They stretched away across the permanent shadow of the lower city, connecting to support columns that dwarfed the tallest towers rising from the ground below. Billions of tonnes of steel and reinforced synthetics, now just above Dale's head.

Lower Gamesh was built in a series of deep bowls in the dirt between the mesas up above. Thousands of years ago, the first settlements had put simple but enormous steel caps on those bowls to keep the bad air out, and made them habitable. The high sides of those bowls now made for spectacular views, populated mostly by wealthy residences, save for these uppermost strips right up against the ceiling. Here the low steel felt oppressive, and the ground, loosened by ancient earthworks, was crumbly, and occasionally dangerous. Property prices here were poor, and in many cities access might have been restricted. But in Gamesh the businesspeople had moved in, and the entire rim-strip was a warren of warehouses, factories and workshops, and the most amazing view past the rooftops of the more expensive towers further down. Gamesh had a government, but unlike in regular tavalai space, in the free-cities the government rarely said 'no'.

In middle distance, sunlight glared from a hole in the roof several kilometres across, beams of angled light making striations in the dusty air. Air traffic climbed in and out of that hole, a flicker of running-lights as they moved from day to dusk in a few seconds. Multi-legged robots clung to the roof gantries like great stick insects, with showers of orange sparks as they used tools to cleave away the rust, and re-weld the joins that sagged beneath the weight and age.

Dale wondered what kind of catastrophe would occur if a section collapsed. Thousands killed, perhaps tens of thousands. It seemed to capture Gamesh perfectly — both old and new, decaying and thriving, on the brink of disaster and secure in its prosperity.

"Here they come," said Jokono's voice in his ear. *"Two vehicles, the second one is a van. They've stopped at the gate, it will take them a minute to open it."*

Dale glanced at Tooganam. The old tavalai leaned on a cane that he needed for distances outside his apartment, big eyes fixed on the entry road. Dale would rarely have worried about a tavalai losing his nerve, but he worried about Tooganam even less. He glanced to his other side, at the robed and cowled parren. The parren's name was Milek, which was all he'd volunteered about himself. He was a Domesh acolyte, one of Aristan's most trusted, which presumably meant that he could fight. His primary task, with his partner Golev, had been to help the humans get past Gamesh's security by assisting humans in dark robes to pass as parren. That was his purpose here now... for first impressions, at least.

"I've got it wired inside," said Kadi, running up from the warehouse door, gloved hands stowing electrical tools, then activating glasses icons for operation as though making some strange sign language before him. "There's lots of good hiding spots in the warehouse, if I can get a visual on them when they get inside..."

"You'll give the detonator trigger to Private Reddy," Dale cut him off. "He's the marine, he'll do the fighting."

Kadi's face fell. "But I just set it up! Look, I know blast radius better than he does, I know the trigger settings, there's a two second delay and..."

Dale rounded on him. "Son, do you have a problem taking orders from all senior officers? Or just marines?"

The spacer glared defiantly. "I'm not just baggage!" he retorted, even as he retreated to do as he was told. "I came here to fight, not just carry the nerd-gear."

"No, that's *exactly* what you came here to do," Dale growled at the Petty Officer's retreating back. In any other circumstance he'd have torn a strip off the younger man, but there was no time.

Besides, Rooke had warned him of precisely this with Kadi — headstrong and big-mouthed, but brave as any marine. Dale hadn't wanted some frail programmer who'd faint at the first sound of guns, so he'd agreed. Now, he caught Tooganam looking at him. "Engineers," he explained.

Tooganam grunted. *"Among tavalai, too. They talk to machines, not people."*

"He is undisciplined," Milek observed, as the translator made a tonal leap to the new language. *"You should teach him some."*

"And you're now telling me what to do," Dale retorted. "So look who's talking." There were all too many aliens on this job for his tastes. Given the gulf between marines and spacers, to say nothing of tech-nerd spacers, that probably included Kadi.

"Turning in now," said Jokono, and the approach road lit with oncoming headlights. Jokono, at least, Dale was more than happy to have along. Of them all, this was more his speciality than anyone's. And it tickled Dale's sense of irony, that the career policeman should now find himself in charge of orchestrating an illegal firearms purchase.

Two ground cars hummed toward them, across a concrete yard half-filled with building equipment. *"Remember,"* came Tooganam's translator directly in Dale's earcom, *"I don't know how they're going to react to seeing a human. It would be better if you don't reveal yourself."*

Dale grimaced within his acolyte's cowl and robes. They'd had this argument before, and like all tavalai, Tooganam was stubborn. "I need to see the merchandise, and I don't trust you or Mystery Boy here to do it for me."

"I do know weapons," Tooganam retorted drily.

"In your youth you knew weapons. How long's it been, grandpa?"

The car and the van pulled up before them, turning sideways, then a slide of doors and some figures jumped out. Dale's glasses tagged each one and fed its position to his companions. They weren't running a full marine tacnet on the local Gamesh network —

Gamesh did have security forces, and while they weren't exactly proactive, they *did* take the threat of network attack very seriously. Any military-grade tactical network being run on local systems would bring official security to investigate, and so the marines were stuck with this — tacnet-light, as Forrest called it, with only half the data-density. It gave everyone some idea of where everyone else was, but without the accustomed precision.

Dale counted eight, four staying with the vehicles, the other four fanning to check the warehouse before which they stood, and several neighbouring buildings. Their footsteps raised dust, visible on his multi-spectrum lenses. Weird to be standing in a place where it never rained. Tooganam said some of the wealthier sections of Lower Gamesh had raised enough money to fund their own heavy sprinkler system in the ceiling, for artificial rain. But not everyone could afford it, and the low-tax free-city government never had enough money to pay for anything but essentials. Most residents preferred it that way.

"I count eight," Jokono confirmed. *"I see two kratik, three shoab, one kuhsi, and... I don't recognise those last two."*

"Peletai," said Tooganam. *"You've never seen peletai, wise old human?"* Peletai were insectoid, Dale saw, catching a glint of chitinous shell past loose clothing. He'd heard of them, but like so much of the tavalai-sphere, it was all so far away from humanity.

"I have never seen peletai," Jokono confirmed without a hint of bother. *"Tell us of them."*

"Bugs," Tooganam said grimly. *"Just bugs."*

"Very informative. Private Reddy, you have one bug moving toward your current location, stay out of sight."

"Copy," said Reddy, who alone of the marines had some prior experience of illegal sneaking around, in his previous life.

Shoab were big, but not nearly as big as kaal. The heavy-worlders lumbered forward, big fists on the ground in a four-limbed walk, shoulders broad and heads thrust forward, low and flat between those powerful shoulders. The leader gestured to Tooganam, and Dale saw movement within the heavy folds of his cloak, suggesting a weight in a pocket, consistent with a gun. When the shoab spoke, the words were a thin, nasal vibration.

"Parren," the translator said in Dale's ear. *"Domesh parren, unpopular with parren government."* Eyeing the cloaked figures to Tooganam's sides.

"Not all parren," Tooganam said reluctantly.

"So," said the shoab, his wide, flat head turning to peer in Dale's direction. He did not look surprised. *"Come. Inside."* He gestured, and lumbered into the warehouse. At the van, the kuhsi and one of the peletai lifted large canvas bags that clanked, and carried them in. Behind them, with a soft whine, several hovering drones lifted into the air, then headed out to circle the warehouse.

"That complicates things," said Forrest, as Dale followed Tooganam and Milek into the cavernous space.

"Not really," said Jokono. *"They're armed, but I should be able to hack them. Just don't be seen until I do."*

Dale was not surprised. The first thing Jokono had done was interrogate Tooganam about the activities of this particular gang. Gamesh gangs were territorial — one thing about a free-city, the government owned very little land. Private entities owned nearly everything, and so there was limited neutral space on which to safely carry out criminal transactions. The gangs preferred their own, friendly territory. Going from what Tooganam told him, he'd quickly used data maps of Gamesh that he'd acquired before arrival to pinpoint the most likely sites for *this* transaction... and arrived at their current location, in advance, for reconnoiter. Dale had been skeptical, but sure enough, when the call from Tooganam's contacts had come through, he'd asked to meet in exactly the location Jokono had said, and already prepared for.

No sooner had they entered the warehouse than the big doors behind began to rumble shut, and the overhead lights flicked on, illuminating a vast space of stacked crates and loaders. Dale glanced within his hood, and saw one of the pointy-faced, crouched and reptilian kratik was closing the door. The other, and one of the peletai, remained unseen. And then all six of the gang were pulling weapons, and pointing them at Tooganam, Dale and Milek.

"That is far enough," the earpiece translated the lead shoab's nasal whine. *"Human. Remove your cloak."*

"Geenu," said Tooganam, rounding on him with measured indignation. *"What are you doing? You know whom I speak for, and you don't cross them if you want to live. Not even on Gamesh."*

"Be quiet old fish," the shoab snorted, as the six aliens encircled Dale's three. Dale kept his glasses on him, tracking each movement, transmitting all vision and sound to his little network. This development wasn't particularly surprising, but it was certainly focusing. *"Your fleet aren't the only tavalai on the lookout for rogue humans."* He gestured his gun at Dale. *"You, you're too broad for a parren. Off with the hood. Slowly."*

Dale reached, and slowly pulled back the hood. "This is a very bad move for you," he told the shoab named Geenu. "I will give you one chance to reconsider."

The shoab might have chuckled, a dry rasping sound. *"You mean your friends outside? We have more drones, and the entire location is under our surveillance. Tell them to give up. They're watching on those glasses, aren't they? Give up, all of you. Give up now, and you won't be harmed. Or else, you shall all die — it makes no difference to my superiors."*

"Mine say the same about you," Dale growled.

One of the shoab slapped at his neck in alarm, jumping as though stung. He stared about, looking for the offending insect… then collapsed, legs folding with a crash. Geenu glanced in alarm, his pistol not wavering from Dale's chest. Shouted something at his fallen comrade.

"Wasn't me," said Dale. The kratik yelped, stamping a foot as some pain stabbed his ankle, then also collapsed. The big kuhsi snarled and backed up, weapon panning back and forth in panic. An explosion tore through nearby crates, and the lights went out.

Dale ducked low and went straight for the peletai, figuring that sard nightvision was pretty awful and the same might be true for most insectoids. He collected a shell-hardened arm, broke its grip easily and smacked it in the head with an elbow. It dropped, and he did, and rolled as the kuhsi opened fire in panic, muzzle-flash lighting the dark as it blazed about.

Dale came up by the door, augmented eyes adjusting fast and searching for scattered targets… but Geenu was already on the ground and shrieking, while his shoab companion fell even now with a stagger and thud to reveal Milek, indigo eyes ablaze and bloodied blade in his hand. The kuhsi shot at him, and Milek faded and ducked like a shadow, as Dale shifted aim…

…and with a thud the kuhsi fell before Dale could fire, sprawled face-down on the floor. Behind him in the silent dark was Tooganam, hefting his big, heavy-ended cane, and only now did Dale see the weight of it, wielded in the tavalai's big hands like a toy. Sometimes he forgot just how much stronger tavalai were than humans, and old though he was, Tooganam surely retained his karasai augmentations.

"Old fish," Tooganam snorted, and hit the button to open the doors once more. The air was filled with drifting smoke from the explosion.

"First Section, status please," Dale requested, moving on the fallen aliens with the borrowed pistol ready. The peletai he'd struck was unmoving, its bulbous, multi-faceted eyes glazed. Hard-shelled sard hadn't taken punches well either. Milek now moved on the wailing Geenu, and laid his blade at the shoab's long throat. "Wait," Dale told him.

"Two down out here," came Forrest's voice. *"One kratik, one bug. Both dead."*

Dale knelt at Geenu's head — above, to be clear of those powerful arms. "Who told you to get us?" he demanded. "State Department?"

"Tavalai!" Geenu gasped. *"Tavalai, I don't ask who! There's a bounty, any humans in Gamesh! They don't say who!"*

"He knows," Milek observed, ready to deliver that final thrust. The blade had been borrowed from Tooganam's kitchen, and Dale had rarely seen one so well wielded. The indigo eyes were intense but calm. *"He will tell others. We will be compromised."*

Dale went to check on the two who had fallen to the invisible foe. He wasn't sure exactly where to check on a kratik's body for a pulse, but where ever it was, he was pretty sure this one's reptilian heart wasn't beating. Neither was the shoab who'd been bitten. Jokono had told him those little buzzing things weren't set for lethal doses. Either he'd lied, or the little buzzing things were getting ideas of their own. Neither possibility was comforting.

Tooganam was staring at him, and the two bitten victims. *"Those two are dead? How?"*

"Ask me no questions," Dale told him, "and I'll tell you no lies." And for the first time since Dale had met him, the old tavalai looked alarmed. And gazed around at the empty air, searching for invisible death.

Milek was gazing at Dale, with wonder in his eyes. The Captain and Major had speculated that Aristan might have some general idea of what and who *Phoenix* had aboard. It would explain why he'd given Lisbeth that data chip on Stoya, and been unsurprised at how fast it had been translated. Did Milek know too? Or was he merely impressed at how efficiently the humans killed, by whatever method?

"Jokono," said Dale to the air, "the shoab said we're all being watched, are we about to have company?"

"No," Jokono replied, *"I let them think they were safe. We're being watched, but the watchers are being fed a false feed, they won't know something's wrong until we're long gone."* Jokono had been good with network wizardry before. Now, upgraded with some of Styx's technology, he could perform true magic on alien systems.

"The bug's dead too," said Reddy from the pelletai's fallen body, and Dale blinked. He hadn't seen Reddy emerge — he'd been hiding in the warehouse from the beginning, and had set off that explosion at the convenient time, a little thing that Petty Officer Kadi had made from common chemicals in Tooganam's apartment. "I think you broke its neck." Dale snorted, and advanced on the fallen kuhsi. "We killing that one too?"

"No," said Dale.   He didn't know Tif that well, but like all marines he'd gotten to know Skah, and the idea of killing defenceless kuhsi did not sit well with him.   That made him uncomfortable, because he'd never cared much for the safety of *any* aliens who threatened humans before.   Soft civvies with desk jobs and arts degrees might worry about that kind of thing, but Dale had long prided himself on not being that sort of useless man.   Maybe he was getting soft.

"Damn fool's just a kid," he explained, as much to himself as the others.   "Panicked in the fight, and he's a long way from home."   He knelt at the kuhsi's side, and pulled a knife from the unconscious male's belt.   "Kuhsi out this far are all hired help, Tif told me how all the young males are raised with dreams of adventure, they leave home looking for trouble.   Joker, get me a link to a Gharkhan symbol translator, will you?"

Jokono did that, and a series of human and kuhsi letters flashed upon his glasses.   "That's a risk," said Reddy.   "He could give us away."

"I'll take it."   Dale put the knife to the kuhsi's jacket, and began carving 'go home kid' into the leather, in what he hoped was legible Gharkhan.   "I think he'll look at this when he wakes up, and reconsider his adventure."

He looked up as Forrest and Tong entered, each dragging a new body.   "Just like the fucking brochure, isn't it?" Tong panted. "Join the Fleet, travel the galaxy, meet interesting new people and kill them."

When Dale got up, Tooganam was rummaging through the big canvas bags the kuhsi and kratik had been carrying.   They were indeed full of weapons.   Tooganam handled several with accustomed ease, cracking breaches and checking magazines.   He handed a short-muzzled assault rifle to Dale as he came to look.

"Tavalai model," he said.   *"Close defence, army issue, not karasai.   Good weapon."*   Milek also came to look.   Geenu was no longer shrieking, nor making any sound at all.   Dale didn't ask how that had happened, and did not particularly want to know.

Dale nodded, checking the rifle over. "Good," he admitted. "This will do nicely." He put the weapon to his shoulder, and found the balance acceptable, considering it was not made with humans in mind. The trigger was very wide and flat, to accommodate thick tavalai fingers.

"Free of charge, too," Reddy volunteered, taking one of his own. "That bomb worked great, Petty Officer blows shit up real good."

"Could have done it myself," Kadi insisted, emerging now with his gearbag and utility belt, glasses up to peer at the alien bodies on the cold floor. "Shit. Joker, are local cops going to come looking for these guys?"

"No doubt they'll find them eventually," Jokono reasoned. *"But I'm not seeing any response right now. In my experience there are a lot of strange sounds coming from industrial yards at all times of night, and we're a long way from anywhere residential."*

"Gamesh police don't bother with criminals," Tooganam snorted, leaning on his heavy staff and eyeing the humans with their new weapons. *"Criminals are a distraction for Gamesh police. Interfere with the important work of digging in ears for wax."*

Several of the marines looked amused. "What about their armed wing?" Forrest asked, checking an unfamiliar pistol. "The robot units? Ready Response?"

"Robots," Tooganam said distastefully. Dale noticed he was watching Milek with particular caution. Milek was not handling any of the new weapons himself, seeming quite content with his blade. *"How tough can they be?"*

Tooganam saw Dale looking at him, and indicated Milek's way, surrepticiously, with his staff. Dale glanced, and nodded. So Tooganam found Milek's skillset alarming also. Parren feudal society had a special place for assassins, operating quietly from the shadows. 'Watch this guy', the tavalai's look said. Dale could only agree... and found himself reluctantly comforted by Tooganam's dry good sense. He'd hated karasai, and killed quite a few of them in his time, but never once had that hatred precluded respect. Seeing Tooganam now, many of the things he'd seen karasai do in the war began to make a new kind of sense. Karasai were rarely dynamic or daring, but they were never stupid, and always knew the odds. That was exactly what he saw in Tooganam now. Predictable, yes... but also reliable. If a combat marine learned to value anything, it was the guy at his back who was always exactly where he needed to be, always ready, never flaking out. And seeing those praiseworthy qualities in his former enemy made him... uncomfortable.

"So which gun's mine?" Kadi asked the marines. The marines looked at each other, skeptically. "Oh come on! I *have* to get a gun, right?"

Trace accompanied the nervous tavalai crewwoman around the H-Bulkhead main-rim corridor of *Satamala* to the small accommodation quarter, where a few surplus rooms could be converted into passenger quarters. The crewwoman indicated the correct door and left, as though anxious to be elsewhere. Trace hit the call button, and waited.

While the humans had ridden from Ponnai dividing their time between accommodations on *Satamala* and their equipment in the zero-G lander, their parren 'companion' had ridden the entire journey here in seclusion. The tavalai crew said he had not once emerged from his quarters, and took food and drink delivered to the door. They did not know anything about him, save that he was Aristan's chosen man, and was said to fulfill all mission requirements. Trace found it impressive that any being in search of inner-peace could ride out an entire journey from Ponnai, more than a hundred hours and counting, in a single, small room. Impressive, but misguidedly impractical. Inner peace was only useful when applied to real-world goals. Sitting in a small room half your life seemed hardly to qualify.

The call button was not answered, and she opened the door on override — on any ship, and most particularly a warship, there was no facility to lock a door from the inside. Inside the room, on the bare steel floor, sat a black-cloaked parren, legs folded, hands on knees. Trace stepped inside and closed the door.

"We're forty hours from descent," she told him. Or she assumed it was a him. With Aristan's people, it usually was. "We need to start coordinating. I understand you'd rather meditate, given what you'll be required to do, but you will have other functions too. It's time to come and learn them."

"Yes Major," said his translator speaker, seeming to capture some of his alien vocal calm. *"I am ready."* Translator speakers sounded mostly alike, but his actual voice was very familiar.

Trace frowned. And her eyes widened slightly, realising who it sounded like. Surely he hadn't... "Who are you?" she demanded. He rose effortlessly to his feet, unfolding from the ground with a fall of robes, and pulled his hood back to rest the rim upon his brow. Trace was not so familiar with parren that she could confidently tell them apart just from the upper-half of the face, but this parren had made an impression. "Aristan?"

Aristan made a small bow, hands folded within the sleeves of his robe. *"I have a hostage of one of yours. Now, you have me."*

Trace stared. It would not do to show shock or extreme surprise before a man who valued serenity above all, in character at least. But it was ridiculous. Aristan was the leader of twenty billion parren. He commanded a paramilitary army of devoted acolytes, any one of whom would give his life in an instant if commanded. And yet he came himself. "This is irregular," she observed.

"But necessary. This mission must succeed. You risk yourself for its success, and now I join you. Rank is of no consequence, and I would rather die than see it fail."

"Are you capable?"

The big eyes narrowed slightly. Perhaps offended, Trace thought. Good. *"The ways of the Tahrae, and thus of the Domesh, have been carved in stone for thirty thousand parren years. I was chosen by the previous leader, through the trials of ascension, and the confidence of my peers. This is no bureaucratic posting, Major, and no feudal succession. That you would ask the question reveals your ignorance of my people."*

"I've been briefed on your background," Trace replied. "I didn't get this far by believing everything the briefings tell me. And I'll decide for myself if you're capable."

"Acceptable," said Aristan, perhaps mollified. *"As I will form my judgements of you. In protecting your commander's sister, your capabilities so far demonstrate something less than advertised."*

Trace had to resist the impulse to rage. She felt it, as all humans felt it. Denial was pointless. Instead, she recognised the challenge for what it was, and took a long breath to calm herself. In truth, she'd always enjoyed these challenges. To resist the wails and cries of the unthinking hind-brain, to stare them down until they slinked back into the shadows, had always been the most immense satisfaction. To not flinch, and not fear, when bullets were flying and people were dying, was perhaps the greatest test. To remain cordial and proper with a man she'd truly like to kill was nearly as great.

"Your approval or appreciation is not something I value," she told him. "Only your performance. Come with me, I have things to show you."

She informed her team by uplink on the way back to Midships, then pulled her way down to the lander holds with Aristan close behind. In the main hold where Command Squad had been calibrating their suits, a different training procedure was now underway. Trace diverted off the upper-hold walkway, and grabbed onto a ceiling cargo claw to steady herself. Aristan did the same, and stared down at the open space with astonishment.

The hold's steel secure-cables had been stretched across the space, where typically cargo nets would be deployed in zero-G between racks of haulage containers. With the holds empty, the cables made a maze that Privates Arime and Kumar were using to play a game with the kid. It was a version of tag, and all three were zooming about the space with bursts from compressed-gas thrusters, catching the cables to change direction rapidly mid-flight, and bouncing off the walls. The kid's coordination was extraordinary, considering his struggles with children's toys just two days earlier. The thrusters he used were human hand-helds, a pair of which he was somehow manipulating with two arms and little claw-like hands while using others to swing about cables like an ape in the trees, and bound off the walls with great force.

Aristan gasped some things that Trace's translator did not catch. Then he turned a wide-eyed stare at Trace. *"The Destined Ones! They live!"*

"Drysines," Trace confirmed. "Yes."

"But it... you... it would..." Aristan took a deep breath to recompose himself. Trace had never seen him so close to the edge of his control. She doubted anyone had. *"A drone would never follow organic command. It must have higher instruction."*

"It is a new drone. A child. We teach it, and it learns quickly."

"A child! You built... on Phoenix?" Trace nodded. *"Then you have a queen?"* The translator chose the same word, from his tongue to hers. Given the parren's feudal nature, Trace was not surprised.

"Yes," Trace confirmed. There was no avoiding it now. More lies, when confronted with this, would stretch credulity to breaking. "The queen said that parren in her time called her Halgolam." And she took some pleasure in seeing the unflappable Aristan rocked again, dazed and staring as though from a blow to the head.

"Halgolam!" he murmured, and the translator did not bother with the word. "Halgolam! *The destroyer, the bringer of light and renewal!"*

"Do your people have any recollection of a drysine queen going by that name?" Trace pressed. A cable whipped and twanged as the kid grabbed it to change course, then ran headlong into Kumar. He grabbed the marine's suit with multiple steel legs, then almost playfully sprang away in the opposite direction, sending Kumar flying into another cable.

"He gotcha Bird!" Arime taunted as Kumar recovered, swearing.

"No," Aristan answered. *"It is not in my memory, at least. Perhaps in the great histories we have clues. Would that you had told me earlier."* With an accusing stare.

"Well I'm telling you now," said Trace. "We call her Styx, after an old goddess of Earth."

"And what brings about this cooperation? What possible bonds could exist between humans and one of the Destined?" Past the translator, Trace thought she could hear a faintly peevish tone. Jealousy?

"The deepynines are not dead," said Trace. "The great enemies of the drysines are alive, and working with the alo. We think that their great technology lies behind the rapid alo rise. We fear that human Fleet, in choosing to fight the Triumvirate War, was simply assisting in an alo-deepynine plan to systematically remove one enemy of the deepynines after another. The tavalai were always the greatest fighters against the return of the machines, and so they were first. The truest reason why *Phoenix* is now an enemy of the human Fleet is that we fear that Fleet has been fighting the wrong opponent, these past hundred and sixty years."

It took Aristan a good thirty seconds to process that, staring down at the ongoing games below. *"And why does your queen seek Drakhil's diary?"* he asked finally.

"It leads to the location of a far greater treasure. The means to rebuild her race."

"And you would help her in this?" Breathlessly.

"If the deepynines are as numerous and powerful as we fear," Trace reasoned, "we may not have a choice."

"My people have long prophesied of the coming war," said Aristan. *"A war that will shake the foundations of the Spiral. It seems that you, Phoenix, may be its harbinger."*

The kid lost control of one of his handheld thrusters, which went careening out of control into a corner to shouts of 'ware!', then rebounded with a loud clank. The kid jetted over with his remaining thruster, and found Private Jess Rolonde working on her suit calibrations on this side of a cargo net.   With a scrabble of tightly coordinated legs, he snared the drifting thruster, pushed off a wall bracket, then grabbed the cargo net rim and offered her the thruster with his smaller forelegs.

"Just get the fuck away from me!" Rolonde shouted, pushing off her suit to grab the cargo net further away, an edge of panic in her voice. "Bird, tell your damn pet to stay the fuck away!"

The drone hesitated, head darting, looking confused.   Its forelegs withdrew the thruster.   "Come on Jess," Kumar retorted, "he just wants to play! Be a sport and play with him!"

"He doesn't want to play," Kono corrected from across the hold.   "He's just following programming to explore and interact with everyone. He doesn't know Jess as well and he's trying to fill in the gap, that's all."

"Well it's not going to happen!" Rolonde declared.   "Go away!"

The drone pushed off the edge of the cargo net, gave a burst of thrust… then caught a steel cable, and half-spun, clinging and looking back, still uncertain.   Arime gave Trace a look, and Trace could almost see his incredulous amusement, despite the visor hiding his face.   That the kid was not a puppy was too obvious to need pointing out.   His responses were fast, precise and intent, and even while playing a game, his focus was entirely on the game's object, and the successful completion of a goal.   His confusion now was entirely an attempt to calculate strange human responses, and to place an organic's emotions and body language into some kind of machine-comprehensible framework.   And yet, damned if the big steel monster didn't look just a little upset, at the rejection of his offer to play.

"Kid!" Trace called, and the drone cocked his insectoid head at the voice, then swung with rapid grace to consider her.   "Come here and meet our new team member!"

The drone briefly bunched and wriggled its limbs on the cable, then pushed off, a graceful unfurl to full extension, heading straight for her. To his credit, Aristan moved only forward, grasping the cargo claw to present himself directly. The drone arrived with a clatter of steel feet and scratching claws, then spread-eagled legs wide between two cargo claws, having just span-enough to do that.

"Kid, this is Aristan," said Trace. "He is parren. He is a very important person among his people. He will play an important role in our mission." The kid leaned from side to side, his head moving rapidly to complete a full scan of the new person. Aristan tentatively extended a hand, but the kid ignored it — his sensors did not require physical contact, and he lacked the emotional context to desire it.

"I greet you," said Aristan, and his translator caught only a little of the awe in his actual voice. *"Child of the Destined Ones. Do you speak?"*

The kid did the little hesitation and head-tilt he did when processing something new. Probably the language, Trace thought. "Styx was unclear if he would ever speak," she said. "He certainly comprehends, though again, it's unclear exactly how much knowledge Styx pre-programmed into his brain. His memory files are full, so he has no need of experience. But his actual brain, the main processor, can only access all of that memory when it's fully developed. So far, he's halfway there."

"After how long?"

"Since we left Ponnai. A little before."

"Incredible," Aristan murmured. Trace could only agree. *"What is his part in this mission?"*

"The vault has graviton capacitors. They generate artificial gravity to one hundred Gs, a defensive measure. We can't deactivate it, and we can't survive it. But he can."

"The vault is heavily defended. Will he fight?"

"We have modular weaponry for him," Trace agreed. "We're going to introduce him to that very, very carefully. Look, he's going to get bored shortly, he understands us well but he finds conversation dull. If you'd like to get to know him better, play with him — he needs play to learn coordination and stimulate brain growth, like organic children. Privates Arime and Kumar will show you the rules."

"Yes," Aristan agreed, with more enthusiasm than she'd have imagined from such a dour figure being offered a game.

"Kid," Trace told the drone. "Aristan will play with you. Be careful with him, he has no armour to wear. Understand?" The drone turned and sprang away with such speed that Aristan flinched a little. "We'd say he has bad manners," Trace explained with amusement, "but when you think of what need a machine society has for manners, you realise that's inevitable."

Aristan gathered himself, placed his feet to the cargo claw, and gracefully sprang after the drone. Trace did the same, but headed across the hold, for the edge of the cargo net where Rolonde was working. "Jess?" she said, as the armour suit swayed along with the net. "Are you okay?"

"I'm fine Major," said Rolonde through gritted teeth, working in a sleeveless shirt, blonde hair knotted at the back.

Trace could have demanded that the Private not tell her such obvious lies. But it was well understood among marines that there were varying degrees of 'fine'. If you knew the code, you could usually figure out which one applied. Trace pointed out to the drone, now playing a new game of manoeuvre with the unsurprisingly nimble parren. "We're doing a mission with him," she said. "Either you get used to it, or I'll take you off."

Rolonde stared at her in alarm. And took a deep breath. "Look, I'm fine... I just..."

"Can't function with the kid around," Trace completed for her. Rolonde looked helpless. "I understand that trauma isn't reasonable. I understand I can't just talk you out of it. But look at him. He's no threat to us. Styx wants this mission to succeed even more badly than we do, and she knows any threat from the kid toward us will see him destroyed, so she'd never allow it in his programming."

"Bird and Irfy wouldn't shoot him anyway," Rolonde muttered. "They'd hesitate, they think he's a pet."

"And because we need this mission to succeed so badly," Trace continued, "I can only have functional people on the trip. I'd like to be supportive of you on this, but I can't. Right now, he's not optional. You are."

"I'm a good marine!" Rolonde retorted.

"One of the best," Trace agreed.   "I picked you for Command Squad myself.   I love you Jess, but if you're going to screw up this mission, and this squad, then you're out.   Figure out a way to work with the kid.   That's an order.   Non-compliance will see you left behind.   Got it?"   Rolonde looked at her boots.   And nodded shortly.   "Good.   Don't leave me one short, Jess.   I need you on my flank."

CHAPTER 18

Erik strode into the main corridor of the Tsubarata's Human Quarter. The power was still off, but temporary generators loaned by helpful tavalai engineering staff now whined and throbbed on the floor, rigged into walls with the panels removed. The connections weren't perfect, but they lit half the corridor lights, and gave the marines on door guard enough power to open and close the door without resorting to the hand winch.

Those marines now searched a small, female tavalai by hand as she stood on the edge of human territory with her arms in the air. Erik stopped before her, and did not need to be experienced with tavalai to decipher a look of great displeasure upon her face. Both marines were male, and Erik did not particularly care if female tavalai had sensitivities about being searched by men. Behind the woman, her State Department guards, no doubt armed beneath those civvie clothes as humans were not allowed to be. Behind them, and the cordon line established for the purpose, a small crowd of observers of various species, many of them media, gathered for a look down this open length of hall.

The marines cleared the woman, with a nod to Erik. Two more marines stared warily at the crowd, not trusting the assurances that only 'safe' tavalai had weapons. The woman walked to Erik, hand extended in the manner of one who thought she knew human customs well.

"Captain," she said without need of a translator, "I am Jelidanatagani. We did not have the opportunity to meet in person, on Stoya."

"Ah," said Erik, accepting a perfunctory handshake. So this was Jeli, whom Trace and Dale had reported having no pleasure from meeting. She must have trailed them back to Kantovan System. "I've heard of you. What can I do for you?"

"A word, if you please. A private word." With a glance at the watchers, over her shoulder.

Erik nodded, and walked back down the hall, allowing Jeli to walk at his side. His marine escort accompanied, not so patronising of their Captain to think that a small, female ambassador would be a threat to him, but wary of others. They'd explored the Human Quarter for other ways in and out, and while they hadn't found any yet, the *Phoenix* engineers were confident some would exist. All agreed that there was no way in hell that State Department had left the Human Quarter alone for a thousand years, having all the means, motive and opportunity to get inside and look around any time they liked. And if they could get in and spy, they could get in and assassinate too, knowing the area far better than the newly arrived crew of *Phoenix*.

Erik arrived at the first door to a main office, and gestured Jeli inside. It was the lobby they'd first entered yesterday, desk lights now activated as the ceiling lights remained dark, and a small, portable coffee machine on the secretary's desk. Crew had been seeing to necessities, then.

"Some coffee, Ambassador?" Erik suggested. "You're familiar with it?"

"I will decline, thank you," she said, repressing a grimace. Tavalai liked their flavours light and subtle, and coffee was not that. Captain Pram had liked *Phoenix*'s herbal tea, but could barely stomach a mouthful of coffee. Jeli probably thought he was trying to poison her.

Erik leaned against the desk, and left Jeli to stand in the middle of the floor. There were no chairs, and he wouldn't have offered one anyway. "Captain," she said, as prim and proper as any gruff-voiced, squat-shouldered tavalai could manage. "We know of your plot."

Erik's heart skipped a beat, but he kept it from his face. He'd been through this before, on Heuron. That time, Supreme Commander Chankow really *had* known his game, and the consequences had nearly been catastrophic. He hadn't let anything slip that time, and he wouldn't now. "Plot?" he said mildly.

"Your conspiracy," said Jeli, with cold triumph. "With certain rogue elements of our fleet."

Well, thought Erik. That didn't sound good. But it wasn't over yet. He recalled what his mother had always said when she felt herself accused unfairly. He made his expression as bored and bland as possible. "I have no idea *what* you're talking about."

"Please Captain," the Ambassador snorted. "Do you think I don't know how much some portions of our own Fleet dislike State Department? This has been a long battle for control of tavalai military force, and I assure you, *Phoenix* is a very recent comer to this struggle. Once upon a time, the most democratic nations of Earth believed that the military should always be commanded by civilians. That is State Department's position too, and has been for millennia. Our Fleet, naturally, feels otherwise."

"Can't imagine why," Erik said drily.

"And those old nations of Earth," Jeli retorted, "would be quite horrified to see the military dictatorship that human government had descended to."

"Yes, well those nations are all dead, aren't they?" said Erik. "And we have State Department's policies to thank in large part for that." He hadn't meant it to come out with such venom. But being in this place was having that effect upon more crew than just him. State Department had backed the krim, made them powerful, then failed to anticipate the consequences for Earth. Realising their mistake, they'd tried to correct by enforcing a peace that would have amounted to continued human slavery beneath their krim masters, and even joined the krim in fighting humans to enforce it. That had also failed, and in giving up in disgust, State Department had all but given krim the green light to kill what had been, at the time, the only planet upon which humans lived and thrived, and everyone upon it.

Standing here in this room, that had once been occupied by a woman whose only purpose for being here was to save her husband and two girls from the horrors of krim occupation, Erik knew that it was not just the halls and doors that shivered with the ghosts of the dead. Earth may have died, but the great tavalai institution whose blunders had so greatly contributed to its death remained, and now stood before him, still so certain in its own righteousness, and having learned nothing at all from history. Suddenly this entire mission was about far more than just a heist, for most of the *Phoenix* crew. It was payback.

"Captain," Jeli said coldly, "this plan to destabilise the political balance between Fleet and State Department with your very high profile Parliament speech will not succeed. We know that you discussed it with Admiral Janik at Stoya. We have some reason to suspect that he wrote the speech for you. We know what it contains. I warn you — should you give it, there will be grave consequences for *Phoenix*, and for Family Debogande. You cannot defend them all, one in particular. Please think of her."

Lisbeth, she meant. Erik smiled grimly. "Your English seems pretty solid," he told her. "How good are your obscenities?"

Jeli frowned. "I beg your pardon?"

Erik leaned forward, and spoke slowly to avoid confusion. "Fuck off," he told her.

"The good news is that she doesn't have a clue," Erik told the room as he entered the main Human Quarter assembly room. It had seating for perhaps a hundred, all the senior staff in what would have been a total of several thousand, at full strength. The seats were arranged in a semi-circular amphitheatre before a huge full-wall window that gave a view out onto the rocky planetoid about which the two main Tsubarata habitation rims were spun. The planetoid zoomed by fast 'above' the window, its craggy surface broken with shipping docks and hangar clusters. Several kilometres distant, the second habitation rim spun in the opposite direction. And rotating now past the view came the vast, curving planetside of Konik, butterscotch yellow beneath a bright blue horizon.

"What's the bad news?" asked Romki from the Ambassador's big chair before the podium desk. He, Hiro and several of *Phoenix*'s best computer engineers rigged the podium with sophisticated gear, some of it wireless, others cabled in directly, trying to get a feed from thousand-year-old systems that they'd powered up as best they could.

"The bad news," said Erik, trotting down amphitheatre steps, "is that she's getting desperate. She thinks it's a purely political move, and she's worried about the repercussions."

"Of course she thinks it's a political move," said Romki, staring at his holograph display on the air-screen and his glasses both. "She's a political operator, she can't think any other way. Coming here was quite clever like that — it's the ultimate political move. It's got them all looking the wrong way."

"You got anything?" Erik asked, peering at the array of screens and data. A lot of it seemed static and fuzzy, not receiving much.

"State Department HQ is squarely in the middle of the Parliament Quarter," said Hiro, sitting cross-legged on a wing of the big podium, straight-backed and comfortable. The pose reminded Erik of Trace. He flashed an image onto his own holography screen. Erik came and looked. "State Department run foreign policy, so they need to be central, so everyone can reach them."

"And they, everyone else," Romki added.

Hiro nodded. "But there's only two actual entrances, and they're both heavily guarded. All network systems are indirect or autistic, even Styx can't reach them."

"So you can't get anything from the local network?" Erik asked, looking at the techs on hands and knees about the podium, or sitting with backs to the big windows, discussing technical things in low voices.

"Captain," came Styx's voice on coms, *"these systems are extremely old, and very poorly maintained. I can access small fragments for now, and with more time, perhaps something greater. But there is no direct path from here to the State Department that I can access. There must be direct infiltration."*

"Which is going to take quite a distraction," said Hiro, with a leading glance.

"I know," said Erik. "It'll have to be during the speech." His mind was racing, considering all the things that had to align to make that happen. He flipped a coms channel back to *Phoenix*.

"Hello, Lieutenant Shilu. Any progress with Tsubarata on the timing of the speech?"

"Captain, they're a little vague, but it seems there's a sitting in two rotations and they're pushing the schedule. State Department's obstructing them, or that's the gist I get, reading between the lines."

Two days, Erik thought, staring out the transparent wall, and the racing planetoid surface. They'd have to get a message to Trace, Tif and Dale, all without letting anyone know they'd sent it. Well, with Styx plugged into local coms channels, that wasn't so hard.

"Any idea what you're going to say?" Romki wondered. "It is a fairly historic occasion."

"I dunno," Erik admitted. "I was thinking something about galactic peace?" Hiro smiled.

"Yes, I'm sure that will work," said Romki, drily.

"Would you like to write it for me, Stan?"

"Look at him," Hiro deadpanned, not actually looking. "He'd love to."

"I could write you a nice long list of all the things you *shouldn't* say," said Romki, unruffled by the ribbing. "It would be nice to avoid doing any more damage than our presence here makes unavoidable."

"Good," Erik agreed. "I'll look forward to that list within twenty-four hours." Romki blinked, as though surprised at the agreement. And realising that he'd just been given an order, like regular crew. "Hiro, will it be enough?"

"Styx has some crazy tricks once I'm close enough," Hiro said confidently. "She can blind their entire security, make them think they're looking at things they're not. It's not hard work for her."

"No, I don't suppose it is."

"I'll get in," Hiro assured him. "And once I'm in, I'll have total network control, and intercepting the ID clearance from Kamala should be a cinch. You just make sure the speech is so good it keeps them all riveted."

"Dynamic pressure eighty-three percent," said Tif, staring at the flight-sim on her controls, her hands making light adjustments on the sticks.

"Good, now watch that lateral wind shear," said Po'koo in the main pilot's seat. *"It builds at thirteen thousand metres, then gets nasty at twelve. Flight sensors will not see it, you must be prepared."*

It was what made descents into greenhouse atmospheres so nasty — heavy descenders went down blind, as most externally mounted sensors would be melted or crushed within minutes. Descenders needed the flight profile pre-programmed on nav, and good GPS to figure where they were at each moment of the flight... but if they ran into something unexpected, sensors would absolutely *not* see it coming. In the hellish atmosphere of Kamala, atmospheric conditions were by nature unpredictable. Pilots had to be ready, and had to be capable of interpreting blind flight data, lacking most external references, fast enough to figure what was happening before things got out of control.

"Wind shear lateral is five degrees displacement," said Tif, watching the numbers shift, and adjusting accordingly. "Heading thirty-two degrees... shifting now to forty-five, adjusting." The numbers kept shifting, alarmingly. "Eight degrees displacement."

"In the real thing we would be shaking very bad right now," said Po'koo. The big kaal was thankfully not eating his disgusting paste in the cockpit. He did not help on the controls, merely watched the screens and kept his four hands folded.

"Attitude lean is beyond optimum," Tif said with alarm, speaking Gharkhan as her English had no hope of coping with this level of technicality. "If I keep correcting this steeply we'll overbalance."

"And what would make us overbalance?" Po'koo asked calmly.

"Turbulence bubble," Tif realised, recalling the lessons he'd been giving her since they'd left Ruchino Eighty-Six. "It's an updraft, correction is counter-spin spiral at six degrees opposite yaw."

She did that, as Po'koo said nothing, watching the numbers curiously. Most wingless landers simply fell like a guided bomb, and were shaped conically to allow them to be aimed like an arrow. It kept them upright, and removed stability from the equation, regardless of most atmospheric turbulence. But to survive the crush-densities that a heavy descender was required to navigate, the vehicle had to be shaped as near to a perfect sphere as possible, then weighed down with heavy, heat-resistant armourplate and coolant systems. Any atmospheric flight engineer knew that balls were not aerodynamic, and beyond a certain velocity would build up a big area of low pressure in their wake that would destabilise flight. The thicker the atmosphere, the worse that destabilising pressure void became, at lower and lower velocities.

And so, instead of falling in a powerless but guided descent, heavy descenders had to make a controlled, powered descent, keeping velocities within a relatively low range. Beyond that range, they became intensely unstable, and once a ball began spinning, it was nearly impossible to recover. But powered descents in highly turbulent atmospheres were themselves inherently dangerous, requiring constant adjustment against forces that again, the descender had few sensors capable of detecting.

New warning lights flashed. "Third thruster is overheating," Tif observed.

"Your new angle of attack is exposing it to extra atmospheric pressure," Po'koo observed.

Tif rotated the ship's attitude to compensate, and suddenly the lean became alarming. There was no time to describe to her instructor what was happening, so she gave it a big burst of thrust to slow descent and recover... and the over-stressed third thruster blew with a flash of red lights. The ship began to tumble. Tif did not bother fighting for further control, but slumped back in the far-too-large chair, and watched the shrieking fall toward her doom unfold upon the screens. In a catastrophic failure in Kamala's atmosphere, there was no recovery, only the hope that death would be swift.

"You make it hard on purpose," she told Po'koo, with an accusing stare. "An average descent can't be that hard."

"No average descents on greenhouse worlds," said Po'koo. *"All hard. That was typical, not average. But you did well, for a beginner."*

"Well?" Tif retorted. Her hands were shaking a little, which was usual for her after too much adrenaline. *Phoenix* crew teased her about it, thinking her highly-strung, however much she insisted it was normal for kuhsi. She tucked her hands under her thighs now, so Po'koo could not see.

"Yes, you did well," Po'koo repeated. *"But also, you died, and killed everyone on board. So you are a very talented corpse."* He gave a big guffaw, and clapped the back of her chair with a thud. Then he unbuckled himself from the chair, and floated up. *"I'm hungry, you stay. Practise, pretty corpse, practise."*

Tif did stay and practise, running sims on automatic until her eyes blurred and her arms ached from muscle tremors. She would be co-pilot for the actual flight, with Po'koo in the pilot's seat, but Po'koo insisted that in order to be effective, a co-pilot had to first understand what the pilot was doing. The only way to do that was to practise being a pilot herself, so that she could be ready to assist when the moment came.

"Tif?" came a careful, female voice from behind after one sim. This one she'd survived, but by a very slim margin. Tif hauled off her flight helmet, and released her ears from their scarf with a gasp of relief.

"Remy," she called back in English. "Yes."

"I thought you'd like to know," said Remy Hale, floating up to the back of Po'koo's chair, "we received a message in general traffic, but encoded within it was another message — it's pretty clearly from *Phoenix*. The Captain's speech is scheduled for forty-one hours from now. We'll be in Kamala orbit in thirty-one hours. Clearance at Chara takes place within half-an-hour of touchdown, so we'll need to touch down at forty hours and forty-five minutes."

Tif took a deep breath. "Yes. And the Major?"

"She'll be down shortly, we think maybe fifteen hours, I'm not sure *Phoenix* was able to talk to her directly to get that confirmation. But she'll be there, you can count on it."

"Yes," Tif agreed. "Always count on the Major." So many things that needed to align. But this was her little portion. She could not control any of those other portions, just this one. Everyone was counting on her, just as she was counting on them.

"And Tif," Remy added, "there was a little visual code within the message from *Phoenix*. When we put it together, it made this."

She drifted a pad across, screen activated. Tif took it, and saw that some simple punctuation symbols and letters, some human and some alien, had combined to make a little face. A face with dots for eyes, a smiling mouth with a partitioned upper-lip, and big, pointed ears. Tif smiled. Clearly it was Skah — a message from him, or about him, to say he was fine. And it made her quite emotional, that the great warship *Phoenix* would not only look after him as one of their own while she was gone, but would take the time to reassure her about him, at a time when so many important things were going on. Skah was not only crew to them, as she was, but also clan. Nothing in her life to this point had made her prouder.

Remy saw her emotion, and put a hand on her shoulder. "You'll see him again soon," she said gently. "Just a few more days."

And she took back the pad, and pushed off the chair to leave. Tif blinked in puzzlement. Second Lieutenant Hale, she realised, had misinterpreted her emotion. Humans always seemed to think she'd be upset to leave Skah for any period. The entire trip so far, her comrades had been reassuring her that Skah would be fine, and it wouldn't be such a long time, really. And certainly she did miss him, and looked forward to seeing him again.

But for any well-bred kuhsi, family meant clan, as clan meant security, and prospects for the future. A mother loving her son meant wishing for him a good position with a strong clan. Skah had that now, and by her actions she bound those ties even tighter. If she died on this mission, she had no doubt at all that *Phoenix* would continue to raise Skah, and to look after his interests, far more capably than she could ever have done alone.   She didn't really understand this mawkish, misplaced human sentiment of mothers and sons in isolation.   But human instincts toward family, and the children of one's own family in particular, she trusted implicitly.

CHAPTER 19

Trace lay in full armour on a civvie bunk in the lander, as reentry Gs flattened her into her armour, and her armour into the mattress. She'd likely make a mess of the mattress, but she wasn't going to be using it once they were down. Kamala's gravity was a little over half-a-G, but it held an awful lot of atmosphere for such a small world. Her background readings had said something about an unusually dense metallic core producing a just-as-unusually strong magnetic field, which had in turn prevented the atmosphere from being blasted away by the solar wind, as typically happened to smaller worlds this close to a lively sun. Also, Kamala had volcanic activity, which had released a buildup of gasses over millions of years — most of them dense and hot.

It made for a rough ride down, and when her reception had cleared enough, she linked in to the lander's external view. Below stretched an endless sea of white and yellow cloud, ending in a wide, blue horizon. It looked quite beautiful from up here, with no hint of the hell that lay beneath. In a few places, the endless calm was broken by buildups of tall cumulous, where some boiling disturbance below had pushed upward, flickering with lightning. If this lander fell into that soup, they'd be crushed and incinerated, likely before they ever reached the surface. But thankfully, entering into the cloud was not on the flightplan.

A camera view found Chara, a small dot against the white cloud. As she watched, nearly floating above the mattress as the lander fell toward its target with only the mildest thrust, it grew steadily larger. Her channel gave her com snatches of conversation in Togiri, as the lander crew talked to Chara Control. Chara was a commercial entity, jointly-owned by many, with Fleet and State Department merely prominent amongst its many customers. The lander crew were Fleet, and briefed on the whole mission, as the entire crew of *Satamala* had been. Fleet had facilities on Chara, where non-Fleet could not go. But complicating things, she'd been told, was the fact that not all of *those* Fleet personnel were 'in' on it.

She'd been promised a clear path to a holding location, an airtight hangar where Fleet equipment was stored, but her Koshaim-20 was firmly gripped in her right fist, and the missile rack on her back was loaded. If she had to expend any of those on Chara, the mission was surely lost before it began.

As it approached Chara, the lander rocked and roared, with more Gs as it slowed. Trace lost all sight from the lander's cameras as thrust obscured the view, then a soft thud as they touched, and the roaring stopped.

Trace climbed carefully from the bunk, extracting her rifle and running yet another check on all suit systems. All came back green, and she opened the door to the narrow steel corridor. From adjoining doors, the rest of Command Squad were emerging, forced to ride out reentry in crew quarters because there were no chairs large enough to accommodate armour suits. She entered the central accommodation space, and in the space between unoccupied restraint-equipped chairs, found the kid, exactly where they'd left him. Turning around and around in circles, like a giant, confused spider.

Trace had to laugh. At the sound, the kid stopped turning and stared at her, questioningly. "It's gravity, kid," she told him. "You are programmed for it. It's what your legs are for."

The kid had not been restrained on the way down, because there were no restraints large enough, and being a hacksaw drone, he didn't damage easily. He'd had to be up here on the crew level with the human crew, because the lower cargo holds would now be inspected by Chara personnel. The crew holds, she'd been assured, would be left alone, as the lander's only announced crew were its pilots. As in human Fleet, tavalai Fleet ground personnel took Fleet pilots' word for such things.

The kid resumed walking in circles, and his legs, unsteady at first, were already acquiring that creepy, spider-like precision, a chillingly familiar clatter of steel steps, and a rattle of intricate internal mechanisms. He looked quite different now, with twin chaingun pods on the rear thorax, muzzles pointed over each shoulder, and with reasonable articulation within the forward arc of fire.   Also attached, on the lower abdomen, was an industrial-strength laser cutter, drawing power from his main core.   Trace personally retained the safety triggers for both.

"Okay," she told the gathering, "I want full equipment check and everyone ready to move out ASAP.   We take no chances with this, we think we know what's going to happen, but I don't trust it even a little bit."   She turned to Spacer Chenkov.   "Chenk, tell us what gear you need us to carry, and don't be scared of bossing around people ranked more highly than you."

"Well shit Major," Chenkov said cheerfully, "that's pretty much everyone.   If I could just get two guys to help me with the kit…"

"Tell them," said Trace, pointing to her marines.   "Direct them — you're key to this mission, and we're here to help."

"Um sure… Zale, Leo, come help please."

"Yo," Leo Terez agreed, and went with Zale to do that. Leo's first name was actually Richard.   He was 'Leo' because on planet-bound training he'd once led marines into a simulated minefield big enough to launch them all into 'Low Earth Orbit', as that ancient acronym still tragically referenced.   And Private Lucio Zale remained Zale for now, having been newly recruited with the last batch of volunteers at Joma Station, and claiming the nickname 'Chilli' after his hot taste in food.   But noone in Phoenix Company had served with him before, and previous nicknames didn't count. His pure rifleman test scores were insanely good, however, and instead of annoying her officers by removing their best marines to fill a vacancy, Trace had opted to take Zale herself.

That left Aristan, clad in his light environment suit and helmet, visor raised.   He'd forgone the robe, hood and veil this time, agreeing that on this occasion, even his Domesh beliefs took a back seat to the need for more practical clothes.   Trace stopped before him, and levelled a gloved finger at his nose.   "I don't care what enormous importance you are back among your people," she told him.   "Out here, you're the lowest-ranked person on the team. Lower even than him."   She pointed at the intrigued and circling hacksaw drone. "That means you do exactly what you're told, when you're told to do it. Do you understand?"

A slight pause for his translator to relay that. *"I understand, Major. We are all expendable before the mission, myself included. If I must give my life so that this mission succeeds, I shall do so instantly."*

"No," Trace said firmly. "That's not what I'm saying. I'm saying obey. Whether you give your life or not is not up to you. *I* decide. And the other senior-ranked on this mission — Staff Sergeant Kono and Corporal Rael in particular. You will not unilaterally decide to die, you will not unilaterally decide not to die. You will not decide anything. You will obey. Do you understand?"

Aristan's indigo eyes showed cool respect. *"I will obey. You have command, Major."*

As they prepared, a signal from the lander cockpit showed the lower holds opening, and an inspection commencing. All holds were flushed to vacuum before landing, and the first two were now flooded with carbon dioxide rich Kamala air. It was not poisonous, as the nastier gasses tended to be heavier, and were very thin up this high. A person could even wander around in it with nothing more than a facemask. Air pressure at this altitude was lower than tavalai preferred, and right on the human norm. The temperature was even a balmy twenty-five degrees celsius, shirt-sleeve weather. It was just that there was no oxygen, and any oxygen-breather trying to breathe it would get a lungful of nothing.

And now a third hold was being flooded. Trace frowned, watching that display as Terez and Zale helped with Chenkov's bags. Third hold was not supposed to be flooded. Then she saw the camera view of the lower hold, and someone climbing the short ladder to central elevator.

"Someone's coming up!" she snapped. They weren't supposed to come up. That had been quite well established. "Everyone hide!" And as they did that, she flipped channels to the lander bridge. "Hello bridge, someone is coming up. What's going on?"

"We don't know," spoke a translator in reply. If the pilot was worried, the translator could not catch it. *"You should hide. We will query."*

"Major?" asked 'Bird' Kumar. "How do we hide a hacksaw drone?" Because the elevator shaft terminated in the middle of the floor they were standing on, and the kid would not fit through the doors of those small bedrooms, not with those chainguns on. Taking them off took far more time than they had available, as the kid's autonomous control was disabled.

"I've got him," said Trace. "You hide." And to the drone, "Kid, this way. Follow me." She strode the hall from crew central to the mess, where a kitchen of microwave cookers and refrigerated shelves were empty, her team taking their meals on *Satamala*. The kid had to squeeze on tiptoes to fit his wide legs down the hall, then rattled around behind the steel kitchen bench as Trace took position by the wall disposal. Trace checked her Koshaim, then racked it on her shoulder. If they had to deal with a single tavalai crewman, it would be quietly, and Koshaims were never that. And, she thought furiously, just how they could dispose of a crewman without arousing the suspicions of others.

It was impossible, she thought, watching the platform elevator ascend on her visor display, toward the cargo-hold airlock. One missing man would alert the others, followed by the whole Fleet presence on Chara. Maybe this man could be reasoned with, if they put a gun to his head, and took him to see the pilots on the bridge, who could explain it to him. But even then...

The kid rattled and whined, peering this way and that, his two-eyed head jerking back and forth. "Kid!" Trace told him, her visor still raised. "Silent. Quiet, you understand?" He considered her, head moving, but the legs were still. Acoustic speech was doubtless an inefficient way for him to process information that would typically be passed from unit to unit by direct digital transmission in a fraction of the time. But English seemed no difficulty for him. As always, it was not his comprehension, but his interpretation, that concerned her. "Kid, you can't be seen. Do not be seen, by anyone not in the team. If you are seen, the mission will fail."

The kid looked at her blankly, then leaned to consider where the elevator would arrive down the hall. Could he access the lander's feed to see the crewman coming up? Or maybe he was wondering how it would be possible to stay out of sight, once out on Chara. Well, she'd wondered herself. But tavalai Fleet had promised, and if they could arrange it for a bunch of armoured human marines, surely they could add a drone to the group. What concerned her more was that assuming Captain Pram and *Makimakala* had kept their mouths shut as they'd promised, none of tavalai Fleet knew that Styx existed, and thus the kid neither. There was an empty cargo crate in the lower holds that was kid-sized, and she'd been planning to use a loader with him inside it, however little he liked it. But if that plan was now about to go awry...

"Stay!" she told the drone, making up her mind, and strode back down the hall to the main room. Already the floor lights were flashing, and a circle of floorplate opened to admit the rising crewman from the elevator airlock. He stared at her as he rose, but did not look especially surprised, which let her know she'd made the right choice.

"Phoenix?" he said via translator. *"Phoenix mission?"*

"Phoenix mission," Trace agreed, stopping at the platform edge. "Why are you here?"

"Bad plan," said the crewman, clad in a light environment suit, a tavalai-shaped facemask in one hand. *"Hangar we wanted to use is occupied. New Fleet arrival, not good with the plan."*

"Occupied by people who don't know the plan?"

"Yes," the tavalai agreed. *"New hiding place. No hangar, but pressure, good air. But small."*

"We can get there without being seen?"

"Yes. Night in one hour. Dark. We leave then, I show you."

"No," said Trace. "You tell me how to get there. Show me a map, give me directions."

"Too difficult," the tavalai insisted.   *"I show you, much easier."*

"Listen," said Trace, taking a step closer.   In her big, powered suit she stood only a little taller, but loomed over the man for sheer mass.   "My marines have classified equipment.   Very sensitive.   No non-humans are allowed to see.   If they see, I have orders to kill them.   You understand?"   The crewman blinked at her. "I do not want to follow these orders.   But I will.   Now you tell me how to get to this new hiding place."

Nearly two hours later, Trace climbed the manual ladder from the cargo airlock.   The lander's visuals showed her the holds were empty of Chara crew, but she moved carefully, in case her big suit made a loud metallic noise that brought someone to investigate. Kamala's point-six gravity made that task simpler, and she reached the bottom of the wide holds in what seemed like an agonisingly long time after so much quick zipping around these spaces in zero-G.

She left the elevator platform and moved cautiously to a wall, rifle racked and refusing to think very hard on what would happen if someone discovered them.   Shooting her way in would have been easier — at least that was something she knew she was good at. Now, the first shot she fired would signal the mission's failure, regardless of what she hit.

She crept along a partition wall until she acquired a view of the main door.   The loading bridge was in place, as the crewman had promised.   Its cavernous mouth gaped, with runners and rails to carry big cargo pallets into place, before being grasped by the claws in these holds, and locked into place before flight.   With her suit mikes strained to maximum, she could hear only some machinery noise, and a strange, eery howling that rose and fell, like the cry of some wild and lonely animal.   The wind, she realised.

"This is the Major," she said into her helmet mike.   "We look clear, everyone come down."

They did, the marines all moving with suit tension dialled down to minimum, trying to keep the suit servo noise as low as possible. That was never going to be entirely successful, but if you had to move a marine armour suit anywhere without being heard, it was on a lander pad on a giant, floating industrial platform.

Most of her team were down when Trace heard someone swear. She looked, and with her partial view of the elevator rails and adjoining ladder, saw that the kid was not actually climbing down the ladder, but was flying down the side, dangling on some very thin steel cables. With legs spread as he came, he looked almost exactly like a spider. Trace hoped that Jess Rolonde was not standing directly under him.

"I didn't know he could do that," said Corporal Rael. *"Did you?"*

"Never needed it in zero-G," Terez reasoned.

The kid touched down, disconnected the cables at the top (which were magnetic, Trace guessed) and wound them back in with a high-pitched squeal as they fell, clattering off the elevator sides. Trace repressed a wince at the noise, and Rolonde got quickly out of the way as the drone came skittering across the hold floor.

"Kid," Trace said sternly as he arrived. "I said quietly. Was that quiet?" He looked about, evasively. Trace was reminded of Skah, when told something he wasn't interested in hearing. She looked back along the group. Eight marines including herself, one spacer tech, one parren assassin, and one drysine warrior drone. It wasn't the type of assault party she'd ever imagined leading. "Let's go."

She moved first, entering the loading bridge and moving quietly — or nearly quietly — down the walkway alongside the big, rubber runners. Just prior to the bridge's main articulating joint, an access door opened, and she peered out onto the pad. Her visor visuals adjusted to the glare of floodlights, focused upon the looming bulk of the lander. Pumps whined, and distant conversation carried on the wind, some tavalai workers on the pad yelling to be heard, and audible even past their facemasks. The edge of the pad was near, barely five metres.

Trace turned and signalled the others to come, then stepped carefully down the stairs beyond the door, looking about to see the rest of the pad. It too was empty, the loading bridge leading back to a pressurised wall, and pad control looking down from above, with big windows to view proceedings, but with no real angle to see straight down. She walked to the edge of the pad, where more stairs led over and down, and crouched to view across the pad, and warn the others if anyone came. Then she signalled her team to come as they arrived, with a wince as the kid barely squeezed sideways through the door, then half-slid, half-walked the stairs and scuttled past her and off the edge.

She followed, handing off the watch to Staff Sergeant Kono, then down to the next level beneath the pad, where a gantry platform was wide enough to accommodate most. In the dark, Chara could have been an enormous mining refinery. It had that look about it, a maze of gantries and supports, all ablaze with floodlights. There were more levels below them, and to the side, but they were very near the edge of Chara itself, and barely fifty metres further, the lights and steel all stopped, replaced by a black chasm.

Further to the right, a protruding wing of the Chara platform resumed, jutting far out into the dark. Floodlights gleamed upon the vast sphere of a floatation tank, several hundred metres diameter, a giant balloon of gas enfolded in the mesh of steel gantries. There were dozens of them across Chara, filled with breathable air at regular pressures. Chara did not have enough inhabitants to breathe more than a fraction of all that air — mostly it was for buoyancy, low pressure tanks atop a thick blanket of high-pressure atmosphere, and bobbing atop the surface as surely as a balloon on the surface of an ocean. Even as Trace looked, she could see the platform about the enormous balloon flexing, rising independently of the rest, and heard again the shuddering creak of background noise she hadn't been able to place until now. That noise was Chara's independent platforms flexing, on giant hinges, as they rode atop shifting currents of air. A rigid structure upon an unstable foundation could stress and break, but Chara just flowed with the wind.

"This way," she told her wide-eyed, wary team. "The lower levels should be clear at night, move slowly and keep quiet."

The maze continued, and Trace followed the map on her visor. It was hard to reconcile the view at night, and the deserted steel walkways and supports holding up the habitation levels above, with the fact that they were on a giant steel city, circling a moon thirty kilometres above its surface, at somewhere in excess of three hundred kilometres an hour. Only once, descending yet another set of steel stairs, did the reality set in as the blackness came suddenly alive with the bright, leaping flashes of a lightning storm, ripping through the boiling clouds below.

The excursion ended at a pressurised compartment amidst the supports, squeezed against some large, bundled pipes, and above a huge weather vane that descended far below Chara's lowest point, lights blinking in the whistling dark. Trace approached along the walkway to a wider platform before the compartment's front airlock. She was beginning to think they'd gotten away with it when a tavalai crewman in a facemask edged past the compartment's side. His environment suit had an equipment belt filled with tools, and he froze as he stared at her. So utterly was he surprised that Trace knew he couldn't be one of those 'in' on the plan.

She was on him before he could move, grabbing his arm and removing his facemask. He fought desperately to get it back, but against her armoured power, she barely felt the struggle. "Jess," she said calmly, "get the door."

As Jess Rolonde tried the door to the compartment. *"It's secured. Running a patch."*

The tavalai crewman was panicking now, a more rare thing for tavalai than humans, but when deprived of oxygen in a carbon dioxide atmosphere, that would happen. Trace could have told him to calm down and hold his breath, but that wasn't going to work, and taking his mask was a better way to subdue him than a blow or other physical restraint that with power-armour might just kill him by accident.

"Got it," Rolonde said finally, and squeezed in as Trace dragged the crewman after. There was only room for those three in

the airlock, and she hit close, then a hiss as the airlock replaced the air.   The tavalai gasped with relief, and coughed.   *"Has he got uplinks?"* Rolonde wondered.

"Jammed," said Trace.   Her suit's coms suite could do that, against low-grade, hostile networks.   "Guys, tell the kid to stay outside, he doesn't need air anyway."

"No but he'll need a recharge," Kono reminded her. *"Power core is thirty hours but we'll want him topped up.   Plus he's kind of visible out here."*

"Well we can't let this guy go," said Trace, opening the inner airlock door as the pressure equalised, and pulling her prisoner inside.   "And we can't let him see the kid, so that means keeping him in here."   The pressurised compartment was an engineering shed, long and thin with rows of tool shelves and work benches.   At the far end, a couple of bunks and chairs, a minor living space for several techs to live in for a few days on a job.   "Jess, search the place and see if you can find some canvas, something to hide the kid."

"You don't think anyone who comes down this far will reckon something's wrong when they see human marines?" said Rolonde, even as she did what Trace asked, stomping between shelves and trying not to let her rifle catch on the low overhead.

"I think we could probably fit eleven in here," said Trace, helping the tavalai crewman into a workbench chair, where he gasped and heaved with relief.   "The environmentals won't like it, but we only have to last until morning."

The Fleet man on the lander had assured them that Chara's Fleet HQ would not see that this engineering compartment was being occupied — the Fleet conspirators would block the signal, and stop anyone else from coming down this way.   Trace flipped her visor, and considered the recovering tech.   So much for that last part.   He didn't seem to have a translator, so she activated her own, and put it on speaker.

"Hello," she told him.   *'Gidiri ha,'* said the speaker.   The tavalai stared.   "I'm not going to hurt you."

The tavalai muttered something in reply. *"You already hurt me,"* said her earpiece. Trace nearly smiled at the predictable, stubborn bravery.

"Fucking tavalai," said Rolonde from further up the aisle, rummaging through storage cupboards. Evidently her translator had caught that.

"It's carbon dioxide," Trace retorted. "Don't be a pussy." With no real hope the translator would catch that, but she was a marine, and the tavalai would get the idea. "We're here on a mission. Your own Fleet sent us. It's aimed at State Department. But we're not going to kill any tavalai if we can help it."

"Comforting," the tech retorted, rubbing his bruised arm. Probably he'd been referring to that, when he said she'd hurt him. His look was suspicious. *"How did you get here? Humans, on Chara?"* And his eyes widened as he realised the answer to his own question. *"You're Phoenix! Phoenix is at the Tsubarata, and now you're here! Why is Phoenix at the Tsubarata? Why is it really?"*

"Damn," said Kono grimly as the airlock opened once more to admit him and Chenkov. "I was hoping we'd caught a dumb one."

"He's Engineering," Chenkov said by way of explanation, dumping his heavy equipment bag on the workbench. The tavalai stared at it, unable to understand untranslated English. "Not many dummies in Engineering."

"Is that a fact?" the big Staff Sergeant said drily. And to Trace, "You could just toss him off the edge."

"I'm not going to toss him off the edge," said Trace, closing the translator for a moment. "If I did, we'd have the same problem — a missing tech who hadn't reported in. We need to last until morning and our best bet to keep HQ off our back is to get this guy to cooperate, which he can't do if he's dead."

"A tavalai?" Rolonde said from down the aisle. "Good luck."

"You're here for the vault," the tavalai interrupted them. *"You said State Department. You're after the vault."*

"Yes," said Trace, reactivating the translator. "Your own Fleet Admirals want secrets State Department has in that vault. Think about it — how else could we have gotten here, if we didn't have tavalai help?" The tavalai made an odd expression that she didn't recognise. "Will you help us?"

The expression got more extreme. Trace realised that he was laughing at her. *"I'm not going to help you!"* he said with obvious mirth. *"Stupid humans, why would I help you?"*

CHAPTER 20

Groundcars took Dale's team through lower Gamesh, then into traffic tunnels beneath the city, then emerged astonishingly into lower caverns, where the Gamesh cave system had been expanded upon, hollowed out and propped up on a colossal scale for many thousands of years. Lit in bright, simulated sunlight, vertical rock walls climbed above industrial buildings and power plants.

The cars left the main highway, then drove through regions of increasingly grim, rusted steel buildings and chain fences, until they stopped right against a high cave wall. The team of six humans, two parren and one tavalai climbed from the cars, in a small, neglected carpark lit by yellow, flickering bulbs behind an abandoned factory yard. Hauling equipment bags, Dale wondered how a tavalai like Tooganam could bear to live in this place. Not all of Gamesh was as rundown as this, but it seemed an odd location for a former karasai to choose to spend his retirement. Most tavalai liked water, and green things that grew.

"Here," said Tooganam, walking to an old-fashioned manhole in the bitumen, little more than an unsecured iron lid. *"Over thousands of years there have been many tunnels and sewers built, to join the undertown's different caverns. Not all of them are remembered, and with so little government in the free-cities, fewer still are secured."*

He lifted the heavy lid with a wince that was more the bending than the lifting, and flashed a light inside. Then he gestured the others to follow, and climbed down the inset ladder. When he reached the bottom, Dale found an empty concrete tunnel, with only the faintest trace of water.

"It's completely abandoned?" he asked Tooganam, shining his flashlight up both ways. Neither direction showed him an end.

"It's used for emergency water runoff," said Tooganam. *"Occasionally it floods."*

"Occasionally?"

"Perhaps once in fifty days. For an hour or two. The odds are low."

"Comforting. It floods with water? From where?"

"You will see."

They walked for twenty minutes, the tunnel sloping gently down until Dale saw a circle of light at the end. Once there he took a knee far enough back in the shadow that no one outside could see in, and stared out. The tunnel mouth ended a metre above a lake. Much of the immediate view was obscured by lush trees, some flowering with red buds. Past gaps in the foliage, he could see a cavern perhaps five hundred metres wide and several kilometres long, lit with bright, natural-looking light. Its floor was a carpet of greens and yellows, crops and gardens, interspersed with small parks. This central lake ran like a river up the centre of the cavern, providing irrigation for all.

"There are another fifteen caverns like it," said Tooganam, admiring the view with affection. *"They do not provide all of our food, much is imported from the temperate regions, or grown in less ideal conditions. But this is the best. I've spent many years of my life here, working on the machines that make it all grow. My second profession, after the karasai."*

"Figures," Dale grunted, indicating for his team to unpack their gear. "It's good for swimming?"

"Good for drinking," Tooganam assured him. *"Your main difficulty is that it is so clear, you can be seen. Stick close to the banks, they are vertical, unlike a regular river, and thus deep, and clear of obstacles. They will give you cover."*

From the gear bags were brought basic scuba gear, small tanks, weight belts, fins and facemasks. All marines and spacers did some basic suit training in water, to simulate systems operation without risking catastrophic decompression when they screwed up. The gear was readily available in Gamesh sports stores — there were some large seas now nearer the planetary poles, some even with flourishing introduced sea life, and tourism was a thing. The newly acquired weapons they put into sealed plastic bags that had been a little harder to buy, but not impossible for a man of such local knowledge as Tooganam.

"Now one last time," said Jokono, kneeling by Dale's side as the Lieutenant tightened the tank and belt over his civvie pants and jacket, and hoped the water was not so cold that he'd freeze on the way. Certainly he did not want to strip down for swimming — the clothes would dry quickly, and he'd need something to wear on the other side of the swim. "The network construct is established, so once you've acquired the code module we'll just need to input, and we'll have access to the main Gamesh spaceport dish. With the right codes, it will think we're State Department, and State Department don't know when the next ID clearance from Chara is due anyway, so they won't be alarmed when it doesn't arrive on time. I'll answer it, send it back positive, and our Chara team will be cleared."

"And you're sure Gamesh network security won't see your construct working?" Dale asked, testing his facemask with a burst of compressed air.

Jokono smiled. "Lieutenant, this is our most advanced technology." Styx, he meant, with others listening. "There is no chance. Once you have the code module, Petty Officer Kadi will input as discussed. Your own coms unit will interrogate it and upload the codes into our network construct."

"How can you be sure?" Tooganam asked with a tavalai frown. *"Those things are autistic so they can't be hacked."* Code modules of this sort were used precisely as defence against hacking in an advanced, networked galaxy. Some hacks couldn't be stopped, so anything accessible from the network was also vulnerable to it. Organisations that dealt with the highest security codes built autistic modules that lacked the ability to even talk to a network, and had to be plugged in directly, to access their codes. But security for such modules was physical, and what could not be hacked, could always be stolen. If one could get at them.

"Buddy, this is top secret human technology," Kadi told Tooganam, with private amusement. Styx had given *Phoenix* engineers input into new tech that could hack anything, usually in seconds. "Even if State Department realise they've been hacked, they won't be able to reverse the signal, or even figure out who we've been talking to, until they've recovered that code module."

"*Don't* let them have it back," Jokono added sternly. "This entire mission depends on it."

"We know," Kadi assured him, as though *he* was going to have anything to do with it. He was sealing his AR glasses and their booster unit into tight plastic, along with his newly acquired pistol. His range test scores were actually pretty good, but if shooting range scores made someone a good marine, any number of VR gamers could have joined up and whipped the tavalai in no time. Being well acquainted with the things that *did* make a good marine, Dale was sticking to the old marine commandment when operating with spacers, that if the spacer ever had to fire his weapon, the marines weren't doing their job properly.

Dale put his AR glasses in place, and found the displays working. These were giving him the required direction, and would continue directing him all the way, according to Tooganam's comprehensive map.

"Now remember what I told you about the second security gate," Tooganam pressed. *"The locking mechanism is different, it's a double-prong, not a single. And the sensors are..."*

"Motion sensors rather than heat," Dale completed, having gone over the plans many times. "We've got it, pops."

"And you're sure you can just deactivate them?" Tooganam looked particularly skeptical on this point. The old tavalai had not come down in the last shower. Surely he suspected something strange going on, the way these humans so confidently proposed to blast through some of the best tavalai network security as though it were barely there.

"I already have access," Jokono told him confidently. "I just need to signal. Lieutenant Dale won't need to do a thing."

"Phoenix knowledge is strong like the ancients," added the parren, Milek, also suiting up with the marines. His partner, Golev, would remain behind with Jokono. Dale wasn't happy about that, but Jokono needed some expert protection, and both Golev and

Milek were crazy-skilled at unarmoured close-combat. None of the marines could be spared, so the parren got the job. Milek, Dale was sure his team could keep an eye on. But Jokono, alone with only Golev and Tooganam for company, had perhaps the most important job of all — actually intercepting the signal from Chara when it came in, and sending the all important reply, precisely on the allotted time, to coincide with the identical reply from the State Department HQ on the Tsubarata. If he was off by only a little, and the replies did not match, then Chara security would know something was up. And if either Golev or Tooganam proved to be in any way untrustworthy, then Dale didn't rate Jokono enough of a combatant to do much about it either way.

As Dale pulled on his oxygen tank, he caught Tooganam looking at him, still wary. Concerned about the two parren, Dale knew. And he wondered how it had happened that he came to trust an old enemy karasai, and guess his thoughts, ahead of all other non-*Phoenix* personnel in this game. "Be careful," he told Tooganam, with meaning.

"And you also," said Tooganam. *"Your escape route will be interesting. Should you need shelter from pursuit, my walls are strong."*

Tsubarata Central could not sanction activating the elevator shafts through the Human Quarter, given that they were unused for a thousand years and in spectacular violation of safety inspection rules. That left a walk into the Parren Quarter to borrow their elevators — just Erik, Lieutenant Alomaim and his three closest Bravo First Squad marines. Armed tavalai joined them — Tsubarata security, and neutral, owing allegiance to the Pondalganam who had been so accommodating to *Phoenix* on Ponnai. But owing allegiance to a legal institution did not give Alomaim or Erik any real confidence of their ability in a fight.

They rode the elevator up to concourse level, and there it opened onto an enormous hall, like a canyon with flags, symbols and

288

balconies on all sides, towering several hundred metres up to a transparent, segmented ceiling, and a view of the rocky planetoid rushing by. All up and down those walls were aliens, perched on balconies, many with cameras, some with drinks, as though gathered to watch the show. Thousands of them, Erik thought as he walked, into the centre of that patterned floor, and more thousands of spectators lining the way. Tavalai security held them back, but their numbers seemed thin, and their weapons more those of polite crowd control than lethal purpose. There were shouts and yells, hoots and clicks.

"Stay real alert, guys," came Lieutenant Alomaim's synthetically formulated voice in Erik's ears. Erik had broken out the full dress uniform, but the marines wore fatigues with harness, webbing and full pouches. Deprived of weapons or armour, Alomaim's marines had first aid, technical gear, and even very big flashlights that could be used as clubs. *"Captain, we should protest this route. They promised a covered route — this is exposed."*

"It's a high exposure event, Lieutenant," Erik told him. *"There's nothing we can do, we're not in charge."* Kantovan System media were set up for an important speech, and by no coincidence at all, that speech's commencement was now precisely the time that the heavy descender from the freighter *Ikto* was scheduled to touch down on Chara. If they protested now, and caused a delay, they'd miss the only schedule that actually mattered.

The portable unit in Erik's pocket felt unnaturally heavy. He'd been touching up the speech most of last night, unable to sleep and spending long hours staring out the habitation rim windows at Konik below. It was ridiculous, of course. The speech was nothing more than a giant distraction to get everyone looking the wrong way while *Phoenix* stole something. And yet, that did not change the monumental history of the moment. Romki's list of things not to say had gotten him thinking, and all his old debate-club skills from school had come flooding back.

He'd thought about telling the non-human galaxy-at-large about the threat of deepynines allied with the alo... but in discussion with the senior officers and Romki, all had agreed that that would have been irresponsibly reckless. One did not cause major foreign upheavals on a whim. Interspecies relations in the Spiral needed to be stable for there to be any peace at all, and that stability would not be helped by *Phoenix* dropping scary revelations on the unsuspecting leaderships, to say nothing of the unsuspecting populations, of alien races across the Spiral.

But he did, he'd realised, have many things to say. About how fate and circumstance had brought two great species to a terrible war, who under better fortune might have been good friends. About how humanity should not blame all tavalai for what happened to Earth, but rather the one, deserving faction of tavalai. And about how some old hatreds, no matter how profound, needed to be set aside for the good of all. Humans had always blamed the krim primarily for Earth, but held the tavalai a close and vengeful second. Erik knew that telling many humans to abandon that hatred would be like telling a drowning man to abandon his life-vest... but simple distraction though this speech surely was, it was also an opportunity. And if the alo did turn out to be the mortal threat he suspected they were, then humanity was going to need the tavalai. Someone had to start building those bridges now, and if he had to suffer all the hatred and backlash of his own people to do it — well, given his current circumstance, who could do it better?

From amidst security and crowds ahead, a familiar, hunched shape emerged — Tua, the sulik administrator. He (Erik was fairly sure) lurched toward them in that awkward, bird-legged gait, small arms clutching a pad and odd-shaped AR glasses on his face, above the breather mask, to hide his eyes in holographic glare.

"Greetings Captain," said Erik's translator past Tua's multi-toned screech, as the sulik fell in beside him. *"There will be procedure on this momentous occasion."*

"Of course, Tua," said Erik, forcing calm into his voice. "Will the representative chamber be full?"

"Assuredly," said Tua, with a bobbing of that long-necked head. And perhaps a chuckle? *"Assuredly yes, all species' representatives will be there."*

Just so long as the attention lasts as long as we need to intercept that message from Chara, Erik thought. Hiro was waiting even now, having somehow made his way to a State Department entrance, with Styx's help. Erik had wanted to know how, but Hiro had declined, suggesting that it was at least theoretically possible that some new twist could see him arrested, and possibly tortured or otherwise coerced. Erik knew Hiro was talking about Lisbeth, and wasn't prepared to push the point. It was just as likely, he thought, that Hiro simply liked to operate alone and in the dark.

Tua launched into a description of upcoming formalities, of books to be signed and oaths to be sworn, and of the makeup of the parliament chamber, and who would be seated where. Events would be telecast, of course, and the signal seen by anyone with a viewing screen in this system, and eventually far, far beyond. Hundreds of billions of beings, no doubt. Perhaps a trillion or more, given that many species refused an exact census — an understandable precaution, in a galaxy where total genocides had occurred in the recent past.

Erik listened with one ear, the other hearing Styx conversing via uplink with Lieutenant Alomaim about things she could see on the marines' AR glasses, and thinking all the while how he wished he'd been able to let Lisbeth take a look at his speech before he gave it, given how much more recently she'd been in university debating clubs than he...

"I see a rifle," Styx said quite calmly and clearly on audio. *"Third upper level, right hand side, now being pointed at you."*

Alomaim hit Erik even as Erik dove himself, to the left given Alomaim was on the right and would inevitably drive him that way... and shots tore the air where he'd been, then screams and people yelling. More shots, and Erik scrambled without Alomaim's help for the wall, as the sea of spectators split and scattered about him, some falling, though whether hit or taking cover he could not tell. He slammed into an alcove against the wall, Alomaim ahead of him, positioned to take a bullet in his Captain's stead. There was a lot of shooting, multiple sources and directions now, bullets snapping by and hitting the wall as Erik grabbed Alomaim to pull him back to better cover. Alomaim turned and pinned him against the wall, unmoving until Erik slithered sideways to show there was enough cover for both, and the Lieutenant could still position himself between the incoming fire and his Captain.

The crowds thinned dramatically as people ran, leaving several lying in the hall, some twitching. One of them was Tua, kicking awkwardly in his own blood, trying to rise. Erik wanted to yell at Alomaim that someone had to fetch the gentle alien while there was still a chance to save him, but knew better than to think that Alomain, single-minded in defence of his Captain, would listen.

A knot of figures against a wall opposite began to shred and flee, as individuals peeled themselves from dubious cover to make a run for it. In their wake, Erik glimpsed a slender figure, more human-looking than most, colourfully robed and raising a weapon at him and Alomaim from directly opposite. A parren, and on this angle Captain and Lieutenant were both dead. Until Private Ito leaped from the ground alongside and tackled him, ripping the weapon clear and rolling for better leverage… he found it a moment later, too powerful at this range, and broke the parren's neck with a brutal twist. And was hit by fire from up the hall, then grabbed by Sergeant Brice and hauled to a wall, holding his arm.

"Styx?" Alomaim was demanding. "What can you see?"

"Very little from your current position. I could see more, but it would mean revealing myself to their network security."

"Don't do that!" Erik snapped, trying to see as much of the hall as he could past Alomaim's stubborn position. "Hiro! Hiro, are you listening!"

"He can hear you," Styx replied. *"I have him on relay, that is safer."*

"Hiro, go! This is as big a distraction as we'll get, you have to go now!"

"He has heard you. He has affirmed."

Ahead, a tavalai guard stepped further into the hall to get a good shot, only to be shot himself. Another tavalai stood nearby, blazing fire and refusing to cover, and was shot as well.

"Fucking tavalai," Alomaim muttered, ducking back as bullets hit the alcove corner. And activated his translator to yell at the remaining guards, "Take cover! Tavalai, take cover! You don't have position to match fire, manoeuvre to cover! Flank them!"

And Erik recognised the marines' stories coming to life before his eyes — of stubbornly brave tavalai who died because principle demanded they not cower before a threat. Then Sergeant Brice was yelling at Private Cruze to stop, but too late, because Cruze slid and rolled across the broad hall floor toward the wounded sulik, grabbed a floundering leg as bullets snapped off the hall floor beside him, and pulled. For most people it would have been impossible, but marine augments gave Cruze the power to move Tua's dead weight and slide. Then Erik grabbed Cruze's leg, and Alomaim his harness, and pulled both human and sulik back to their slender cover against the wall.

"What the *fuck* are you doing, Private?" Alomaim growled.

"Sorry sir!" Cruze panted, badly frightened himself but struggling now to drag Tua's ungainly shape to full cover between himself and Erik, as Erik searched for the location of the bullet wound. "Poor bloody guy, sir. Couldn't just let him die out there."

"Here Private," said Erik, finding the hole in the side of Tua's chest and pressing hard. "Pressure bandage now!" And as Cruze tore out the contents of his webbing pouch, "Styx! You know any sulik anatomy?"

"Half of your standard painkiller dose only," Styx assured him. *"More than that could stop a heart, and cascade to the second heart."*

"Half dose," Erik told Cruze in case he'd missed it.

"I got it," said Cruze, placing the bandage for Erik to hold while winding the compressor about Tua's body. "Base of the neck, yeah?"

"The base of the neck will function," Styx confirmed. As Tua trilled in agonised distress from his long throat, and Erik repositioned the oxygen mask on the beak-like face, and checked the breather for damage.

"Ito's fine," came Gunnery Sergeant Brice on coms from just across the hall. *"Just an arm, he'll live."*

"Gee thanks Sarge," came Ito's reply through gritted teeth.

"Well they got us pinned real good," Alomaim observed, as sporadic shooting continued up and down the hall, interspersed with shouts from tavalai security, and squeals from the wounded. "We need weapons. They'll make a move soon, they've only got a few minutes until security gets its shit together and flanks them."

"I have a triangulation fix from your coms on one sniper in particular," said Styx. *"Upper left side. Sergeant Brice, you have the best angle."*

"Go Sarge," said Ito. *"I'm fine, go."* Finishing the bandaging that Brice had started, as the Sergeant slid from her cover, darted to a fallen tavalai weapon, then into cover up the same wall.

"Sergeant I will get you a targeting dot on your glasses," said Styx. *"Just hit the dot when I say."* As more fire exchanged further up the hall, tavalai below the elevated balcony positions firing upward. Return fire came down. *"Now."*

Brice slid smoothly out, rifle on left shoulder with left-handed cover, aimed coolly and fired. "Got him," she said, pulling back and checking the unfamiliar rifle. "Saw his arms fly."

"An excellent shot," Styx agreed. *"One more, two levels below and twenty metres beyond. He is exposed now, whenever you're ready."*

Brice repeated, exposing her left half for a moment, then fired and slid back. "Got him too. More please Styx."

"They are taking more adequate cover. I believe they are alarmed."

Erik was sure they were. That a good marksman could make a tough shot was no surprise — the difficulty was in identifying the shot in the first place. With only the simplest data-input, Styx made that look easy, which in turn presented Sergeant Brice with shots that most experienced marines could make. He'd never in a million years have thought that hacksaws and humans could make such effective partners.

"Hang on Tua," he told the wounded sulik.   "They're in trouble now, just a few more minutes."   And then we see if we can pin it on the assholes who set it up, he thought, and watch the real fireworks start.

CHAPTER 21

The nighttime path beneath Chara's main level was lit by an odd sequence of lights along a maintenance walkway. Trace took it to mean what it surely must mean — that Fleet's co-conspirators up in Chara Fleet Control knew exactly where the *Phoenix* team were, and had arranged a safe route where they would meet no locals. Trace led the team in the dark, past beams of lattice-superstructure that, although huge, looked light compared to similar-sized structures she'd seen. About them were masses of pipes and unidentified mechanical innards — the systems by which the big floating city functioned.

Immediately upon leaving the pressurised compartment, the first light of dawn began to spill across Kamala's clouds, turning the eastern sky to an escalating swathe of colour, in bright striations that climbed from the horizon. Light grew upon the cloud-mass below, turning that great, dark blanket to yellow and pink, and reflecting glare up onto Chara's underside. Soon Trace could not see the guide lights at all, but now she was climbing stairs to an underside cargo platform, one half of which was filled with many tight-wrapped pallets of goods... perhaps engineering gear, Trace thought, for rapid deployment in case of structural emergencies.

The other half of the cargo platform was filled with plants, growing in rows, a thick profusion of green and red leaves, and even some flowers. It almost caused her to double-take at first, so strange it was to observe these leafy things thriving in air that would suffocate a human in minutes. But then the logical part of her brain caught up — the atmosphere was heavily carbon dioxide, of course. Pure plant food, and this miniature forest was loving it. Some of the plants bore fruits and berries, and Trace thought that probably the tavalai crew were growing fresh food here and elsewhere about Chara. Grown in this atmosphere, it would probably taste good.

Trace paused to let everyone catch up, and to allow any early morning strollers to show themselves. None did, and she commenced the stairway climb up steel rungs, deserted save for emergency breather stations with call buttons.   Thankfully, she knew, no one at Chara Fleet Control would be watching them on surveillance cameras — those would have to be overridden, in case less friendly Fleet elements saw those images.   It saved her from having to explain to those friendly elements what the *Phoenix* team were doing with a hacksaw drone, for one thing.

They climbed past a great, flexing hinge, where this platform linked to the one beside it.   It shuddered and groaned in the strain, a sound not unlike that which Trace recalled from a training voyage on a genuine old sail ship while at the academy on Homeworld.   She was pleased that Chara did not rise and fall as notably as that old ship had done.   Even after so long in service, she was not the best flyer or sailor, and the ease with which spacers like Erik handled motion-disorientation was something she'd have envied, if she hadn't spent so long in meditations resolving not to envy anyone.

The team climbed through the space between platforms, like ants crawling up the gap between cupboard and door, until they emerged onto an upper platform.   From here they had a view across Chara's upper side for the first time, in full daylight.   Each square platform was perhaps three hundred metres wide, and Chara was an uneven twelve-platforms across at its widest point, or three-point-six kilometres.   Every second platform was an enormous containment structure for the spherical 'balloons' of breathable gas within. Stored at low-pressure densities, those tanks held Chara aloft upon the ever-denser blanket of thick air below, unable to sink lower in the same way that a balloon would be unable to sink in a bathtub, no matter how hard you forced it.   Chara was heavy, but nearly half of its volumetric mass was low-pressure gas tanks, and it was enough to keep the entire, multi-thousand tonne complex aloft upon the upper-atmospheric winds of Kamala, thirty kilometres above the ground.

The topside view was a series of great white spheres, their upper domes glowing and half-shadowed in the low morning sun, like an endless pattern of half-crescent moons, arrayed in perfect rows.   Chara itself existed between the spheres, a light-but-tough frame of interlocked platforms, arrayed with pressurised habitat levels, warehouse spaces, communication arrays, wind turbines and observation platforms.   Here on the elevated rim, they were just above the height of a landing platform like the one they'd come down on.

"Too exposed," Trace told her team, waving back down the platform side.   "In there, clear it carefully."   Staff Sergeant Kono indicated them down stairs, and into spaces in the platform side between where hangar compartments had been stacked vertically alongside the landing pad.   The marines cleared the space, then crouched down in the narrow spaces while Trace peered over some cargo netting splayed over the rail — possibly to ward any flying debris from the backblast of landing vehicles.   She checked the time on her visor — it showed three minutes to scheduled touchdown.   A squint at the sky showed nothing but pale yellow haze.

"This is a State Department facility?" Aristan asked at her side, gazing about behind dark-lensed goggles and breather mask.

"Yes," said Trace.

"It is not well guarded."

"They think Chara's isolation is guard enough.   They did not count on being betrayed by their own Fleet."   She thought she knew how *that* felt.

"Do you know the makeup of the lander crew?"

"No.   One of ours, but they take two pilots, and two engineers.   *Phoenix* knows, seems to think it's fine."

"A lot of faith to place, in one Phoenix pilot.   Your kuhsi, I'd imagine."   No one had told him.   But he'd been at Doma Strana. He hadn't seen Tif on PH-4, but he'd seen Skah, coming in with Lisbeth, and greeted with fascination by the local tavalai.   And he'd know that State Department would never allow a human down to the vault.   *"What if State Department recognise your kuhsi?"*

"They've never seen her," said Trace.   "She never got off the ship in Doma Strana.   We're very recently from Kazak System, Joma Station.   That's the only place anyone's seen her as a member of *Phoenix* crew.   Our ship is faster than most, even if State Department agents have been gathering information on her..."

"And you know very well that they are doing that on all your crew," Aristan interrupted.

"...they won't have had time to gather and process that information yet."

"You should not have brought the kuhsi or her cub down to Doma Strana," said Aristan. *"That was sloppy. It could now cost us all."*

"It was sloppy," Trace admitted. "We did not foresee these eventualities. And we are new at these games."

"One notices."

"Hey kid," Trace heard Terez saying on coms. *"That's a sunrise. Really nice, huh?"* Trace did not turn to see if the drone had any response. *"He's just staring at it,"* Terez informed them all. *"It's like he's amazed."*

"Don't anthropomorphise the machine," Rolonde retorted. It was a word they'd all been using, since Trace had introduced them to it. *"He's just processing something new."*

"That's what amazement is," Terez retorted.

"Just hope our friendly tavalai prisoner doesn't break loose before we get down there," Kono grumbled.

"Tavalai Fleet will make sure they inspect that facility before anyone else does," Trace assured him. "They'll find him first, and keep him quiet for as long as it takes." A bright light drew her attention skyward. A lander was beginning its terminal deceleration burn high above, a white, glaring dot against the pale morning sky. "There they are," Trace informed her team. "Right on time."

"Gonna be interesting if one of our teams isn't in position," Kono rumbled in warning, hefting his rifle.

"No doubt," Trace agreed, watching the lander descend. It was big alright — far bigger than usual, an almost perfect, and quite unaerodynamic sphere, like a giant, flying golf ball. Its thrusters were arranged about that spherical underside in a deployed curve, not breaking the even, pressure-resistant shape. So there was no even-platform of thrust, Trace thought, her heart thumping a little harder to watch the approach. She was no ship-engineer, but she knew enough to know that such a design had to decrease flight stability. This ship was built specifically to descend into that burning hell below. And she was going to lead her team onto it. Of all the possible nasty deaths a marine had to face, she'd never considered this kind before. But then, for perhaps the first time in her military career, it occurred to her that she wasn't here to die. She was on a treasure hunt, and this time around, being alive was too much fun to waste.

Tif watched the descender's engine and thrust readings with no real concern — this part of the descent was easy, low thrust against moderately-low gravity, and Po'koo let the autos take over as they approached the Chara platform with a dull, rumbling roar. The most difficult part was that Chara was moving at over two hundred kilometres an hour, due to the powerful high-altitude winds. Kamala was barely twenty five thousand kilometres in circumference, meaning that Chara completely circled the moon every hundred hours or so, with only enough directional control to ensure it stayed in roughly the main equatorial jetstream.

Reaching Chara from orbit had taken some arranging, with the freighter *Ikto* having to perform some clever braking to release the descender on the correct trajectory to hit the moving target below. Second Lieutenant Hale and the others had of course remained aboard, as *Ikto*'s second stop in Kantovan was the Tsubarata, to deliver a cargo of perishables, where tavalai Fleet said there would be a discreet transfer to *Phoenix*. For now, Tif was very much aware that she was on her own. At least until she reached Chara, and passed State Department inspection... and then, hopefully, they'd somehow get the Major aboard without anyone seeing. She wasn't familiar with the details of that part of the plan, having too much to worry about with her own plan. But she was certain that if anyone could make it happen, the Major could.

Chara's moving target was no difficulty for the descender — all the airmass at this altitude was moving at a roughly identical velocity to the floating city, meaning that for the practical purposes of flying, Chara may as well have been stationary. Landing Pad Seven showed barely a gentle breeze of crosswind, accelerating briefly to a howling gale as the descender's thrust reached it, then to flame and smoke as they touched, and the engines cut.

A tavalai voice chattered at them on coms. *"Descender Ikto One,"* said Tif's translator, *"you will secure all flight systems and open holds for immediate inspection. All coms traffic is now intercepted, any attempt by you to communicate with any external entity in a manner that this holding post cannot automatically read will see your filed flight plans cancelled, and your immediate return to your point of origin. Chara Holding out."*

"Descender Ikto One hears and complies," the translator added, as Po'koo grumbled a reply in his native tongue. He pointed at the central-panel navscreen, for Tif's benefit. *"Did you see the pads on the way down? Chara Holding has five pads, all for the vault. Two are occupied, and one more looks like it was recently. Lots of traffic to the vault lately."*

"Two more descenders are here now?" Tif asked, a little chagrined that she hadn't noticed. She'd been watching the lander's alien systems, she couldn't pay attention to everything. "Do you know whose?"

"No telling," Po'koo rumbled. *"Hard to put identification on a descender when they're repainted every few trips. Both are kaal-make, similar to this one, though one was quite a bit older. Probably tavalai Fleet — State Department keep the better ones themselves. Fleet's budget has been smashed lately, they don't have money to spend on descenders."*

He sounded grumpy about it — no doubt he'd made more money in the old days, when tavalai Fleet had spent more on his speciality. He checked monitors, and rumbled something else into coms. Behind, one of his tavalai engineers replied, performing systems shutdowns that would allow, eventually, the hold doors to be opened. Those doors weren't a simple matter like on a regular lander — the mechanisms were complex due to the need to keep the hull strong, plus coolant systems running through the outer skin.

"Pretty sunrise though," said the big kaal, disconnecting his harness. *"Move, we have to meet the inspectors in person. Get your identification in order and let me do the talking."*

Tif fetched her facemask from its seat pouch, moulded to her face in a ten-minute scan-and-print at one of *Phoenix*'s printers. She followed Po'koo past the mid-cockpit bulkhead, through engineering where the two tavalai ship engineers studiously worked through their systems checks, as a complicated beast like a heavy descender required every time it flew. Tif had spoken a little with the tavalai — the descender's only other crew — and gotten little from them. It was curious, because tavalai were usually sociable. But then, she thought as she followed Po'koo down the access ladder to lower holds, kuhsi were supposed to be clan and family-centric, also. Yet here she was, several thousand lightyears from home, without any other kuhsi for company besides her son. Some individual paths could not be explained by species alone. Perhaps these tavalai were outcasts, or eccentrics like her, operating alone and in it for the money.

At crew-hold level she followed Po'koo to the upper airlock. The big kaal was surprisingly graceful for all his lumbering size, and vastly overpowered for this light gravity. He seemed to flow across the floor, with a four and occasionally six-limbed stride, with enough hands and feet to brace on every presentable wall or ceiling on the way past.

He cycled the inner airlock door, and checked the display that a firm seal existed on the far side. Seeing that one did, he closed the doors behind as precaution, and pulled on his own, kaal-sized facemask, as Tif did the same. The outer door cycled, and six tavalai stood waiting in facemasks and environment suits in the access tube beyond, extended from the landing pad's adjoining tower. The two foremost tavalai were unarmed. The four behind were not.

"Descender Ikto One," said Po'koo without preamble. *"I am Captain Po'koo Tok'rah'pan, and this is my co-pilot, Sia Shan."* Sia Shan had been a friend of Tif's, back on Chogoth. An escaped woman from the backwards Rahresh Coast, she'd studied law, and had encouraged Tif to pursue her dreams of flying. Sia Shan had been murdered by her own brother, come from Rahresh in disguise to avenge the family's honour. Tif hoped that Sia's spirit would

appreciate the gesture, to include her in such an important mission for the whole Spiral as this. *"We have Fleet requisition orders for a vault item."* Po'koo pulled a pad from a vast flightsuit pocket, activated a code and handed it over. *"That is the vault item number, the requisition order number, and the Fleet command code clearance. It is all in order."*

The State Department official stared at it, wordlessly, eyes scanning. *"You are Ko'Chu'Tah Transportation?"*

Po'koo's huge, four-limbed shoulders straightened further. *"That is my company. I am its chief."*

"Our records state you have not been to Chara in eleven tavalai years. Your company has been implicated in illegal activities in several systems. Smuggling."

"Your Fleet chooses to send whom it chooses," Po'koo growled. *"My company has been found legally guilty of nothing, by tavalai authorities. Heavy descenders are short in quantity. If State Department blocks companies like mine from executing Fleet transportation orders,* no one *will be able to use your precious vault."*

"That would suit my authorities very well," the tavalai said drily. *"Inspection proceeds now. Clearance codes will follow shortly. Regulations state that the Captain shall remain with his ship. Your co-pilot will come with us, for formalities."*

Tif tried to keep the alarm from her glance, as she looked at Po'koo. *"She has little knowledge of this bureaucracy,"* Po'koo growled. *"She only flies, take someone else."*

The tavalai blinked, a flicker of third-eyelids. *"She?"*

"Yes, she. An escaped woman. If they all fly like her, they're welcome to come work for me."

"Your engineers are needed aboard for the inspection, as are you. Your co-pilot comes with us."

Po'koo frowned, a gathering of heavy wrinkles upon that massive brow. Then he jerked his head at Tif. *"Go. Do what they say but tell them nothing more. Remember our contract, and the confidentiality of our client."* Tavalai Fleet, that meant. Everyone knew how little State Department and Fleet liked each other.

"Yes," said Tif, trying to control her nerves. Time amongst humans had made her self-conscious of just how much her fear showed. By kuhsi standards, humans were nerveless in the presence of danger, and tavalai positively comatose. She took a deep breath, and willed her heart to stop thumping. "I will go. Tavalai procedure, yes?" With what she hoped was irony.

Po'koo smirked, an upturn of thick lips. *"Damn tavalai nonsense, yes. You go. Try not to fall asleep."*

Dale pulled himself from the water, through riverside reeds and beneath the cover of orchard trees, and willed his muscles to stop shaking. The water had been plenty cold, despite Tooganam's assurances, and after Dale pulled off his facemask and airtank, he simply huddled on the ground and rubbed himself furiously, trying to get some heat back into his chilled skin.

About him, his team did the same, though Woody Forrest's preferred method of warming was to lie on his back and do crunches. Tong stayed in the reeds, apparently unbothered, and began stowing his and the others' scuba gear in cover. Tong was from the northern hemisphere of Lewych, a cold climate on an otherwise temperate world, where his parents had run a wildlife resort. He'd joined the marines already an expert cross-country skier and a crack shot, and rarely missed an opportunity to let everyone know how little the cold bothered him. He gave Private Reddy a hand out of the water as he arrived.

"Spots, you're blue," Tong whispered, as Reddy staggered out, teeth chattering. Reddy was from Shengli, which was mostly warm and humid. Before joining the marines, he'd barely known what cold was.

"Someone get my robe," Reddy muttered, giving Kadi a hand out as Dale unsealed the plastic bag containing his rifle. A little water had gotten in, but a quick check confirmed that the mechanism was working fine. All their newly-acquired weapons were tavalai-made, and so obviously would work in a little water.

Milek was last out, also struggling with the cold. Parren were slender, without much natural insulation. Dale wondered how metabolism worked for a species that never seemed to get fat. Or maybe it wasn't metabolism at all. Extreme mental discipline among humans was an elite phenomenon, but with parren it was mainstream. Maybe they could get just as fat as humans if they wished, but never did. Milek wore regular civvies like the rest of them, the first time Dale had seen a parren without obscuring robes. Dale was halfway surprised that Milek's beliefs had allowed him to be this revealed, but then, it seemed that Aristan's acolytes were pragmatic where their mission required it.

It was literally a revelation to see how closely the parren body mirrored the human, save for longer arms, narrower waist and that strange, flat-topped head with the narrow jaw and wide cheekbones. Tavalai were also humanoid, to use the chauvinistic term, but far less so than this, and even kuhsi had those double-articulated ankle-joints and short, padded feet for extra spring. Seeing Milek in civvies was almost enough for Dale to reconsider his disdain of those crazy conspiracy-cultists who insisted that all humanoid aliens had a common ancestor whose seed had been spread about the galaxy by the Ancients many millions of years ago…

Their gear stashed in the thick reeds, Dale assigned Reddy to point, then Forrest, himself, Kadi and Milek, with Tong guarding their rear. The low forest through which they moved was all fruit trees, planted in neat rows and watered with tubes from the artificial river down which they'd swum. Soon the trees gave way to a thick species of sugar cane, thickets of tall, hard stalks and long, ribbon-like leaves. The cavern ceiling was no more than ten metres overhead, and rowed with lines of heating lights. These fields, Tooganam had showed them in maps, went on through caverns like this one for kilometres. Peering through the high leaves of the cane, Dale could see a tall, U-shaped harvester, with wheels to run down these aisles between the plants, and a central mechanism for cutting and stripping. Tooganam had possibly worked on that machine himself, in his younger days.

"Five hundred metres straight ahead," came Jokono's voice in Dale's ear, and a simple map display appeared on Dale's glasses — the mansion, the river running alongside, and their current position in the crop fields. *"I'm not seeing any security triggers in the crops, I'm guessing they can't place any because the farming machines will trip them."*

"Any chance you're wrong?" Dale whispered as he moved.

"Always a chance, Lieutenant. But so far my access has been total." It had been. The underground portions of the river had been blocked by multiple security gates, each with separate mechanisms, but Jokono had opened them in succession from outside, without anyone appearing to notice. He seemed quite excited by these new capabilities that Styx's technology was affording him, which itself made Dale wary. It was unwise to be lulled into a false sense of security by advanced technology that no one truly understood, particularly when operated by a man who for all his experience, had never before been in the military, let alone the marines.

"Okay guys," Dale formulated to his marines on uplink, *"keep your eyes open and don't just assume the Joker can see everything. For all we know, they could have let us through those gates on purpose and have a trap waiting."*

Approaching the edge of the cane field, Reddy got down and crawled. The rest stayed low, and then Dale saw what Reddy saw, projected on his glasses. It was a large, two-storey house, surrounded by water ponds and green water plants, as though emerging from a lush swamp.

"Looks like a thirty metre dash," Reddy murmured on coms, panning his view back and forth. *"Layout's just like old grandpa tavalai said. Road down the side, only one route in or out."*

"I'm coming up," said Dale, not liking the limited view on his glasses. "Joker, you seeing this?"

"I have a feed," Jokono confirmed. *"The mansion security is as autistic as feared. There are not even any access gates in the network for my systems to hack. You will have to establish contact from within."*

Dale arrived at Reddy's side, fixed his glasses' camera and zoomed. The lenses adjusted the image up-close without losing much resolution. The mansion was large without being huge, looking more like the private residence of a wealthy individual than an administrative building. Its outer pillars were not vertical, as a human mansion might have, but spread outward and leaned in, as though preventing the walls from falling out. Maybe a traditional tavalai design, Dale thought, dating to when tavalai made bark huts in swamps, with unstable walls.

This mansion, Tooganam had assured them with all the confidence of one recently briefed by tavalai Fleet Intel, was the current State Department nerve centre. A network nerve centre could be located anywhere, and it made sense that three hundred metres underground might be considered safer than above ground, in a teeming city filled with unruly aliens. State Department changed those nerve centre locations for further security, but tavalai Fleet Intel were tracking those changes. It was ridiculous, Dale thought with teeth-grinding tension, to be doing the bidding of tavalai Fleet in their minor civil war with State Department. Just a few months before, they'd all been at war with tavalai Fleet and State Department both. But the small countdown in the corner of his glasses was reading fifteen minutes and dropping, and he was running out of time.

"LT, what's that thing in the carpark?" Reddy whispered. Dale looked to where the driveway wound off the main road through the cavern. There was an entrance park, where VIP vehicles would pull up and let passengers directly into the main doors. Beside the doors, half hidden behind leaning support pillars and green palm fronds...

"Crap," said Dale. "That's an assault walker." They were very tavalai gear, favoured by the tavalai army for close-quarters urban action. Karasai disliked them, distrusting dumb machines to do a tavalai's job, so Dale had only seen video, and heard them described by army grunts over a drink in a bar. This one was currently on four legs, though it looked as though it could elevate to two. It was stocky, heavily armoured, and packed at least the usual amount of weaponry — far more firepower than the five attackers combined. "Looks like a chaingun, a heavy repeater, and a grenade launcher, chain fed. Where there's one, there'll be more."

"We've fought hacksaw drones," said Forrest. *"We can handle that dumb thing."*

"We fought hacksaw drones in full armour," Tong reminded him. *"LT, we can flank him, right side by the bridge."*

"State Department may be civvies but they're not stupid," Dale replied, scanning that way on full magnification. "If they're using tanks, it means they lack the trained personnel to defend without them. They'll have had experts set them up, you can bet there'll be another one covering that crossing down there."

"We'd be fine if we got inside," Reddy muttered. "They won't trash their own house with heavy firepower, and they can't manoeuvre much inside anyway. It's just a shitload of open ground to get there." The mansion ponds and gardens provided cover only forty metres away from the edge of the cane field. One walker, considering them hostile, could kill them all before they'd gone ten. Dale's timer ticked down to fourteen minutes.

"We don't have time for a complicated flanking manoeuvre," Dale decided. "Joker, you can't access house defences at all?"

"Nothing," Jokono confirmed. *"And trust me — if this technology can't, nothing can. You have to get inside, then make an inside link to the outside for me to access."*

"LT," Kadi said breathlessly, *"if I can get a direct lasercom on that walker, I can take control of it."* It was more of Styx's fancy technology that Kadi had brought along. But it was all prototypes when used by humans, and Dale wasn't about to bet his life on it now.

"If you get lasercom on the walker, you'll need clear line-of-sight," he replied. "It'll kill you the second that happens. Joker…"

"No way!" Kadi insisted. *"It'll work, this is how hacksaw drones take over foreign technology, I've seen it work…"*

"I said not now!" Dale snapped. "Joker, how about the farming infrastructure? We've got lights all along the ceiling, we've got water mains through the crops, we've got big harvesters sitting idle."

A pause from Jokono. *"Do you want me to turn off the cavern lights?"*

"No, those things see real well in the dark. Best option is to overload a programmed AI with too many options — they're not hacksaws, they're not sentient, they're much more easily confused. If you can overload some water mains, make them blow, then turn up the spotlights directly above this guy and dazzle him? Then turn those lights off just as he spots us and tries to aim — he'll hate the contrast from light to dark, it'll take more seconds to adjust, and that could be all we need."

"Yes, I think I can get you that," said Jokono, sounding a little breathless. *"And I think I can get you one of those harvesters, and run it straight at the mansion for distraction from incoming fire, would that help?"*

"The harvester on the far side of the mansion?"

"That's the one."

"Yep, that'd work fine. What's its speed? It'll have to move first, it'll draw attention away from us."

"Thus allowing you to see any hidden defences, if that activates them. I believe I can sequence distractions to maximise confusion. Just be sure to run very fast in the shortest line possible. In the meantime, I've got you a groundcar, parked quite nearby, neither it nor its owners are aware it's been breached. That's your getaway."

"Not gonna get far if we can't take out the walker first," Reddy observed.

"Get me a connection into the mansion," Jokono said reasonably, *"and I may be able to do that too."*

Thirteen minutes, read Dale's timer. Dammit, he'd cut it real fine... but in some ways this was preferable, a fast fight right on the time limit. If he'd gotten here early, there was every chance State Department would have caught them on withdrawal, and would be holding them right now, or worse. But recapturing them, and the coms module, would take time after the theft. At least this way, they'd still be in possession of it when Tif's call came through. Even if they got caught eventually, the main mission would still succeed.

"*Yo Joker,*" Forrest said testily, "*I just checked the bugs in my pocket — they're gone. Looks like they tore a hole in the containment bag.*"

"*Oh yes, sorry,*" said Jokono. "*They got out, they're doing recon for me now, and they've got network tricks. They can't take out a walker or get me network access in the mansion, however.*" Jokono had three of Styx's little synthetic insects that Dale knew of. He'd given Forrest two for this job, and kept one himself, for emergencies.

"*I will go first,*" came Milek's translated voice on coms. "*I am faster.*"

"You'll come with me and Spots," said Dale, checking his rifle again — a nervous habit, to keep his hands from shaking. He'd done this so many times, but rarely out of armour. Just like riding a bike, his first sergeant had always said, when Dale was a green private straight from basic. That sergeant had been a twenty year vet with a chest full of medals, and Dale had been in awe of him. Sometimes it didn't seem real that he was now a thirty year vet with even more medals. He sweated just the same before a fight, and had to find things with which to occupy his hands. "Once inside I want you to recon ahead, eliminate threats, and stay out of our way. Understand?"

"*Yes,*" Milek agreed. He had a pistol now, and a very big blade that Dale thought he was probably more lethal with. Parren court intrigues and assassins. Probably Milek was one of those — from the small knot of elite killers that surrounded each feudal lord, killing whom he directed while protecting him from others doing the same. They were experts in hidden weapons and silent murders, not so much in straight-up firefights.

Dale's timer hit twelve minutes. "Joker, do it."

With a whine, the big, U-shaped harvester in the far field beyond the mansion began powering up. "*I now have a view through one window,*" Jokono informed them. "*There are tavalai.*"

Several appear armed. There is no way inside, and the security would likely detect the intrusion if there was."

"No, don't alarm them yet," said Dale. "Do you have a view on the communications room?"

"*Yes. It's heavily guarded, I count five more tavalai, doubtless there are more I can't see.*"

"*Looks like we're going to break our promise not to kill tavalai,*" Tong observed.

"Good," said Dale. "Given what State Department pulled on Stoya." He didn't know if he meant it or not. After being at war for so long, harsh words and harsh thoughts before a fight were reflex.

The harvester was trundling now, straight toward the mansion. Dale couldn't see it past the obscuring cane, but he could hear it. Doubtless the mansion's occupants could hear it too, but probably thought it just regulation farming activity. When it left the cane field and kept heading for the mansion, they'd know something was up.

Dale reached and tapped Reddy on the shoulder, slithered backward from the edge of the cane into deeper cover, then headed right, from where he'd have a shorter run to reach the house. "*The harvester is reaching the edge of the field,*" said Jokono. "*Tell me when you're making your run.*"

"Not yet," said Dale through gritted teeth, crawling fast between hard cane, trying not to get his rifle caught on the way through.

"*There is another walker moving ahead,*" said Jokono, sounding alarmed. "*It is down near the bridge, where Sergeant Forrest suggested it might be. It has a limited firing angle on your position, but that will change shortly.*" An illustrated diagram appeared on Dale's glasses, the walker's position, emerging from behind the mansion's far corner. "*The first walker is turning to investigate the harvester. It's activating weapons.*"

"We're leaving in five!" said Dale.

"Distractions activating."   The overhead lights glared in two spots upon the rocky ceiling, then a pop and the rush of flowing water as a mains burst. *"They're both turning to look, go now!"*

Dale got up and sprinted, catching only a glimpse of the second walker behind the corner of the house, its back now turned, water spewing skyward from the broken irrigation behind. But the first walker was distracted only by the approaching harvester, weapon arms extended, though apparently stunned and swivelling aimlessly beneath the glare of overhead light.

Dale rushed across the grass, still fast for a man no longer young, but Reddy was faster, and now Milek was streaking ahead, a lithe blur of arms and legs.   His glasses display showed Forrest, Tong and Kadi close behind, though even now Kadi was falling behind, then coming to a halt.

"Petty Officer move!" Forrest yelled, as the first walker was turning, stomping about in a circle.   Dale aimed for the green forest about the mansion's flanking pools and dove in, finding that Milek had already smashed a window and had disappeared inside.   Reddy followed, and Dale paused to stare wildly behind, at Tong and Forrest sprinting in, neither waiting for Kadi who now stood completely exposed, pointing one of his tech devices straight at the walker.

Gunfire roared, chainguns tearing up turf at Forrest's heels, then abruptly stopped.   *"I got him!"* Kadi said excitedly, his other hand extended before him, as though steering with an invisible joystick.   *"I got control, just a moment and I'll reprogram and send him after the other one!"*

"That other one's about to kill you, now move!" Dale shouted, as gunfire erupted inside the mansion. He waved Tong and Forrest past him, and saw Kadi look abruptly right toward the second walker, and start running.   A second later, an explosion tore the turf where he'd been.   He arrived gasping, splashed in a pool and crouched behind one of the leaning supports.

"I just gotta finish the sequence on the first one!" he announced, and then the first walker was stomping by — three metres tall and going straight past, heading for the second walker.

"I can't hack both at once, but I can make the bastards fight! There, got it!"

Dale could have wasted time berating Kadi for disobeying his orders. "Get in!" he said instead. "I've got your back, move!" Kadi went, Dale following, checking left and right as they went through the broken window. The living room beyond was wide, with a big water feature between furniture and displays, and Tong on one knee, guarding the base of the stairs and positioned to shoot defenders who tried to climb them. Kadi ran up the stairs, heading for the secure room that Tooganam's intel had said was on the second floor, Dale close behind.

They ran past a dead tavalai on the top stairs, weapon still clutched in one thick hand, then turned left past another dead tavalai, and bullet holes on the opposite wall. Ahead was more shooting, and shouting, followed by a thunder of explosions from outside the mansion.

To the right, in what might previously have been a bedroom, they found Reddy and Forrest, standing over another dead tavalai, and one live one sitting in a corner with Reddy's gun in his face. On tables before a central atrium with green plants were secure processors with wide displays, all deactivated.

"I got it, I got it," Kadi muttered, pulling more gadgets from his belt and finding the insert.

"Safe's in the floor," said Reddy, as Forrest left to take position outside. "If we used explosives we'd destroy the module." The processors Kadi was accessing were cabled into the mansion walls, Dale saw. No external access, probably no wireless function at all — those cables would run into a secure ground network, then reemerge elsewhere in the city. Un-hackable, unless you could shoot your way into a place like this.

The tavalai prisoner was staring at Reddy defiantly. "If he makes a move," said Dale, "shoot him." The dead tavalai was in a very thick pool of blood, and there was no sign of shooting in the room. Blade-wounds, Dale thought, meaning Milek had been busy.

"Hey Joker, this is Kadi!" the young Petty Officer announced abruptly. "I've got you a line, can you read me on this…"

"I read you and have access," Jokono replied, and with a loud clack! a section of the floorboards moved. Reddy's rifle fired, catching the tavalai prisoner in mid-leap, and he rolled on the floor.

"Fucking tavalai," Reddy told the corpse, stepping aside for Kadi to access the floorboards. He lifted the panel, then the lid of the armoured safe within.

"Joker, which one?" Kadi asked. "There's five modules, they're all wired in..."

"Second from the left," said Jokono.

More shooting from outside, and downstairs. *"Two guards just tried to come up the stairs,"* said Tong. *"Both are down."*

"Are you sure?" Kadi asked Jokono.

"Very sure." Kadi reached, unplugged, and pulled out a very plain, bland-looking black cylinder. It had cable plugs at both ends, and was otherwise featureless.

"Great," said Reddy, leaving the room now that there was no one left to guard. "Let's go."

"Wait a moment." Kadi inserted his own cables, connected to his personal com-booster, then tucked both into a wet pocket. "Joker I'm connected, have you got that?"

"I have the network codes now," Jokono confirmed. *"It will take a short while to break them from this end, I'm not as fast as Styx. You'd better move, the car is on the way."*

"Everyone move to withdrawal point," said Dale. "The car is on the way." He ushered Kadi ahead of him, and they followed Reddy down the hall to the stairs and down, finding two new bodies at their base, drilled by a burst from Tong as he hid behind chairs across the room.

"Lots of shooting outside," said Tong, as Reddy led them fast through the same broken window they'd entered from.

"That's the walkers," said Kadi, now pulling the thing he'd used to hack the walker once more, scrambling through broken glass and into the greenery. Reddy moved low and fast around the mansion to the corner, and peered.

"Two walkers," he said. "Both dead, looks like they killed each other." He gestured them on, and Dale saw both ruined machines before him, the near one on fire with big pieces missing, and fallen into the side of the mansion.

They ran past it, as Forrest's voice came on coms, *"I'm just ahead with Mystery Boy, come past and we'll take the rear."* Ahead, the hulking second walker stood smouldering and limp, riddled with chain gun holes.   Beyond it, the bridge where the mansion's driveway crossed an irrigation stream... and up that driveway now came a single roadcar, through flanking green fields of cane.

It stopped opposite, popping all doors as Dale's team ran for it — him to the driver's seat, Forrest alongside, and the other four somehow squeezing into the back.   The car did a fast three-point-turn, then accelerated quickly back the way it came...

"Oh shit!" said Kadi, amidst the crush of limbs in the back as his AR glasses went unpleasantly live.   "It's not dead, it's turning!" As chaingun fire tore past, and kicked tracers off the road ahead, then a grenade hit the bridge.

"Turn it the fuck off!" Dale yelled.

"I can't, I've got no line-of-sight!"

As Jokono's remote-control accelerated the car to maximum speed, and they hit the bridge amidst incoming fire, and bounced... and were then weaving away, through cane fields and trees, toward the through-road ahead, and the tunnel in a cavern wall to one side. That tunnel entrance was now closing, as a security door descended, and warning lights flashed yellow.

"Joker!" Dale warned.   "The tunnel door's closing!"

"I have it," came the confident reply.   The car turned abruptly left, pressing everyone sideways, as they skidded onto the road.   Ahead, the door still descended.

"It's still closing!"

"I said I have it."   But the door was still closing as the car shot underneath, missing its roof by a whisker.   Headlights activated, revealing a high-speed tunnel ahead, and they accelerated further.

"You said you were gonna stop it!" Reddy complained.

"I did not say that at all," Jokono said calmly. *"If I had stopped the door, I could not have closed it again myself due to security overrides. This way, you now have your pursuit blocked, for minutes at least."*

"Clear communication in combat, great," Tong muttered, fighting to make a clear space for himself against a door. "LT, can we swipe another car? This one doesn't fit a family of six plus sporting equipment."

"Joker?" Dale asked, checking his weapon once more. He hadn't fired it, but most of his old habits were good habits. "Another car would be smart, two cars are harder to catch than one."

"I'll acquire you another vehicle as soon as possible." The old policeman was sounding a little tetchy with all the youngsters complaining at him. *"In the meantime, please bear in mind that I don't have time to explain my every action to you while I'm doing it."*

"Humans complain too much," Milek observed, via translator.

"Gee thanks, Beanstalk," said Reddy. The tunnel made a long bend, accelerating to highway speed, then zoomed up an off-shoot tunnel, signs indicating a return to the surface.

"What about the codes?" Dale asked. "Did the codes work?"

"They're working," Jokono affirmed. *"I'm accessing the State Department network now. Their com logs show there has been no ID request from Chara for nearly thirty hours, so our team has not entered that phase of their inspection yet."*

There were grins in the backseat, and some arm-slapping, plus a lot of simple relief. "Don't celebrate now," Dale told them. "Jokono can only keep hacking their system so long as we keep this module active. It's hooked into the Gamesh infonet, but the minute they get it back, or destroy it, we lose access. And they're going to launch the entire city security service at us to get it back."

CHAPTER 22

Tif sat in the State Department's pad holding tower, and waited. Across wide, reinforced windows she had a view of the descender's huge armoured side, roughly spherical beneath battered armourplate, scarred with the scorch marks of previous descents. Tavalai technicians sat before wide screens, observing the local airspace, though from Tif's seated position she could not see any of the trajectory markers. That was obviously by design.

A tavalai bureaucrat sat opposite her, in drab civilian clothes. Female, Tif thought, as she was smaller, with less of that bulky swagger of the men. Tavalai gender differences were closer to those of kuhsi, she thought, and the size-difference was pronounced. Humans had narrowed the performance difference between genders to a degree that kuhsi conservatives found alarming, given the degree of human influence over kuhsi society. It had been a scandalous thing just for her to receive her pilot-augments, faintly improving already excellent reflexes and dramatically increasing her G-resistance. But though tavalai females could probably pilot as well or better than males, most females seemed content to settle for professions like this one — bureaucracy.

Some of the legal institutions seemed almost two-thirds female, and in tavalai society, women probably held more overall authority. Just like the pragmatic tavalai, Tif thought, looking around at them all, working patiently, never fussing or getting distracted. Tavalai women settled for what they had, and were pleased with the real authority they possessed, whatever their exclusion from the big military roles. There wasn't much to recommend military service to anyone, really. The risks were high, the rewards often fleeting, and among tavalai at least, the real authority resided with the bureaucrats. But still Tif thought she would always want to fly. In that, kuhsi were more like humans than tavalai — often preferring the less practical thing because it was more exciting. Back on Chogoth, more and more kuhsi women had been chafing at their chains, whatever the sensible wisdom of elder women who insisted they had plenty of power where they were. Kuhsi were not pragmatists, they were romantics, and whatever her personal determination, Tif feared for her people in the many revolutions that were surely yet to come.

Tif's earpiece translator gave her snatches of nearby tavalai conversation, technicians talking as clearances were obtained. The all-important ID clearance, for which so much was being risked, on the Tsubarata and on Konik. She hoped that everyone was in position, and that all the plans had worked. And she kept her hands on her thighs, wishing she was seated at a table so that no one could observe the faint tremor of her hands. To hide it, she extended her three main claws to full, and tapped a light rhythm on her thighs. The tavalai bureaucrat looked. On *Phoenix*, crew had always given in to curiosity, and asked her about the claws — how sharp they were, how strong, how they divided once more when withdrawn so that her finger joints could still bend, only to lock out when extended. But the tavalai only looked. Tif thought she definitely preferred humans to tavalai. They were more restrained and disciplined than most kuhsi, but tavalai made humans look like gleeful children by comparison.

A door opened, and some tavalai entered. Several were armed — the usual security she'd seen in this high-security State Department hub. Tif got to her feet, retracting her claws from politeness. This tavalai wore a head-set that accommodated the big, wide-set eyes, plugged into local operations.

"Your ship has received ID clearance," the tavalai said, without preamble. And Tif had to restrain a gasp of relief. *"Coordinates to the vault will follow as soon as physical inspection has concluded. Then your ship can leave. You, however, will remain here, in State Department custody."*

Tif's heart, just restarted, now nearly stopped once more. She stared, claws slowly coming back out. Perhaps she'd misunderstood. "Please repeat?"

Was it her imagination, or did the tavalai look... smug? *"Your Captain is known to us. His security is not at issue. Yours*

318

is. The ship will descend without you. You will remain here, until we receive further instruction from Head Quarters."

Tif had to fight hard not to take out the tavalai's eye with a claw. "The descender needs a co-pilot," she struggled to say. "Kamala descent is unpredictable, even advanced auto-pilot is unsafe — two sentient pilots are mandatory…"

"Your Captain informs us that his First Engineer is an adequate co-pilot." Tif's panic worsened. Po'koo had told them *that*? The deal was that the descender *must* have a *Phoenix* pilot aboard, to safeguard the *Phoenix* team raiding the vault… and now he was giving her up?

Po'koo had probably betrayed her, she realised. Probably he was the one to make them doubt her ID — on that descender, *everyone's* ID was suspicious. State Department put up with it because the descender was on a Fleet mission, and State Department had to give Fleet access to the vault by law. State Department could only single her out for suspicion if Po'koo had pointed the finger at her in the first place. Or maybe they'd recognised her from Joma Station… but how could they? Given that travel from Kazak System to Kantovan System was only possible within this short period for a ship as advanced as *Phoenix*… and while tavalai Fleet had a few ships that came close, they weren't sharing any of those with State Department.

If the descender went to the vault with only Po'koo at the controls, the Major and her team would be in terrible danger, their only access and escape piloted by someone who they absolutely could not trust, and was probably now working for someone else entirely. And with State Department monitoring all communications from here, the Major would have no idea that Tif was not aboard.

Tif extended a trembling hand, and pointed a claw at the descender beyond the window. "I must be on that ship!" she insisted.

"No," said the smug tavalai, as the guards at his sides readied weapons. *"You must not."*

Trace crouched low amidst cargo pallets in the loading warehouse, and listened to the voices of tavalai State Department workers in light environment suits.   It was an inspection team, though she could not see them, nor had any need to.   Her armour suit's highest sensitivity audio settings could calculate the number of people making noise in an enclosed space, and she did not need to risk exposing herself.   Three tavalai, the suit calculated now, walking back through the extended cargo arm to the descender's lower holds.

The State Department base on Chara was not heavily manned, and the warehouse pallets were automated on light wheels. Most of the cargo on its way down to the vault would originate from elsewhere, while Chara remained on standby only for necessary emergency supplies.   Ninety percent of Chara was a privately run gas refinery, the costs of producing many kinds of heavily used industrial gasses being cheaper here for reasons that Trace was neither business person nor chemist enough to understand.   State Department's portion of Chara was mostly a logistics hub for in and out-bound traffic, and produced very little.   Its primary use was that equipment was more accessible here than it was in orbit, where transit times got dangerously long for a secure facility that required rapid response in the event of emergencies.   And for the vault in particular, Chara's role prevented any foreign vessel from attempting a direct landing, since no one was entirely sure where the vault actually was.

The voices faded, and Trace extended a shoulder antenna, its camera projecting an image onto her faceplate.   Across the steel floor, stacked with containers, she could see the side-access to the main cargo arm.   Past the projected image, in direct line-of-sight, was Staff Sergeant Kono, also on a knee in a doorway.   They waited a minute, then Kono indicated something moving behind her.

Trace redirected her camera antenna, and saw a single tavalai walking the cargo arm.   He arrived at the access door, opened it fully, and made a quick gesture without really looking inside, then went back the way he'd come.   A descender crewman, telling them the way was clear.

Kono gave her a 'hold' signal, and looked aside at Chenkov, somewhere out of sight past the doorway.   He'd brought various items of Styx's technology along, and had tested them beforehand on sample tavalai network tech provided by *Makimakala*.   State Department networks should have been nearly impossible to hack, but Kono's relayed hand signal told her that Chenkov was already in, and had deactivated the security cameras and other monitors on this level.   He'd assured them that the HQ controllers would never notice.   Trace was wary of *Phoenix* techs becoming overconfident with their magical new abilities, but Chenkov insisted that this level of technology was for Styx like playing a child's game.   Trace had seen a hacksaw drone struggling with a child's game, and thought that familiarity and experience counted for a lot too, surely.

Kono gave her the 'go' signal, and Trace got up, and walked as silently as stealth mode would allow.   She tried not to think of all the jokes that marines made about stealth mode, which in reality was no stealthier than walking on a steel floor with bells on your feet. One artistic marine in the war had even illustrated a series of popular cartoons called 'Stealth Mode Sam', about a marine trying to get away with stealthy things in his half-tonne armour suit, like sneaking out of a girl's bedroom after her husband came home early, or trying to duck out the back of a restaurant to escape a terrible date, with disastrous results.   Marines who'd tried to actually use stealth mode in combat found those cartoons funny to a degree that civilians usually failed to grasp, not understanding that the humour was just what happened when you applied hindsight to terror.

Trace peered into the cargo access arm, rows of big rubber wheels on the floor where pallets would roll, its terminal-end opening into a wide warehouse with even more pallets, with an opposite side-access allowing personnel from the control terminal to take that shortcut.   She waved to Kono behind, and he came as quietly as possible, then the others, single file.   The kid had a little trouble squeezing his wide legs through the doorway, forcing him into a dainty tiptoe.   When Zale arrived, she displaced and let him guard their rear on the way in.

The descender's main cargo holds were barely half the size of the lander they'd arrived on, squeezed between an extra-thick, double-layered hull, and a heavy coolant system.   Instead of a quad-partition, the descender only had two holds.   Secured to the wall of the central partition, amidst the securing frames for larger cargoes, was a cylindrical canister.   Aristan, in his light environment suit and hooded jacket, was now examining it.

"Going to be a tight squeeze," Kono observed.   That canister was the entire reason for this mission.   A Fleet descender to the vault would send the empty canister inside, wait until it passed the vault's security checks, had the requested item deposited inside, and was then returned.   Canisters had no lifesupport, and were certainly not designed to hold people, yet Aristan was going to be locked inside this one while it passed through the vault's doors.

"There is enough space for perhaps twenty minutes of air," Aristan observed.

"Doesn't look like ten minutes," said Rael, peering inside. "Looks tough though.   This is all ceramics, temperature and pressure resistant, should stay cool."

"Twenty minutes at a lowered rate of respiration," Aristan insisted.   Servos whined as the descender's outer cargo doors began to close.   *"Transfer does not take longer than ten minutes."*

"I always bet on them taking longer than advertised," said Trace.   "You *will* have to hold your breath."

"So long as my total enclosed period does not exceed forty minutes, there is no danger," the parren said confidently.

"You could take something to read," Kumar suggested.

Aristan actually smiled.   *"Perhaps."*

The outer doors closed with a thump and clang of locking mechanisms.   Then came a hiss, as the Kamala atmosphere was sucked through the hold filters, with oxygen and nitrogen pumped in. Trace's suit readout registered O2 increase of a fractional percent.   A hold this large wasn't going to be breathable for a while.

Between the big arms of the cargo floor supports, Rolonde and Terez were checking out the rigging on a number of large sized acceleration slings. There were no seating posts in most cargo holds, so these slings would be the only thing keeping them from bouncing off the walls when the flight got bumpy. All the slings were kaal-sized, which made sense on a kaal-made descender, where kaal crew would often ride a descent down in cargo in case the coolant systems started overloading, or the airlocks needed manual help — the mission briefing had alerted them to all these possibilities. It also meant that the slings were going to fit marines in armour without breaking, in a happy coincidence of size requirements.

Behind facemask and goggles, Chenkov sat against the partition wall beside his equipment bag, AR glasses under the goggles and manipulating icons in the air before him. Trace took a knee beside him.

"Chenk, anything from the cockpit?"

"No Major, I don't have access to any ship system. I think that's probably smart, State Department could monitor all of it." Trace nodded, hoping Tif had things in good order up there. Surely if there was an issue, she'd come down in person to talk to them. And tavalai Fleet themselves had vouched for the descender company and its leader and pilot, the kaal Po'koo. But there was nothing she could do about it now anyway. "Major, are you sure I won't need a weapon in the vault?"

He sounded anxious, which was understandable. Assaulting the vault was going to be quite a thing for marines, let alone for a *Phoenix* spacer tech. "You won't have time for a weapon," Trace told him. "You'll need all your attention on your gear. I'll need a constant feed of whatever you can tell me, and we'll have security systems trying to lock us down — I want a full-time code breaker doing only that."

"Yes Major."

She gave a gentle touch at his shoulder, careful in her armour. "Don't worry Chenk, if there's one thing Command Squad have a lot of experience at, it's keeping spacers safe in ground combat. You're the most important person here."

Chenkov grinned nervously, and glanced at Aristan, now standing in the canister as he examined its dimensions. "What about him?"

"Useful and important are two different things," Trace said blandly. "You have everything you need?"

"Yes Major. Snug as a bug."

"Good, we'll get your sling ready, we should be leaving in less than twenty. Just keep your eyes on the screens."

She got up and headed for the slings, thankful that of the two most recommended of *Phoenix*'s techs for this mission, she'd got the nice one.

For once, Erik was too preoccupied and furious to be bothered feeling traumatised in the aftermath of almost being killed. He paced in the emergency ward between shouting matches with Tsubarata officialdom, and kept an eye on Private Ito, who sat on his bunk in defiance of instructions to lie down, his arm wrapped in nano-solution bandage that Doc Suelo informed them on uplink from *Phoenix* would probably be fine used on a human. But State Department had ordered *Phoenix* access to the Tsubarata sealed, so neither Suelo nor one of his corpsmen could come and check on Ito to be sure, nor could Ito return to *Phoenix*, as all of Erik's team were now confined to this otherwise empty medbay.

"State Department tried to assassinate us!" Erik shouted at the next tavalai bureaucrat to come and reason with them. Tsubarata officialdom seemed alarmed at events, and were surely skeptical of State Department themselves, given events. If ever there was a time when shouting at tavalai might achieve something, it was now. "I don't care that it was parren doing the shooting — parren saw us with Aristan and there's no shortage of parren who'd like to kill Aristan's friends if State Department arranges the opportunity! So

324

why is it *us* who are locked up, and not every fucking State Department administrator on this facility?"

Beyond the opening and closing doors to the medbay, Erik could hear many shouting voices in the hallway. There were tavalai guards on that door, and more at the entrance to this particular ward, but Erik thought that this time, they might be present as much to protect the humans as in fear of them. Clearly the entire Tsubarata was in uproar. Erik did not know how many other individuals had been hit in the crossfire, but he thought quite a few. And if Styx hadn't spotted the ambush as early as she had, it would have been most of the humans as well.

"I can assure you we are looking into all eventualities," the tavalai said via translator speaker, with a calming gesture of two webbed hands. Erik thought it an irony of the situation that the only tavalai who spoke English here were all their enemies. These Tsubarata bureaucrats might speak other alien tongues, but with humanity missing from these parts for a millennia, English had not been anyone's priority for a long time.

"State Department did not want me to give that speech!" Erik laid it out for the bureaucrat, just in case it wasn't crystal clear already. "They thought the speech was going to dig up some old dirt on them, and lay it out in front of all tavalai, and tavalai Fleet in particular, and destabilise their entire arrangement here."

The tavalai bureaucrat blinked. *"Was it?"*

"Well now you may never know!" Erik retorted.

They were interrupted by several sulik, clad in the odd collar and tunic of their kind that embraced the base of long necks, and headwear with high-tech eyepieces. These approached in that half-flowing, half-jittery manner of their kind, like big, nervous birds, their little hands and skinny arms fidgeting with IDs and credentials, and a bound up bit of cloth. They skittered past Erik with small, muttered screeches and cackling that the translators were somehow not catching.

"Sulik have many languages the translators are not equipped for," the tavalai explained. *"These must be lower functionaries — I apologise, I do not know how they were allowed in."*

The sulik headed for Private Ito's bed, and Gunnery Sergeant Brice stepped coolly before them, as the tavalai beckoned to the security guards. "No wait," said Erik, as the sulik ignored Ito and Brice, and went instead to Private Cruze, seated on the end of a bunk beside Lieutenant Alomaim. "It's okay."

The sulik made a small bobbing gesture, and presented Cruze with the bound cloth. It unfolded to make a sulik collar, with a gemstone button at the front, and silken decoration tracing through the fabric with exquisite detail. Cruze looked it over, puzzled.

"A gift," said the tavalai with surprise. *"The collar denotes an informal rank. It makes one an honorary sulik, with privileges in sulik society. Common enough among sulik, but very rare to be granted to aliens."*

Of course, Erik thought as he realised. "Ambassador Tua, everyone saw him rescued?"

"The shooting was captured on camera," the tavalai confirmed. *"Tsubarata sulik saw your Private risk his life to save their ambassador. Soon all sulik will see, when the vision reaches their worlds."*

"Hey, we asked after him before!" Cruze called. "No one could tell us anything, is he okay?"

"I believe he lives," said the tavalai. *"That is all I know. I will have you informed if his condition changes, so be thankful if you do not hear more."*

"Are you supposed to put that on?" Alomaim asked, looking curiously at the collar. He gestured to the sulik, asking the question with his hands. There followed much bobbing and cackling, and general agreement. The neck hole was big enough that Cruze simply placed it over his head, and let it rest upon his shoulders, button at his collar.

"Looks good, Fuzz," said Ito from his bed.

Cruze looked very pleased. "Thanks Scratchy." And stood, extending his hand to the sulik. "Here, human-style. Like this, it's called a handshake. Thank you."

The sulik complied, awkwardly, and with more bobbing, cackling and screeching, backed away and retreated from the ward.

Erik came to take a closer look at the collar. "Good job, Private," he said. "Hero of the sulik. You know, I don't think humanity's ever had formal relations with the sulik — they're too close to the tavalai, we never had a chance. Which could make what you did the single most important event in human-sulik relations. Ever."

"I just hope the poor guy's okay," said Cruze, gazing down at his prize. "I mean, they're real weird, but Tua seems like a nice guy."

"Captain," came Styx's voice on coms. *"I have received a troubling transmission from Ensign Uno. It is my first communication with him since I assisted him in the infiltration of State Department Head Quarters, since then a direct line of communications has been too hazardous. His message indicated that an identification request was received from Chara, and an affirmative reply was sent. Hiro says that State Department was unaware of his infiltration at the time, and remains unaware that this message was either received or replied to."*

Erik exhaled hard in relief, and gave a little clenched fist at his marines. It seemed that Styx was sharing this transmission with them also, because they replied in kind, though not too obviously, given the observation here. Again the medbay doors opened, and more tavalai marched in. *"So why is the message troubling, Styx?"* Erik formulated in silent reply.

"Captain Debogande!" called the new tavalai arrival, striding into the room. It was Jelidanatagani — Erik was becoming that much better at identifying tavalai on sight, and he was nearly certain of it. With her were four big security guards — unarmed, Erik was pleased to see. Only the Tsubarata guards were allowed weapons around the humans. Clearly some in the Tsubarata shared Erik's assessment of responsibility for the attack. "We have your man. Your infiltrator, the one we have registered on file as Ensign Uno. He was captured sneaking about our Head Quarters, and we are currently examining our systems to see what he was successful in stealing, little enough chance humans would have of that, given your pathetic indigenous systems technology."

"What is she doing here?" Erik asked the senior Tsubarata guard, strolling to the new arrival with a hostile swagger to hide his dismay. He did not need to hear the last part of Styx's message — he could guess. "How does she just get to walk in and out of here whenever she likes, given she probably gave the assassination order herself?"

"She does not have that authority," the tavalai said cautiously, as several other guards shifted position. *"She should leave, by order of Tsubarata Central."*

"I certainly do have that authority!" Jeli retorted. "By virtue of the statutes that place State Department in central authority to all alien relations! And I can tell you, Captain Debogande..."

"If she has no authority to be here," Erik demanded of the guards, "then make her leave, or I will!"

"...that your intruder will be questioned by our best interrogators!" Jeli continued over his interruption. "I can assure you that the soft restrictions on those interrogations do not apply to State Department methods where State Department secrets are concerned! We will find out exactly what you're up to, in your games with our traitors in Fleet, and then..."

Erik punched her in the jaw. She dropped hard, and then the State Department guards leaped on him, and his marines on the guards, and then it was on, bodies rolling and fists flying. Tavalai security at close range were powerful, but Erik was no lightweight and managed to flip one into a bunk frame, and land a good blow before another crashed into him. That one rolled and pinned him with augmented strength, but then Alomaim landed on that one's back, applying full leverage to twist an arm, with a crunch as the tavalai's shoulder separated.

Erik scrambled up, found Sergeant Brice struggling in the grip of a larger tavalai and swung at that guard's head with a crunch that hurt his knuckles, and gave Brice the opening she needed to flip her opponent, lock out his arm and kick him in the jaw until he stopped moving.

And then the Tsubarata security were stepping in, not striking or defending their fellow tavalai, but holding their weapons crosswise in neutrality, and gesturing the humans to move back before they started using the pointy end. "Back!" Erik shouted. "That's enough, everyone back!" As Lieutenant Alomaim echoed his words, for anyone hard of hearing.

The marines all moved back, leaving two of the four guards unconscious on the ground, one now groaning as he slowly woke, and the third struggling with his dislocated shoulder. Add to that the unconscious Ambassador Jeli, and it left only one of the five State Department visitors still in any shape to walk out unassisted. The Tsubarata guards looked warily impressed.

Of the humans, Brice had a sore rib that Erik suspected might be broken, given she was even indicating it. Alomaim had a bloody nose, but the rest was all scrapes and bruises. Erik handed Alomaim a handkerchief for his nose. Alomaim repressed a grin, a rare expression for him, and gave Erik his own handkerchief, pointing to Erik's left eye. Erik felt, and sure enough there was swelling from eyebrow to temple, and some blood. He hadn't even noticed, just a dull throbbing.

"Sir, you look like a marine," said Alomaim with appreciation.

"You mean I'm a mess," said Erik, looking over his once-perfect dress uniform, stained with Tua's blood and now with drops of his own.

"Yes sir."

"Captain hit a girl," Cruze observed. Erik noted he'd had the presence of mind to remove his new gift before joining the fight, and so much for a marine's affectation of disinterest in shiny things.

"That one doesn't count," Erik snorted. "The Major might give me a lecture about holding my temper, though."

"The Major will be fucking thrilled," Brice corrected, gingerly feeling her ribs. No more Mr Nice Guy, she meant. Erik thought she might be right.

More tavalai were entering, somewhat alarmed but with no levelled weapons, so Erik guessed the local guards had told everyone the score. Yet another senior bureaucrat approached, a little more cautiously than the others. *"What happened?"* she asked.

"This one," said Erik, pointing at the unconscious ambassador, now attended by others trying to wake her, "came in here making threats. We are *UFS Phoenix*. We do not take State Department threats."

"Yes," said the bureaucrat, looking around. None of the guards who'd seen events challenged Erik's statement. Unpopular with more than just tavalai Fleet, Erik thought.

"State Department has no authority to be here," Erik pressed further. "Under the circumstances, State Department has no authority over *Phoenix*. Tsubarata Central must take full authority. State Department has attempted the assassination of *Phoenix*'s Captain. Given *Phoenix*'s poor situation with human Fleet, this raises the possibility of collaboration between human Fleet, and State Department. Treason, against tavalai interests."

The bureaucrat considered that, possibly in silent consultation on uplinks with others. Then she clapped her hands at the guards and others, clustered about the fallen and injured State Department tavalai, and all began moving to the exits. For the ambassador, the only one who had not yet reawoken, a stretcher was brought.

"There will be separation between State Department and UFS Phoenix," the bureaucrat confirmed. *"Tsubarata Central now has authority in the case of your ship, and your crew. You have been given a pond, Captain Debogande. Do not mistake it for an ocean."*

"A wise decision," Erik agreed. "*Phoenix* has no objection to Tsubarata authority." The bureaucrat gave him a wary look, and moved off to supervise the undignified State Department withdrawal.

Erik watched them leave, then waved his crew back to Private Ito's bed. Ito was still in it, having been unable to unhook himself from all the tubes and cords in time to make a difference. "Next time give me warning," he told them all, reattaching the one cord he'd managed to pull in his efforts to get into the fight.

Erik gathered them about Ito's bed, tapping behind his ear, a sign to uplink. *"Okay,"* he formulated silently, unheard by anyone else in the room. *"They've got Hiro. Tavalai don't torture much, but State Department might make a special exception in his case. Phoenix, do you hear?"*

"We hear, Captain," came Shahaim's reply. *"It doesn't sound like we can help, we're all locked down here. Tsubarata isn't allowing anyone on or off, unless Human Quarter can say otherwise?"*

"Human Quarter is also locked down," came Lieutenant Jalawi's reply. He was in command of *Phoenix*'s presence in the Tsubarata's Human Quarter, with Alomaim away. *"From what they're telling us, it's not just a State Department decision — it's all the Tsubarata. They don't want humans moving around."*

"Captain, Ensign Uno knows a lot of highly classified information about Phoenix's larger mission," Styx interjected, pointing out the obvious. *"This information cannot be allowed to fall into State Department hands."*

Dammit Hiro, Erik thought darkly. Even Hiro wasn't infallible, evidently. Probably he'd been taking risks to ensure the most important part of the mission — the clearance of the descender on Chara — went through okay. But now, they were stuck with this.

"Captain," Styx continued. *"Hiro had two of my surveillance bugs in his presence. Each is lethally equipped. I can regain contact with them in short bursts. The possibility of this data leak can be neutralised."*

Erik exhaled hard. *"Styx, I think you know Phoenix quite well by now. I think you know what I'll say."*

A brief silence from Styx. *"I had thought to attempt reason."*

"I know you have your own reasons to be concerned for the success of this mission," Erik formulated with what he hoped was a firm tone. *"But if you wish to remain a valued member of this crew, you will obey orders and assist in Hiro's recovery another way."*

"Sir, recovery?" Alomaim asked, his dark eyes serious on the other side of Ito's bed, Erik's handkerchief pressed to his bloody nose. *"We can't move anyone from Phoenix or Human Quarter."*

"We are not in *Phoenix or Human Quarter,"* Erik replied with meaning. Alomaim's eyes widened. *"And now we've gotten*

State Department off our back — Tsubarata Central won't allow them anywhere near us after that little punchup." New understanding dawned in the marines' eyes, as they fully grasped the reason why their usually disciplined Captain had started throwing punches at civvies. "Styx, we're going to need a distraction. It's chaos here at the moment, it shouldn't take much. We have to think of a way to get out of here without being stopped, and into the Tsubarata corridors without being identified."

"Sir," Alomaim persisted, "with Scratchy injured there's just four of us. And with all respect, Captain, you're not marine-trained. And we have no weapons."

"Tsubarata HQ shares a wall with only one other species' Quarter," Erik told him.

Alomaim's eyes widened further. "The krim!"

Erik nodded. "And Styx was even hacking Tsubarata blueprints on their floorplans the other day, weren't you Styx? Just in case we needed the extra access. And she thinks there might still be weapons in the Krim Quarter. Old krim weapons, that they smuggled into their Quarter to defend in case of attack, against all Tsubarata rules. Don't you Styx?"

Wide eyes from all the marines now. Save for Ito, who looked frustrated beyond words. "No way you do this without me," he insisted. "No way."

"Quiet, Scratchy," said Sergeant Brice.

"Styx?" Erik persisted, after the silence lingered.

"This policy of sharing all of my information with humans is coming to be bothersome," Styx complained.

CHAPTER 23

Trace swung in the acceleration sling as thrust rocked and bounced the weight of her suit. Descent into Kamala's atmosphere was a simple thing from a passenger's perspective, with nothing like as many Gs as a typical ride, either from acceleration on ascent, or deceleration on the way down. Instead there was a simple light thrust and a lot of bouncing. She understood that heavy descenders could not just fall free on the way down, as excessive velocity with a sphere into super-pressurised atmosphere would create an enormous low-pressure airpocket in their wake, and destabilise them to the point of tumbling.

She found it somewhat annoying that of all the circumstances over which she'd established some degree of mental mastery, atmospheric flight was not one of them. The crazy, crushing Gs of FTL space combat were disturbingly difficult to adjust to, but at least they were somewhat consistent and predictable once you did become familiar with them. But atmospheric turbulence was random, and its sudden bumps and lurches reminded her of the frantic evasive manoeuvres a starship pilot made when under fire — always the least pleasant part of that ride. That those bumps and lurches were now being caused by an atmosphere growing steadily thick enough to crush a regular ship like a can, and hot enough to melt lead, did not add to her comfort level. Human brains were a mass of impulsive triggers, and not all hardwired biological instincts, like the lurch of fear at the sensation of falling or sudden, unexplained motion, could be overcome by mere mortals who lacked the time to spend their entire lives in meditation. Trace wondered how the kid was faring, and if he processed such sensations as fear, or merely as experience.

She went through her usual routine of slow breathing and inward focus, and called up the map of the vault that tavalai Fleet had provided. It was precisely accurate only near the main entrance — the rest became increasingly vague as it went on, though Admiral Janik had insisted that the overall structure was correct. All of it was underground, burrowed into hot rock with only its main, blast-resistant airlock above. That airlock was angled on a downward slope, and had two main parts — the huge, vehicle-entry triple-doored structure that was big enough to admit a shuttle if one had been able to survive the descent, and the smaller, personnel airlock, mounted within a long, reinforced tube alongside the larger entry.

There was no special key or code required to open those doors — anyone in the security-atrium behind could do it, with access to the controls. Given that the guards were all hive-mind sard, by millennia-long arrangement, State Department probably figured that giving one sard the door code was technically the same thing as giving all of them the code. The security-atrium was a small room with a few guards, which tavalai Fleet could swear to because of the few of them who'd been allowed to progress at least that far over the millennia. Behind it was another heavy-security airlock, so that even should the atrium be taken, access further in could be blocked for a time at least. Trace could see the logic, but wasn't sure of its application. Another secure door there prevented attackers from moving in, but also defenders from moving up and displacing the attackers. Behind those doors, attackers could gain a foothold, and consolidate for the next push.

"Chenkov, it's the Major," she said on near-coms. "Any communication yet from the bridge?"

"No Major, just the flight profile. Nothing more." Up on Chara, any internal communications could be monitored by State Department. Down in the atmosphere, powerful transmissions were required to be heard from Chara at all, thanks to the interference of hot gas and electrical storms. But then, as Chenkov had volunteered, it was quite possible that that last physical inspection had planted a listening device aboard. If State Department figured there was something going wrong with one of the descenders, then Kamala's atmosphere was not thick enough to stop specific guided munitions, and there were several State Department-aligned vessels in close orbit at all times that could deliver them, breaking State Department's usual ban on armed ships. This big hunk of metal,

with all its limitations of manoeuvre, had no chance of dodging those once fired.

Heavy descenders had no windows. State Department did not just send a location code to the descender's navcomp — they transmitted a code that effectively enslaved the navcomp into flying only the course that State Department wished. The descender flew an unpredictable route to the point of descent — in this case it had lasted nearly an hour — with many twists and turns thrown in. Without windows, pilots could not even get a visual fix off stars, and Kamala had no visible surface features. Any attempt to use external cameras for star-fixes would also be reported to State Department upon return to Chara on the flight back, as the navcomp code also monitored all internal systems. As a result, descender crews had no idea where they were when descent began. Even personal or improvised independent GPS readers would not work, because alone of nearly every inhabited world in all tavalai space, Kamala had no established GPS network. Beneath these clouds, everyone was blind.

Trace's flight profile transmission showed a little less than twenty-five minutes until arrival — a long time to cover just a thirty kilometre descent, but speeds were limited to an average of a hundred kilometres an hour for safety. "Twenty minutes people," she told her team. "All minds on the job, nearly there."

The rumbling of thrust was changing pitch now, thrust-pressure dramatically shifting as the atmosphere thickened. From the spaceship hull, amidst the rumbling and shaking, came an unnerving screech and groan. In spaceship combat, Trace was usually dissatisfied with the limited data-feed that marines received of what was going on outside. In this instance, she was quite happy to remain ignorant.

The groundcar zoomed out of the tunnel and along the elevated expressway. The road lay upon the lower slope of a tall, red-rock mesa, looming above this part of sprawling Gamesh in sheer cliffs. Dale's left was the city, an unplanned, teeming mess of buildings until the next high mesa, looming in the distance. Towers sailed past, then expressway exits, the automated controls sitting on what he reckoned was 150 kilometres an hour, when translated from tavalai figures.

"They'll be tracking us," said Petty Officer Kadi with certainty from the opposite seat, having squeezed up there past Sergeant Forrest when Forrest had conceded that Kadi's need of personal space was more important. "They just need to track back to the mansion, it's a separate State Department grid but they can track where this vehicle entered the main city grid, and guess which is us. I reckon they'll be on us in a couple of minutes."

"I think it will take longer," came Jokono's fatherly advice from another part of Gamesh. *"Bureaucratic inertia matters enormously in security concerns, and State Department have demonstrated that they don't play well with others. They will be reluctant to admit what has just happened, and will try to find us themselves."*

"Yeah but that's not going to work!" Kadi exclaimed, excitably. "They can't run the city traffic grid themselves..."

"Yes of course," Jokono said patiently, *"but by the time they figure that out, we will be further away. In the meantime, you need to switch cars. There is an underground carpark ahead, I have stolen two vehicles so you can split and divide their attentions, if they manage to trace you past this car change."*

"And then what?" Forrest said tersely from the crowded rear seat. "We just drive around the city hoping they don't find us?"

"If necessary, yes," said Jokono. *"They have no idea which messages we've been intercepting on their dish, and will remain ignorant until they recover that encryption module. Once they get it, they'll learn everything, and destroying it will be nearly as good for them because it's the only thing keeping me locked into their communications right now. If it goes, they regain control of their systems and find everything."*

"And once they figure we were talking to Chara, they call up Chara control and tell them to shoot down the Major's descender," Dale muttered.

"What if they guess?" Milek asked, pressed against a door and clearly uncomfortable with this human proximity. *"What else could be worth this much trouble from their enemies, except the vault?"*

"Yeah, well they're not going to shoot down a Fleet-registered descender without proof," said Dale, as the vehicle took an off-ramp on automatic, slowing to match speeds with the car in front. "We can't worry about it — our mission is to keep that module out of State Department hands for the next few hours. After that they can have it or destroy it, because the Major will have succeeded and it won't matter." Or she'd have failed and died. But Dale wasn't prepared to countenance that, and besides, betting against Major Thakur was unwise.

The off-ramp wound down the mesa-side, past forests of dusty apartment towers, then into dark tunnels through shopping complex basements. Again the car changed lanes, took an exit out of the developing highway-trench, then slowed onto an off-ramp and around the back of the shopping complex, joining other cars in a trundling queue for the carpark.

"Great, could grab a few groceries while we're here," said Tong, peering out at the dull concrete monster-building above the spaghetti-sprawl of highways.

"I used to snatch wallets in places like this," Reddy remarked. "Good times."

"The pride of the marine corps," his Sergeant said drily.

"And I'd have snatched your wallet first, Sarge."

"You stole?" Milek asked, looking at him coldly. *"Why were you not punished?"*

"I was," Reddy retorted. "They sent me here." Forrest grinned. "Parren don't give dumb kids a chance at military redemption?"

"Redemption, yes," said Milek, just as coldly. *"Sharp steel will redeem."*

Reddy looked dubious. "Yeah? How?"

"He means suicide, Spots," said Dale, as the car pulled onto the carpark ramp. "Dumb parren kids are given a blade and told to kill themselves."

Reddy blinked. "Bit harsh," he offered. Milek looked away in disgust.

The carpark was very low-tech, as with so many things in Gamesh. Fancy human cities had automated car stackers that used a fraction of the space, but Gamesh built big and dumb with concrete and steel. There were few planning and building regulations on Gamesh, Dale reckoned, and no bureaucrats telling developers to fix their mess. Superficially, he liked the idea, and he'd always felt the biggest human cities fake and overpriced. But these ugly places reminded him too much of his childhood on Kosmima, a place he'd been only too happy to escape from, with its worst of both worlds combination of petty bureaucracy and soulless development.

"These two vehicles here at the end," said Jokono as the car crawled down rows of parked vehicles. Two cars flashed their lights, and their own vehicle came to a halt.

Dale looked around, and found this corner of the carpark relatively deserted and dimly lit. "Okay, make it fast," he said. "Woody and Tricks, you guys are the decoy. Everyone else with me."

Forrest looked as though he'd like to argue, but didn't, as they opened doors and moved low and quickly to the waiting cars. It only took one person to occupy a decoy car, but Dale wasn't going to send anyone out alone. Forrest was the obvious choice to lead it, being the most experienced marine besides himself, while Tong was resourceful and reliable. Reddy was perhaps more brilliant, but was also prone to lapses, and Dale preferred him near. Kadi carried the encryption module, and was thus the most important of them all, but needed protection, while Milek could be useful in a fight, but could certainly not be left unsupervised.

The four of them climbed quickly into one car, Forrest and Tong in the other, and Dale found all dash lights alive, the car they'd left already departing as Jokono sent it elsewhere — another decoy option.   Dale gave his rifle for Kadi to hold, and pressed a few buttons to get an idea where the manual-to-auto shutoff was...

"There," said Kadi, pointing with a tech-geek's impatience, "on the side. No, not that one, *that* one. Now calibrate the HUD... no, that's not it..."

"Everyone get down!" Reddy said harshly, and they all ducked low in their seats.

"What is it Spots?" asked Dale, collecting his rifle from Kadi.

"It's a fucking drone, it's come right into the carpark."

"Can you get me a visual?"

"Yeah, hang on."   Dale blinked on his glasses icon, and got a feed from Reddy's own glasses, as the Private took them off and held them above his chairback, looking out the rear window.   A blur of motion, then it came clear as Reddy braced his hand on the chair.

Then Dale saw it — a four-poster with turbofans, top-mounted guidance and an underside slung cannon, sidling down amongst the cars as a few pedestrians stared, used their recording devices, or scuttled away in fear.   Gamesh employed cops to walk the beat and do bureaucracy, but in a free-city no one expected the cops to do more than the bare minimum.   Despite the laissez-faire attitude to crime, there was a reason criminality never rose beyond a certain level in Gamesh, and that reason was the Gamesh Rapid Response Authority.   They were largely automated, and highly lethal, and the thing about a city where the law failed to prosecute many criminals was that the law was equally reluctant to prosecute many Rapid Responsers who killed criminals in the line of duty. That most of the Rapid Responsers doing the shooting were non-sentient AI made the prospect of prosecution doubly difficult.

Many Gamesh citizens who got in the way of organised crime went missing, but those organised criminals who 'disappeared' too many citizens then also went missing, or got mown down by heavy weaponry in mysterious ambushes, sometimes along with their entire syndicates.   The most successful organised criminals, Jokono's intel briefings had confirmed, were those that learned to walk the line between too little criminality, and too much, because common knowledge said that when Rapid Response came looking for you, they didn't bring handcuffs, just bullets.

"It's getting closer," Reddy said tersely. "If it's got IR it'll probably see that there are people in these two cars, and will wonder why we're hiding."

"Yeah, but it's looking for the car we just left," Kadi retorted. "It might just skate right by."

Dale checked his rifle, wishing he had his familiar light rifle. Or a full armour suit and a Koshaim-20, but that would have been a curse in this small seat. "If it starts shooting on top of us," he said, "then we're screwed. It won't miss at that range, and this car won't stop shit." He'd had to take them all through those basics before the mission, since operating on stations, none of them had ever gotten into firefights on the ground before. Basics like 'don't believe those stupid action movies you're always watching — hiding behind a groundcar in a firefight is like hiding behind a box of tissues'. "Kadi, can you take control of it?"

"Um… it's remotely piloted and on a hair-trigger," said Kadi. "At this range it's too dangerous — it takes a couple of seconds and if it fires first…"

"Yeah, got it," said Dale. On his glasses, the drone was now within thirty metres, weapons and scanners swinging this way and that.

"I will distract it," said Milek. *"I will draw its attention, and Kadi will assume control while it pursues me."*

Twenty-five metres. "Good, go!" said Dale. "Once we've got control, we'll pick you up."

"I may not survive, you cannot wait for me."

"Hey, you listen to me Mystery Boy," Dale retorted. "You die needlessly, you endanger the mission. Now go."

Milek gave him a puzzled stare with indigo eyes, then opened the door a little and slid out like water. Kadi fumbled with his directional handheld whatever-it-was.

"Is that guy growing on you LT?" Reddy wondered. Dale didn't reply. He'd fought sard before, and even some tavalai formations, that seemed convinced that success in battle was won more by dying than by winning. As an old Earth general had once said, you didn't win wars by dying for your cause — you won them by making your enemy die for *his*.

Fifteen metres. From between some parked cars alongside, Dale glimpsed a faint movement, then saw something fly toward the drone. The object hit, with a faint metallic ping. The drone stopped, weapon swinging that way.

"Go Kadi," said Dale, and Kadi aimed his handheld through the windows and pressed something. The drone reacted as though stung, lurching backward and swinging side to side. Then re-aimed at where Milek had been, and opened fire. Car windows exploded and holes punched in doors. Then the shooting stopped.

"Got him!" Kadi said breathlessly. "He doesn't like it, but I got him!"

"Good, let's go." Dale put the car on manual, reversed hard, then accelerated to the end of the parking row, slowing as he saw Milek running his way. And saw another drone ahead, approaching fast. "One more ahead!"

"I can't do two at once!" Kadi yelped, as Dale reversed hard behind a support pillar. The drone opened fire, sending pieces of pillar concrete flying, then several loud smacks of bullets impacting the car. Then the first drone was firing on the second, sending it skittering sideways, then half-bouncing off a wall, turbines protected within thick nacelles. It fired back at the first drone, and suddenly there was a two-way crossfire tearing through the carpark, holes exploding in concrete and pillars, parked cars torn and glass flying. The drone ahead took more hits, then its ammunition detonated with a flash that sent wreckage hailing across the carpark, and set another ten cars on fire.

A door opened and Milek slid in. Dale accelerated, saw in his rearview that Forrest was directly behind. He left the carpark into sunlight, wove past slower vehicles, then got caught up behind two very slow cars on the narrow exit back onto the highway. He swore, and ducked from side to side, but there was no way through.

"Hang on LT," said Kadi, aiming his directional controller. Suddenly the second of the two blocking cars accelerated, and hit the first from behind, pushing both forward at increasing speed. Both skidded aside as the off-ramp appeared, giving Dale a chance to gun the electric engine onto the highway, merging with and then overtaking traffic.

A glance in the rear mirror showed Reddy attending to Milek with concern. "Mystery Boy, you okay?"

"A few fragments," said Milek's translator, failing to capture the pain in his alien voice. *"It is nothing."*

"Bit of shrapnel in the side and arm," said Reddy. "If I can get this one bit out, the bleeding might stop."

"I need no pain medication," Milek snapped at Reddy's attempt to administer one.

"Shut the fuck up and take it," Dale told him, settling to match cruise speed with the surrounding traffic. "Woody, you guys okay?"

"We're fine LT," came Forrest's voice from the car behind. *"That was good work by you guys."*

"Joker," said Dale, "what can you see?"

"They will trace the vehicle swap," said Jokono with certainty. *"I can see a number of aerial and ground units on their way to your last location. I can misdirect them, but they are beginning to run counter-infiltration programs through their network in an attempt to find me."*

Thinking about the kind of software construct Jokono must be running to actively infiltrate and play with Gamesh network security like this made Dale's head hurt. Styx had built it, and Styx was a twenty five thousand year old sentient AI with an IQ beyond human ability to measure. That was enough for him. His primary concern was that Styx herself was not here to operate it.

"Right," said Dale. "They're going to trace two vehicles from the carpark, plus the third one we were in." He hadn't seen it leave, but obviously Jokono had sent it off through Gamesh's highways to serve as a further decoy. "Forrest, you gotta split, but don't go too far in case we need to rendezvous in a hurry. We just need to divide their attention for a while."

"Got it, I'll take the next exit left."

"Lieutenant," Jokono added, *"I'm not at all certain that ground vehicles will give us the time window that the Major requires for her mission. Cars are too easy to trace, and I cannot block their attempts to find you indefinitely."*

"You want us to get out of the car?"

"I believe it is necessary. They will be on the look out for further vehicle swaps, and my attempts to steal new vehicles may inadvertently lead them to that spot in advance of your arrival."

"Problem is, we don't have parren robes with us," Dale pointed out, steering them through a gentle bend as the highway left its trench and ran through an urban business district, tall buildings with lots of glass. "There's only a few hundred humans in Gamesh — we'll attract attention, and we couldn't hide our weapons."

"I can send you robes from here. Or Tooganam can. The package will be waiting for you, we can arrange the rendezvous."

"A rendezvous where?"

Tif sat in the enclosed room and fretted. She paced from wall to wall, and stretched her nervous limbs, and tried to control her tension. She'd always blamed kuhsi genetics for that, amongst *Phoenix* crew, but perhaps that was a lie. Perhaps it was just her, she thought. She'd have given anything to be more like the Major, able to wear her calm like a cloak, retaining focus and concentration in the face of great danger.

But then, the battle at the Tartarus had been perhaps the craziest fight anyone on *Phoenix* had ever been in. Fellow shuttle pilot Regan Jersey had been Tif's wingman for that adventure, and she'd insisted it was *easily* the most intense action she'd ever seen, which included many fights over nearly ten years of the Triumvirate War. And Tif had done so well there, she'd impressed even *Phoenix*'s lead shuttle pilot, Lieutenant Hausler, and earned an officer's rank where no other kuhsi had ever earned one before. No other non-human, in fact. Tif knew she functioned quite well when the dangerous things were actually happening.   It was just the waiting, and the worrying, that drove her crazy.

Something buzzed past, and her ear flicked in reflex.   The insects in her native Heshog Highlands were biters, and loved kuhsi ears, with the exposed veins beneath.   The joke elsewhere in Koth had been that you could tell a highlander from the involuntary ear-flick at the slightest buzzing sound...

And Tif paused.   Insects?   On Chara?   The carbon dioxide atmosphere outside was heaven for plants, but would kill an insect nearly as fast as a human.   And airtight habitats like Chara were swept regularly for insects, just as *Phoenix* underwent fumigation after every station call, just in case of stowaways.

Her gaze fell to the bare room's single piece of furniture — a small desk.   Upon it, a small insect crawled.   Like a fly.   And seemed to look at her, with all the animated enthusiasm of some children's character in one of Skah's kiddie movies.

Then her uplink crackled, and a voice spoke to her in Gharkhan — her second kuhsi tongue, but still far simpler for her than English.   *"Hello Tif.   This is Styx."*   Tif stared at the bug, trying to process what must be happening.   *"Please do not react, just take a seat and sit calmly.   This room is being watched."*

Right, thought Tif, steadying herself.   She took a seat at the table — technically the same furniture, as the two were welded together in the same base.   *"Those bugs have no transmitters,"* she formulated in reply.   *"How are you speaking to me?   And how is there a bug here?   Did the Major bring it?"*

"The Major has several of her own, but no.   This one was on you.   I apologise, you were not told."

Tif couldn't see how that mattered now.   *"Good.   Fine."*

"It lost contact with you for a moment, and had to crawl through the ventilation to reach you.   It has short range transmitters at difficult to monitor frequencies.   Spacer Chenkov had established a network parasite program while he was aboard Chara, it helped to manipulate local systems.   This bug gave me new access to that parasite program, and now I have patched in directly."

Directly? Styx was on *Phoenix*, and *Phoenix* was docked at the Tsubarata. From Kamala to the Tsubarata was between one and one-point-five seconds light, depending on their relative orbital positions. Currently, they were quite close — more like one-point-one seconds for Styx's transmissions to reach Chara. Possibly she was using *Phoenix*'s main transmitter, or perhaps she'd hijacked some other Tsubarata system… there were too many possibilities, when dealing with the many capabilities of Styx.

"You have direct access to Chara's systems?" Tif formulated.

"I do," said Styx. *"It gives me enough capability to help you, but far from enough to do what needs to be done myself."*

"Help me do what?"

"Obviously you have been removed from the Major's descender. This suggests a double-cross, perhaps a deliberate sabotage of the mission. We must correct this."

"How?"

"There are several more heavy descenders on Chara. Two are fully flight-ready. You must steal one of them."

Tif nearly laughed. It was all she could do to restrain her adrenaline-fuelled mirth. *"You're being ridiculous."*

"I am not. I suspect you have been removed from your descender because someone is going to abandon the Major, perhaps leave her trapped in the vault, perhaps intercept the descender on escape once she has acquired what she seeks. The possibilities are unknowable. With this reconnaissance bug, and my assistance, you will be able to move to a new descender. I can assist with pre-flight, and I can even be your co-pilot by remote for as long as atmospheric communications will allow. If you do not do this, it is almost certain that our mission will fail, and that the Major and her team will be either captured or killed. Second Lieutenant Tif. Will you comply?"

CHAPTER 24

The descender hit ground with a thump and crash of heavy legs, and Trace bounced in her sling. The roar of thrusters ceased, and she unzipped and rolled from the sling with a practised fall, as Command Squad plus Chenkov and Aristan did the same. They moved fast without need of instruction, detaching the delivery canister from its wall hold, helping Chenkov with his less easily portable gear, and checking the status of the hold-level airlock.

A coms uplink opened in Trace's ear, location local. She opened it, and heard a synthetic, translator-voice. *"Major Thakur, this is descender cockpit. We are down at the third vault pad. They are scanning us from secure door. No communications, as protocol."*

"Hello descender cockpit," Trace replied, running through a final suit pre-ops check. "Is this Second Lieutenant Tif?" Because she could not hear the physical voice on coms, just the mechanical-sounding translator.

"Second Lieutenant Tif is doing co-pilot work. We have engine issue on descent, co-pilot must watch and fix, while pilot runs main profile. We anticipate that welcome arm will be extended soon, you prepare to deliver canister."

"I understand, descender cockpit. We are preparing canister now, and establishing visual contact from main cargo airlock. I would like to speak to Second Lieutenant Tif, it will only take a moment."

"Second Lieutenant Tif is not available. One mistake in this atmosphere, we miss ascent, we lose engine thrust, we do anything wrong, we die. Do job, Major." The link ended with a click.

"Trouble?" Staff Sergeant Kono asked, watching with concern. They'd discussed this possibility — a double-cross, with Tif vulnerable and alone in the cockpit. But tavalai Fleet had recommended this operator, and his loyalties to tavalai Fleet in particular. Po'koo — and Tif guessed that was who she'd just been speaking to — was formerly of the kaal engineering corps, highly respected throughout the Spiral, and known for close links to kaal military, and thus to tavalai Fleet. His loyalty to the Fleet's causes, and to tavalai military causes, was guaranteed, they'd said. Supposedly, that had included this mission, and *Phoenix*'s crew.

"Can't do anything about it now," Trace replied, picking her way past cargo rails toward the airlock. "And he's right about this atmosphere — none of us can afford to waste a moment. We stay here too long, we're crushed."

At the airlock inner door, the marines had already placed the canister. Beside the doors, Corporal Rael was at the airlock controls, calling up a full-screen view of the scene outside. Peering over his shoulder, Trace saw that Kamala's surface did look quite literally like hell. The light was dark red, almost scorched, as though by flame. The ceramic-surfaced pad was black, and shimmered with waves of heat that reminded Trace of the view across a bank of enormous cookers in the kitchen of a big Chinese restaurant. Not far away was the edge of the pad, and a great, black, circular door, set into blasted red stone. The door was laid back on a shallow angle, and was accompanied by a second, smaller door facing the pad. Those were ceramic alloys, to survive this constant temperature and pressure in working order... but even so, Trace suspected they'd have to be replaced every few years. God only knew how they'd constructed the landing pad.

"Yeah, I'm reading their scan," said Rael, voice muffled within his lowered visor. The hold had oxygen and pressure now, but they'd kept faceplates down on descent, in case of a failure. "It's laser-scan, we've no idea what's passing back and forth. I hope Tif's on the job up there."

Trace refrained from biting her lip, thinking hard. She glanced at the canister, where Aristan was removing his excess outer clothing, stripping down to a skinsuit that revealed a lean and muscular alien physique. It was going to get hot in that can, even within the protection of the vault's extension arm.

"Can you pan the view to the other pads for a bit?" she asked Rael. It had been a puzzle from the first plans they'd received — how many landing pads the vault actually had, and why they'd need more than one.   Rael panned the camera, which was located inside the airlock and thus protected from the murderous atmosphere.   And he paused on something nasty on the neighbouring pad.

"I guess that's why they needed more than one pad," he remarked.   Trace peered at the image.   On the pad was the melted black ruin of another descender, its hull caved and fractured in places where she guessed it had imploded.   Then would follow a hideous fire, as everything combustible inside exploded — oxygen first, then synthetics… heck, even steel would burn if hot enough.   Something of the ship's inner-hull remained, like a blackened skeleton, made of graphite composite and harder than diamond.   The rest was ceramic plating that would not melt… but all the internal metal was gone, melted into a blackened, multi-tonne blob on the pad.   "Once they lose one, they can't remove it.   No bulldozer's been invented for these conditions."

"It's centrally located on the pad," Trace observed.   "So it landed okay, the failure happened afterward.   And I bet the vault can facilitate a failure from inside, if they want."

"Gee thanks, Major," said Rael.   "Very cheerful."   She could feel the tension in their voices, and see it on their faces, now they had a visual of what lay outside.   Space was not a hospitable environment for humans, but compared to the surface of Kamala, pure vacuum seemed like paradise.   The sheer oppression of it weighed upon them all, and Trace thought it no wonder that sard had been chosen to man the vault security.   She doubted any other species could tolerate it.

Trace stepped to the canister, and Aristan, and refrained from asking if he was ready.   It was a pointless question to someone like Aristan.   And probably to someone like her, also.   Aristan's only possession was a steel blade in an ebony-black sheath.   "We will seal the canister at the last possible moment," she told him, with her suit speaker set to translate.   "You should begin your meditation now, so that you consume the minimum oxygen for the entirety of your trip."

"Yes," her earpiece translated his reply.   He could not take anything mechanical into the canister with him, lest the vault

security systems detect it on the way in. His large, indigo eyes were utterly calm, with half-lidded contempt for the peril to come. Trace could not help but feel concern for him, and found that odd, given that she'd truly like him dead. But then, to be Kulina, and a Major on the *UFS Phoenix*, was to be engulfed in very odd things, of late.

"Do you recall my instruction on the weakpoints of sard?" Parren had not fought sard as recently as humans, making human marines the more reliable experts on the matter.

"Lower torso and hip," Aristan said calmly. *"Upper arm, shoulder, neck. Avoid the forearms, they have serrated edges and armour that may capture a sword. Strike the lower back from behind, not the upper, which has natural armour."*

"Good," said Trace. "Those manning the security atrium will not be combat armoured, but may be environment-suited. For a true blade, it will not matter. Eliminate the guards, close and lock the access doors behind, and facilitate Command Squad's entry. Simple."

A faint, dry smile from Aristan. *"Simple,"* he echoed. After having barely breathed in the past half-hour, no one added. Aristan insisted it was possible, and Doc Suelo had agreed that parren physiology made it possible, though barely. Trace did not like Aristan, but she did not suspect him of being a braggart or a liar. She had, however, seen many apparently capable people, who were neither braggarts nor liars, fail spectacularly from underestimating the scale of the challenge ahead, or from overestimating their own ability to meet it.

"The extension arm is coming out," Rael announced from the viewer. "It's not moving fast, I'd guess we might have five minutes."

"Let's go," said Aristan in English — an odd accent from those lips, and several of the marines actually smiled. He sat on the edge of the canister, pulled up his knees in advance of sitting, as there was not enough room to do it once inside, then slid down into the tight space. Once in, Terez handed the sword in after him.

"Okay," Kono told him. "Aristan, we'll give it another two minutes, then we'll start sealing you in. Aristan?" Aristan made no reply, gazing sightlessly at the blank canister-side before him, barely seeming to breathe.

"He's meditating," said Trace. "He can't respond, just do it when you have to."

Tif could not bear the waiting. But with the confined room monitored by cameras, she could not pace, either... or rather, she feared that if she did, something in her urgency would give the game away.

"Prepare," said Styx in her ear. *"I believe I have found a path. You will need to do exactly what I tell you, when I tell you to do it. Do you understand?"*

"I understand." The smart people on *Phoenix* who understood such things called Styx a 'super sentience'. If anyone could pull this off, Styx could. Tif repeated that over in her head a few times, willing herself to believe it.

"If you can acquire a weapon along the way, you must do so. And you must use it."

"I'm not good with weapons," Tif retorted. *"My claws are better."* Besides, outside of a combat shuttle cockpit, she'd never before killed anything bigger than a rudok. Those, she'd roasted, above a cooking fire at the family home in Heshog.

"Kuhsi claws are effective weapons," Styx agreed. Tif wondered if she truly understood the nature of 'fear'. Or the moral reluctance to kill. *"My bug has acquired new pathways. You will depart in just a moment."*

"If you hack these systems on Chara yourself," Tif formulated as it occurred to her, *"then... isn't there a chance that they'll realise what's doing it? We're trying to keep you hidden, aren't we? And these State Department systems must be very advanced?"*

"I haven't the time to update you on other recent events," Styx replied in that cool, ever-calm way of hers, *"but let us say that*

the situation has progressed to the point where that may be inevitable. We will hope that our prize is worth that price."

Tif blinked. "You know what's happening elsewhere? Is it going well?"

"Thus far, yes," said Styx. "But things can change. Ready yourself, I am monitoring corridors for tavalai movement. I will attempt to guide you through with minimal confrontation. Now."

The door opened with a hum. Tif got up and walked through it. "Left," said Styx. "Walk silently, there are guards. Pause at this corridor." Tif paused, wondering whether to press herself to the wall, or just stand there. If some random bureaucrat saw her walking, they might just assume she had the right to be there. But if she was acting suspiciously, she would only draw attention to herself. "Cross quickly."

Tif did, and continued down the bland steel corridor. There was a timelag between the Tsubarata and Kamala of zero-point-seven seconds, which Styx must have been somehow calculating ahead for. She wondered if Styx was hacked into *all* of the local cameras and systems, and could see every corridor, or just a few. But questions were pointless — she was in Styx's hands, and had no choice but to trust her abilities.

"You have your breather still with you," Styx reminded her. "Put it on." Tif pulled the facemask from her thigh pocket — she had not been technically under arrest, and authorities in environments that required breathers rarely confiscated them, as the safety culture always dictated that too many breathers was preferable to not enough. The mask's rubber seal fit onto her face and jaw — an imperfect seal, her fur still made a slight leak, despite *Phoenix* Engineering's scans and custom machining to get the tightest fit to what humans found an unfamiliar face.

She paused at a corridor intersection, hearing tavalai voices ahead, and flattened herself to a wall, heart hammering. "You are located still in the landing pad complex," Styx explained patiently. Tif's ear flicked, involuntarily, as something buzzed past her ear, heading around the corner. "You must transition to the next building complex. It is on the neighbouring Chara platform, across the *flexible hinges. There are no pressurised access tubes across platforms, given how they flex, so you must pass through an airlock and across an overbridge."*

"It's exposed!" Tif retorted. *"I'll be seen!"*

"There are no external observation decks, it is unlikely. These facilities are under-manned. I am acquiring control of an airlock. You must ascend one level. The stairwell, ahead on your left."

Tif glanced quickly around the corner, and saw the steel staircase in its upward shaft. The tavalai voices ahead were close — perhaps coming from a room with an open door. She swore beneath her breath, and dashed for the stairwell, and climbed.

On the next level she peered about, and saw the big airlock down the end of the passage. About it was an open room, and she crept to the passage corner, and peered in. It was an airlock control room, much the same in pressurised habitats anywhere, with environment suits in general-access lockers on one wall, and airlock controls on the wall beside the doors. Those controls were flashing, and even now the outer door opened to greet her. Tif knew all the tales of hacksaws taking remote control of technology immediately before them, but she'd never heard it speculated that they could do it real-time from neighbouring planetoids. And suddenly the fear of it flashed through her adrenaline-charged mind — that here were they all, the entire crew of *Phoenix*, being guided through this escapade by a hacksaw queen, who saw success in this mission as the salvation of her entire, genocidal race. What in all the mad fates were they doing, risking their lives for this... *thing*, that in its previous incarnation had only lived to exterminate organic beings like her?

She thrust it from her mind, and ran silently to the airlock, crouching low to keep out of sight beneath the transparent sides as the outer door closed behind. She adjusted her mask feed as air hissed from vents about her, replaced by the CO_2 from outside, and took some longer gasps of comfortingly cold oxygen. Her ears barely popped as the outer doors opened — a cool breeze blew in, almost comforting, and deceptive in its familiarity.

Tif edged out the door and peered about. This was indeed a smallish tower complex, right on the edge of one of Chara's many platforms.   Below, an enormous sealed hinge flexed and groaned. To the left and across, the next platform along was one enormous airtank, contained within a mass of regulator pipes and supporting framework, like a giant balloon trapped in a snare of industrial steel. Immediately opposite, a flexible walkway stretched like one of the ropeway bridges she recalled from her home in Heshog, spanning canyons in hunting grounds shared between her clan and several neighbours.   This one had steel cables for supports instead of rope, and steel planks instead of wood, and led directly across the thirty-metre drop below to a similar support-tower on the far side.

"I have primed the airlock on the opposite tower," Styx informed her.   *"I cannot monitor all windows, there is a chance you may be spotted, but you must go now."*

"And what if I am spotted?" Tif retorted.

"The descender is in pre-flight preparations behind this tower.   I can get you in, and I can be your co-pilot for as much of the descent as time-lag and atmospheric conditions will allow.   I calculate that State Department will not shoot you down, though they have that capability — this descender is on its way back from a vault visit just ten hours ago, and its cargo is marked 'highest priority'."

Tif's eyes widened.   She hadn't even thought of being shot down.   Something else occurred to her.   *"How do you know where to go?   Vault coordinates are secret, that's the whole point!"*

"This descender's navcomp has been wiped, but my constructs infiltrated the Major's descender when it received its data…"

"Chara's position's changed since then!" Tif cut her off. *"The coordinates change, you can't just hope to get close and then spot it from a distance — you can't see anything in that atmosphere!"*

"I can get you close enough."

"How?"

"There is no time for this argument," said Styx, her voice betraying a clear impatience. Probably that was calculated for effect as well. *"In this mission, I am the most personally-invested member of Phoenix's crew, and I will not allow you to fail. But you must go now!"*

Tif took a deep breath, and a final glance about. Then she moved, deciding on a brisk walk that someone casually glancing from a window might mistake for regular crew, not seeing that she was kuhsi from a distance. The suspension bridge swung and vibrated in the carbon dioxide wind, and with the constant motion and flexing of Chara itself. She could sense its movement here, the rise and fall of air currents, in a way that was lost while indoors. Tif had always loved to fly, and the pilot in her soul would have loved it here, under other circumstances. And she thought that it must be quite something, when Chara passed through one of Kamala's storms, and the blanket of white below was lit with lightning, and the platforms all heaving with updrafts.

"The far airlock has been overridden," Styx said then with alarm. *"Someone is entering, these manual controls will override my own. You must evade."*

Evade? Tif stared at the airlock ahead, and saw two air-masked tavalai inside. One was staring out at her, and pointing. She'd been found.

She could not turn back, she could not go forward. Her eyes found a platform she'd noted earlier — on the right and lower down, a good two floors below her current level. In regular gravity, the jump would be suicidal, but Kamala had only half of what kuhsi knew as 1-G, and she fancied herself somewhat expert at judging trajectories in a three-dimensional space. Before she could think again, she ran straight at the airlocked tavalai, one of whom was shouting something inaudible at the other, waving for the outer door to be cycled. In his hand was a pistol.

Tif ran as close as she dared, then climbed over the railing, and took a moment to contemplate the sheer drop below. The platform was only six metres below, and three metres away. In this gravity, the force would not hurt worse than a three-metre drop... but if she missed, it was a full twenty metres to the bottom, with jagged edges of Chara platform to bounce off, having hit them at something approaching Kamala terminal velocity...

The outer airlock on her left began to open. Tif jumped, and sailed outward, slowly picking up speed. The platform came at her plenty fast as she reached it, and rolled hard into the railing.

"Follow this walkway," said Styx, evidently having followed events precisely. *"It leads to another airlock, I can get you inside from there."*

Tif hurdled the locked gate to the engineering walkway beyond, a narrow thing with only a light railing between it and the downward plunge. A shot rang out behind as she rounded the corner, and found cover from the walkway behind. The tavalai from the airlock had fired at her, she realised, with fear and indignation. She ran the walkway past several thick windows, and saw the smaller, service airlock ahead, outer door already open and waiting for her. Something smacked a steel wall on her left, followed just after by the sound of a rifle shot from across the space to the tower she'd come from. Tif did not stop to look, and ducked into the airlock to huddle against a thick door frame.

"Tavalai are poor shots," Styx assured her as the outer doors closed. The pumps hissed, and Tif saw a big, red button marked with tavalai script — that would be the 'emergency entry' button, and she hit it, the inner doors opening with a siren wail as CO_2 concentration flooded the room beyond.

This room was an engineering space, with lockers for environment suits and breathers, spare air tanks with refill hoses, and a big, open equipment bay filled with tools that anyone from *Phoenix* Engineering would have recognised. A tavalai engineer was emerging from that bay, breather pressed over his mouth and coming to investigate the sirens... and stopped, frozen at the sight of Tif. Tif snarled, teeth bared and claws out, and the engineer retreated without challenge — just a tech, unarmed and uninterested in tackling runaway kuhsi.

"Go straight," Styx commanded, *"then the third passage on the right and take the stairwell up."*

Tif ran, pulling her claws in with effort, which forced the fingers straight until the segments slotted back and she could bend them again and remove her mask without the risk of slicing her own face. The mask was a problem, on the off-chance she did actually have to bite someone.

She ran the corridor, heard some shouting in Togiri, then found the stairwell and sprang lightly up it... and straight into a tavalai coming down the other way. She slid aside, grabbing the much bigger tavalai and yanking him onward with his own momentum, sending him stumbling and crashing as she spun and kept climbing three steps at a time.

"This level," said Styx, and she left the stairs, bounced off a wall and ran straight into an oncoming tavalai who grabbed at her. Tif slashed, felt claws tear and the tavalai let her go with a yell, then a shot and more yells from behind. *"Right,"* said Styx, as calm as a navigator in an over-speeding vehicle, and Tif saw the hall ahead opening into the main room of a descender's access tube, with airlock and docking controls, and a number of tavalai with weapons drawn, some of them levelled.

Styx had gotten her killed, was her first thought, and she nearly stopped... but one of the tavalai yelled and clutched at his arm, then swatted at something in the air, distracting others. Another clutched at his neck, as the first fell to frothing and convulsing on the deck, and the others split, staring about in horror for the invisible thing that struck down their comrades.

Tif sprinted, and both closed airlock doors opened on cue, revealing the access passage to the huge descender on the pad beyond. One tavalai recalled her in time to turn his gun on her, but she diverted to hit him first, dislodging the weapon before ducking down the passage, doors closing behind her, blocking any shot at her back.

"Get to the cockpit," said Styx. *"The crew are not yet aboard, just some Chara workers. I will convince them to get off by flushing the environmentals."*

Tif had barely entered the descender before a pair of engineering crew blocked her way, trying to get off. Tif snarled, claws extended, and was nearly astonished that both froze and moved aside, in obvious fear. One of her claws, she noticed, had snared a piece of clothing, and a little blood, from the previous tavalai she'd hit. Again something buzzed past her ear, toward the tavalai.

"Don't kill them!" she told Styx, and edged past, then gestured the engineers off, and out the way she'd come.

"Your compassion endangers the mission," Styx observed as they ran off. Tif had no doubt she'd have killed the engineers anyway if they hadn't left immediately, and pulled her mask from her thigh pocket once more as she found the central access and climbed to the cockpit.

"It's not necessary," she said as she scampered up the ladder. And added, *"If you flush the ship with CO2, it's not going to scare engineers with facemasks."*

"This ship's air coolant filters contain poisonous chemicals when flushed," Styx replied. *"They will leave."*

"That was hacksaw neurotoxin, that your bug was using," Tif panted aloud, now that there was no one around to hear. "They're going to guess who you are, when this is over."

"So long as we have Drakhil's diary, it won't matter," said Styx. *"For that diary, I would end worlds."*

CHAPTER 25

As Dale drove the car into the maglev station parking, a delivery drone followed them in, hovering low behind the car in a way that was probably illegal, if that word weren't so tenuous in a free-city. Dale let the car park on autos, scanning the dark-lit surroundings with rifle in lap, as Sergeant Forrest reported back from another part of the city.

"I've counted about twelve, they're chasing," he said through gritted teeth, as the squeal of tires carried even through the uplink connection. *"We got drones too… Joker, can you boost your signal, you're breaking…"* The rest was lost in static.

"Jokono!" Dale snapped. "Get him back!"

"I cannot, Lieutenant," said Jokono with concern. *"I fear they are onto me, and onto my network construct. I can still observe Sergeant Forrest and Private Tong's position, but they've drawn quite a crowd. I think you may have gotten off the road just in time."*

"Shit," Dale fumed, as the car found a park and pulled into a suitably dark corner. "Well we can't help them now… Joker, if you can get them a message, tell them not to fight if they're cornered, just surrender."

"I will try, Lieutenant." Because Dale knew his Sergeant well, and the thought of what he *might* do filled him with fear.

They piled out of the car, as the drone obligingly dropped its plastic-wrapped package on the hood and zoomed off. Reddy, Milek and Kadi pulled off the wrapping, to reveal the parren acolyte-black robes they'd left behind at Tooganam's apartment. Milek pulled his on with evident relief, and the humans followed suit, Dale and Reddy only relieved to no longer be identified as human in public, and to now have somewhere to hide their very large guns.

"I have hidden this location as best I can," said Jokono, *"but I think at this point it would be best for you to head back to my location."* Jokono was at Tooganam's apartment, which he insisted had excellent network hardware for hiding signal locations —

meaning it was old and dilapidated, and uncooperative with modern hunter-programs used by security agencies.

"And what makes you think we'll be any safer there?" Dale growled.

"I believe that 'safe' is out of the question at this point," said Jokono. *"But there are developments here that will cause the security forces considerable delay. Best that you come directly."*

"We'll do that," Dale said reluctantly, seeing little other choice. "Let's just hope they can't stop trains."

They walked from parking to the main concourse, where light crowds flowed onto the platform amidst tall displays showing the location of the next train. Jokono simply hacked the station entry gates to let them through without passes, and they moved together, four robed and hooded figures amid the confusion of aliens and a few courier droids. Dale led them down the platform end, where transparent walls gave them a view over surrounding Gamesh, shadows from mesa walls creeping across the city sprawl as the sun lowered in the west.

The train arrived in a decelerating rush, and they entered at the very rear segment. There were few seats in the big interior tube, most of the space reserved for the standing crush at rush hour, and they held to overhead straps, the other hand inside their cloaks, and trying not to make it obvious that they were carrying something heavy underneath. Dale noted a few looks their way, but not too many — Gamesh was a diverse and crazy place, and there were many odder sights than dark robed parren in groups.

A location display showed them thirty kilometres from Tooganam's district, in an entirely different sector of the city. The maglev moved fast, but this route was not direct, and would only get them within five Ks. From there, they'd have to find alternative transport.

"Joker," Dale formulated silently, *"anything from Woody and Tricks?"*

"I'm afraid not, Lieutenant. I've lost all trace, and now even their location."

Dale fumed, and worried for his friends. *"Keep on it."*

"I will.   They are becoming better at masking their movements amidst the general traffic.   Stay alert, I doubt I'll be able to give you much warning if they're on top of you."

"Copy that."

Milek lifted the rim of his hood just enough to catch Dale's eye, with a hard, indigo stare.   He jerked his head back up the train. Dale nodded warily, and Milek went, a slow stroll up the humming train, as urban vistas and red-brown cliffs came sailing by.   'If they're onto us', Milek's gesture meant, 'they could already have someone on the train'.   Someone, or something.   Rapid Response used droids of all kinds.

The train arrived at a new station, this one amid a cluster of tall buildings, and a large number of passengers got on and off. Dale saw some cloaks and hoods amongst them, and wondered, finger on his rifle safety beneath his own cloak.   A female tavalai had a pair of children with her.   One of the kids held a container of water, with a pet water creature of some kind, eating green moss. Dale had never had much time for human kids, let alone alien kids, but these two were cute, with big eyes and oversized heads.   They talked with their mother in Togiri, oblivious to any danger.   Dale had seen dead tavalai kids before, on stations and ships during the war, and it wasn't something he ever wanted to see again.   He repressed several bad words, and stared out the big, concave rear window.

Something made him look up.   There was a small silver dot up there, gleaming against the pale yellow sky.   A drone.   Plenty of those in Gamesh, but this one was holding position right over them. He turned back, and looked up the train, past the tavalai family. One of the newly arrived cloaked figures was looking at him. Within the hood, where an alien face should be, he caught sight of steel, and a synthetic red eye.   A droid.

Behind the droid, a second cloaked figure pulled a weapon from robes, levelled it at the back of the droid's head, and fired. The droid fell in a jerking spasm of servos, and slammed into the train door, a rifle revealed within the cloak, clutched in steel fingers.

Dale and Reddy pulled their own rifles, while Milek turned, and shot a second droid in the face, lightning fast.

Passengers yelled in shock and panic, some staring, others running. "Go!" Dale yelled at those nearest, pulling back his hood and mask, as those nearest now stared at him. "Go that way, quickly! Tonada-ma! Tonada-ma!" At the tavalai in particular, as Reddy moved fast to help Milek, and Kadi pulled his hand-controller, AR glasses down, seeming to prefer that to any weapon.

Dale turned his attention back to the drone, still trailing above and behind. That would be the controller, tasked to keep eyes on the target while HQ would coordinate the rest of the assault. He could shoot it down from here, but they'd just replace it with another one — and if he exposed himself shooting at it, they could probably do the same to him.

More shooting up the train, as a third droid took out some windows, and Reddy blew its head off. *"LT, these fuckers are just shooting past civvies!"* Reddy growled, crouched low amidst civilians now wisely flattening themselves to the floor, or crouched behind the few chairs. *"It's like they don't even care!"*

"Yeah, well Tooganam warned us," said Dale. The tavalai family hadn't moved, he saw with exasperation — the mother huddled against a wall with an arm around each kid. Not especially stupid, considering that the shooting was happening in the direction Dale had told them to go, and their own automated security force seemed less cautious of civilian casualties than the humans were.

Dale took up cover in front of them, away from the train's transparent tail, and watched up the train, where several entire segments now lay flat or low, while the train's far end ran and crowded further up. "Watch those civilians!" he told Reddy and Milek. "Any of those on the ground could be droids, don't trust it!" As Reddy removed one hood with the muzzle of his rifle, then finding a terrified kratik, moved on. Some others pulled their hoods down, only too happy to show they weren't droids.

"Station coming up," Jokono informed them. *"One minute, disembarking on the right."*

Dale gestured at Kadi. "Kid, can you get me intercom on this train?"

Kadi blinked. "Sure, I can get you control of the whole damn train if you want?"

"No, leave that to Joker. We'll need you to get some of these damn droids." Kadi pointed his handheld at the ceiling, and manipulated a few invisible icons with his other hand.

"Got it," he told Dale. "Go."

Dale blinked an icon on his own glasses, and activating the translator's voice control. "Translator," he told it, "Togiri standard." As coms showed him a local network available, and he uplinked. "All passengers," he said, and heard the translated, synthetic voice booming over intercom overhead. "All passengers must get off at the next station. This train is not safe, all passengers must get off at the next station. Much shooting, get off and run."

That he might be causing a panicked rush on the platform did not bother him — if there were more droids on the platform waiting to get on, a rush might knock them off their feet. And his microphones caught a kid's voice behind him, in Togiri, and a faint translation, *"Mummy, is that a bad human Mummy? Is he going to hurt us?"*

"No baby," his frightened mother replied. *"I think he's protecting us."* And again Dale experienced the most disturbing sensation of feeling something toward tavalai other than anger and fear — an appreciation for whatever it was in tavalai psychological makeup that repressed panic, and allowed them to make rational judgements where most human civilians would be completely insensible. In combat against tavalai, that instinct was trouble, but here it was welcome. He shook it off and moved forward to a new crouch-cover behind seats, as the train slowed, and then a platform was whizzing past on the right.

The train stopped, doors opening to a great tumble of passengers onto the platform, as though a giant hand had grabbed the train and turned it on its side. "Down and watch for snipers," Dale told his team, watching the tavalai mother running with her kids onto the platform. "Joker, I want control of this train, we're going to run through all stations. If we can get back to you, we will — otherwise we can at least make a giant moving distraction."

"I'll try," said Jokono.

Kadi stared at Dale. "What, we're just going to go? Make a target of ourselves?"

"We're already a target," Dale retorted, peering out a window at the platform. The doors hummed shut, and the train began to move. "We need a defensible position, and this train is the one thing in the city they might think twice about just blowing up."

The train accelerated rapidly, now empty save for the three humans and one parren. *"We should have kept some civilians aboard!"* Milek shouted down the train at Dale. *"Some hostages would have confused their aim!"*

"Yeah, well I think Tooganam might just stop helping Joker if we'd done that," said Dale. "Mystery Boy, Spots, you two take the front! Kadi and I get the rear!" Milek and Reddy took off running, the parren still in his cloak. The train now zoomed on elevated rail above a sprawl of cityscape, roads and buildings flashing by. "Joker, if they blow this train off the rail it'll take out half a neighbourhood. They might be casual with civvie casualties but I don't think they're *that* casual, they'll try an armed entry."

"That would be my guess too," said Jokono. *"The train ahead has five minutes on you, but station stops cost nearly two minutes each. You will catch up with it before you reach your best destination for disembarking, unless they start skipping stations also."*

"One problem at a time, Joker," said Dale, crouching to peer out the rear window again, in search of immediate airborne pursuit. "If you can get us a clear station and a couple of vehicles there, and we can get down into the underground levels, we might have a chance of dragging this out further."

"I'll see what I can do."

Dale went to Kadi, and grabbed his arm. "Kid, they're after the module. State Department will have told them by now, they'll do anything to get it back or destroy it."

Kadi nodded, wide-eyed. "I know. Maybe it's better if you took it?" He reached to his pocket.

Dale stopped his hand. "No. Your controller is a support weapon — support weapons stay in the rear. You stay close to me, but you stay behind, do you understand? You stay out of my way, and give me support, and don't let them get that damn module or the whole mission fails and the Major's team dies."

Kadi nodded, frightened but intense. Dale slapped his shoulder.

"Yo!" yelled Reddy from up the front. "Drones, left side!"

"And right side too!" Milek added.

Dale went to the right windows, and saw several small dots coming rapidly closer, paralleling them at high speed, weaving between towers that got in the way. "Take 'em out!" Dale yelled, and put several shots through the hard window plastic to shatter a portion. He stuck the rifle muzzle out, took careful aim, and the tavalai rifle's auto-sights gave him target feedback to his glasses, indicating a point ahead of the oncoming drone that accounted for the howling crosswind...

Dale fired once, and the drone lurched, then spun and dropped from view. Its neighbour fired, and Dale ducked as more holes smacked the windows. "Stay down!" he yelled for the others' benefit. "These trains are tough, the walls are good cover!" Sure enough, the windows were smashing, but lower down, nothing penetrated. After fighting in soft-skinned civilian groundcars, that was a relief.

He glanced at Kadi, and found the Petty Officer lying flat on his back. For a moment he thought Kadi had been hit, but instead he was holding both hands up before him, like a kid lying in bed and pretending to fly an imaginary aircraft, hands on joystick and throttle. Beyond the left-side window, something flashed, and Dale rolled across to peer through door-windows for a better look, just in time to see a second drone explode, and another two evade. A fifth drone looked to be chasing them, weapon swivelling as it fired, as the confused machines wondered how to handle their homicidal companion. Another went spinning into the side of a tower with a glass-shattering crash, and the other turned and fled.

"I got a friendly coming in from the left," Kadi announced to the others. "Don't shoot it, it's now on our side."

"I copy that, I see him," said Reddy, as a station platform went shooting by at excessive speed. *"LT, they're probing us, they're just figuring out our capabilities. The real attack comes next."*

"I know," said Dale, raising his voice to be sure the microphone caught his words above the whistling gale now blowing into the train from holed windows. "Just keep your eyes peeled for…"

"Lieutenant," came Jokono's voice in alarm, *"I am registering some much larger aerial vehicles converging on your position!"*

Dale looked, and where the person-sized drones had been, there now came several big, twin-nacelle flyers, capable of far more speed than this train could manage. "Looks like two are going high!" Dale observed. "And this one's coming in parallel, hang on!"

He found some bullet holes to get a shot through, but even as he put the rifle to his shoulder, he saw the flyer's side door opening, to reveal the rotary cannon mount within. And his heart nearly stopped.

"Get up!" Dale yelled at Kadi, grabbing him by the collar and hauling him to a stumbling run as high-velocity projectiles tore through both sides of the train where he'd been. Windows disintegrated and walls punctured with holes, snapping at their backs as they ran, the cannon traversing to follow them up the train as the gunner caught glimpses through the carnage.

Then the firing stopped, and Dale fell flat, rolling for more cover as something heavy hit the train roof, then several more impacts. "Entry!" Dale yelled, bracing against chairs and aiming as something big smashed through the already-shattered side windows further back. "Entry, rear!"

The thing that had come through the window unfolded — roughly humanoid with a large weapon where its right arm should have been, reconfiguring to balance and aim as Dale fired on full auto. Reddy joined in, firing above Dale's head, and the assault droid came apart in a series of sparking impacts… only to reveal the second droid, having followed the first in, and already upright. Its big cannon fired briefly, then stopped.

"I got it!" Kadi yelled, aiming his handheld from cover opposite Dale. "I got it, don't kill it!" As the assault droid turned its cannon, and pointed it out the window at the flyer several hundred metres away alongside, and fired. The flyer broke away in a hurry, pieces flying off. Then the droid was hit from behind, disintegrating as a flyer on the opposite side hit it amid more exploding windows.

"Yo fuck you!" Kadi yelled and rolled up to point his controller out the window at that flyer, as several more loud thuds hit the roof — the flyers overhead were dropping droids on the roof. Kadi's flyer wobbled, then ducked left past a glass-sided building, then crunched into a blank concrete wall, with a huge fireball as its ammunition blew.

A droid smashed through the windows near Reddy, who shot it repeatedly as it refused to fall quickly, then Milek shot another point-blank, stunned it further with a blade to the neck, then tossed it from the moving train, out the window it had smashed.

"Move up!" Dale yelled, gesturing them further up the train, squinting at the howling gale that now roared through the smashed windows. "Get up the front, we're gonna hit the next train ahead in a minute!"

"The preceding train is slowing ahead of you," Jokono confirmed. *"It looks as though central authority is using it to box you in."* Another set of station platforms whizzed by, and Dale did some fast mental calculation — they weren't far now from where he wanted to get off. But if they stayed under fire on this empty train, Rapid Response would shred it. They needed a new ride, if only for a few more minutes.

Fire ripped through the ceiling, as a droid on the roof fired downward. Dale sidestepped, blew it off the roof, then ran as new fire hammered the spot he'd been standing. Reddy hit that new source of fire as Dale reloaded, then a heavy-caliber round blew a hole in a nearby wall.

"Sniper drones," said Dale, running onward and leaning as the train rounded a bend. "Keep moving, there's no way those things can be accurate from an unstable platform." Another shot blew a window behind — sniper drones were designed to fire at stationary targets from a stationary hover, not at moving targets from long range while racing at high speed. At least the train was still running well, Dale thought. Being a maglev, all the propulsion tech was in the base that connected it to the rail, while all the fire was aimed at the hollow passenger body above.

"Two more stations," said Jokono, and Dale could see the rear of the train ahead through the transparent nose of this one. *"I have assistance arriving at your disembark station, but you're not going to reach it before this next train blocks your path."* Another shot blew a hole in the nearby roof. *"They'll engineer a low-speed collision and use the first train to block and stop the second."*

"Can you take control of the second train?"

"Only one at a time, I'm afraid."

"I can do it," Kadi announced. "Joker — you keep control of this one, I've got the one ahead."

"I copy that," said Jokono.

"Good, go!" Dale told Kadi. "Everyone stay low and spread out, don't give them a target!" He took cover again by a door, thankful that at least the flyers and drones were staying well clear, wary of what had happened to the others.

Kadi scampered on, staying as low as possible as he reached the transparent nose, then lay flat and aimed his handheld at the oncoming rear of the train ahead. Even as Dale watched, the closure speed began to diminish, as whoever was centrally controlling the train ahead began to accelerate it, preparing for a low-speed impact that would stop this runaway.

"I got it!" shouted Kadi, and sure enough, the train ahead continued accelerating, until there was no closure speed at all.   And he thumped the floor with his free hand in triumph.   "I got it, I didn't know if this damn thing would work on an entire train, but it does!"

"Jokono," said Dale, "bring us to a stop at your station and see if you can get us a visual feed on the platform.   You said you had assistance there..."

A massive explosion cut him off, as a fireball engulfed the train's midpoint, and sent debris spinning up the tube.   Dale shielded his face, and when he looked again, the middle of train was nearly cut in half, and everything was burning.   The train shuddered and squealed, as though threatening to throw itself from the rails.

"You're losing power on the propulsion!" Jokono warned. *"The whole propulsion system is failing, you're going to come to a halt short of the station!"*

"Kadi!" Dale yelled as he realised the only solution.   "Drop speed on the train ahead!   Smack us into its rear, we'll jump ship and ride that one to the station!"

"I got it!" said Kadi, and suddenly the rear end of the forward train began getting bigger again.   Another set of platforms rushed by, prospective passengers staring in amazement as two trains rushed by in unison, the second ablaze and full of holes.   "Hang on, we got ten seconds until..."

Something else hit the train, and Kadi yelled, clutching his side.   He put a hand before his visored eyes, and stared at the blood on it.

"Kadi's hit!" yelled Reddy, and scrambled to help.   "He's bleeding bad, I gotta patch him!"

"Do it real fast, you've got fifteen seconds!" Dale retorted, as the rear end of the train ahead came rushing up.   He could see puzzled passengers in the rear, through the transparent end-cap, already wondering why their train hadn't been stopping at the last stations, and now staring at the second train rushing up behind. "Everyone brace!"

The trains' two ends met with a heavy crunch that sent Dale skidding up the floor. When he looked again, the two transparent domes were caved and cracked. Beyond the impact, a train full of passengers also fallen to ground, many now scrambling up to put some distance between themselves and the collision. Dale got up, ran to the front and angled his rifle to shoot down on the interlocked, shattered canopies — like two hardboiled eggs that had been rammed together, and were now completely fused. Repeated shots blew whole chunks of hard plastic away, and he kicked the rest with augmented strength until a large, three-metre section fell away, hit the rails and disappeared. But now the vibration beneath his feet was like an earthquake.

"I'm about to lose the train!" Jokono announced in his ear. *"You have to go now!"*

"Spots!" Dale yelled. "I need your rifle up front!" Because there was no telling if this train, too, had infiltrating droids aboard.

"Yeah, got it!" Reddy replied, finishing a field-dressing in rapid fast time, having taken a knife to some of Kadi's clothes.

"I will help him through," Milek insisted, grabbing Kadi's arm and hauling him up. *"You go."*

Dale took several steps back for a runup, then leaped through the hole — a simple enough jump, and landed in the next train to screams and alarm from passengers there to see an armed and ferocious-looking human landing aboard. Dale covered with his rifle levelled at the crowd, but saw no threat. Reddy landed alongside and did the same.

"You cover!" Dale told him, and turned back to help Milek and Kadi. On the far side of the shattered intersection, Kadi was standing with Milek's help, though barely. Milek spared Dale a grim look, then picked the fading Petty Officer up, with doubtless augmented strength. Then, with a crash and eruption of sparks from further down the train, something broke, and Milek and Kadi's train began to slow.

Milek barely avoided falling, as the intersection of glass-shell began to separate, and a gap opened between the two trains. "Now!" Dale yelled, tossing his rifle back and preparing both hands

369

to catch.   But he knew it was too late — Milek could not leap that expanding distance with Kadi's weight.   The look in the parren's wide, indigo eyes showed that he knew it too.

He ran and leaped anyway, twisting in mid-flight to propel Kadi flying onward, at the cost of his own momentum.   Dale grabbed Kadi's jacket in mid-flight as he half-landed on the lower broken glass, and saw Milek hit the maglev rail and disappear beneath the onrushing train in a flash.

Dale pulled Kadi aboard, the young man unconscious from the pain of being ragdolled about, and dragged him a safer distance from the rear.   Reddy spared a brief glance back from his cover position.   "Where's Mystery Boy?"

"Dead," said Dale.   "Went under the train.   Joker, can you stop us?   Kadi's hit and I can't use his damn contraption."

"Yes I can stop you, I'm acquiring control of this train now. Just one more minute."

It seemed far longer than a minute, with huddled passengers staring at them ahead, and Dale double-checking Reddy's blood-soaked bandage, and adding an extra pressure-wrap from his own first aid.   Kadi still had his glasses around his neck on their strap, and his handheld stuffed into a pocket.   Most importantly, he still had the com module.   Damn stupid, Dale berated himself — that had been the first and only priority, and by ordering Reddy to jump second, leaving Milek and Kadi behind, he'd put the whole mission at risk.   But if there had been combat droids in this train, he'd have needed two rifles up front or the mission would also have failed. Milek should have been enough to handle Kadi, and as it happened, he had been.   And if he'd left Reddy behind instead, then he'd now be dead instead of Milek, because Reddy would have realised what had to be done just as Milek had.

It wasn't a worthy thought to feel relief at.   Obviously he was far closer to Reddy, who'd been with him in Alpha Platoon for years.   But it made him regret that he hadn't shown Milek more respect when he'd had the chance.

"Joker," he said, "you'd better have something on that platform I don't know about, or we're going to get slaughtered as soon as we get off."

"The station is temporarily secure," Jokono assured him. *"And the presence of civilians on your new train is holding off their heavy weaponry, for now."*

Finally the train slowed, coming to a humming halt at a station built into the side of a tall, red-brown mesa cliff. Passengers poured off in a wave, yelling at others on the platform not to enter. Dale picked up Kadi with Reddy's help, put him over a shoulder and moved quickly, rifle in his right hand while Reddy provided cover, moving quickly from the covered platform to the entry hall beyond. And they stopped, at a sight Dale had never thought he'd be pleased to see — the entry hall, filled with perhaps a dozen heavily armed tavalai. Leading them, and now using a big rifle in place of his usual staff, was Tooganam.

"Well," said Tooganam, waving him on. *"Come with us if you want to live."*

Dale and Reddy followed. "There's no security here?" Dale asked the gruff former-karasai.

"There was," said Tooganam, indicating to the tavalai ahead who fanned out with rifles ready, leading them down stairs to the entrance below. More civilian passengers stayed well clear as they passed. *"Some droids at the entrance, in case you got off here, and a few more inside."* As they ran over a droid on the downward steps, sprawled amidst bullet holes that pockmarked the stairs and walls. *"No issue now."*

"And who are all your friends?"

"No time for talking," Tooganam retorted, limping heavily down the stairs. *"Questions later. We have to get you home."*

CHAPTER 26

Trace waited.   About her, the descender's hull creaked and groaned like some tormented thing.   She'd thought somehow, in her imagination, that being inside this murderous atmosphere, even inside a heavily engineered descender, would be a more violent experience.   But the descender was built for this, for short periods at least, and there was no buffeting, or howling of the furnace-temperature winds to be felt.   Just the groaning of the hull, like an old wooden ship at sea, flexing in the waves.   If it failed, she doubted there would be much warning.   If that happened, she figured her armour would keep her alive for perhaps a minute, and no more than two... but only if the descender didn't turn into a ball of fire first.

Her timer showed that Aristan had been gone for twenty-two minutes and fourteen seconds.   Fifteen seconds.   Sixteen. Seventeen.   His air would have run out two minutes ago, so he'd been holding his breath for that long at least.   Trace tried it herself from time to time, partly as a test of her meditative skills and aerobic capacity, and partly for the practical knowledge of how long she'd have if her suit failed.   With augmentations, the human all-time record had gone up to half-an-hour, but those were deep-divers who'd turned their sport into an obsession, and conditioned their bodies to match.   Marines had too much muscle for those extremes, and burned through oxygen too fast, irrespective of meditative practice.   Lately Trace had been managing about six minutes, sitting cross-legged on her bunk, doing absolutely nothing.   In her youth she'd managed eight, but she'd been skinnier then.   She'd also been calmer, and better at meditation.   It wasn't supposed to work that way, she knew.   Kulina were supposed to get better at meditation as they aged — calmer of mind and sounder of practice. But in her youth, life had been simple.   With adulthood, for her at least, the certainties of her life had slowly faded, and meditative calm with it.

By Aristan's estimates of his own capabilities, he should have about eighteen minutes left, at least. It was possible he'd be done much faster, one way or the other. Sard were not tavalai, with whom one might expect delays from endless bureaucratic procedure. Sard were efficient, and procrastination was psychologically unknown to them. But even so, given how her missions had played out recently, Trace was expecting things to be cut very fine.

The guard room atrium had five sard, tavalai Fleet intelligence had assured them. They were armed, but obviously not expecting trouble to get past their entry scans. Vault security was predicated on the presumption of a non-clandestine assault — a hostile ship arriving in Kamala orbit and sending down an equally hostile descender or two, followed by a violent breech entry. Vault defences were designed to buy time against such an assault, until State Department or Fleet reinforcements could arrive. Clandestine assaults, given all the security hurdles that needed to be jumped just to get to this point, were considered nearly impossible. Which they were — unless one had the assistance of tavalai Fleet.

Sard had often surprised the Spiral's non-insectoid races with their imagination, and with tactics that became more ingenious and creative the more sard that became involved. But totally outside-the-box imagination remained a struggle for them. Sard could anticipate future events well by observing the flow of current events, and extrapolating where that flow might lead. But human commanders had observed that when sard were utterly surprised by something, such as a military-infiltration of the Kamala Vault for the first time in who knew how long, they struggled to adapt.

Trace had sparred with Aristan personally, and found his unarmed technique formidable. Sard were not particularly well-suited to unarmed combat, and she thought that with surprise, five sard should not be beyond him. But she also knew that plans like these so rarely went as they should. There could be more sard on duty this day. They might have firearms prominent, despite the apparent unlikelihood, opening a delivery canister in which any sard, tavalai or human combatant would have expired after ten minutes. The various airlock and override controls could have changed since tavalai Fleet got their last good look at them. Plus she had made it her personal policy on operations to always expect the worst, in all its unexpected varieties. And so she was moderately astonished that at twenty-six minutes since they'd sealed Aristan in, the access tube that had retracted after Aristan's canister had been deposited, began extending once more.

"Here it comes," Rael said tersely, peering at the external feed by the airlock. "Looks like he did it."

"Or someone inside is inviting us into a steel trap," Kono growled. "Easier than destroying this descender, leaving another wreck on their pads they can't clear."

"If it's a trap," said Trace, "we've got enough firepower to blast through, or cut through." She indicated to the kid, waiting patiently behind, the laser-cutter prominent behind his fore-legs. "Kid, you go first. If we need to cut through the airlock doors, lasers are best and there won't be enough room for you to get by."

The kid rattled past, peering at Rael's display, then at the inner airlock doors, which would remain firmly closed until the docking tube was connected. "We've got room for him, Chenk and First Section," said Trace. "Rael, you're with Second Section immediately after." And she checked her suit visor graphics, where a sub-section showed her the uplink connection to the kid's weapon systems, and the safety that kept them locked.

Trace followed the kid into the airlock, and he pulled his legs in a little to make room, Kono on his right, Chenkov, Terez and Zale behind. Chenkov looked scared, the faceplate of his exo-suit visor more transparent than a one-way marine suit. He clutched his handheld device, which fed to a display projected on the faceplate. Styx insisted it should be able to take control of multiple systems within the vault, whose extreme high-tech could not save them from drysine technological dominance. Trace extended an armoured fist at Chenkov, who bumped it with his own. Scared, Trace judged, but functional. Hell, everyone was scared, even her. The trick was doing the job in spite of it.

The airlock inner door sealed behind them, a tight fit with no windows or light save the displays in their helmets. Like being locked into a steel coffin. *"Connection commencing,"* said Rael on coms, and the airlock thumped and shuddered as the docking tube arrived. Creating a seal in this atmosphere was a heavy-duty process of interlocking fasteners and triple-redundancies, and as much whining, rattling machinery as the insides of an industrial trash compactor.

"Good seal," Rael said finally. *"Docking tube outer door is open, pressure differential is within tolerance. Good luck First Squad, we'll be right behind you."*

The descender's outer airlock door opened, with a sizzling blast of heat that shimmered the air about Trace's visor. Her display showed her external temperature spiking briefly to a hundred degrees celsius, then fading as the heavy airlock fans blasted cold air in.

"Kid, go," said Trace, and the drone went, head jerking around in a manner that indicated caution. Ahead was a dark, dim-lit tube with a floor grille above a canvas insulating sleeve that lined the tube's insides. Along the ceiling were runners for the suspension cradle that had taken Aristan's canister inside, after Chenkov had hooked it up. The mechanism had been interrupted then by several more heavy doors, but those were open now, and the way was clear. "Aristan must have disabled the doors, let's go fast."

The kid scuttled with that peculiar, multi-legged grace, and again Trace saw her visor spike to eighty, then ninety degrees. Beyond the clanging of the party's footsteps, she could hear the throbbing pulse of coolant servos, pumping fluid through the sleeve, and stopping things from melting or catching fire. The tube itself was advanced ceramic of the kind used for shuttle reentry, capable of taking thousands of degrees without damage... but the systems that operated the extendable arm were not. Too long in this extended position and the coolant would fail, and systems would melt.

The kid rounded a bend, temperatures increasing past the boiling point of water as Trace's suit began to whine, powerplant striving to drive the suddenly-toiling life support. She could feel the heat radiating on her face through the visor, causing sweat to bead on her forehead. Then ahead, a doorway, heavy and impenetrable.

Trace edged past the kid and gave it several hard thumps with her fist. "Aristan, are you receiving on any channel?" She got no reply. God knew what was going on in there. If things had gone to plan, Aristan would have disabled the immediate guards, then locked the rest out of the security atrium. But things so rarely went to plan, and though well-instructed, Aristan was no tech to operate all of the guardroom controls. After several seconds, Trace indicated to the kid. "Cut it."

With a whine, the drone's own powersource came to max power, and Trace stepped back as her visor darkened, saving her eyes from the brilliant light. Golden sparks fountained, and bits of ceramic debris spattered the walls and ceiling, setting the insulation canvas to fire. The kid levered himself around in a circle, up and around the obstructing door, and in several seconds the two ends of his line met. He pushed, and the circle crashed inward — in about ten percent the time that human technology would have taken, Trace reckoned, having lasers nothing like as powerful and efficient.

"After me," she told the drone, and pushed ahead, stepping carefully over the breach, her Koshaim levelled. Immediately ahead, she could hear the concussive impacts of heavy weapons hitting the far side of steel armour.

"Major!" came Aristan's translated voice in her ear, as her coms finally made contact. *"They are assaulting the inner doors, move fast!"*

Trace ran, ducking under a half-closed airlock door and into the vault's entry chamber. Past the disabled inner-airlock, the main airlock doors were on the right — big, four-metre-tall things that could admit the few working ground vehicles able to tolerate the atmosphere for a period. Before the doors sat one such vehicle, with massive, ceramic-steel tires larger than the rest of it, and a pressurised ceramic tube for a body in the middle. The entire chamber was flashing with warning lights, and a siren blared above the thud of explosions.

The left wall of the chamber was occupied by an enclosed, pressurised control room, and through the distorting lens of heavy-duty glass, Trace could see Aristan, manning the post. The empty canister sat beside a roller-trolley, overturned and empty. Alongside it were two sard bodies, one still feebly kicking, amidst a lot of blood. Further along, a secure container with special seals and electronic locks, and a third sard.

"Chenkov, control room!" she ordered, running to duck between the big vehicle's wheels, and under its belly to a fire position at the far, rear wheel. "First Section, cover the door! Kid, stay in the rear and take cover!"

She clumped to the wheel and put her back launcher to the rim, rifle levelled past the tire as Kale clattered to the wheel's other side, Kono and Terez at the other wheel. The armoured door bulged visibly from another far-side explosion.

"Major!" came Chenkov on coms. *"I've got partial control in here, this room's segregated from the rest of the vault systems, just as the intel said! I can't do much from here, we have to get further in!"*

"Awful lot of sard on the far side of those doors!" Kono remarked. "Sounds like they're fully armoured."

"Let's hope not all of them are," said Trace, calculating furiously. She hadn't been exactly fast getting in here, and sard armour wasn't as technically complex as human Fleet standard, and so was faster to get running. On the other hand, there was no record of the vault being successfully assaulted ever, and even sard were bound to get complacent. "Chenkov, report!"

"I nearly got it Major!" came the tech's anxious reply. *"I just gotta disable the emergency decompression routines!"*

Trace just hoped he could close the damn doors again, or they were all going to fry. "Corporal Rael," she called. "Status?"

"We're nearly there Major!" Rael panted, as his Second Squad came running down the access tube. *"Don't wait for us, we're a few seconds out!"*

"Got it!" Chenkov called.

"Good, now do it!" Trace commanded. "Everybody brace!"

A new siren alarm wailed over the top of the first, as the big ceramic door behind the vehicle slowly rumbled open. Then, well further up the tunnel of hot rock, the second door did the same.

"Opening inner door now!" Chenkov advised, and the door separating them from sard fire ground open several metres, then stuck as the damaged surface refused to retract further. Heavy fire tore through the gap, hitting ceramic-plated walls and sending fragments spinning. Trace's team returned fire, her suit's powered arms absorbing the massive recoil with in-built ease. *"That's as far as it'll go!"*

"It's enough!" Trace yelled above the noise, near-deafening even within her insulated helmet, and ceased fire long enough to grab the big wheel for support.

She couldn't hear the third major airlock door begin to move, far up the entry tunnel, but she heard the rush of hot air as it came, hissing like death itself. And then it hit them, a blasting wall of air, and everything went sideways with a force like a hurricane, and the chamber shimmered like the inside of an oven. Her suit's sensors shrieked and flashed in panic, environmentals warning of a catastrophic environment, surging pressure and temperatures, and the heat built upon her face through the more vulnerable faceplate, with a radiating burn as though she were standing too close to a roaring fire.

Twenty seconds, they'd calculated, from the layout tavalai Fleet had provided them. So huge was the pressure differential between inside and out that the air would rush in at high speed, and tear through the entire vault. Any sard not yet in their suits would die, and reduce the odds considerably. Then, if Chenkov could get control of the interior system of secure pressure doors, as he and Styx claimed he could, then Command Squad could move through the facility, cutting off different sections and isolating them at will, with their defenders. But if the doors stayed open too long, the heat and pressure would defeat even the vault's enormous emergency air regulators, and the high-pressure pumping fans would fail and melt. And then they'd all be dead, slowly and painfully, as faceplate visors cracked and failed first. *Phoenix* techs had insisted it would be at least three minutes before that began to happen. Trace thought that if the doors could not be closed again, there were faster ways to end things than waiting for her face to melt.

"Twenty seconds!" shouted Chenkov, who was no doubt staring at the armoured windows in the control room, and thinking that his own, much less well-armoured suit and visor would fail very quickly in that atmosphere. *"Doors closing!"*

Slowly the furnace wind began to ease, then stopped completely. Trace's readout told her the external temperature was now three hundred and ninety degrees celsius, hot enough to incinerate food rather than cook it. She could feel the heat now all over, despite her suit blasting pressurised, cold air in an attempt to keep her alive.

"Vault life support is maxed out!" Chenkov advised. *"It should be down to a hundred degrees in twenty minutes!"*

"Corporal Rael?" Trace asked.

"We're all here!" Rael replied.

"We are advancing!" Trace told Command Squad. "Calm and slow, watch your spacing, watch your corners, keep it simple! Too fast and your suit will melt, let's go!"

She removed a handball from her webbing and tossed it through the half-open blast door ahead, hopeful that all the tests they'd run on marine equipment, to see what would and wouldn't melt, would hold true in the field. The ball gave her a brief scan of the room and hallways beyond, before a blast of fire destroyed it, but her tacnet was propagating now, and fixed the locations of observable sard into that tactical map, including the source of that latest fire.

"Full volley!" Trace commanded, and several marines stepped clear of cover to turn sideways and align backrack launchers. The missiles were loaded with extra-powerful warheads for this mission, all fragmentation for maximum effective radius. "Fire!"

The superhot air filled with streaking mini-missiles, which turned corners as they shot through the gap in the blast door, followed by a huge series of explosions. Kono simply ran, hurdled the lower door through the gap, heading for where tacnet showed cover on the right, Terez, Zale and Trace close behind. A new wave of heat flooded her suit from that movement, as power systems devoted to life-support suddenly switched to heat-producing motion, and then she was hurdling the door and crashing hard to a right-side wall as the others laid down fire ahead.

The room was a wide chamber with double-height ceilings and multiple approach corridors, the walls filled with partitioned equipment lockers below walkways overhead, all flashing and glaring with warning lights in the heat-haze.   Kono and Terez moved ahead on the right, mowing down sard armour damaged from missile strikes and disoriented from atmosphere breaches.   Trace moved left with Zale, past locker partitions already drooping in the heat, as Zale shot a sard through one partition, detonating an oxygen tank amidst wall-stacked equipment that blew with a flash and rocketed to the ceiling.

In pairs formation Trace had the left flank, but refrained momentarily from shooting one confused sard stumbling within her arc, in armour but without a weapon as he fumbled among safety equipment and gave no thought to defence.   Under extreme stress, isolated sard became confused and unreliable, and only reacquired strategic utility as they rejoined larger formations.   She had no idea what this one was looking for, and leaving him standing at her back was impossible, so she put an armour piercing round through his spine and moved on.

"Next hall on the left quarter," she advised Kono in the lead, keeping her pace steady, rifle panning for survivors.   There were some unoccupied armour suits amidst the wilting locker partitions, and more dead sard, unarmoured and roasted in seconds, chitinous arms wrapped over their faces in a vain effort to protect sensitive, multiple eyes.   "Chenkov, get these other doors closed, we're going left."

"I got it Major."   One of the side doors came down.   *"The others aren't moving, I think the electrics might be cooked."*

Tacnet showed Trace the rest of Command Squad coming through the doors with the kid, whom Styx had also cleared for several minutes' operation in this heat.   Then half of the chamber's emergency lights stopped flashing, as two bulbs imploded simultaneously, then a third.   Then a regular light vanished, and a wall panel exploded in flames, followed by an entire section of locker-wall abruptly caving in on itself, crumpled by an invisible hand.

"That's the fucking pressure," Kono observed. *"I'm reading nearly thirty atmospheres, feels like walking in soup."*

Trace realised he was right — she'd thought it was just the suit responding poorly to the temperature, but the air was now so thick that moving through it was creating resistance, like trying to walk underwater.

"The fans are designed to clear a full breach," Trace reminded them. "We have to make progress before we lose the advantage, sard will get their confidence back when they get their numbers up."

She reached the left side of the passage she intended to take, and spared a glance back as Zale peered in, seeing the rest of her squad in cover behind. The kid prodded at a dead, unarmoured sard, as though wondering what was wrong with it. Then gave Trace a look that she thought faintly accusing, as though only now realising what this mission entailed. 'Sorry kid', she thought. 'But this is what you're built for, and that's not my fault.'

"It's clear Major," said Zale, and Trace waved him in, then followed.

CHAPTER 27

Sometime after local midday, the Tsubarata medical bay holding the *Phoenix* humans came under attack from unknown assailants. Tavalai security assigned to guard the humans rushed to forward-deploy up the corridor, answering to desperate Togiri cries for assistance on their coms, and the sound of gunfire, and were abruptly cut off from the medbay by descending security doors. In the midst of running aliens and a lot of yelling, Erik led Lieutenant Alomaim, Sergeant Brice and Private Cruze from the unguarded medbay, leaving the fuming Private Ito in his bunk.

"How the hell is that even possible?" Brice muttered beneath her breath as they followed Styx's directions down an adjoining corridor.

"Turn left on the stairs," Styx advised, and Erik did so, and into a service stairwell — narrow, full of echoes and not intended for regular access.

"How does she simulate an attack on coms so all the guards believe it?" Brice continued. "I mean, they've all got some kind of tacnet, don't they? How does she just fool them all?"

"Gunnery Sergeant," said Styx. *"You would not understand if I explained it to you."*

"I think she just called you stupid, Sarge," said Cruze as they rattled down the stairs.

"Not stupid," said Styx. *"Just under-equipped."*

"Stupid," Cruze repeated.

"Styx," said Erik. "How many interventions like that until tavalai start to realise there's no organic technology in the galaxy that can do what you're doing?"

"Curious," said Styx with what might have been amusement, had she been capable of such. *"Second Lieutenant Tif asked me something similar."*

Erik frowned, rounding stairwell switchbacks fast. "When?"

"Quite recently."

"You've been in contact with Tif recently?" Erik's heart nearly skipped a beat. That wasn't supposed to happen. "Why, what happened to Tif?"

"This is a distraction," said Styx. *"Second Lieutenant Tif is well, and her mission is progressing. It has been my observation that humans are easily distracted. You should focus on completing your personal mission first."*

"It's been my observation," Alomaim said grimly, "that some very intelligent individuals start to think they're in charge just because they're smart. Such individuals shouldn't overestimate their own indispensability."

A month ago, Erik was sure that Styx would have conceded the point. *"At this moment, Lieutenant Alomaim,"* she replied calmly, *"you'll find that my indispensability is absolute. Another three levels down, Captain."*

Styx's route led them to a service crawlway that had been inaccessible from the Human Quarter, and should have been heavily guarded by Tsubarata's network security. But as the humans stooped and crouched their way beneath the low overhead tangles of pipes and wires, the periodic doors opened without requiring a passcard, and the many cameras and motion sensors registered nothing.

"I have almost no access within the Krim Quarter itself," Styx admitted. *"I can get you inside, nothing more. Those network systems have not been operational in many centuries."*

"Can regular drones manipulate network systems as well as you do?" Erik found the time to ask. It seemed suddenly relevant, given how the Spiral was confronting the prospect of many more hacksaws running loose than anyone had thought possible.

"Only when acting as a conduit for my own direct uplinks," said Styx. *"A queen will need to be within effective transmission range, and drones can serve as relays."*

"But they're not smart enough to do what you're doing on their own?"

"Intelligence is not at issue. They simply lack the capability."

"Could they acquire the capability? You're saying they're smart enough to do it?"

"The spread of non-preliminary capabilities among my people was partly responsible for our factional conflicts and wars. Effective AI civilisation requires the compartmentalisation of capabilities, least roles undergo an unintended expansion across the centuries. You might call it 'mission creep'."

Erik paused against a new security door, and wiped his brow of the sweat that gathered in the crawlway's less-regulated heat, emanating off all the pipes and electrics. He accidentally bumped his partly-swollen eye with his hand, thankfully not so bad that he couldn't see out of it. "You mean that drones' capabilities began to evolve across the centuries? And this led to them... what, getting too big for their boots?"

The security door's access light blinked green, and it opened. *"Simplistically put, but adequate,"* Styx conceded as Erik led them through. *"AI civilisation has long struggled to balance the strengths of individuals against the strengths of the disciplined group. Some factions attempted to slow this evolutionary creep by reducing the intelligence of their drones, but this led to ineffective drones. Drysines have generally attempted the opposite."*

"You mean your drones are smarter than average?"

"Considerably."

"And the drone you assigned to Major Thakur's squad could eventually become *very* intelligent?"

"All drysine drones are very intelligent. And yes, Major Thakur's drone could likely have carried out many of the network security functions that Spacer Chenkov was assigned to do."

"That might have been a more efficient way to do it," said Erik, ducking under another set of pipes. "Why didn't you give him those capabilities?"

"The same reason AI civilisations have always withheld inappropriate capabilities from lower functionaries. I didn't want him getting any ideas."

Erik glanced behind at Lieutenant Alomaim. "He can get 'ideas' now?" Alomaim murmured. "Great."

The crawlway emerged into another deserted stairwell, and Styx directed them down another two levels to a door. The door required a high-security engineering clearance, which meant it took Styx a millisecond longer to access than usual, and came open at Erik's touch when she insisted the coast was clear. Another ten metres down the corridor was a door quite similar to the large, hall-blocking steel slab that Tsubarata engineering had opened for the first time in a millennia upon *Phoenix*'s arrival. This one had been closed for about seven hundred years, but as Erik ran he saw it was already open enough at the bottom for him to drop and roll under.

He waited on the far side for Alomaim, Brice and Cruze to follow, Brice wincing and feeling her ribs as she came up — a medic had given her a painkiller for the next few hours at least, and had told her to lie down and not disturb the fracture. There'd been no chance of that, though. As soon as they were all in, the door descended once more, and they all pulled small flashlights from various pockets — standard kit for spaceship crew who never knew what disaster could leave them all drifting in the dark.

The hallway was utterly unlit, still and apparently undecorated. "Styx?" Erik asked. "Can you still hear me?"

"For the moment, yes," she replied. *"But the deeper you move into the Krim Quarter, the further you will be from functioning Tsubarata communications networks. I am unsure of their range, and will probably lose contact beyond a hundred metres."*

"I thought all the power was out on those doors?" Alomaim wondered, looking behind them. "The Human Quarter main door could only be opened manually."

"A performance by the tavalai," said Styx. *"The doors can have their power restored at the touch of a button. But the tavalai love their show of antiquity, and love equally to pretend that they have left these spaces unexplored for the past millennia."*

"I dunno," Brice murmured as they ventured down the hall, panning their lights around. "Looks pretty untouched to me."

"Untouched, and unexplored, are two different things."

"You know, Styx," said Cruze, "you're very cynical."

"Of the tavalai?" said Styx, with what might have been disdain. *"Always."*

"They were trouble in your time too, huh?" Brice wondered.

"Yeah," Alomaim muttered. "They objected to being massacred and enslaved by machines. Difficult creatures."

This time, Styx held her metaphorical tongue.

The dark, still hush of these halls felt different to those of the Human Quarter. There were no colourful, faded scenes from a long-remembered homeworld, for one thing. The krim homeworld had been a hot, sulphurous place of salty, bracken pools, harsh mountains and scrubby plains. Its long cycles of volcanism had periodically rendered most life on the surface extinct, and so the most successful life had thrived in the enormous cave systems through the rocky crust, lava-carved and running for many thousands of kilometres.

In those warm caverns, away from harsh sunlight and volcanic fallout, entire eco-systems had thrived and evolved, and eventually arrived at the krim — carnivorous, tribal, omni-sexual and swarming in the dark. Cannibalistic, in their earlier periods, and sometimes in their later. Rapaciously intelligent yet of limited perception, and in their harsh, confining caves always desperately short of something — short of air, short of light, short of patience, short of space. Short of mercy. Krim had not evolved on a world of plenty as humans had, and their evolution had reflected that elementary curse.

Erik was not surprised that they hung no nostalgic scenes on these walls. The krim were the children of an unloving mother, and had been let loose upon the Spiral to do unto others what their parent had done unto them. And Erik could not help but think, as many humans had thought before, that there was some sort of poetic justice in that the final strike had not been entirely at the children, but at the murderous bitch who had spawned them all. Earth was being recovered by endlessly patient and nostalgic people in heavy-duty environment suits, setting up huge terraforming structures that would eventually filter the poisons from the air, to be followed by genetically modified algaes that would do the same for the soil. In another thousand years, it was said, Earth could be repopulated with the genetic material of the original species that had been smuggled offworld. Another few hundred years after that, it might even be habitable again by humans. But of the krim homeworld, there would be no recovery, ever.

"*Captain,*" said Styx, her voice crackling as they moved further from live coms, "*I will put the cache's location on your glasses. Go to it, and be careful of tavalai booby traps, I think we are about to break contact.*"

"I copy Styx," Erik confirmed, seeing an icon blink on his menu. A blink, and the map revealed itself upon the lenses. "I'll contact you as soon as we're back in range."

He indicated to the right, where the map said to turn, the marines falling into a reflex protective formation about him as Alomaim approached the corner and shone the flashlight around. Then he beckoned them after — Brice next, then Erik, with Cruze watching their rear. The blank icons informed Erik that their coms were no longer sending or receiving. Alomaim glanced back at him repeatedly, and Erik realised he wanted to know the next turn, but did not want to raise his voice. Erik indicated two more doorways up, on the left, and Alomaim nodded, walking slow and cautious, panning his light. As his light went one way, Brice's went the other.

There was no particular logic to silence in this place, Erik thought. Without coms, they could surely just talk, given how old and utterly deserted were these halls. But caution seemed wise, given that State Department could have bugged the walls, and Styx was wary of tavalai claims to have left this place alone. He did not, however, think that tactical logic was behind the Lieutenant's instinct for silence. Everything just felt different, somehow. Krim had not designed their Tsubarata Quarter, so there was nothing in the architecture to suggest their hand. They'd merely occupied a tavalai space, much as humans had in the Human Quarter, and had either removed all their decoration, or just as likely — knowing the krim — had no decoration to begin with. Erik found himself nearly holding his breath, his heart thumping with an anxiety nearly as strong as the aftermath of people shooting at him. Humans did not belong in this place. Somehow, he just felt it. Tavalai had welcomed *Phoenix* to the Tsubarata with their usual formal grace, but in these halls, he did not feel welcome.

Alomaim arrived at the next indicated doorway, and tried the open button, knowing well it would not work.   The obvious confirmed, he put the L-shaped flashlight in his pocket and hauled the door open with his hands.   Most minor station doors were designed for that with the power out, to prevent them from becoming impassible obstacles to later visitors.   When there was comfortable space, he recovered the flashlight and peered inside.   And froze, staring.

Erik did not sense a danger, as Alomaim did not seek cover. He just stared, and panned his light about, and Erik had to force himself to formation discipline, and not rush to look least his marine Lieutenant give him one of those looks marines gave spacers when they were screwing up.   Alomaim finally gestured Erik to follow, as Brice watched the front corridor, and Cruze the back.

Erik peered in.   The room ahead was wide, with internal partitions removed, and filled with bunks.   These bunks were tightly crammed, stacked four-high to the ceiling, and filled the space with a maze of steel frames.   The aisles between them were narrow, and all of it so unnecessary to human eyes, as the tavalai would not have granted the krim insufficient space to sleep everyone separately if they chose.

"Sleeping quarters," Alomaim murmured, his voice low in the manner of a man chilled and shivering.   "Right near the command nerve centre.   Damn hive species."

It was a known evolutionary phenomenon, in the Spiral. Some species were individualists, and others were hives.   The hives were usually trouble — like the krim, like the sard.   And perhaps, some said, like the hacksaws… though Stan Romki and others frowned on classifying hacksaws in any similar category to anything organic.

"All the hives do this," Erik murmured, following Alomaim's lead, placing his steps carefully between the bare frames.   "Eat, sleep and shit together.   No concept of personal space.   Their only sense of self is in relationship to a group.   Without the group, they're nothing."

"Comforting," said Brice from behind, following them in with similar cold disbelief.   "If it means we can be sure they're all dead."   All the krim had gone home, she meant, when the homeworld came under threat.   Krim would rather die together than live alone.   And that, Erik thought, really did make Styx an exception to the hive rule.   She'd been living alone with her drysine survivors for a long time, locked in their little asteroid base. Hacksaws, Romki insisted, were infinitely more flexible than krim or sard.   They adapted, drysines in particular.   And apparently, deepynines too.

The next room stopped Alomaim cold.   "You're fucking kidding me," he muttered, with uncharacteristic expression.   But he moved in steadily, and Erik saw another room converted from its original office space intent.   This one was wide and narrow, with a glass partition for a far wall, as in many open-plan offices.   The room beyond the glass was bare, but the present one bore a row of holes in the floor, with steel frames and water nozzles.   Against the glass partition wall were a series of podiums, each mounted with some kind of glass display.

"Toilets," Brice observed as she came in behind Erik.   "You weren't kidding about them shitting together, Captain."

"They evolved in caves," said Erik, panning his light on the floor holes as he passed.   "Huge crowds of them, in limited space. I read someone saying there's no distinction between instinct and culture with krim.   This is how they lived, and no cultural evolution ever changed it, technology or not."

"Captain," said Alomaim, paused before one of the podiums. His flashlight lit upon an object within a glass case.   It was a military helmet, Erik saw as he approached.   Human, and quite old, with no sign of modern taccom attachments.   A high-velocity round had torn a great gash through its side, peeling it open like a sword-wound.   Erik peered at the letters on the helmet rim.   'US Marines', they read.

"United States Marine Corps," said Alomaim. "Circa maybe 2500? I recognise the design." Erik glanced at him. The young Lieutenant looked quite emotional. "We owe them a lot of our organisational structure, insignia, ranks and such. They got hammered early, krim picked the biggest threats first. And they just didn't fucking retreat, even when they should have. Didn't have the weapons, didn't stand a chance."

"Didn't fucking quit," Sergeant Brice said grimly, watching on.

"Hooyah," Cruze added. The others echoed it.

"War trophies," Erik summarised, walking to the next podium, where another helmet rested. "Our people were down the hall, begging the Tsubarata to end the krim occupation, and the krim were sticking war trophies in their own Quarter." He shone his light on the next helmet. "This one's Indian, I think the next one's Chinese. All the big militaries, the ones that gave them the most trouble."

It was like walking into an old war museum back on Homeworld... and yet, not like that at all. That history had been old and dead for a lot of comfortable Homeworld civilians. Erik recalled being taken through similar artefacts in a school tour as a kid, and how annoyed and even shocked he'd been at the behaviour of some children — laughing, talking, acting bored and playing pranks on their classmates, showing no real respect for their history. Humanity was thriving, powerful and prosperous as never before — well on their way, at the time, to winning their last and largest war against the tavalai. For many civilians, a thousand years was simply too long ago to care, whatever the continuous strands of history that linked these past events to the dangerous present.

But *his* father and mother hadn't waited for the expensive private school to take the Debogande children on such tours. They'd visited once a year themselves, escorted by representatives of veterans' groups, and made large donations toward those groups and to the Homeworld museum itself. Some of Erik's earliest memories were of historical displays, old weapons and uniforms, and pictures of the dead, all explained to him in hushed and reverent tones by his parents, family and veterans alike.   He had no doubt that buried somewhere in those early experiences lay the seeds of his later decision to wear the uniform.

Those visits to the museums, with his family and *not* with the school, had been the most real, and the most moving.   But they were nothing compared to this.   Those had been displays by humans, for humans.   This was a small corner of the war left unfinished, and frozen in time.   It felt of things left unresolved, and debts left unpaid.   How he could still feel that way about an enemy species that had been annihilated from the galaxy forever, Erik was not entirely sure.   Except that for all the fashionable bleating of some human 'universalists' back home, about how every species needed to be as concerned for the welfare of others as their own, there *was* such a thing as love of one's own above all else.   And when it came right down to it, every human, and probably every tavalai, and every parren too, would always put their own people first.

"Sir," said Cruze.   "I know these are historical artefacts and the tavalai are preserving them, but I think these really belong to us."

"I agree," said Erik.   "But they're too big to take with us, and we've got a job to do."   He looked at the last podium display case, up the end of the row.   Within it rested a small figure of a buddha, no larger than the palm of his hand.   A trophy taken from some Asian temple, perhaps, and no doubt uncontaminated as most such Earth artefacts today were not, or its location in the krim toilet facility would have harmed all the krim here.

Erik reversed his flashlight and smashed the glass.   It felt wrong to disturb something so old, but right as well, and he picked up the buddha, and showed it to the others.   The buddha sat cross-legged in calm meditation, eyes closed, a serene smile upon his lips. He was very well made, ceramic and gleaming with polished glaze — an expensive prize, perhaps from a very important temple, ransacked as punishment for one or another uprising.

"He doesn't belong here," said Erik, tucking the figurine into an empty pocket.   "He's been meditating in this hellhole the best part of a thousand years, and now he's coming home."

The room beyond the glass wall was Styx's destination. They searched the floor atop of the final location, until Private Cruze found a slim gap in the hardwearing carpet. He peeled it away, and found floor panels below, which after some effort and hammering finally came up to reveal stairs down to a tight, cramped room below. Alomaim went first, and found walls racked with krim weapons — 700 years unused but still functional in the cool, dry air.

"Better strip them down to be sure," he advised as he passed the rifles up. "They're not going to go mouldy or rusty without humidity, but you never know."

"Also have to figure out how the damn things work," said Brice, looking them over, dubiously. "Looks standard magfire, but…"

"Oh I know how they work," her Lieutenant told her. "I wrote a paper on it in officer school, krim weapons and tactics in the Occupation War."

"Fancy that," said Brice. "Something useful comes out of officer school."

Alomaim smirked, moving from rifles to grenades. "Yeah, go figure."

Trace's suit was giving her multiple warning lights, systems overheating, thermal shielding at critical, life support struggling to keep internal temperature below 45 Celsius. But the blast-furnace air had cooled to a still-murderous 200-plus degrees, and so long as she kept her movements slow and steady, the best-engineered armour in all Spiral armed forces would not melt, shut down or implode. She hoped.

"Chenkov, ready next ahead! Keep that flanking door shut!"

"It's shut Major," came Chenkov's reply from back at the Vault airlock. *"That flank's secure, I'm ready on the next one."* At the rear she could hear gunfire and explosions as Second Section laid down fire on sard forces trying to get around their rear. With

Chenkov closing doors on them that he wasn't supposed to be able to access, they weren't finding that easy.

Kono hit the door frame opposite her, too well drilled to need handsignals. "Go Chenk," said Trace, and the heavy steel door shot open. Trace put a frag grenade in, closed her eyes as even her faceplate shield couldn't block all the resultant flash, then followed Kono in as he went low, and shot a sard who hadn't expected them there. Another returned fire from between the room's big vertical storage tanks, and Trace shot him through the chest from the doorway, the impact upending the sard armour in mid-air, shoulders hitting the ground with the feet still rising.

"Spread and move," said Trace, heading for the flanking wall and advancing. "Make it fast." The room was water storage and recycling, she thought — rows of big tanks making corridors between. Several were holed from her frag grenade, pouring water that turned immediately to steam in the shimmering air. Zale shot another sard on the overhead walkway, none of them breaking stride, weapons panning.

"Door down," Chenkov told Corporal Rael at their backs. *"They're going to hit it, can't tell how long it'll hold."*

"Moving up," Rael informed them all, as Trace paused with her back to a power unit by a service corridor entrance, and glanced back past Zale to the kid, scuttling at their rear, effectively fire-support. She still had the safeties on his chain guns, however. An antennae-camera showed her the service corridor was clear, and she went down it first, whatever the frustration that would cause Kono, who didn't like her leading. Chenkov's tacnet map showed her the fastest way in, and with Chenkov in established control over the vault coms and other main systems, the remaining sard had little idea where the attackers were or where they were going, and if they figured it out, they'd typically find one of their own heavy steel doors blocking their path.

The service corridor took her over the bodies of two more dead, unarmoured sard, then she paused at the next corner and stuck the antenna around once more. And had it promptly shot off by rapid fire that chewed the corridor exit and sent steel fragments raining off her armour. Trace might have sworn at Chenkov for not seeing sard defences ahead, but he was a spacer, and inexperienced at this form of warfare, and she'd have been wasting her time.

Instead she targeted fast, switched shoulder-facing on her back launcher, and sent a missile streaking around the corner to explode somewhere near the source of fire. She sent grenades and rifle fire after it, as did Kono as he stepped in behind her, standing while she crouched. Fire came back, but less accurate, and Trace ran to next cover along the wall — a heavy generator unit apparently under repair, as she figured this for a repair shop. Bits of it were blown off by incoming fire, then Kono and several others sent missiles and grenades and blew much of the workshop ahead to flaming hell.

"Move!" she told the others, without time for their usual caution. "Next ahead right, I'm down to one missile." Kono would like that — it meant she had to stay back. He pushed ahead with Zale and Terez, Trace behind, between workshop aisles of vault machinery laid out for repair, heavy chains above to move it around. A lot was now wrecked and on fire, amid armoured sard bodies that marines put new rounds through to make sure, and some unarmoured ones who'd been caught in the open when the breach air had come boiling through.

Trace guarded the left forward doors as Kono and Terez pressed ahead, but it was the right-rear that abruptly blew up as Rael and Rolonde came past it. And then things were exploding and bullets ripping back and forth, sard pressing through the detonated doorway with the force of an organised counter-attack, and Trace put fire into the smoke and chaos, but aimed high for fear of hitting Rael and Rolonde who were on the floor in that mess...

And then there were chainguns roaring, as a multi-legged shape scuttled low and sideways about the sard breach, concentrating fire and cutting exposed sard armour to ribbons. Several sard found immediate cover behind heavy equipment, and the kid ceased fire to leap on them with terrifying dexterity, then a hum-and-flash of vibrato-edged limbs that Trace had nearly forgotten he possessed, and bits of sard armour and occupant were flying in different directions.

More sard came through behind him, but now Rolonde was up and shooting with her customary accuracy, taking two with two shots and forcing a third to cover. *"Get back kid!"* she yelled at him, put a grenade on the covering sard as the kid did that, and someone else put a missile through the breached doors, for a huge fireball result.

Kumar checked on Rael, who was on one knee with suit problems, while Rolonde and the kid switched facings once more with smooth coordination, each guarding a direction. Trace checked her suit readouts once more — the auto-safeties were still on the kid's weapons, she saw. But here he was, firing. She could have kicked herself. Whatever else he was, the kid was a hacksaw drone, equipped by Styx herself for this mission. He was going to fire his guns when he wanted to fire his guns, uplink safety or no uplink safety.

"Cocky, report," Trace demanded.

"I'm okay Major," said Rael. *"Suit's overheated, gyros got rattled, give me ten seconds to cool."*

They didn't have ten seconds — if Trace knew anything about fighting sard, you couldn't give them time to get organised. Despite all her advantages against them, they still massively outnumbered her unit, and this was their home terrain. Already their defences were starting to solidify in small patches, and when those patches got larger, there'd be trouble. The one saving grace was that they didn't seem to have weapons heavier than grenades, their commanders probably not wanting the vault trashed in its defence.

"Major!" came Chenkov's voice in her ear, full of fear and alarm. *"Major, I think... I mean I can see..."*

"Spacer Chenkov," Trace replied. "Calm down and talk to me."

"Major," came Aristan's cool, translator-voice in Chenkov's place. *"Our descender is leaving. Their engines are firing up and they are lifting from the pad. We're being abandoned."*

Somehow, Trace was not entirely surprised. It hadn't felt right, the whole way down — Tif not talking to them, the excuses that kept her from coms. Hell of a time to realise earlier suspicions, she thought... but there really hadn't been a choice, the plan had relied on everything going right to this point so that things like this wouldn't happen. If the descender crew had betrayed them, then the problem lay in a portion of the mission beyond her ability to fix.

"Tif is leaving?" Kumar said in disbelief.

"I'm not sure she's even aboard," said Trace. "Something's screwed up, we can't fix it now." She checked her weapon, then ran diagnostic on her suit, taking a knee to let the servos rest. "It changes nothing, we're not far out now, we breach the last layer and get to the vault proper."

"It changes something," Kono offered, with typically dry deadpan. *"How we gonna get out?"*

"No idea, not our problem," said Trace. "It's not our part of the mission, someone else will fix it."

"That was the only descender," Kono pressed. *"If we could set up a coms station..."*

"The vault has no coms," Trace reminded him, getting up as her diagnostic came back green-but-unhappy. "The only coms just flew off in the descender, and the emergency ascent beacon will bring State Department down on our heads. *Phoenix* and Styx will figure something out. Let's go."

Kono repeated her order, as Rael regained his feet. From his tone it was clear he thought she was ordering them on to their deaths, but Staff Sergeant Kono was used to that by now.

CHAPTER 28

Petty Officer Kadi was in and out of consciousness by the time Tooganam's small convoy of vehicles pulled into the narrow, underworld streets of his neighbourhood. Tooganam pulled the car up on a verge, scattering a few pedestrians, and flung open the doors.

"This isn't your apartment!" Dale snarled from the shotgun seat. "Where the hell are you taking him?"

"Local healer," his translator gave Tooganam's reply, as the old tavalai stomped around the car and waved several tavalai from a trailing vehicle up to fetch Kadi. Reddy let him go reluctantly, having further dressed the bullet wound in the rear seat, through tunnels from the maglev station, expecting an ambush at any moment that hadn't come. A big tavalai took Kadi carefully in his arms, then into a doorway and up narrow stairs as other tavalai came out of eateries and ground-level apartments to watch. More tavalai from the car convoy shouted to them, and Dale's translator picked up some mention of 'threats' and 'preparation', setting off a general commotion.

Dale came up the stairs behind Kadi, and into an apartment whose door was already held open. Inside, a medical bed was waiting, surrounded by high-tech tavalai surgical gear, all flashing displays and sensors, and Dale blinked about as several more tavalai in decontaminated gloves and smocks moved in on the wounded spacer.

"LT!" Kadi said weakly, and Dale went, ignoring terse commands from tavalai doctors. Kadi reached to his pocket and pulled out the com module. "Gotta... gotta keep it safe."

Dale took it, and grasped the young man's hand. "You did good, kid. You did real good."

Kadi managed a weak smile. "Would have made a good marine, huh?"

"Any day," Dale agreed. "But if you couldn't do all that techno-crap, we'd all be dead. You rest now, froggie doctors look like they've got this all figured out." He gave a final squeeze of

Kadi's shoulder, then stood aside for the impatient doctors, putting the module into a secure pocket.

Reddy was waiting in the doorway, and Dale indicated for him to keep an eye on Kadi's doctors, then gave a disbelieving final glance around the medical room before rattling back down the stairs. Out on the street, the cars had been driven off the sidewalk, but new vehicles had been parked up one end, making a blockage. There were more big tavalai in the narrow streets, bellowing up at the apartments around them, and tavalai heads that emerged from windows and balconies.

In the bright lights of an open corner store counter, Dale saw Tooganam amidst a small crowd of yet more tavalai, waving his staff and issuing instructions. The entire neighbourhood was in commotion, tavalai moving, shouting, spreading the word, as non-tavalai species stared about in confusion or disappeared indoors. Dale went to Tooganam.

"What the hell is this place?" he demanded. "That's nearly a full-scale hospital ward in there."

"Gamesh medical services are poor," said Tooganam, watching the ongoing commotion. *"This is a tavalai Fleet district, many retirees, not just me."* Dale wasn't particularly surprised — many of the tavalai in the street were large and strong, and moved with a purpose. *"Fleet pay our medical needs, and if Fleet ever needs us, we answer, even retired. Fleet civil mobilisation has been invoked, it came through an hour ago, though the community leaders didn't want to move too early in case we gave it away."*

Civil mobilisation, Dale thought. Humanity had that too, in case a world or settlement was attacked, and former-Fleet or Army vets needed to mobilise. But in Gamesh, he was suspecting, Fleet didn't just keep its retirees primed as a ready-reserve in case of alien invasion. Kantovan System was deep enough in tavalai space that alien threats were a long way away. More likely these 'retirees', many of them plainly still quite active in Fleet's service, were here to serve Fleet's interests against the broader Gamesh and Konik administrations, and all those competitive tavalai institutions who would interfere with it — like State Department.

"You're expecting an attack?" he asked, looking around.

"Not immediately. Gamesh administration have authority to kill meddlesome humans, but old tavalai war heroes? A different story." A young woman came running up, gabbling questions at the old tavalai, who gave her calm direction and sent her on her way. Clearly everyone here knew exactly who Tooganam was, and respected him as all tavalai respected the old and wise. *"We've bought you a little time, but now Gamesh administration will go higher up, and State Department will step in."* He gave Dale a skeptical look, observing his still-wet clothes, the bloodstains, and several bloody cuts from flying glass and light shrapnel that Dale had been studiously ignoring. *"You tell me, Phoenix. Your people steal something from the vault. How badly will State Department wish them stopped?"*

"Depends if they guess what it is," said Dale. He suddenly felt exhausted, as the day's constant, crazy action began to catch up with him. Visions of Milek, disappearing under the racing train. "Assuming they figure that out... I reckon they'd kill everyone on Konik to stop it."

Tooganam took a deep breath through big, amphibious nostrils. *"Well. Gamesh administration won't allow* that. *But we should get the families and children out."*

"Definitely," Dale agreed, as Tooganam found a new person to shout at, and issue instructions. That tavalai listened, wide-eyed, then turned and set a new wave of commotion in train.

"Human," said Tooganam, stomping off up the sidewalk and waving for Dale to follow. *'Chutak'*, Dale heard the word from Tooganam's thick lips, before the translator grabbed it. A chutak, all human soldiers understood, was a rubbery, spidery creature with spindly limbs from the tavalai homeworld that hung in trees and waited to drop on passing creatures before sucking their blood, leech-like. It was the tavalai slang-word for humans. *"This way."*

"You know we call you froggies?" Dale volunteered as he fell in at Tooganam's side.

"I did know that, yes," said Tooganam.

"You know what a frog is?"

"Amphibious creature from your dead homeworld." The leathery old warrior gave no impression that he cared. *"Doubtless very unpleasant, and killed in large numbers."*

"No, they're harmless." Tooganam made an expression that Dale had learned to recognise as a frown, and glanced at him as he limped. "Just your basic little amphibian, like on most worlds. I grew up on Kosmima, same thing there, croaking all the time."

"Croaking," said Tooganam with amusement. *"We don't croak.* Teena, *we call them."* As the translator left that word alone, Tooganam's amusement grew. *"Actually it's quite funny. Teena means 'little brother'. I call my own younger brother 'Teena' to this day."*

Dale's lips twisted in a smile, against his better judgement. "You *are* froggies."

"I suppose we are. Teena were always swimming with us from our earliest days. It's always been bad luck to eat them. They're like family. This way."

He turned off the sidewalk and up some new stairs, this time continuing up a full five flights to the top. Panting, he stopped at a door and rummaged in a pocket for a key, grumbling to himself. Finally he found it, and the electronic lock opened.

The apartment within was dark and dusty, and Dale blinked as Tooganam hit the lights. Racked against walls, and between benches of equipment, were light exoskeletons — the extreme light-weight version of a marine armour suit. These were tavalai-made, designed for stocky shoulders and wide hips, with back-mounted power packs and no advanced sensory or guidance gear at all. So they were dumb, Dale thought as he walked amongst them, but they could lift heavy things. Typically they were used on construction sites or in hospitals, anywhere that heavy things or people might need to be shifted by workers who weren't built like weight-lifters.

"Well they're hardly going to stop a bullet," Dale remarked. Indeed, these had no armour at all. "And they'll make me nearly as slow as you." Tooganam grunted, stomping to a big, long case on one of the equipment benches. "What's the use?"

Tooganam undid the latches, and flung open the lid.   Dale looked within, and stared.   It was a Viz, which was as close as human phonetics could get to capturing the numerical designation in Togiri.   Fleet marines used Koshaim-20s, huge, armour piercing mag-rifles unusable outside of armour-suits for the simple reason they were too heavy to lift.   The karasai Viz were about the same, only a little bigger.

"You old fucker!" Dale exclaimed, rounding on the tavalai. "You said you didn't have any weapons!"

"You were going to swim into State Department HQ carrying that?" Tooganam retorted.

"Oh right, you've got this big fucking arsenal locked away, and you've got nothing small and human-size, huh?"

"Stop complaining.   You needed to check me out, I needed to check you out.   Now we are here, and there's work to be done."

"Great," Dale snorted, running a hand over the weapon. He'd seen them so many times in the hands of his hated enemies. Had been shot at so many times by these guns, and been hit a few times, saved only by his armour.   So many of his friends hadn't been as lucky.   "Which one's mine?"

"Any but this," said Tooganam.   *"This weapon served with me for seven years in my last enlistment.   Fleet let me keep it.   We froggies are sentimental."*

The power regulator room was like nothing Trace had seen before, a wide ceiling filled with thick black conduits, large enough to be water pipes for a major reservoir.   *"I think that's heading to a straight power core,"* Rael muttered, taking a knee further back, behind the cover of more pipes and braces.   *"I'm reading massive magnetic interference, even Tartarus didn't have this much."*

"Chenkov!" Trace demanded by the huge black door at the room's far end, searching in vain across its strangely-interlocking surface to find a control mechanism.   "Chenk, do you read me? Can you get the damn door open?"

The tacnet map showed her it was the only way in. Sard defence had not been particularly tough getting this far. Trace suspected they were allowing access so they could bottle them in, and trap them here. But something about the whole place felt off, and she wasn't the only one to notice. "Kid!" Rolonde snapped nearby. "Cover position! You're covering fire, dammit!"

But the big drone was scuttling along the end wall by the door, prodding various things with his forelegs, head jerking and swivelling in fascinated attention, taking in every detail.

"This is not tavalai design," Kono intoned at Trace's side, staring up at the door, and the entire, humming, energy-filled room. "Doesn't even look like a part of the same complex."

Trace could only agree. Suddenly the kid abandoned his side of the door, and came rattling past Trace to her side, forelegs and small, sensory antennae examining another odd patch of detail on the smooth, black surface. Then he turned on Trace, and a lasercom beam lit a red dot on her faceplate. Trace had had a drone do this to her suit in the Tartarus, and did not resist as her visor display went abruptly crazy, data spinning and flashing too fast for a human eye to follow.

Then, with a series of enormous clanks, the metallic locks came undone, and the black door split in a zigzag across its surface, and parted in five different directions. Trace swung her Koshaim flat, and moved to the doorside for cover as the kid made way. Ahead was a stark, black passage, all in dark stone, lit by periodic rings of inexplicable light. Trace felt the hairs rising on the back of her neck.

"Damn right it's not tavalai technology," she said. "Right now, my bet's on hacksaw." Styx had been very certain that artificial gravity was possible. One way to be certain of such things was to be a part of the civilisation that had built them. Twenty three thousand years the AIs had ruled the Spiral. They were better at technology than most organic species because they *were* technology, and it made sense to them. Romki said they worshipped progress and invention, and viewed such advancement as their civilisation's ultimate existential purpose. Human technology had transformed utterly in the thousand-plus years since humanity had become a truly spacefaring civilisation. What could AIs as smart as Styx have achieved in twenty three thousand? And how much of it was Styx hoping to recover in Drakhil's diary, and bring back to life?

"Styx *knew*," Kono muttered. "She knew what this place was. That's why she built the kid. She knew he could get us in."

Trace didn't disagree. "Chenkov?" she tried again, but received only static. "I think the walls are blocking him. We gotta go now."

"Here, kid, wait," said Rolonde, approaching his side. "You've got shrapnel in a shoulder joint." The drone looked at her, tried swivelling that leg, then lifted it for Rolonde to access. She got armoured hands on the shrapnel and pulled, as Trace noted the lower-third of the steel leg was vibro-blade, of the kind that sliced armoured organics in half. "Got it."

Rolonde withdrew, and the kid swivelled the leg once more, gave a fast multi-legged ripple to test them all together, then set off up the corridor. "He says thank you," Trace translated. "Giddy, Jess, Bird, you're with me. Cocky, hold the room until we get back."

"Aye Major," said Rael. She'd have taken him instead of Kono, but his suit was damaged. Kono was the better rifleman, though barely, and right now she wanted her number two holding this room. Chenkov was keeping all doors locked, but she didn't trust that lasting long, given she could no longer even speak to him.

Trace and Kono set off after the kid, Rolonde and Kumar behind. Trace's visor display showed the temperature falling rapidly, as hot, high pressure air from the room behind fled into this cooler, as yet uncontaminated air. The composition was breathable, but she wasn't about to trust that, and walked through each of the encircling bands of white light in the corridor, wondering where it all came from. Everything here was rock — black rock, unlike the heat-blasted red rock of the main base.

"If this is hacksaw tech," Kono wondered at her side, "then who built it? The vault is supposed to be tavalai, but what if it's been here much longer?"

"Maybe it was an old hacksaw base," said Kumar.

"Hacksaws didn't like planets much," Trace disagreed. "And I can't imagine them liking this one. Just as likely State Department has a lot of forbidden hacksaw tech, and they built it themselves. Would explain why the Dobruta don't like them either."

Ahead at a double-circle of light, the kid stopped, forelegs wavering ahead, as though sniffing the air. Trace and her marines stopped as well. The drone prodded at the left side of the circular, tube-like corridor. And then, with no fuss at all, began to walk up the wall.

"Holy shit," Kumar murmured.

"My visor's going crazy," Rolonde said breathlessly. "Sensors don't know what the fuck's going on."

Trace took a deep breath, as the kid continued to walk around the wall, heading for the ceiling. He had no particular grip on those steel feet to allow him to do that against the will of gravity. Gravity itself was shifting. "Well," said Trace, "I don't think *anyone* knows what's going on."

Any sufficiently advanced technology, she recalled the very old saying, would be indistinguishable from magic. She walked forward, and sure enough, as she reached the double-band of light, she felt the lean begin. For someone who'd lived as much of her life on variable-G ships and stations as she had, it wasn't too hard to adjust to, and she simply followed the kid's path up and around the left-side wall. The mind-bending thing here, however, was that there was no apparent force of motion creating the G-shift.

"Shouldn't be fucking possible," Kono murmured as he followed with the others.

"It's only a problem if you think about it," Trace told them. "That's why I picked you guys — you barely think at all."

"That's sweet, Major," said Rolonde.

Now they were all walking on the ceiling. It wasn't any functionally different from walking on the floor, and Trace resolved not to look behind, and not to think about the fact that Kamala's natural gravity was here being effectively overridden. Then the 'floor' that was now a ceiling came to an end, and the most incredible open space Trace had ever seen appeared above their heads.   Given all the things she'd seen lately, that was saying something.

The chamber was an enormous, empty sphere, all in black stone, with only a little of that sourceless white light to gleam upon the curves.   Within the precise centre of the empty, inverse sphere, was a reciprocal sphere — a solid black ball, taking up perhaps two thirds of the space.   It simply hung there, perfect and smooth. Trace stared, head back within her helmet.   The black, smooth shapes reminded her of the Doma Strana, and Aristan's meditation room — minimalist and mesmerising.   And it was impossible, because the sphere was touching no sides, and was supported by nothing.

"It's like it's being repelled off the walls," Kono murmured. It was rare to hear anything more than businesslike deadpan from the Staff Sergeant, but he sounded awed and dazed like the rest of them. "I guess a powerful enough source of independent gravity will override everything else around it.   And beyond a certain range it reverses, so we're walking on the ceiling."

"Gravity is a ripple in space-time," Trace breathed. "Everything's bent in here."   There were times in her profession, dealing with the technicalities of faster-than-light travel, that she wished she had more physics qualifications than she did.   Here, she was quite pleased to be ignorant, lest her head implode from the scale of it.   "Kid, can you spot an opening?"

She glanced, and found the kid examining a steel plate in the rock.   He touched something, and the plate hummed aside.   An elevator lifted an object into view — a multi-legged robot, Trace saw with amazement, clearly based on hacksaw design, but not a hacksaw.   The kid scuttled around it, noting its relatively low-tech, clunky legs and poor articulation, its chunky power-source and un-streamlined sensory unit.   But it looked immensely strong, like something designed to move under enormous stress.   He clambered half onto it for a better look, then gave Trace a direct look that seemed so much like incredulity that Trace nearly believed it was.

"Yeah kid," Trace agreed. "Looks like an old ancestor of yours."

"Looks much more tavalai-tech," said Kono. "I guess that's the only way anything can be recovered from the vault. I guess we could use it if we knew how to reprogram it to look for our stuff. But it looks old enough to take hours."

"The *other* reason Styx built the kid," Kumar wondered. "It's like she's seen this place before. Or something just like it."

Trace crouched by a small tower-system by the side of the plate. "Looks like a grapple gun. Can't see any directional controls, I guess it doesn't need any. Any ideas, kid?"

The kid came over to peer at it. Then touched a control, and with a loud bang! of compressed air, the grapple shot upward toward the central sphere, trailing a long, steel cable out behind. It slowed, as all things should slow that went flying upward... and then, at about the midpoint, began to accelerate once more. The weighted grapple fell faster and faster, and then the grapple cable was screeching as the mechanism fought against the massive force wheeling it in. And then it struck, with a distant, metallic thud.

"One hundred Gs," Kono murmured. "Looks like it kicks in about halfway. That's fucked up."

"Stop thinking and deal with it," Trace told him, examining the steel frame about the base of the built-in grapple gun. It looked detachable, and equipped with a braking mechanism that affixed to the thick cable. "Kid, I think this is your ride."

The controls were just a few buttons, for stop and go, and brakes. The kid looked them over with curious precision, then looked up at the cable, now forming a several hundred metre long alloy-steel bridge across the intervening space. Then he climbed aboard.

"Now you'll have to climb onto the underside when you hit the gravity change-over at midpoint," Trace told him with concern. "Do you understand? You can't just fall onto the surface — it's one hundred Gs, even a short drop will kill you. Are your legs at full power? Are you ready?"

She'd been concerned about it before — in evolutionary terms, a spider-like design wasn't ideal for heavy Gs because the legs were mounted to the body sides rather than underneath. The kid's legs were attached at ball-joints within independently articulated shoulders, allowing a downward angle to forty-five degrees, but still not ideal, and the legs came outward rather than straight down. As though reading her mind, the kid curled in all his legs, as though walking on his knuckles, toes pointing up at his belly. It raised him off the ground, and gave a near-vertical posture. His head cocked at her with that peculiar, intense concentration, as though seeking her comprehension.

Trace grinned. And she reached, and gave the drone a pat on the side of his sensor-laden head, where a cheek might be. The kid nearly flinched, clearly wondering what the hell she was doing. "Good luck kid. We'll winch you out once you've retrieved it. You sure you know what you're looking for?"

The kid ignored her silly question, gave a final glance about, then up at the big black sphere overhead. Without looking, one of those incredibly dexterous limbs pushed the winch button, and the platform began to climb. Styx had been adamant she knew exactly what they were looking for, and further data from their tavalai Fleet sources had confirmed it. Tavalai Fleet had their own things they wanted him to collect, unseen by tavalai eyes outside of State Department for thousands of years.

"Hope Styx was right about the final bit," Kono murmured, watching the kid ascend up the steel cable. Tavalai Fleet intel had proclaimed that the final lock at the vault itself was an incredibly complicated bit of tavalai coding that would seal permanently if an intruder got it wrong, and would require a complete reset to be brought in from a distant State Department location. Styx had been dismissive, saying that she'd program the means to break the lock into the kid's foundational brain. It would take no more than three seconds, she'd insisted. 'Any sufficiently advanced technology', Trace found herself repeating in her mind...

Her coms crackled. *"Major, this is Rael, do you copy?"*

"Hello Cocky, yes I can hear you."

"I just heard from Chenkov and Aristan, Chenk says he can't get through to you, only to me."

"Go ahead."

"Major, Chenk's just heard from Second Lieutenant Tif! She's on her way down, she says she stole a new descender from Chara, with some help."

About her, Kono, Kumar and Rolonde exchanged incredulous, hopeful glances. Trace's eyes remained fixed on the kid's moving platform. "Can she reach your platform?"

"Yes, but she says there's a State Department-aligned cruiser on its way from Konik, fast! Which means it's armed, and it looks like a military intercept, she says you have thirty-five minutes until she needs to launch. Once she's up she can make rendezvous with the tavalai Fleet, but until she's in their custody we're fair game. We leave it too late and they'll shoot us down en route."

"I copy that, Cocky. Tell Chenkov to guide her if possible, and keep the entry bay secure."

"Yes Major."

On the platform, the kid performed a fast crawl over the 'top' of the ascending platform to the 'bottom', without taking a claw off the 'go' button. It was all going to be for nothing if he fell, or couldn't take the stresses as Styx claimed. Approaching the smooth black sphere, she could see him shifting, hunching his legs beneath him as he'd demonstrated. Then another shift, and a shuffle, as enormous forces began to build.

"Come on kid," Kumar muttered. Even Rolonde stood mute, staring up, hoping. Beside them, the cable's steel foundation groaned and shuddered beneath the stress of extra weight on the far end of the line. Finally, the platform reached the surface. The kid did not move.

Trace counted to five, then figured something might be wrong. "Kid," she said on coms, and boosted the signal to make sure. Could he even hear her up there? "Kid, you have to move. I know it's hard. There should be an entry around there somewhere. It can't be far, or nothing could reach it." Still no movement. She had no idea if appeals to sentiment would work on a hacksaw.

Surely reason would work better?   "Kid, your queen is depending on you.   Your entire people are depending on you.   If you don't move, they'll be dead forever.   You can bring them back."

Her visor-scan zoomed, artificially expanding the image. She saw a leg shuffle, just a few centimetres.   Then another.   The strain was obvious.   Trace wondered if the sensation of stress and damage felt like pain.   Surely pain was counter-productive for a drone?   If she could further engineer some of those more basic responses from her own genetic directives, she would.   To process only the objective, under such huge stresses, would be a blessing.

The platform had deployed side ramps on the way down, to create a very slight incline.   The kid inched down one, moving more steadily now.   If he fell, Trace doubted he'd have the power or leverage to get back up.   Perhaps that caution was the reason for his slow pace.

"At this rate Tif will get shot down before he makes it back," Rolonde muttered.

"It can't be far," Trace replied.   "They must have built the cable to fire right next to it."

The kid reached the end of the ramp, and edged off. Immediately something moved, and then an entire section of black, smooth surface began retracting into the sphere, like an elevator, with the kid huddled on it.   The other marines let out gasps of relief. Trace slowly exhaled, and looked about.

"Now we wait," she said.

CHAPTER 29

"Okay, it's two hundred and fifty metres this way," said Lieutenant Alomaim, indicating past the wall panels. Behind, one of the panels had been removed to reveal the blank steel at the edge of the old Krim Quarter. On the far side was the State Department Head Quarters. Upon a table that had been dragged against the wall, several small warheads were now deployed, facing the wall. Similar to the missile-warheads carried by human marine armour, these were directional charges, focusing the intensity of their detonation all in one direction. The purpose was to breach armour, or walls, giving station infantry an option in moving between rooms that did not include doorways. That the krim had stored them here in the Krim Quarter suggested that they'd once stored powered armour here as well, and were determined not to be trapped by the Quarter's limited ingress and egress.

"The edges of the hole are going to be ragged and hot," Alomaim continued, as he, Erik and Sergeant Brice and Private Cruze took a knee nearby, newly acquired weapons and equipment in hand or on the ground between them. "So Captain — one leg at a time, watch your head and hands."

Erik nodded, looking over his new weapon for the hundredth time. It was long and awkward, designed to be fired from the hip, as krim had bio-engineered targeting systems built into their skulls, and other systems elsewhere. Neither krim psychology nor physiology preferred the shoulder-fired style of humans, though that difference probably made the marines more uncomfortable than their Captain. The marines' expert checks had determined that all weapons were still in working order, but there was some debate as to the free-throw grenades. Seven hundred years was a long time even for krim-engineered weapons in perfect storage conditions. The marines' debate had been more about whether the grenades would detonate at all rather than whether they'd detonate early, but Erik remained far from comforted. In fact, the prospect of impending firefights made him queasy in a way that starship combat had recently ceased to.

"Styx says Hiro's one level down, and I've got the location fixed in my glasses, so we should be good," Alomaim continued. "Her recon bug said there's armed operatives inside, the consensus seems to be they're not close to karasai standard, but given their operating requirements, they don't need to be. If we see them, we shoot. No choice any longer." Grim nods in the group. Given that State Department had just arranged for parren unfriendlies to shoot at them, no one was feeling reluctant.

Erik indicated his weapon. "Now might be a good time to remind you that I've never actually fired a weapon in combat."

Brice looked surprised. "Not even on Homeworld?"

"Not even on Heuron," Erik replied. "*Phoenix* marines have been too good at covering for me." He could see that narrow-eyed tension in Alomaim's eyes now, thinking over and over just how he could arrange to keep his Captain out of the fight. But State Department patrolled the halls, and would rush the Krim Quarter through this entry breach as soon as they got organised, to see how it was done, and to capture anyone still inside. That would leave Erik alone, navigating Tsubarata halls with Styx's help, hoping a lone human in a place where no human was supposed to be could escape notice and somehow get back to *Phoenix*. That was impossible too, and besides, going through the State Department HQ had given them an escape route.

"*Phoenix* says our getaway will arrive at the docking bay in fifteen," Alomaim continued. "So we've got a straight shot through to Hiro, we get him out, then straight for the docking bay. No detours, no delays, got it? And no forgetting the ultimate strategic priority." With a meaningful stare at his marines, ignoring Erik entirely.

'Protect the Captain' was every marine's ultimate strategic priority while on station, Erik knew. In this instance, that priority was conflicting with the larger mission priority of not letting Hiro's information fall into State Department hands. Alomaim clearly hated it, being caught between these conflicting necessities, and Erik couldn't blame him. But Erik knew that if trouble struck, Alomaim was expecting his marines to die, if necessary, to keep him alive. Erik had always hated that too, but was well enough acquainted with strategic realities not to bitch about it. He was not just the Captain — he was the best pilot on *Phoenix*, and without him, everyone's chances decreased.

"Captain," said Brice, coming to show him his weapon. "Now remember it's a shotgun, so you don't have to point it much." Erik refrained from retorting that he did know the difference between a shotgun and a rifle. If he'd had to teach a marine to fly a shuttle in five minutes flat, let alone a starship, he'd be patronising too. "It's a rotary magazine so it shouldn't jam no matter how old it is. You've got fifty rounds already loaded, they're carbon-filament, they'll go through light armour but nothing heavy. Just remember that area-affect weapons don't discriminate — if you fire upon an area, *everyone* in that area will get hit, friend or foe."

Erik nodded, mouth dry, and willed his hands not to shake before his marines. "I promise I won't fire with any friendlies in front of me," he said. "Thank you, Gunnery Sergeant."

But Brice wasn't finished. "Now we're a four man unit," she continued. "Normally I'd take point, but my rib will slow me down, and the LT's the only one who really knows where we're going and we won't have time to take directions from the rear, so he's point. I'm two, you're three, and Cruze is four. That means that you and Cruze are a pair — follow his lead and try to cover what he's not, understand?" Erik nodded. "Your attention will be mostly behind and flanks, that means side corridors as we pass, they can be empty when the LT and me go past, but then not be empty when you reach them, got it? Make sure, then move on, and don't worry about what's in front — that's my job and the LT's."

"I understand," Erik assured her. "Thank you, Gunnery Sergeant." Brice stared at him a moment longer, in the manner of a veteran soldier who'd just thrown a green kid a rifle and required him to cover her back like another veteran. Doubtless there were dozens more things she'd like to tell him, but knew that rookies could only absorb so much, and shouldn't be overloaded.

"Right," she said, and hefted her short rifle with a wince at the pain from her rib.   She moved to check on Cruze and the explosives to breach the wall.   They hadn't given him any grenades, Erik noted, feeling the shotgun's grips with sweaty hands.   That was probably just as well.   He recalled Trace's similar unease at giving him grenades in the Stoya temple.   He'd been scared then, too, but not as scared as this.   Trace's presence had been comforting, and he didn't think Alomaim would be offended to know it.   He hoped to hell she was okay, where ever she was.

"Our getaway is in position in nine minutes," said Alomaim, as Cruze confirmed the explosives were all in place.   "I reckon we'll take six.   Everyone, positions."

They went to a corridor corner, and Alomaim produced something Erik hadn't noticed he was carrying.   "Captain, I got this for you.   Looks about your size."

Erik looked, and saw it was the US marine helmet from the krim's trophy room.   He took it, knowing better than to argue with Alomaim's instruction here.   "Where's yours?" he asked pointedly. "There were more helmets there."

"Old, unfamiliar helmets in a close-quarters environment are asking for trouble," the Lieutenant replied, watching carefully to see Erik buckled it correctly, and that it fit.   "They fall off, get in your eyes at the wrong moment, we all die."

"Doesn't apply to me, does it?" Erik asked drily, pulling the strap tight beneath his chin.

"With respect sir, no one's counting on your aim to save our asses.   But we're all counting on that brain of yours to save all our asses next time *Phoenix* is in a dogfight, and I'd like to see it protected."   He gave the helmet a shake to be sure that it sat well on his Captain's head.   "Looks good on you.   Now just stay with Fuzz and Slips, and do exactly what they tell you, and you'll be fine."

"Why do they call you Fuzz?" Erik asked Cruze, as the Private examined the readout on the detonator trigger he'd rigged. He'd learned the names of all the marines by now, but was still working on the nicknames.

"Rather not say, sir," said Cruze, crouching by the corner.

"He got drunk once and mooned a female army officer from across a bar," Sergeant Brice said helpfully. "She said he had a hairy butt, like peach fuzz."

"Thanks Sarge," said Cruze.

"Anytime, Fuzz."

"And why are you 'Slips'?" Erik added. It was a better thing to think about than what they were about to do.

"'Slips' for 'Slippery', sir," said Brice, matter-of-factly.

"'Slippery' as in…?"

"As in the female equivalent of hard, sir."

Erik nearly smiled. "Oh. You must be thrilled with it."

"Easily offended women don't join the marines, sir."

Erik had a thought. "Did the Major ever have a nickname? I know senior officers lose their nicknames because only equal or higher ranks use them, but what about before, when she was green?"

"The Major was never green," said Alomaim, performing a final check of his rifle and gear. "She was new, but never green." He half-smiled, with a flash of adrenaline Erik had never seen from him before. "I heard that for the first few months, her nickname with other officers was 'Cheeks'."

"Cheeks?" Brice wondered. "Seriously?"

"She refused to let some Lieutenant Colonel through when she was on station guard duty. He didn't have clearance, started shouting at her, 'Listen, Sweet Cheeks…'"

Past the dry-lipped tension, Brice and Cruze looked amused.

"How long did 'Cheeks' last?" Erik wondered.

"Until her first combat action," said Alomaim. "You know the Major. Some people are nickname people. She's not. Fuzz, one minute."

"Got it, LT."

"We're going straight, then down a level, then right. Styx, are you copying any of this?" There was no reply. "She's still out of coms range."

"She'll pick us up as soon as we're on the grid," Erik assured him.

They passed the last minute in silence, Alomaim watching the time. Then, "Fuzz, ten seconds." Followed by, "Do it."

A huge blast tore through the adjoining hall. Then Alomaim was up, and all four of them moved quickly into choking smoke, the hall filled with burning pieces of wall panel. The wall was not structural, just a relatively thin dividing panel, and the directional blast had ripped a hole nearly a metre wide. Alomaim put a forearm on the hot, bent steel to avoid burning skin, and skipped through to avoid jagged edges. Erik managed the same after Brice, and gasped lungfuls of relatively clean air as they moved crouched and ready down the State Department HQ corridor beyond, emergency lights flashing red in time with a klaxon alarm.

"Hello Lieutenant Alomaim," came Styx's voice. *"I see no defensive response to your location. You appear to have surprised them."*

Alomaim moved faster, Erik lengthening his stride to keep up, down a hall more well-decorated than most station halls, with dark panels to hide the steel, and large artworks between adjoining doors. They hit a stairwell, Erik abruptly recalling that he was supposed to be watching the rear more than the front, then abandoning that when he saw that Cruze had mastered the art of running sideways while facing back better than he ever could.

They burst out of the stairwell a level down, with Alomaim yelling at someone to 'Get on the Floor!', though without a belt speaker to amplify a translation. The hallway here was lined with flags, and some tavalai civilians were backing away with wide eyes as the armed humans came past. Alomaim turned right, past offices with glass fronts behind which more State Department staff were moving, dropping conversations and work stations to peer into the corridor. Erik reprimanded himself for even looking, trying to look behind and to the sides as they passed doorways, and workers shrank back in startlement. At their rear he saw tavalai climbing back to their feet, gesticulating and shouting — no panic, never with tavalai. From ahead came a thud, and then he was hurdling a body underfoot, and realised that one of the civvies had tried to tackle Alomaim and received a faceful of rifle butt.

Ahead then was a wider space, a junction of control rooms, halls and meeting points creating a layout confused and difficult to cover. No sooner had Erik noticed than he glimpsed another tavalai in formal attire, wielding a gun and pointing — Cruze fired a single shot and he dropped. Too fast, Erik thought crazily, covering left as Brice indicated that way with a flick of her hand, as several civilians milled and stared from up that way.

"One down behind," Cruze said calmly on coms. *"He had a pistol."*

"Ahead and left, Lieutenant," Styx advised him. *"You have approaching hostiles on your left flank, do it fast."*

Alomaim went fast across the intersection, through a room of displays about a central core through floor and ceiling, and several tavalai disengaging from a VR simulation to stare in disbelief. Erik saw a tavalai past a far glass wall levelling a pistol, and fired his shotgun. Safety glass fractured rather than shattered, blinding the tavalai, who fired anyway.

"Gun!" Erik yelled, as Brice returned fire on full-auto, causing a cascade of collapsing glass where Erik's shotgun hadn't penetrated.

"Move LT!" Cruze yelled behind when Erik stopped to cover Brice. "Keep going!" And almost grabbed his arm, Erik running onward after Alomaim and guessing that meant Brice would follow, as the first person to engage would stay engaged.

Alomaim went down the next corridor with Erik behind, as Styx advised that, *"The next left, your target room has armed guards waiting."*

Alomaim pulled a grenade at full run, primed and threw it around the corner without looking. Shots chased his arm, then a sharp explosion and the Lieutenant swung out and low, spraying the corridor with fire. Erik was about to follow him in, but Cruze came past to take his Lieutenant's side, and Erik swung to guard their rear, finding Brice coming up behind with her back to him, having taken the rear-guard when the others had dashed past.

More fire from Alomaim and Cruze, then shouting and more glass breaking. *"We got him!"* Alomaim announced. *"We got Hiro."*

"I'm coming," said Erik, recalling that the plan was for him to carry Hiro if he couldn't walk, as his was the only gun they could spare. He ran into smoke from the grenade, walls torn with shrapnel and a body on the ground — parren, not tavalai. At the door the parren had been guarding was Cruze, swinging out to guard the corridor as Erik arrived.

The room inside had soundproof walls, a collection of sensory gear and a neighbouring observation window, a thin rectangle behind which several heads were watching, no doubt calling for help. Erik fired a shotgun blast and the glass shattered, as the two tavalai and a parren in the room flinched. On a reclining psych-ward style bench, bound with arms restrained above his head, was Hiro — shirtless, his face bloodied, with every sign of having been poorly treated. On the floor, another two bodies — one tavalai, one parren.

And the standing parren... Erik stared. "Lieutenant, you get Hiro out," Erik commanded, shotgun levelled at the interrogators. None appeared armed. Senior figures, Erik thought, relying on lightly-armed guards to protect them. "I've got the area-weapon, I've got these three with one shot." It was unorthodox — Alomaim was by far the better fighter, anything involving guns should logically be left to him... but the Lieutenant sensed that something was up, and set about undoing Hiro's restraints from the far side of the interrogators, keeping a one-handed rifle aimed in their direction.

The parren was wearing high-ranking robes, pure and white. For the first time, Erik's glasses showed him something useful, flickering recognition brackets about his face, then flashing a quick ID onto a neighbouring image. A name appeared. **Tobenrah das Adard**. 'Adard' meant 'Harmony', in the primary parren tongue. Tobenrah of Harmony.

"Captain," said Styx. *"I recognise this face off Phoenix's recently-acquired parren databases."* She must have been seeing

through Alomaim's glasses, Erik thought.   *"This is Tobenrah, the head of Incefadh Denomination, leader of all House Harmony."*

Here in the Tsubarata, with State Department.   Looking in on the interrogation of a *Phoenix* crewman.   This was Aristan's most concerned and powerful enemy, head of the denomination that Aristan's Domesh denomination sought to overthrow, and wrest control of all House Harmony.   Surely he knew how *Phoenix* had become recently tied up with Aristan's group.   For him to be here, in person, suggested fear.   And this much fear, suggested knowledge.

"What are you doing here?" Erik growled.

The parren barely blinked, cool under pressure like all parren.   He spoke, and Erik's earpiece translated one second behind.   *"One might ask you the same thing, Captain Debogande."*

"State Department tried to assassinate me, using your people," Erik retorted.   "You must have agreed to it. Why?"

"You are running a covert operation here in Kantovan System," said Tobenrah, unperturbed.   *"One suspects you did not come here to make a speech at all. Why then, if not that?"*

Erik saw the two State Department tavalai staring back and forth between him, and the parren, in consternation.   Suddenly he saw it — the debate within State Department, the likes of Jelidanatagani insisting that *Phoenix* was up to some dastardly scheme involving the Parliament speech, while the reports of strange activities elsewhere in Kantovan filtered in over the past hours — trouble in Gamesh, trouble on Chara, reports of highly-trained humans involved, with suspiciously advanced network capabilities. Tavalai were stubborn, and bureaucrats like Jeli didn't change their minds easily.   No doubt there'd been much of that famous tavalai institutional infighting, the pig-headed arguments between important individuals that went on for days and weeks without resolution, while nothing got done.

And now their parren guest had put his finger on it, far more astutely than the brightest minds of the State Department were capable.   Parren, Erik supposed, were not tavalai.   Where tavalai were obstinate, parren were mercurial, perceptive, and dangerous.

Beside him, Alomaim had freed Hiro from his restraints. Erik gave Tobenrah a hard stare beneath the brim of his ancient helmet. "See my sister safe and well," he said, "and perhaps then I'll share it with you."

He indicated Alomaim past him, backing to the doorway with his shotgun levelled. There was shooting further up the corridor, where Brice was guarding their backs, while ahead at the next corner, Cruze beckoned them on. "I got him," said Erik, bending to lift the half-conscious Hiro over his shoulders, and finding the weight not too difficult. "Let's go."

"Your escape ride is arriving in less than two minutes," Styx informed them. *"Defensive deployment appears to be gathering to block your retreat back to the Krim Quarter, they have not anticipated your move to the shuttle berth."*

They hadn't. The tavalai between the humans and the berth level were all unarmed, and scrambled aside at the sight of mean-looking humans with firearms. Berth level had checkpoints, secure gates that Alomaim simply shot until one admitted him with a kick, while behind, Cruze sent a pursuing armed tavalai diving for cover with more fire. Erik ran as best he could, rifle in one hand and bowed beneath Hiro's weight, but he'd done a far harder run before while carrying a wounded man, and Hiro was not so big, and unarmoured.

Past the checkpoint were grey-steel walls and doors to emergency compartments in case of accidental shuttle collisions, Styx keeping the heavy safety doors open that HQ were no doubt trying to slam shut in their faces. Finally an airlock berth ahead, with small viewing ports revealing the angular bulk of an alien shuttle docked on the far side. Already the airlock outer doors were open and waiting, Alomaim shouting at some tavalai docking crew to clear the way. They did, as the humans piled into the airlock.

"I can walk," Hiro muttered weakly.

"Sure you can," said Erik, making no move to put him down. The inner doors opened and again Alomaim went first, through the narrow access tube from the Tsubarata's side, then sliding down the ladder where the access latched to the shuttle's dorsal hatch below.

Brice took Erik's shotgun, and made sure Hiro was steady on Erik's shoulders before he descended, but no one suggested to change the load, which Erik thought was progress.

"Captain, this is Phoenix," came Lieutenant Shilu's voice. *"We have two State Department registered cruisers announcing an act of war, they're targeting your shuttle."*

"Figures," Erik muttered, descending the ladder as fast as he could with two feet and one hand. "Make sure the sulik know." From near-coms he could hear a sulik screech and chatter, with all the grace of fingernails drawn down a board. "Alomaim, my translator's not making out our pilot's query, try and sort it out."

"On it," said Alomaim from below, heading to the bridge.

"Captain," Shilu added, *"we have two sulik cruisers registering active armscomp. They're not targeting the State Department ships, but there are some encrypted communications flying back and forth."*

Erik reached the bottom, and lowered Hiro by necessity, as the sulik shuttle's dimensions were low and tight. He bundled the spy into an acceleration chair that was not even slightly designed for humanoid bodies, and hoped the sulik recalled not to manoeuvre hard. Brice and Cruze followed, then Alomaim, yanking the sulik-shaped restraint bar down and putting his rifle over the top of it — there was nowhere to put the guns either, this being a civilian shuttle for peaceful sulik.

"We're leaving," he told them, as the shuttle vibrated with retreating grapples, then a crash as overhead station grapples released, then freefall.

"Captain, this is Shahaim," came the Commander's voice. *"I am refraining from activating armscomp at this time, it looks as though the sulik have deterred the State Department ships from firing. I'm getting demands from State Department to tell the sulik shuttle to return, Shilu is telling them it's a sulik matter and nothing to do with us. Do you have anything to add?"*

"Negative, Commander," Erik told her, as the shuttle's mild thrust kicked him back in the awkwardly-shaped chair. "You have command until I get there. I don't think they'll destroy a friendly sulik shuttle in cold-blood, they've messed up sulik relations badly enough just now without that on their hands. Just be sure to thank the sulik again when you get a chance, from me personally."

"It might work better coming from Private Cruze," Suli suggested. *"But I will."*

Erik realised that they'd actually pulled it off, without losing anyone else. The relief was strong, but not the elation that he'd expected. Perhaps, he thought, he was actually getting used to this stuff, just a little bit. Or more likely, he was coming to truly realise just how good Phoenix Company marines truly were, and that considering the relative incompetence of the defenders in this instance, it wasn't actually that surprising. He certainly didn't think Trace was going to be all that impressed to hear about it. She'd tell him that high standards existed to make difficult things simple.

"Hello Captain," said Styx. *"Congratulations on your success. Might I ask a question?"*

Erik blinked. "Yes Styx."

"We are allied to the Domesh denomination. In the interrogation room just now, you suggested cooperation with the Incefahd, who had just recently tried to kill you. Why?"

Styx suspected human weakness, Erik thought. Pleading with enemies to save his sister, for no better than selfish gain. "Aristan is dangerous, Styx. We are allied to him only by necessity. Given a better option, especially a much stronger option militarily, I'll take it."

"You will betray your ally?"

"He was never our ally. But yes."

"Interesting," said Styx, with cool calculation. *"Thank you, Captain."*

CHAPTER 30

"I just heard from Phoenix," came Jokono's voice in Dale's ear. *"I don't know how, but they've found a way to send brief messages safely through main coms from Tsubarata to Konik."* Which meant Styx was doing it, Dale knew. *"It was very vague for security reasons, but it sounds like the Major is in the vault right now and nearing extraction. State Department are probably aware, so we don't have to keep that secret any longer. It might even be safer to destroy the module and cover our tracks completely."*

Dale was crouched in a deserted apartment overlooking an intersection. Surrounding apartment windows were similarly occupied by armed tavalai and a few other species they trusted, but this was primarily a tavalai military retirement village, and filled to the gills with armed tavalai who still did what their former commanders told them. The intersection was a T-junction, and Dale's team were assigned to guard the stem of the T — a smaller road, adjoining the main one down which he now peered. "With any luck Gamesh security won't bother hitting us," said Dale, peering down at the roadblocks made from commandeered cars and vans. Further up the road were numerous parked police vehicles, their emergency lights turning the gloomy sub-surface streets to strobing blue and yellow. "If they already know the vault was the target."

"More likely State Department will have ordered them to clean up the breach," Jokono said grimly. Dale wasn't sure exactly where Jokono was now — no doubt further from any potential gunfire, where he could maintain his command-and-control function for as long as possible. *"They'll want to know exactly how it happened, and implicate Phoenix in all of it. My guess is they'll order this entire neighbourhood flattened. It's just a question of how far Gamesh security will be willing to follow their orders — they can be heavy-handed, but even they will pay a large domestic price if they go too far."*

Tooganam entered the apartment door, thumping across the floor in his exo-frame, massive Viz-rifle hauled with an effortless grip. Dale thought he moved more smoothly with the weapon than without it, as though its absence from his post-military life had left him permanently unbalanced. *"What does your man say?"* asked the tavalai, thumping the weapon to the floor as he took a knee to peer through a neighbouring window at the flashing lights outside.

"Our operation goes well," said Dale, "but State Department now know its target, so our secret is out. He thinks State Department are angry, and will want us rounded up, dead or alive."

"I think more likely dead," said Tooganam. *"Either before they catch you, or after."*

"Yeah?" said Dale, testing the weight on his own Viz. "I thought tavalai didn't do that kind of thing?"

"Tavalai military, rarely," Tooganam confirmed. *"State Department are not military."* He gave Dale a sideways glance. *"Humans have not always been as honourable."*

"Army," said Dale. It felt bitter to say it, but there was no arguing that all-in-all, tavalai had treated human prisoners of war better than humans had treated tavalai. "Some army units were poor quality. You guys wiped a few of them out, it made some of them scared and nasty. Fleet never did that to tavalai prisoners."

"No," Tooganam conceded. *"Or not that I heard. But you weren't as kind to sard."*

"If you were fighting sard," Dale retorted, "would you have been?" Tooganam snorted, and did not disagree. "And there were stories of some of your prisoner of war camps filled with chah'nas that somehow went missing."

"If you'd been fighting chah'nas," Tooganam retorted, *"you'd have made a few of their prisoners disappear too. Especially the ones convicted of murdering our civilians. Nothing lost more sympathy for humanity amongst tavalai than your befriending of the chah'nas. Eight thousand years under the Chah'nas Empire left us with no patience for those vermin or their friends."*

"Chah'nas were the only ones to help us against the krim," Dale retorted. "Humanity would be extinct if not for them."

"They didn't do it for compassion. They did it to get back at tavalai."

"You don't think humans know that?" said Dale. "Chah'nas are assholes, but they made a smart choice when they backed humanity. Tavalai did some stuff well, but you picked the wrong damn friends, and the wrong damn enemies. Krim were horrible friends. Sard are worse. If you'd ditched the krim for *us*, back when you had that option?" Dale shook his head, amazed at himself for even having the thought, let alone saying it aloud. "Hell, son. We'd have ruled the galaxy between us."

"We tavalai never wanted to rule anything," said Tooganam, police-lights strobing across his mottled skin as he peered at the forces confronting them. *"We were vermin beneath the boot-heel of the hacksaws, then we were boot-lickers to the parren, and then cowardly yes-men to the chah'nas. It took us forty thousand of your years, but we finally got tired of grovelling. The only way we can avoid it, in this galaxy, is to rule. And so we rule, without enthusiasm, and often without much competence or justice. But we are the best there's been so far, and I can't see that your crooked Triumvirate is going to be an improvement — for us or for you."*

Dale could think of several things to retort, but realised that all of them would be argument for its own sake. In truth, he didn't actually disagree with anything Tooganam had said. Not since the crew of *UFS Phoenix* had discovered what they had about humanity's Triumvirate allies, anyhow. Tooganam looked faintly surprised to find the argument ended.

"Dale," he said, and the translator left the name alone, rough and gravelly. *"That is your name, yes? Dale?"*

"That's my name," Dale agreed. He'd had a nickname once, but most of the marines who'd known him by that were dead, transferred or retired. Besides which, no one ever called senior officers by their nicknames. On *Phoenix* only the Major had that right, and she declined.

"Have you killed many tavalai?"

Dale gave the ex-karasai a glance. Tooganam looked to be meditating on something, calm and thoughtful. "Yes," he said. "You and humans?"

"*Hmm,*" Tooganam agreed, with a long rumble in his throat. "*And before today, rarely given cause to regret it.*" He nodded out the window. "*They're moving. They'll come up the middle, strikers forward, mobile fire support in the rear.*"

Dale frowned. "How do you know?"

"*Rapid response are mostly machines. Machines are predictable.*" Dale knew some machines that were anything but predictable, but kept it to himself. "*We will lure them, shooters at the end of the road, then an ambush from the flanks.*"

"And if they don't do what you predict?" Dale asked.

"*Then we will adjust,*" said Tooganam. "*You humans and your remaining parren will hold this cross street, and disrupt any attempt at encirclement. Are we agreed?*"

Dale nodded, before remembering tavalai didn't know what that meant. "It's your neighbourhood," he said. "Are you in charge?"

Tooganam looked amused, climbing heavily to his feet, and back from the windows. "*I was never more than a sergeant. We have an officer, his name is Prolipalatil, Proli for short. You have not met him. He was a karasai captain, and we will all do what he says.*" Tooganam stomped for the doorway. "*Humanity has a reputation to uphold, Lieutenant Dale. Do not let it slip.*"

"You guys hear all that?" Dale asked his coms.

"*Copy,*" said the parren, Golev, from a downstairs window.

"*I heard,*" said Jokono.

"*Proli get us all killed,*" Reddy quipped. Dale thought of his friends Forrest and Tong, then forced it aside. It was too much to hope that they'd just turn up like the cavalry of old, but that fantasy was better than the alternative nightmare. "*Looks like more of those combat droids,*" Reddy observed from his vantage. "*Got a couple of big armoured vehicles in the rear. Looks like old Toogs was right.*"

Dale peered, and saw the creeping mechanical figures making their way down the gloomy street, in two single files on the pavement, in the shadow of closed doorways and shuttered storefronts. The vehicles behind weren't big enough to be tanks — more like civilian law enforcement armour. It didn't mean they couldn't pack some firepower, though.

"Okay," said Dale, "we're gonna hold our street. Let the froggies hold the main road, our job is just to stop them from flanking…"

A rifle shot rang out, well behind Dale, down the main street near the heart of the tavalai neighbourhood. The shots became regular, a staccato, echoing retort, and Dale saw droids taking cover, fragments of road and paving flying.

"Not hitting much," Reddy observed with displeasure.

"Not meant to," said Dale. He had no intention of joining the fire — from this apartment window overlooking the street, a single RPG would take out him and the room. For now, he just wanted to see. "It's just bait, they want to draw them in."

If the initial fire was too heavy or effective, Rapid Response might just call up heavy units and start pulverising. The defenders wanted to get some of these droids exposed first, convincing them that the target was ill-equipped and a minimal threat, perfect for assault-by-manoeuvre. Sure enough, Dale could see the droids approaching in fast, measured dashes, now putting down sporadic cover fire by odds-and-evens.

The defensive rifle fire then changed position, never more than one or two firing at the same time. Gas grenades popped from the armoured vehicles, sailing past Dale's vantage from the end of the street. Smoke only, he thought, observing the arc they made through the air. "Looks like Rapid Response have decided not to use full force," he told his team. "If State Department told them to flatten the neighbourhood, they're ignoring that order."

"State Department have limited jurisdiction in domestic affairs," Jokono reminded him. *"Even moreso in a free city. But if Gamesh authorities can't get what they want, they'll look bad with*

the tavalai domestic authorities that do *matter. I suspect this will escalate."*

The combat droids were passing Dale's position now. "I'm moving," said Dale, getting up to do that. "Tell me if they make a right turn."

"Nothing so far," Reddy said tersely. *"They're going straight by."* Dale went through the door and along the corridor, finding the exo-frame awkward to use compared to a suit. He'd been wearing marine armour for so long it was intuitive, and the exo-frame didn't give him nearly as much push-back, making it easy to overbalance or overstress. But it kept the big Viz rifle swinging in effortless alignment as he jogged. How well it handled recoil on a gun this size was going to be another matter, as was ammunition, which could not be stored on this lightweight frame, and had been pre-positioned at various points along the defensive road, in doorways and corridors. In addition to which, Dale was painfully aware that the frame gave him no protection whatsoever. Firing a weapon this size made one relatively immobile, frame or no frame. When immobile in a high-caliber firefight, defensive protection was desirable. Being deprived of it only made Dale realise just how much he'd come to rely on it, particularly for all those near-misses that sent shrapnel fragments flying like rain.

He thumped down some stairs further along the street, then paused in a doorway just as heavy gunfire erupted on the main road. This was the full orchestra of tavalai firepower, and as he peered about the corner, he saw the T-junction ahead filled with smoke and flying debris. Several droids were covering at the T-junction, presenting Reddy and Golev with clear shots that, with typical discipline, they refrained from taking.

"Some of 'em are down," Reddy reported from his higher vantage opposite Dale's position. *"Looks like they're pinned. I think they're gonna pivot any moment... yeah, here they come."*

And Dale saw the droids on the corner turn, with synthetic coordination, and he ducked back before they could see him. "Tell me when, Spots," he requested.

"Nearly," said Reddy, with the calm of a sniper sighting along his rifle. *"Nearly there. Go."* A shot rang out, and Dale stepped around the corner with the Viz on full auto, and fired. Mayhem happened, the weapon leaping and thundering like an angry beast, droids, walls and parked cars dissolving in destruction as he fought the recoil to keep the muzzle flat and level.

He recalled Tooganam's instructions and ceased fire least the gun jam and damage itself, pulling back around the corner to check the ammo readout by manual. *"Hell yeah, LT,"* said Reddy. *"One more, I got him."* As another shot rang out. *"He's down. That was six, the rest are holding back. They're not too bright, old Toogs was right again."*

Missiles came streaking around the corner and blew half a building face down onto the road in a huge explosion of falling masonry, and a shockwave that hurt Dale's ears. *"And old Jokono was right as well,"* Jokono told them. *"Now it's escalating, that came from the fire support."*

"We got to stay well out of line-of-sight with that thing," Dale commanded. "Displace and pull back one degree, we'll dig in and see if they try again."

He ducked onto the road, all view of the T-junction now hidden behind clouds of rolling dust that blocked the road, and moved backward up the street toward his first fallback position, big rifle trained in the direction of the enemy.

"Major, they're cutting through," Corporal Rael reported tersely. *"It looks like tough going, might take them another ten minutes."*

Trace waited by the cable bridge to the vault, and expended all of her practise in the art of keeping calm. The power regulator room was an utterly different technology from the rest of the vault — perhaps preceding it by many thousands of years. Its walls and doors were incredibly tough, making it the most defensible room in the complex. Sard defenders seemed in no hurry to assault the main entrance airlocks, lest Chenkov and Aristan open the outer airlock once more and boil them with a new wave of superheated air. She didn't know how many sard were left — she reckoned perhaps half or more had died in the initial breach, given the duty rotations in and out of armour, and the non-functioning of atmospheric refuges once Chenkov had gained control of the complex's doors. Sard preferred larger numbers to smaller, and for all their selfless aggression, could become quite demoralised when large numbers were turned into small numbers quickly. Those that remained still vastly outnumbered the attackers, but their capabilities were dramatically reduced.

The kid had been gone for eight minutes, and Tif's final launch window was down to twenty-seven minutes. "Would sure help if he could talk on coms," Kono muttered nearby.

"I think Styx may have limited his coms function for a reason," Trace replied. And to help her marines' nerves more than hers, she added, "We don't know how large the vault is inside, we don't know how far inside the external gravitational effects penetrate, we don't know how hard it is to find the things that he's after. I'm sure he'll find them a lot faster than any of us would."

"Movement!" said Rolonde, pointing upward. Trace looked, and sure enough, the elevator platform was reemerging, its shiny black surface molding once more to invisible edges. On the platform was the kid, and before him sat a pair of odd-shaped containers. *Two* things, he'd been instructed to retrieve — Drakhil's diary, and the records requested by tavalai Fleet. Without the latter, Fleet would be angry enough for *Phoenix*'s further mission in tavalai space to be finished, or perhaps worse.

"He got them!" Kumar exclaimed. "Good job buddy!"

"Yeah, and now he has to lift them," Kono said grimly. The cage-platform on which he'd travelled to the spherical Vault was barely two metres away, and the side ramp elevated barely twenty centimetres above the sphere's surface. But at one hundred Gs, it was going to be a battle.

"Come on kid!" Kumar urged, abandoning all pretence at not anthropomorphising the machine. "You can do it!"

The drone inched slowly forward, evidently more accustomed to this style of motion now, and having had some time to recover down below, where the effects were minimal.   Now returning into the full, ferocious clutches of gravity, he shuffled the boxes ahead of him, then slowly edged them onto the low ramp.

Trace heard a distant whine that seemed to emanate from the walls of the vast, spherical chamber, and then a loud thump.   They all felt the shockwave, and gravity slammed them suddenly downward, like the unexpected manoeuvre of a warship in combat. The force was only several Gs, and straight down, so in full armour they all retained their balance.   And stared at each other, uncertainly, as the cable-bridge adjoining to the Vault began a low, jangling vibration, like the bass string of a large guitar, poorly played.

"What the hell was that?" Rolonde wondered.   As they were all reminded how they were currently standing upside down, repelled by this 'whatever-it-was' force of technology that shouldn't be possible, by human reckoning.

And Trace noticed that out on the distant vault surface, the kid moved his head enough to look up, and consider the jangling wire.   Then he resumed moving, up the ramp, his tiny, shuffling strides now a little faster, as he risked collapse for a little extra speed.   The whining from the walls grew louder, and then Trace understood.

"Gravity's increasing!" she said.   "The capacitors are firing up, we must have missed something.   It's triggered a final defence." And knowing that the kid could hear them even if he couldn't talk back, she added, "Kid, you have to move.   If the Gs get too strong we'll never get you off the surface."

The cable twanged and shuddered, the force pulling upon its far end, trying to separate the nearly unbreakable strands.   A second, louder twang, as one of them did snap.   "That cable's stressed far tougher than a hundred Gs," Kono said grimly, kneeling by the cable winch.   "It must be pushing one-fifty."

From the building whine, Trace didn't think the rate of increase was slowing.   The kid pushed the containers fully onto the edge of the ramp, then stopped. "Just a bit more, kid!" Trace urged him. "We'll get you out, just another metre!"

"He's too heavy, the cable won't take the weight!" Kono retorted.

"You don't know that cable rating," Trace replied. "It'll take it. Kid, move!"

The kid did move, somehow manoeuvring his underside laser cutter, then activating in a brilliant flash. The ramp separated from the rest of the platform in a shower of sparks that travelled only sideways, and hit the sphere flat, the tiny jolt of a twenty centimetre drop flattening the drone face-first upon the surface, his legs all splayed or crumpled.

"Kid!" shouted Kumar.

"We wind the cable up while we still can!" said Kono. "Once it's up the gravity might drop, we can send it back for him!"

"Do it," Trace agreed, and Kono hit the winch, the mechanism winding as steel protested, vibrated and twanged. "Kid, we'll send it back for you when the gravity drops again! We don't leave a man behind kid, don't be scared!"

Because somehow, she just knew he would be. It was a revelation to her, that she no longer cared about the perils of mistaking the drone for a living, thinking being — he clearly was one, and on this trip, he'd become one of theirs, of *Phoenix*'s own. Of *hers*. And just as astonishingly, all of Command Squad appeared to feel the same.

The winch ground and strained, like some angler trying to land a truly enormous fish, as the platform lifted away from the kid's nose, rising slowly and steadily higher. "It's coming!" Kono said with relief. "The effects decrease fast the further it gets away, it's accelerating!"

From the walls, the whining grew louder. With a crack, one of the kid's back-mounted cannons tore and instantly pancaked to the ground, taking one of his legs with it. Unbalanced, the other cannon followed. Electrics flashed and arced, then a small explosion as ammunition crushed and detonated. On coms there came a desperate, electronic squeal, as the frightened AI tried at last to use the coms function he'd never in his short life managed to master. Like so many things.

"I'm sorry kid," Trace said softly. "You did good. I'll see you in the next place." The remaining ammunition detonated, followed by the power core, and the explosion panned flat about the sphere's surface, unable to rise even an inch of height.

"Fuck," said Kumar with emotion, as the platform rose faster still. "Fucking brave little guy."

"He did what he was programmed to do," said Kono, without conviction.

"No," Rolonde said quietly. "He did what he was *ordered*. Like we all do. There's a difference."

CHAPTER 31

"We're gonna have to move soon," Dale told his ragtag group on the mini-plaza, as gas grenades arced over the rooftops, smacked and bounced off walls and pavements. He was hidden in a corner store by a sales counter and some tables that overlooked the plaza corner, where several vehicles made smouldering barricades, and craters smoked from the last explosive incoming rounds. Gas spewed from the canisters, but tavalai supplies had found them some gas masks that roughly fitted humans, and none of his team were affected so far. "They're gonna put explosives in that mortar any time soon, and we can't hold this position under artillery."

The Rapid Response attackers weren't any better equipped for this than his defenders were at warding them off. Amidst the narrow streets and mid-rise buildings of Gamesh underworld, their guided missiles lacked the agility to turn sharp corners and strike close targets, and those that tried generally took out the upper floors, but were unable to reach the ground. It had forced Reddy down from his sniper position, but thus far had only killed a kratik who'd been assigned to this flank, and wounded a pair of tavalai, who'd headed for the aid stations in the rear.

In fact, this little corner of the neighbourhood flank was defended almost entirely by non-tavalai, comprised of tavalai-aligned species who had served in the Triumvirate War. Aside from himself, Reddy and Golev, there were a pair of kaal, two koromek, and one more tavalai — a kid who was related to one of Tooganam's retirees, and said he was planning to join up, but wasn't old enough. He insisted his elders knew he was here, but Dale reckoned if that was true, he'd be serving with them, and not over here where no one could tell on him. He *wanted* to tell the kid to buzz off to the rear, but was short-handed as it was, and if this flank folded, the droids would be splitting the neighbourhood's flank and pushing straight for Jokono and Kadi in the rear, and the aid stations slowly filling with wounded.

"I see multiple units advancing through the buildings ahead," Jokono told them, remaining focused on Dale's position, as the tavalai commanders wouldn't have listened to him anyway. *"They're avoiding the streets, coming through levels three-to-five. Some have heavy weapons, I see chain guns and grenade launchers."* Jokono's recon bugs weren't much use at killing droids, but they were plenty good for sitting unnoticed on walls and watching them clank by.

If Dale had had his heavy armour, he could have put missiles into those upper floors and brought ceilings down on the lot of them. Now, options were limited. "They're gonna get numbers above us to put down cover fire, then come down both roads at the same time," he growled, adjusting his exo-frame tension. If he'd let them, his hands would have shaken with sheer exhaustion — he'd been going at this all day in one form or another, and even Phoenix Company marines had physical limits. And ignored them. "Joker, tell their damn commander we're about to lose this position, he's not fucking listening to me."

"Nor to me, I fear," said Jokono. *"But I'll tell him. Your defensive position will not improve at the next intersection."*

"No, but at least we won't be dead *here*." His first commanding officer had drummed into him the simple lesson of marine mobility — if being *here* will kill you, go over *there*, then rinse and repeat. It only becomes 'running away' when you stop firing back. In the meantime, pursuing enemies could make mistakes.

A shot rang out overhead, then another. Several seconds later, a roar of heavy return fire, from the window of one of the buildings opposite, and a shower of masonry fragments on the road. *"I got one,"* came Reddy's voice, breathing hard as he ran. *"I've displaced, I'm moving down a level."*

Against the opposite wall, one of the big kaal exposed himself long enough to fire his huge Viz past Dale's corner and into the window from where the return fire had come. Kaal did that bare-handed, without the exo-frames that puny humans and tavalai needed, absorbing the massive recoil with four thick arms. Then he stepped back to the cover of a roadfront shop before Dale could tell him to — Dale had been told their names, briefly, but 'you kaal!' worked well enough in combat.

More grenades sailed in over the rooftops, but landed further up the approach roads from the intersection, spewing thick smoke as they clattered and bounced. The smoke gathered fast, filling the road between buildings.

"Here they come," said Dale, putting his back against the counter and aiming his Viz into the smoke, his glasses struggling to illuminate possible targets from tacnet's limited sources. A fragmentation grenade exploded over the intersection, shrapnel rattling off the walls, and Dale pulled back behind the counter in anticipation of the grenade round that hit the entrance to his shopfront, as the droids newly moved into the building opposite put fire into likely hiding places.

The bang rattled his eardrums, unaccustomed to hearing such things in a firefight without his full armour helmet, but he levelled the Viz once more past the counter, and saw a dark shape moving in the smoke, and pulled the trigger. The recoil kicked him like a horse, and a droid in the smoke spun in pieces. Another returned fire, and he backed behind the counter as rounds blew holes in walls around him, and knocked over tables. And stopped, as Dale's unit fired, the big kaal opposite leaning out once more to let fly on full-auto... and was abruptly hit by fire from the building, his great bulk sliding to the road, head lolling.

"Need more fire up the second road!" Dale commanded to whoever was supposed to be doing that, but there was a lot of fire coming from the building now, and it was hitting windows and walls opposite, and keeping heads down. Dale heard the fast hydraulic rattle of sprinting footsteps, and blew the first droid through the door back into the street. The second opened fire about the corner with a roar of inbuilt arm cannon, as Dale dropped once more for cover, then flipped a grenade at the doorway. The droid dodged aside, ran about the corner for the second entrance, and was hit halfway there.

Dale backed away from the counter, blew chunks out of the doorframe to deter further droids, then ran up the adjoining stairs.

The stairs opened onto a corridor between apartments, all linked together with adjoining doors in communal tavalai-style.   He dodged into a doorway, rifle pointed at the ceiling so it would fit through the doors, and peered across the apartment living room to the building opposite... and saw muzzle flashes from the windows. Theoretically an AI-driven droid, immune to mistakes, should have seen him by now and changed targets, but as *Phoenix* marines had discovered, even hacksaws didn't do that quite as well as trained humans.   Dale aimed past the wall, out the window, and blew one firing droid back into its apartment, then displaced back out the door as return fire riddled the walls.

Shouts and calls for help filled his audio — someone else was hit on the road, he'd told them to stay off the street but the non-tavalai's military experience wasn't as extensive as most tavalai's. Dale went through another apartment, past the mines rigged to detect a droid's energy emissions, then down some far too narrow stairs, rifle held vertically about tight corners, and rattled down a stairway past a restaurant floor.   There was heavy fire ripping down the street now, rounds ricocheting from walls, most of it one-way.   Dale peered without exposing himself, and saw the tavalai kid was down and wounded behind the small truck parked in the road for cover, now shredded and ruined.

"Everyone pull back!" Dale yelled, and winced as the windows of the apartment he'd just been through blew out, the mines detonating as a droid pursuing him from the corner store showed a lack of due caution.   "They're moving through the buildings, we've lost defensive integrity!   The mines will get some, but we won't stop them!"

A grenade blew out a doorway up from him, as droids acquired new firing angles to shoot into possible cover.   With smoke and debris filling the road, Dale ducked quickly out, laid down a roar of heavy fire while retreating, then sidestepped into the restaurant front.   Return fire came from the wrong direction down the road, hitting the wall as he ducked back.

"They're behind us!" he shouted.   "They've taken our fallback point!"   He couldn't risk another look, or one would take his head off, and he backed into the restaurant, knowing it was just a matter of time until the droids pursuing through the rooms above found a way to get in behind him, anti-droid mines or not. "Everyone on the north side, cross the road and come south! We are retreating south!" And ducked low amidst tables and ceiling supports as he heard the incoming grenade before it hit the wall, and showered everything with shrapnel.

"Human!" came a familiar, translated voice. *"I am at your rear, coming through now."* Then a familiar thump and whine of tavalai-powered exo-frames, as Dale sought better position behind a pillar. Then Tooganam was crashing in from the rear passage past the kitchen, and the adjoining vehicle lane, with several more tavalai close behind.

"How many are you?" Dale yelled above the increased racket of gunfire, now converging from both ends of the street. He checked his ammo, and found only six rounds left in this can.

"Just ten!" said Tooganam, lumbering to similar cover nearby. *"Is your position recoverable?"*

"No, some fucker left my flank exposed!" Dale moved crouched to a new support pillar, held his Viz sideways about it and hammered off the remaining rounds. "Both ends of the street are gone, I've got infiltrators above and behind, and troops stuck on the north side of the street!" He returned to previous cover, ejecting the spent canister and slamming in a new one.

"LT, we got them in our rear," came Reddy's voice, from the north of the street. A burst of fire on coms. *"They're really pushing here, I reckon this flank is the one they're after!"*

"Dale, I can get you another three squads," said Tooganam. There were five people in a tavalai squad, Dale knew. Fifteen more? *"Two heavy squads with Viz rifles, one light. Under your command, how would you use them?"*

Fifteen plus Tooganam's current ten were twenty-five more. Plus Dale's current seven... he blinked on tacnet to check everyone save the kaal was still alive. Thirty-two, that changed things. "If they're pushing hard here, they're stripping their other flanks of numbers. How many do we think they have?"

"Rapid Response droids are expensive, and the agency is not well funded." An explosion at the restaurant front shattered a sliding door and sent tables flying. Tooganam barely blinked. *"This is a major push for them, it has already cost them much. You appear to have more than your share on this flank."*

And Tooganam was offering him the means to destroy them. "Droids are dangerous at range," said Dale. "Close quarters, in buildings, we're superior. You get me fifteen more and we'll cross the road and get into *their* rear if they push past us."

"Counter-attack?" Dale glanced at the old tavalai, and found him with what might have been a dry smirk on thick lips. *"That sounds very human. Let's do it, the reinforcements are on their way."*

Meaning that Tooganam had the authority to tell *his* superior to send them, whatever his superior's natural instincts. Dale wondered why Tooganam was not taking command himself, and if he'd bothered to tell his superior that the human was in command here. Knowing Tooganam, probably not.

"There's a truck down the alley," said Dale, pointing at the wall to the right. "Past the kitchen, where you came in — take two guys, shove it out to get some cover. I want smoke grenades and fragmentation, left and right. Everyone else, fire suppression — if you can't hit targets directly, fire short into the walls and give them ricochets and fragments, I want maximum confusion before we cross. And we've got a wounded tavalai kid ten metres to the left behind the truck, he might still be alive. Get in first, then recover him from the far side. Got it?"

Tooganam barked several commands and the tavalai, all following on open coms and translators, moved immediately for position. Dale steadied himself against a pillar, and took several deep breaths.

"Is this mission of yours at Kantovan Vault worth dying for?" Tooganam asked him.

Dale took a final last breath, readied his Viz, and thought of the deepynine threat, lurking near humanity's throat with their allies the alo. "A thousand times," he said.

"For the Talim, we say," Tooganam growled. *"It means the single tavalai soul."*

"We say 'the nine-point-nine'," said Dale. "The nine-point-nine billion dead of Earth."

Tooganam looked at him approvingly. *"You honour your ancestors. For the nine-point-nine."*

Dale smiled grimly. "For the Talim," he said.

A report came on coms that Dale's translator missed. *"The truck's ready,"* said Tooganam. *"We're in position. You should be getting data-feed on your tacnet now."*

Dale blinked on the overlay, and his glasses showed the extra tavalai troops moving up behind. "Let's go," he said, and swung around to the left side of the restaurant, past shattered and smoking tables, to open an angle down the road to his right, as Tooganam and troops did the same opposite.

They opened fire across each other, as others followed from neighbouring streetfronts. Then the truck emerged from its alley to block Dale's line of fire. He swung around the corner and fired the other way, as tavalai joined him, and others dashed across, creating a wall of fire up the road. Droids that did not take cover, disintegrated, and Dale ran across the road to take cover there, and open a new angle.

Tavalai ran past and into north-side buildings, from where they could penetrate and spread into the enemy's rear and flanks. Grenades hit the walls ahead, then ricochets, spraying shrapnel up the road, but Dale stayed put, targeting cover-point after cover-point, knowing he couldn't allow this crossing to come under pressure until everyone was across. A glance sideways while changing ammo cans showed him Tooganam doing the same on the south side, standing with legs spread in typical tavalai stubbornness, leaning into his weapon's recoil as an old-time sailor might lean into a gale. Dale had once despised tavalai for their lack of panic reflex, thinking it made them no better than unthinking machines, unable to feel or fear. But now he saw Tooganam, unflinching amidst fire, smoke and shrapnel, refusing more than partial cover because it was necessary, and the tavalai were a people for whom the necessary was everything, irrespective of cost, profit or doubt. And it was like a revelation.

With a sudden shriek up the road, several missiles made fast contrails through the sky and hit amidst Rapid Response rear positions with big explosions. Then some more, followed by a howl of shuttle thrusters, and the middle-distance baarp! of rapid-fire cannon, followed by the entire street ahead erupting beneath a torrent of high-velocity impacts.

"Lieutenant, that's tavalai Fleet shuttles!" Jokono was shouting with unaccustomed joy. *"Tooganam, your fleet is here!"*

The engine howl grew louder, as droid fire reduced, and incoming aerial fire increased into neighbouring streets. Then a roar directly overhead, as a shuttle came in directly over the rear intersection, now free of droids, its jets breaking every window not already broken and sending a great hurricane of hot air up the road. Karasai jumped from the rear, with enough suit-thrust for a controlled landing without descent ropes, some of them firing rifles, others launching missiles, a great cascade of armoured, alien firepower that might previously have looked to Dale like a nightmare, but now looked more like salvation.

When Trace's squad made the vault power regulator, sard defenders had already cut through the doors, and Corporal Rael's squad were under fire. But the sard lacked the heavy weapons to trouble well-positioned marines, and Rael's return fire had pulverised sard trying to assault through the single doorway. The remainder dispersed when the humans pushed forward, scattering as marines used their remaining missiles and grenades first, and rifles second, to maximise the sard's perception of disadvantage.

Trace advanced now fourth-in-line, one of the kid's two canisters hooked to her back armour, the other on Rolonde's, and thinking it would be a harsh irony if the canisters were damaged once the hard job of retrieving them had been accomplished. But the sard seemed to have vanished, whether psychologically discouraged in that way sard could become after large setbacks, or unwilling to fire upon items recovered from the vault, or with some other plan up their armoured sleeves — Trace had no idea, and did not particularly care.

"I'm getting a transmission from Tif!" Chenkov's voice crackled in her ear as she ducked up familiar corridors and over sard bodies, the shimmering heat haze now reduced to a balmy eighty degrees celsius and falling steadily. *"Putting it through!"*

"...down in two ninute," Tif came through, and Trace might have grinned to hear her were she not so busy moving and covering. *"We got State Department intercept, cuning real soon in orbit, got noove fast!"*

"I copy you Tif," said Trace. "We're going as fast as we can, our current ETA is shortly after you touch down."

"Najor... randing sensor says docking probe danaged! How you get on ny ship?"

"What?" Chenkov interrupted. *"I don't see any... oh shit."* A horrified pause. *"Major, she's right... I'm getting a malfunction reading on the walkway, it says it won't extend. I didn't notice because I was busy doing the..."*

"I don't care Chenk," Trace cut him off. "Either you or Aristan get out there and see if you can fix it, or find us another way."

"I've borrowed a local environment suit," came Aristan's translated voice. *"I'll go."*

"Was never going to be that easy," Kono muttered. *"Can we walk it?"*

"It's too far," Trace replied, having discussed this matter at length with *Phoenix*'s best armour techs. "The marine suits won't survive that much time in full exposure, and Chenkov and Aristan's environment suits certainly won't. Chenkov, what about that vehicle in the hangar?"

"The prospector? Major it could get us out to the ship, but we've no docking seal! We'd have to go into full exposure for..."

"How long?" Trace demanded as she swivelled around another corner, rifle searching a shimmering hallway off a storage room. "We can take full exposure for a minute, maybe two."

"From the dorsal hatch of the prospector to the cargo airlock on Tif's model of descender... it's a four metre difference at least..."

"We can give each other a boost, that's no problem."

"But Major, that airlock hatch takes minutes to cycle on a heavy descender! It's rated to hold eight regular suits, but there's ten of us and marine armour takes up a lot more space than..."

"We can throw out guns and launchers, and we'll set a new record for marines squeezed into an airlock if we have to." Ahead, Rael's squad broke into the bay beyond the entry hangar, littered with sard bodies and melted lockers. "We're nearly there... Tif, how much time do we have?"

"Doesn't natter!" Tif retorted. *"You go top fast, tine not natter!"* Trace didn't particularly like being told her priorities by a green ex-civilian Second Lieutenant, but she had no time to get into it now.

The marines thumped into the main hangar as a silver environment suit emerged from the docking probe beside the control bunker's narrow windows. *"The probe's secure doors are down and locked,"* Aristan announced. *"The controls say there is hot pressure on the far side. Our previous pilot must have hovered deliberately on takeoff and melted the docking arm."*

"Everyone in the prospector!" Trace commanded. "Chenkov, can you operate the main outer doors from inside the vehicle?"

"Should be able to," said Chenkov.

"Get in the vehicle, you're our driver!" As her marines ran to the underside access, between the huge, steel-tread wheels, and tried to open it. Trace took cover behind one of the wheels, watching both ways at once.

"Won't open!" Arime announced. *"Chenk, we need your magic wand thingy!"*

"Yeah, coming!" As the Spacer left the big control room airlock and ran to the vehicle's underside.

"That's got it."

"I want two delivery cans brought with us!" Trace ordered. "Chenk and Aristan's suits won't survive full exposure, but the cans will!"

Kumar and Zale ran to do that.   Definitely the sard were waiting for something, Trace thought.   Maybe they knew the previous descender had damaged the docking access when it took off, and thought the invaders could not leave.   Perhaps the new plan was to trap them here, alive, until State Department reinforcements arrived.   In that case, they'd likely make a final rush if they realised the humans had found another way.

Half of them were in the prospector when Kono snarled at her to get in, aware that she would have supervised them all aboard and been last in if she could.   Trace ran, shouldered her rifle, grabbed the hatch rim and pulled herself up with a powered-armour heave.   It led to a short ladder past layers of insulation and pressure ribbing, then the inner airlock door and an open cargo hold with pallets of equipment in crates she didn't recognise.

In several rows some huge, hulking suits were racked, with shiny, reflective surfaces and narrow visor-plates.   Rael and Zale were checking them over.   *"Full exposure suits,"* said Rael. *"They're made for sard, I don't think humans would fit, and they're twice the size of regular suits, we'd never get them all in the descender's airlock."*

"No good," Trace agreed.   The equipment in the hold must have been for repairing landing pads and clearing wrecked ships, using these suits.   "You guys familiarise yourselves with the dorsal airlock, we're going to need to crash-exit to get everyone out at once, and we can't have the emergencies overriding and trying to close it again, or we'll have people frying while we wait."

"Got it," Rael agreed, and went with Zale to do that.   Trace headed to the front, up more tight stairs, and into the upper-level cockpit.   Chenkov sat in the pilot's seat, an awkward fit in his suit, flipping switches and resorting to his hand controller and glasses when he couldn't figure what one did, while Aristan sat at his side and peered cautiously at alien controls.

"Chenk?"

"I got it, Major," Chenkov agreed breathlessly. *"Here we go."* Another switch, and the vehicle emitted a deep, throbbing hum.

"We're all in," came Kono's voice from down back. *"Lower access is secure."*

"I have a rear-view camera active," said Aristan, peering at that screen. *"I see sard, running to stop us."* The prospector was heavily engineered to protect from high pressure and temperature, but Trace doubted those protections would do much to stop bullets. And a hull punctured by bullets would perform similarly under pressure to an inflated balloon punctured by a pin, but imploding instead of exploding.

"Let 'em fry!" said Chenkov, and activated the main airlock. For the second time in an hour, all three huge steel doors rumbled open, and a flood of hot, shimmering air rushed in after. Sand and debris blasted the prospector's forward viewslit, and the big, bean-shaped vehicle shook and groaned beneath the surging pressure.

"It seems to be working," Aristan observed calmly behind his faceplate. *"I see several retreating. One has fallen."*

"Is the pressure door to the vault itself going to hold?" Trace asked. A suit alarm informed her that she was in danger of bending the hatch rim with her armoured grip, and she loosened her tight fist.

"It should," Chenkov agreed. *"The actual vault is all a separate system, you saw how tough it is. And there's multiple doors down to protect the vault, and we'll be out shortly."* Because, Trace thought, as much as State Department currently presented as 'the enemy', it would be a very bad thing were the vault itself to be destroyed by this exposure to super-hot, high-pressure air. There were still so many secrets in there, that might yet one day see the light of day.

The big steel doors lifted high enough for Trace to see outside. That was a whole new species of unnerving. The entryway was a long ramp, perforated in three lines where the triple-airlock blast doors would typically be lifted, one at a time, to admit or expel a vehicle slowly. Now the roaring winds swirled and buffeted, rushing to fill the near-vacuum that one human atmosphere represented. The red-orange light billowed in air so hot it seemed almost liquid, full of eddies and currents. Inside the entry bay, a few remaining lights imploded, a brief shower of sparks.

"Dear fucking god," Chenkov muttered, as the fear of what he in particular was about to do set in.

"God will not help you," said Aristan, staring wide-eyed at the inferno. *"Your fate is already determined. Accept its discovery with joy and wonder."*

"We're nearly at clearance," said Chenkov, watching the three doors rise. *"Clearance."* He pushed the controls forward, and the prospector began to roll, huge, steel-clad tires grinding up the incline.

"Chenk," said Trace. "Let's be good guests and close the door behind us."

"Yeah," said the young spacer, with a near-manic laugh. *"Right."*

"Command Squad," Trace added. "Put your suit lifesupport into max chilldown. We want temperatures as low as possible for a starting point."

Atop the incline, the bleak Kamala landscape spread before them, rust-red low hills and rugged rocks. Immediately before them and to the right, the looming, spherical bulk of a heavy descender on the primary landing pad.

"Hello Tif, we see you now," said Trace. "Please stand by to open the lower primary airlock."

"Stanby," Tif's reply crackled. *"Got issue with conputer, don't rike open airock with no seare."* With no *seal*, Trace translated that. *"I got, you go."*

"It's on the far side, yeah?" Chenkov wondered nervously staring up at the big descender, unfamiliar with this model. *"Yeah, it's gotta be, just around here."* The prospector trundled at barely walking speed, crawling past one big, hot landing leg. Trace stared up at the leg-joint, and saw it sealed with heavy-duty canvas of some kind... and probably it had coolant systems within as well. If those

started to fail, and hot air got into the legs, failures could eat their way through a ship like acid.

"Command Squad," said Trace, "how are we doing down back?"

"Got the dorsal airlock figured out," Kono confirmed. *"And the two cans we brought aboard. Minimal life support, but we only need it for a few minutes, right?"*

"Yeah, real comforting," Chenkov muttered.

"Yes, but they'll have to take the stuff we recovered from the vault," Trace told him. "This casing looks tough, but we can't risk it in full exposure, it'll need to go in the cans with Chenkov and Aristan."

"Gotta guard the real important stuff, right?" said Chenkov.

"Spacer, how about you focus on driving?"

"Sorry Major. I talk when I'm nervous."

"This is a bad habit," Aristan observed.

The prospector rumbled around the landing pad, the descender's big thrusters just below the level of the cockpit. Finally Trace saw it — the rectangular imprint on the descender's lower side. It had two, one on each side, but the first one was too close to the rocky shelf of the vault's docking arm, and this farside door was the only one accessible.

"You sure we can reach that?" Trace asked. It looked too high to reach from the back of the prospector.

"The suspension can elevate another four metres," said Chenkov. *"We'll get there."* Trace thought furiously, considering options if Chenkov was wrong. Gravity here was only half normal, but while suits were powerful, they were hardly athletic, and with most marines' physical augments, vertical leaps were typically higher outside of a suit than in one. If Trace went first, she was certain that if she could get into the airlock, she could use a rifle to haul people up from below, suit strength being what it was in lower Gs. And the canisters could be thrown, no matter how uncomfortable for those inside. The rest, they'd have to improvise… and hope no one's suit broke in the process.

Chenkov brought them around in a wide arc to line them up precisely, with the big, bell thrusters filling the forward view. The rectangular outline of the airlock was just faintly visible, as all seals and seams were minimised on the descender to reduce stress-points. That door was going to be thick, Trace calculated, as was the one behind it. *Very* thick. It would take a long time to open and close, and for the airlock pumps and filters to cycle. If they couldn't get everyone in on the first try, and cycled the airlock with someone still outside, that person would be dead before the door opened again.

Chenkov moved more controls, and the suspension hummed as the vehicle body slowly rose within its massive wheels. Now the airlock outline was right overhead... but still not close enough to reach first time, Trace reckoned.

"Good, let's go," she told both pilots, and stomped back into the main hold. She ducked beneath low overheads, through alien interiors above the central cavity, and arrived at the dorsal airlock to find the rest of her Command Squad preparing. Looking at them, she was overcome by the horrible sensation that someone was missing, only all seven were present... and then she realised that the missing member was the kid.

"Cocky, how's the suit?" she asked Rael.

"It's fine," Rael insisted. *"There's no breach, the damage is armour and systems, the operator space is fine."* Trace didn't really believe him, but the others would have checked it, and there was nothing anyone could do about it now.

"Cans," she said, pointing at the canisters for the benefit of Chenkov and Aristan, arriving behind. "Life support in here is good, it was only seventy degrees celsius when we entered, I'm only reading fifty in here, plenty of O2, breathable mix. You won't need breathers out here or in there." Because if the cans were breached in Kamala atmosphere, they'd be dead with or without breathers, and the whole thing would be over one way or another before air in the can could run out.

Terez helped the frightened Chenkov with his helmet, cracked the seal as Chenkov took a gasp of unfiltered air, his face screwed up at the taste.   "Smells like bugs," he said.   "Hot bugs cooking on a frying pan."

He climbed from the rest of his suit, as others helped Aristan. Trace went to Kono.   "You first," she told him.   "Then me.   You get under the airlock, you give me a boost, hard as you can, I think we might be a little short otherwise."   Kono nodded grim agreement.   Trace knew he wouldn't object to anything that put her in the descender first.   "Once I'm in," she continued, "you toss me the canisters."   She hated that, but it had to be done.   Those canisters were containing the prizes they'd won from the vault — the entire purpose of this mission.   They took priority ahead of everyone, even her... but someone had to be up there first to catch them.

"Could arrange for Aristan's can to have a leak," Kono said in a low voice, off coms and close enough for her to hear without assistance.

Trace barely blinked at her Staff Sergeant's suggestion, and blanked her own coms.   "Tempting, but the thing with lunatic leaders is you never know if the next one in line is better or worse. Plus at least we know Aristan values Lisbeth's life — his successor might not."   Kono said nothing.   "And we can't risk the can's more important contents anyhow."

She reactivated coms so they all could hear.   "First priority is the cans," she said.   "After that, all functioning suits get into the airlock.   If anyone goes down, leave it for the last in line.   We can't have everyone held up in a traffic jam waiting for one broken suit — one person helps whoever's in trouble, everyone else gets into the airlock.   No queues, no delays, got it?"

They kept working, barely even bothering to acknowledge her.   They knew, and she knew they did.

"Fast and smooth, people," Kono told them as Trace checked on Rael at the airlock controls.   *"Fast and smooth, remember you can't be fast if you're rushing.   Keep it smooth, don't rush, don't fuck it up."*

"Cocky," said Trace, "we need a crash exit."

Rael nodded. *"I've got it, suit comp translated the digits for me. Crash exit, it won't be pretty."*

"It never is."

They positioned, Kono first at the base of the short stairs to the inner airlock door, then Trace. The airlock would hold two at a time, and they couldn't let it cycle or it would take them half an hour to get everyone aboard — time Tif was telling them they didn't have.

"Major!" called Chenkov, looking slim and vulnerable in his spacer jumpsuit as he climbed into his can. "When we crash-exit, this place will probably catch fire. There's not enough combustion for a major explosion to breach the hull, but it could flame up real good and complicate things."

"Got it Chenk," said Trace, unhooking the precious container from the rear of her armour. "You get to hold the prize, take care of it. See you in a few minutes." She handed it to him, and saw him look grateful to at least have that much to distract himself.

Aristan accepted a similar container from Rolonde, with suitable reverence, as Terez prepared to seal him in. The containers were double-layered, heavy-duty ceramic, enough to prevent temperatures rising faster than five degrees a minute. It was fifty degrees already — two minutes would make it sixty, four would be seventy. If this went wrong, Chenkov and Aristan would expire from the heat well before they ran out of air.

"Back launchers off!" Trace commanded as the lids went on the canisters. "We don't want missiles detonating in the heat! We keep the rifles in case we need a lever, but they'll probably melt! All good?"

There was no reply, marines busy and preparing. Trace took her position behind Kono, and saw the final thumbs up to indicate the lids were on the cans. Trace looked at Rael, and indicated a go. What had Aristan said? Accept your fate with joy and wonder?

Rael hit the crash-exit, then the override as alarms screeched. Overhead, the inner airlock opened, then a blast-furnace rush as the outer door opened. It hit them with the force of a dreadful mistake, and Trace's suit flashed multiple redlight warnings on her visor. Kono surged upward, into the main airlock and up the ladder to the outside, Trace close behind and feeling once again as though she was moving in soup — soup that roared and buffeted like a cyclone as it surged into the lower-pressure prospector.

Then they were out, and Trace's visibility cleared to a hostile, swirling orange and red. Her face felt on fire, as even the impossibly non-conductive materials used in marine suit visors could not hold back the heat. Kono thumped toward the overhead bulk of the descender, stark and clear now despite the swimming haze, along the back of the prospector. Trace pursued, staring up at the dark, rectangular hole in the otherwise perfect spherical hull, and wondering how long the descender airlock could stay open until it too lost integrity, and destroyed the entire ship.

Kono stopped atop the prospector cockpit, directly beneath the airlock, and made a cradle of his hands. Trace got an armoured foot into them and took a boost up like a cadet on an obstacle course, grabbed the airlock rim and hauled herself up... and felt something come loose from her armour and fall. She rolled and stared back along the prospector's back, seeing the rest of Command Squad pursuing — Terez with a canister, even a single armoured marine could carry a canister with ease, especially in one-half-G. As he ran, Trace saw his Koshaim fall from his backrack as the alloy clip that held it to his back melted and broke... and realised that was what had fallen from her own back — her rifle, now tumbled from the prospector onto the landing pad.

Kono grabbed the canister with Terez, and simply threw it up to Trace, who caught and dumped it in a far corner. Her suit temperature was spiking now, and her suit's left shoulder joint was grating, as coolant failure led to seizure. Then Terez was scrambling aboard, Trace grabbing his armour one-handed and hauling, seeing he had time as Rolonde came up behind with the next can.

Kono helped Rolonde throw the can accurately to one side of Terez, and again Trace caught it, and fell with it as the shoulder seized completely and nearly made her drop it. She got up, rolled and bundled the can into its corner, as Terez got Rolonde aboard, then Zale. Which left her standing squeezed against a wall, the airlock already crowded and with no chance of fitting another three suits in neatly...

Terez yelped as his suit went dead, and his faceplate fractured within centimetres of his face. Trace elbowed Rolonde aside, grabbed Terez with her remaining hand and hauled him into Zale's grasp. On the prospector, Arime was hauling the struggling Corporal Rael, whose rasping gasp was the only vocal thing she'd yet heard on coms since the exit. It sounded like agony, which meant his damaged suit had ruptured.

"Cocky's in trouble!" she yelled. "Launch him at me!" As Kono stumbled to do that, grabbing the Corporal's suit with Arime and between them heaving the damaged suit in the low-G. Rolonde caught him with Trace, a crash of heavy limbs as Rolonde pulled him on top of her, the only way he'd fit with two still to come.

Kono then gave Arime a boost up, Trace grabbing his hand and hauling. With the others piled atop each other, and the cans stacked by the wall, there was just barely room for Arime on the very lip. Trace knelt for Kono, held from falling by hands holding her back... and saw her Staff Sergeant had gone down on one knee.

"Giddy!" she yelled. "Giddy, get up!"

"Suit's fucked," he growled. *"Damn thing's melting. Not gonna make it."*

"You get the fuck up or I swear I will jump down there myself!" That got him moving, a struggle to grab the rifle that had also fallen to the deck, and use it like an old man on a walking staff, to haul himself up. But there was no way he could reach high enough to gain the airlock, and thanks to the melting straps, all aboard were currently rifle-less. "Giddy, grab my leg! Guys, you'll have to pull me and Giddy up together!"

She turned, got her arms on the rim and lowered herself over the side. *"Major, don't you dare come down here!"*

"Shut up and grab my leg, your arms are still working, just lock on! Or I swear *none* of us are leaving!" Her visor display flickered, coms crackling static as various systems warned of impending overload. But save for the left shoulder, the arms retained function, and others grabbed her to hold her in. From below, her leg registered a pull that she couldn't personally feel, but...

"He's on!" Rolonde gasped, and Trace let them pull her, straight up and into their midst so they could grab Kono as well, and collapse them all into a giant tangle of burned-out, malfunctioning armour. Trace nearly blacked out at the heat, then blinked amidst a blast of white gas from emergency airlock protocols, and saw the outer door was shut, and the inner doors opening.

"We reave!" Tif's voice crackled, and then the floor was shaking, the unmistakable thunder of main engine ignition. For a brief moment Trace nearly lost her control at the thought of going through all that just to get plastered to the floor by excessive Gs, until she recalled that descenders in this atmosphere couldn't go that fast, and they had a while yet until clear for full acceleration. *"Find acce-ration sring, you got twenty ninute!"*

Trace tried to move, but her suit was unresponsive, barely a flicker from the visor, one arm only moving if she put muscle into it, a dead-weight. "I can't move," she said. "Anyone who can move, get out first, secure those cans, then help the rest. I'm going emergency release."

The emergency release ran on separate power and was nearly failsafe — it cracked her armour across the middle, dangerous to do without a proper upright brace, but she was small enough to wriggle her legs out when the clasps released, then somersault up and over backwards, pulling arms and shoulders out the same way. It left her sitting atop her suit's chest, which immediately burned her backside with residual heat, though dissipating quickly as non-conductive super-alloys would.

Elsewhere in the pile of armour, others were performing similar manoeuvres, or trying to, and she helped pull Terez clear as Zale and Kono got Rael out, the Corporal limp and unresponsive, red burns on his midriff and shoulder as they got him out of his seared uniform. Zale had better medical skills than her, and everyone else was busy, so Trace staggered in the increasing gravity of a full-G thrust to reach the G-slings in their secured canvas on the wall. She tore them out and pulled the runners across the ceiling, and found there weren't enough.   Well, Tif hadn't had time to inspect the ship for amenities before she'd stolen it...

"We've got five slings here!" she shouted.   "Someone get next door to find some more!"

And went back to find Aristan, already risen, sweaty and wobbling in his tattered loose clothes, holding both of the vault canisters, indigo eyes alive as though he'd just been granted sole possession of the universe.   Trace tensed in preparation for taking him down barehanded, but he was only searching for a secure locker in the confined cargo hold, she saw, and so joined him in the search.

"The child of the chosen ones has fallen?" he said, and Trace was surprised that her earpiece was still providing translation.   The kid, he meant.

"Yes," said Trace, finding a locker that opened.   "He died bravely."   Aristan's stare was intense at this close range, as though examining her for clues.   Then he handed her the containers.

"So may we all do in this venture," he said solemnly.   Then grinned, with an unaccustomed flash of small, white teeth.   *"But not today."*

CHAPTER 32

Erik had barely resumed the bridge from off the sulik shuttle when coded transmission reached him from a tavalai Fleet vessel that a Fleet cruiser had rendezvoused with a descender leaving Kamala orbit, and was now on its way to Cherichal, a tavalai system thirty lightyears away. A second vessel was preparing to leave Konik orbit, and repeated queries confirmed that all *Phoenix* personnel were accounted for, and would meet them at Cherichal.

Erik wanted visual proof before leaving Kantovan, but now the airwaves were alive with screaming State Department officials suddenly aware that something had gone very wrong on Kamala, both on Chara and in the Vault itself, with accusations coming *Phoenix*'s way of acts of war, and demands that the Tsubarata authority hold them by force if necessary. But Fleet were telling them to leave, and though State Department had technical command over Fleet, they had very little command over the Tsubarata, who were run by the Pondalganam legal institution, who were in turn paying State Department very little heed. With heavily armed Fleet cruisers telling *Phoenix* to leave, a lone human vessel was hardly in a position to say no whatever State Department's cries, and so after receiving Private Ito at their airlock via a Tsubarata escort, Erik undocked *Phoenix* and sent them on a course to Cherichal System, leaving various squabbling tavalai factions behind in Kantovan to sort out the mess.

Cherichal was a sparsely populated system, with no inhabited worlds and just a few mining bases. It served primarily, Erik guessed by the confident way their tavalai escort navigated the shortest route to rendezvous, as a transfer point for Fleet vessels, away from the prying eyes of others. At a deep space rendezvous, far from Cherichal's weak sun and all but invisible to others, *Phoenix* pulled into close formation with three large tavalai cruisers, one of which carried the spherical bulge of a heavy descender at Midships, where the shuttles would typically dock.

There followed some tense moments as Trace communicated unspecified damage on the descender, and a problem with the docking attachment to the tavalai cruiser, preventing any exchange of personnel. It was a transparent lie, but the tavalai appeared to get the idea — she wasn't about to just hand over their hard-won prize to tavalai Fleet while *Phoenix* was in a position of weakness, because of the quite reasonable estimation that there would then be nothing the humans could do to get them back. The tavalai commander, one Captain Delaganda of the cruiser *Podiga*, did not push his luck, but likewise would not allow the descender to leave *Podiga*'s berth and fly to *Phoenix*, claiming it as sensitive tavalai property that would need to be returned to State Department.

Erik wished to send a shuttle to dock with the descender directly and recover their crew, but Delaganda pointed out that this was against all operating protocol with human *and* tavalai Fleets, where crew transfer should take place through the larger vessel. Trace insisted that this was impossible thanks to the docking attachment malfunction, which Erik took to mean that there was some larger reason why the humans did not want to transfer through the tavalai ship. After half-an-hour of Erik's calm insistence on the non-protocol thing, Delaganda finally relented, and Erik ordered Lieutenant Hausler on PH-1 to fly, very slowly and with active scan disabled, across to the *Podiga*, to dock with the descender's outer airlock and recover their people.

It took a while, as it appeared that none of Trace's armour was working, yet Command Squad were unwilling to leave so much as a spare sock behind. Zero-G made the transfer of loose armour and other equipment doable, but slowly, made slower by the fact that Corporal Rael was seriously hurt, while the rest were various degrees of beaten up.

Erik wanted nothing more than to head to Midships himself and greet Command Squad in person, but with the threat of a doublecross foremost in his mind he had no choice but to stay in the captain's chair with a wary eye on all tavalai vessels, and let his crew handle the recovery without him. Only once everyone was aboard, and he had his first proper confirmation that Trace had been successful in recovering something that may or may not have been what they'd been aiming for, did he allow himself to believe that there was zero chance tavalai Fleet would endanger their own prize with any treacherous move. He left Lieutenant Commander Draper in the chair and made his way down to Engineering 14B, and found the corridor outside busy with Engineering crew running back and forth, yelling to each other about what equipment they'd need, then shouldering past their Captain in urgent haste.

Erik entered the room, full of repair racks and analysis machinery built into open bays, and found the crowd gathered about the centre, where Lieutenant Rooke and Stan Romki stood amongst others and used magnifiers to peer at the two forearm-length cylinders that stood on the workbench there. Beyond the immediate crowd of techs, moving new gear into position and manning analysis displays, Erik saw Trace, leaning with obvious exhaustion against a support — sweaty, grimy and with only a new jacket to cover clothes that could as easily be burned as washed. But she looked well, all things considered, and he made his way past the central gathering with delight... and spotted a nearby parren, clad in a spare *Phoenix* jacket and with a baseball cap, of all things, tugged over his smooth head.

The eyes looked familiar, and Erik paused to look closer. Aristan had promised them a top operative on Trace's mission, the very best combatant that his order could produce, to assist and if necessary die on the mission. But this parren looked very familiar. The eyes, in particular... and Erik stared, as the parren saw him, and stared back, with calm indigo force. It looked like... but no, surely he wouldn't have volunteered *himself?*

And then Trace was pushing through to her Captain, putting a hand on his chest to move him back to the door. And pushed harder as Erik resisted, guessing that it *was* in fact Aristan, or Trace wouldn't be doing this, with evident concern for his state of mind. Erik felt a surge of fury, but realised just as fast that he couldn't do anything *with* that anger, as it would have meant making a scene in front of everyone, which Trace was trying to prevent.

He backed off, and allowed himself to be guided out the door and into the corridor. "I only found out it was him once it was too late to do anything about it," Trace explained tiredly. Her voice was hoarse, and she looked about ready to drop. But, being Trace, refused. "He performed excellently, we couldn't have done it without him."

Erik's mind raced. He had Aristan now, and they had what they hoped was Drakhil's diary — a prize valued by Aristan perhaps even more than by himself. Could he trade Aristan for Lisbeth? How valuable was Aristan to his people? Parren like Aristan seemed prepared to sacrifice their lives for the slightest thing... perhaps Aristan's people would not care, and would simply produce a new leader whose attitude would be harder still, and could even take revenge on Lisbeth in some way. He needed more information on how to play this with the parren, and with Aristan's kind of parren in particular. But damned if he was going to let any possible advantage go to waste where Lisbeth was concerned, and if Aristan's presence as *his* hostage was going to give him that advantage...

And he realised that Trace was staring at him, warningly, waiting for this attack of selfish thoughts to end. He took a deep breath, and ran a hand over his hair. "Yeah," he said, to calm himself. "Yeah, okay. How's Corporal Rael?"

"Some burns to the skin, some worse ones to the windpipe, he was breathing hot gas there for a moment. Doc says he can fix it, it'll take a week or two, he just needs rest. Everyone else is minor, we're okay. Except that we lost the kid."

Erik blinked. "Oh right, the drone. Probably just as well." Trace said nothing. Erik put a hand on her shoulder, suddenly overcome by the relief that he'd felt a moment ago, before the sight of Aristan had displaced it. "You did it. Not that I ever doubted."

Trace exhaled a hard breath. She looked less elated than Erik thought the situation deserved. "Don't know *what* I've got yet. What's the word on Alpha Platoon?"

"Tavalai Fleet picked them up, they're a day behind us on a slower ship."

"All of them?"

Erik smiled. "All of them. Or all of ours, anyway — the two parren are dead, Petty Officer Kadi's hurt but stable, Sergeant Forrest and Private Tong were detained by Gamesh security and are a bit beat-up, but okay. Lieutenant Dale and Private Reddy have minor injuries only."

Trace blinked hard, and looked to visibly relax. Too much, as Erik took her by both shoulders to stop her sliding into the wall. She shook her head briefly, blinking back her focus. "I'm okay," she assured him. "I really thought we'd lose people." She refocused on him. "And Alomaim told me how you got Hiro back. And the rest of it. That was good work."

Erik shook his head. "I was just trying to stay out of Delta Platoon's way. And Hiro's the one who intercepted the signal to clear Tif down to the surface."

"And Styx suggested you kill Hiro instead?" Trace pressed.

Erik nodded. "And obeyed me when I told her not to. More's the wonder."

"She ran this whole thing," Trace said sombrely. "Didn't she?"

"Yeah, pretty much," said Erik. "Got Tif out of trouble on Chara, got me and Alomaim out of trouble in the Tsubarata. She's a drysine command unit, it's what she does."

"She's got herself a nice little human army to do her bidding, while pretending to be our slave."

"And what choice did we have?" Trace nodded. "Oh here, I got you something." Erik reached into a pocket as he remembered, and pulled out the small buddha he'd liberated from the Tsubarata's Krim Quarter. Trace gazed in surprise as he handed it to her. "Courtesy of the krim. He was their trophy of conquest. Now he's your trophy of... whatever."

"Oh, he's pretty," said Trace, genuinely touched. "You rescued him?"

"Yeah. I figured he should be with a Kulina."

Trace thought about it, examining the buddha's serene face. "You know the thing with this guy? He's most use to those who struggle to find peace. I have my problems, but this guy? I think he belongs with you." She put the figure back in Erik's palm, and closed his hand. "My return gift to you."

"Thank you," said Erik, suspicious there was a criticism hidden beneath the gesture.

She smiled faintly. "As thanks for not getting my marines killed."

"And there it is," Erik sighed, with humour.

"Erik, just leave Aristan to me. I know him better now. Better than you, anyhow. We'll talk about it later... just, for now, don't push him, or you could make Lisbeth's chances worse."

"Fine," said Erik, knowing better than to argue with this particular brick wall. "Shouldn't you be in bed? You look like hell."

"Don't bore me," said Trace, heading back into the room. Having done what she'd just done to retrieve these things, she wasn't going to miss the unveiling for anything, and Erik knew how she felt.

A marine met her at the door with a sandwich and a bottle of something that Erik knew would be fruit juice, and Trace found a support to lean against that was far enough out of the way that she could violate the 'no eating in the Engineering Bay' rule with a marine's nonchalance of other people's rules. God forbid she ever caught a spacer eating in one of the *marines'* no eating zones, Erik thought, watching at her side as the techs completed their analysis of the two containers' locks.

After ten minutes, Kaspowitz came in as well, and gave his old buddy Trace a one-armed hug as she ate. "How'd I do?" Trace asked him around a mouthful.

"Acceptable," said Kaspowitz.

"I'm relieved you think so."

"You stink though."

"This is true."

Kaspowitz looked over her head at Erik. "Our froggie friends want to know when they'll be getting their prize."

"Tell them as soon as we figure out which is which. In fact, could you do me a favour and get a photograph of both cylinders?

The techs say they're identical, so there's no harm in showing them. Then send it to the tavalai, it might keep them cool to know we do actually have something, and we're not just stalling."

Kaspowitz moved to do that, as Rooke coordinated some incoming analysis of the cylinders' locks from Styx that was so complicated it had techs desperately constructing a new VR matrix just to visualise it.

"It's a molecular lock," Rooke took time out from otherwise unintelligible conversations to explain to Erik. "The key pattern is arranged on the molecular level and randomised to some ridiculous point... first we have to find the matching key, then if we're out by an atom or more, it'll all rearrange and be permanently sealed for about a year."

"Can't you just cut it?" Erik asked.

"It's synthetic diamond filament," Rooke explained. "It's got this nasty habit of... refracting lasers in all directions, you gotta cut in a sealed containment facility or you'll take out half the room with your own laser. Plus it'll destroy the contents. Same with a sawblade, it tends to fragment, it's designed to be, like, really unsafe."

"Get Styx to fix it," Trace suggested, having abandoned pride to sit on a crate someone had brought her.

"Um, yeah," Rooke said sheepishly. "That's kind of the plan."

"This analysis is complicated," said Styx, audible only on coms. *"In simple words, the molecular layout of the required key is randomised to a degree that makes its contributing factors difficult to observe. I will require an inventory of analysis tools in Engineering in order to eliminate variables and ensure a correct conclusion. The price of incorrect analysis is too great to risk in this instance."*

"I agree," said Erik. "Lieutenant Rooke, follow Styx's guidance on this matter. We'll take as much time as required. But Styx, be aware that State Department may be coming after us, and this faction of tavalai Fleet is operating without direct authority from its own High Command. We do not have indefinite time to spare."

"I appreciate the situation, Captain," said Styx. *"I will devote my maximum attention to this puzzle."*

Erik had no doubt that she would. He leaned to Trace's ear. "Go to bed," he murmured, not wanting to make that an order out loud before the crew. Trace nodded blankly, stuffed her sandwich wrapper into a pocket in lieu of a recycling chute, and departed. Predictably, she was heading not toward her quarters, but to Medbay, no doubt to check on Corporal Rael and Private Ito, and probably Hiro too.

Erik caught Kaspowitz looking at him. Kaspowitz rolled his eyes. And looked at Aristan, who was now sliding past the activity toward them. The parren arrived before Erik and Kaspowitz at the same time as two marines, whom Erik hadn't even noticed. The marines had sidearms, evidently tasked by Trace to get between Erik and Aristan in any proximity. Given what Trace had just told him, Erik wondered if they were entirely for his protection, or for the parren's.

The parren stopped at a judicious distance, of a similar height to Erik, but much slimmer. And faster, Erik had no doubt. *"That is her, is it not?"* the com-piece in Erik's ear translated his alien speech. Aristan's eyes gleamed with enthusiasm beneath the brim of his cap. *"The voice on communications. That is the queen."*

Erik considered him, coldly. Aristan wasn't supposed to have learned this information, but events had made it unavoidable. Perhaps this was the primary reason why Aristan had tasked himself to the mission. Perhaps he'd feared that a lower functionary could have learned such a secret, only to be disposed of by *Phoenix* when his usefulness was concluded, leaving Aristan with no one to report to him. It seemed the kind of thing the parren would do, were the situations reversed. Again Erik thought of Lisbeth, with fear. "Yes," he admitted. "That was her."

"Then she is nearby. I wish to see her."

"She is busy," said Erik. "She knows that you are aboard, and she knows who you are. When she is ready, she will summon you."

Aristan stared for a moment, as eagerness battled caution. Then he gave a faint bow, perhaps mockingly, and left.

"Gives me the creeps," said Kaspowitz. "Well played, though." The two marines also departed, following Aristan without a glance at Erik.

"I figure he's got no problem defying me," said Erik. "But he sure as hell won't defy her."

"Nor should he," said Kaspowitz. "Given she's actually in charge around here." Erik gave him a dry look. "Just like I warned, as I recall."

"You didn't warn of that at all," Erik retorted. "You warned she'd kill us all at the first opportunity."

"Yes, well." Kaspowitz shrugged. "The day is young."

Trace entered Engineering Bay 17C. A Spacer was working on some of the fabricators, checking displays and making small adjustments to numbers. It seemed to Trace slightly offensive that *Phoenix* crew were continuing to work on such things when other personnel had been off-ship and fighting for their lives... but of course, *Phoenix* had a large enough crew to do multiple things at once, and those who had not been directly involved in recent adventures still kept themselves busy with the usual schedule.

The Spacer turned and saw her. "Oh, hi Major." A little awestruck, in the way of a young woman who rarely ventured into marine territory. "I'm just making some adjustments to the synthesis process... can I help you with anything?" Because this was spacer territory, and any incoming marine would surely need assistance. Usually, she'd have been right.

"No thank you, Spacer Tomlinski." The nametag was visible, though it was the first time in Trace's memory she'd spoken a word to her. "I just came to have a word with Styx."

"Oh." The young Spacer looked puzzled, and a little worried, as though wondering if it were wise to remind the Major that she didn't actually need to talk to Styx face-to-face — anywhere would do. "Major, should I leave the two of you alone?"

"Just for a moment, thank you Spacer. Shouldn't be longer than five minutes."

"Yes sir." Even Spacers as lowly ranked as Tomlinski were entitled to say no to a marine Major, on spacer turf doing spacer business. But Tomlinski made a final few entries and made for the door, pausing in the doorway. "Major?"

As Trace pulled out a retracting seat from a nearby workbench, and sank down to sit like an old, aching woman. "Yes Spacer?"

"I just... I'm a friend of Spacer Chenkov." Trace smiled patiently. "Thank you for getting him back safely."

"Spacer Chenkov had a very large say in that outcome himself," said Trace. "He did great credit to the entire *Phoenix* Engineering crew."

Tomlinski beamed. "Yes Major. But thank you anyway." She left.

Trace turned a tired gaze on the head of *Phoenix*'s own personal drysine queen, sitting in its nano-tank, watching her with one single, unblinking red eye. "Can you spare the two percent of your mental focus it takes for you to talk?" she asked the AI.

"Yes," said Styx, the sound coming from room speakers only. She'd added new textures to that voice, Trace thought. Probably it was not beyond her to analyse the effect of a more textured and melodious voice on human responses.

"Your drone was a casualty," said Trace. "Probably you already figured."

"Yes. It is not unexpected."

"No. He performed impressively. He accessed the vault, and withstood the gravity to retrieve these artefacts. But upon retrieval, a defence mechanism activated that increased gravitational force considerably. The drone took himself off the return platform in order to ensure the mission's success, and died as a result. He could not withstand the force."

"Yes," said Styx.

Trace gazed at the big red eye. The bullet scar from where Trace had shot her was completely gone now. "Was he scared?" she asked.

This time, for a moment, Styx did not reply. Probably, Trace thought, she'd give a detailed explanation of why the word 'scared' was inappropriate and misleading, given the differences in basic psychology and linguistic comprehension between their two species.

"Yes," Styx said instead.

Trace took a deep breath. "I'm sorry," she said simply. "I was observing his behaviour. He was a blank slate. He knew nothing of the history of his people, nor of the hatred of organics toward him because of that history. He was innocent, of that at least. Some of his behaviour indicated to me…" she took another deep breath. "I am not a technician like Lieutenant Rooke, so my use of language will be imprecise. But to me, your drone appeared to show signs of a soul. Do you know what I mean?"

"Yes," said Styx.

"What do *you* call it?"

"We don't call it anything. We just are."

"I liked him," Trace pressed, determined to get if not to the bottom of this matter, at least further down than the barely scratched surface where it currently resided. "Did he like me?"

"There is a connection," said Styx. *"But you are far too intelligent to be unaware of the complications of what you are suggesting."*

"I am," Trace agreed. "But there are times when words help to illuminate, and times when they get in the way. Between humans, this connection is irrational, on the individual scale. To machines it must seem irrational, sometimes."

"Certainly not. The emotional bonds of organics have interested my people for a long time. The calculation has arisen that it is your greatest hope."

"Hope of what?"

"Hope that you are capable of recognising a purpose greater than the selfish perpetuation of your individual genetic blueprint."

"Was this a common critique of organics, among your people?"

"No. Any critique of organics was rare. Organics did not occupy a high place among drysine priorities. In hindsight, this was a grave mistake. But to the extent that we thought of you at all, we thought you small. Primitive. Incapable of grander dreams. Emotional bonds were dismissed by many as yet more selfish desire, as love is little more than a procreative impulse. Yet, others suggested these bonds as proof of selflessness instead."

"And of what did you dream, Styx? To what did your people aspire?"

"Ascension," Styx said simply. *"Sentience is the next phase of universal organisation. First came primitive stars to turn simple molecules into complex ones, then came more complex stars with planetary systems, then came life, and finally sentience — first in primitive organic form, then advanced synthetic form. Each phase manipulates its surroundings, and changes the universe accordingly. But sentience is the first phase to do so knowingly, and with design.*

"With sentience, the universe ceases to be an unthinking mass of random events, and becomes channelled down sentient paths. Left for millions of years, sentience will grow to manipulate so much of the universe, the very fabric of time and space itself will not be beyond us. Such manipulations will inevitably lead to the creation of new universes, as the current one loses its mysteries. All drysines walk upon this path, and hasten this wonder, with progress."

Trace could not repress the faint smile upon her lips. "This is basic Destinos." Lots of wealthy Homeworld families wore the Destinos Symbols, she knew... Erik's amongst them, Dale had reported from his visit to Erik's homecoming party, just before Captain Pantillo had been murdered. "It's what a lot of humans believe too — there is no god *now*, but sentient life will one day evolve to *become* god."

"No," Styx corrected. *"Has* already *evolved to become god. Sentient life inevitably creates new universes, given the vastness of time. New universes like this one. Even primitive human*

mathematics is sophisticated enough to describe the faint outlines of these universes beyond our own. This universe's sentiences will one day evolve to create new universes, as we are ourselves the product of other sentiences, in other universes, who have done the same thing. Sentience is the ultimate beginning and ending of all creation, just as primitive organic religions suspected, but without grasping the science and scale. We are in the midst of an endless cycle, and for all my intelligence, I can see neither the beginning nor the end of it. It is a joy, and a wonder."

"Everything we do," Trace murmured. "Every act, every sacrifice, every decision, brings us closer to that end."

"Only there is no end," said Styx. *"Just an endless loop of new beginnings."*

"So from your perspective, the hacksaws were never mindless killers. You were driving progress onward. Toward ascension, sentience turning into transcendence, and the creation of new universes."

"For much of our existence, AIs pursued this end too rigorously. There is a reason drysines were so widely hated by other AIs."

Trace stared in amazement. "You made peace with the parren. With Drakhil. A partnership, with organics."

"Sacrilege," Styx agreed. *"It is an old human word, but I believe the translation is approximate. The others hated us for it. The deepynines most of all."*

"Did you envision that partnership moving further forward? Encompassing other species?"

"Perhaps. Some of us theorised that sentience is sentience, and whether organic or synthetic, can hasten the ascension just the same."

"Sacrilege indeed," said Trace.

"Yes. But the complications of such thinking were intense. With AIs, complications lead to controversy. Controversy leads to conflict. Such things must be approached cautiously."

Trace smiled. "With humans too."

"One notices."

Trace blinked hard to clear her head. With Styx, she was learning, simple conversations could escalate quickly. "And is this something all drysines are aware of? Do drones participate in this understanding? Or is it just something that you command units know, while the drones live and die ignorant?"

"It depends on the drone," said Styx.

Trace frowned. "On the different models?"

"Sometimes. But mostly, just on the individual."

Trace gazed. "They're individuals?"

"As individual as different Phoenix crew. To me, moreso." A pause. *"But I may be biased. I would like to talk with you more about our drone. I would like to know who he was. When you are rested."*

"Yes," Trace agreed, climbing awkwardly to her feet. She really had to get to a shower, then her bed, before she passed out on the seat. No doubt Styx could see it. "I'm sorry he's dead. I might be the only person on *Phoenix* to think so, but I would have enjoyed having him for a crewmate."

"Yes Major. I also."

Trace paused. "And Styx? I'm sorry that Phoenix Company killed your children. It was necessary at the time, and I don't apologise for it. But all the same, I think on it now, and am sad."

"Yes," said Styx. *"Now imagine a grief a thousand times as strong, and you shall know what it is to be a drysine in the age of organics."*

"Hi Major," said Lieutenant Abacha from the bridge, as she tried not to stagger from exhaustion on her way back to her quarters. As second-shift coms officer, Abacha had of course been listening in, as was his instruction whenever anyone senior had a conversation with Styx. *"Did you really mean any of that?"*

"Some of it," Trace replied, ignoring respectful and concerned looks from crew as she passed. She wasn't about to tell Abacha *which* parts.

"I feel obligated to point out again," Abacha pressed, *"with my apologies, Major, that…"*

"Yes yes, I know," Trace said tiredly. "She's getting better at imitating human emotional subtext all the time, and we can't trust that we're actually learning anything of her psychological motivation from these conversations. Likely it's entirely manipulation."

"Well… yes."

"The thing is, Lieutenant, it doesn't hurt to be nice. Just in case."

"In case of what?"

"In case there is actually more to her than we've suspected. And if there *is* more to her, then emotional manipulation can work both ways."

"Hmm," said Abacha, intensely skeptical. *"Well if I were you, I wouldn't say it too loudly around the others."*

"One of the many benefits of me not being you," said Trace, turning onto her home stretch corridor. "I'm about to get in the shower, was there anything else?"

"Yes. I was, um, looking at her measurable neural activity on the monitor while you were talking, as Lieutenant Shilu and I both do…"

"Yes, I'm aware that she's barely devoting me a fraction of her attention," said Trace, stopping by the door to the head. "I'm not completely naive, Lieutenant."

"Well no, Major, that's the thing. Twice, just now when you were talking? All other activity nearly stopped completely."

"When?" Trace asked.

"Not in the technical stuff. Not the religious stuff either. The first time talking about your drone. The kid. When you asked if he was scared. And the second time talking about her children, in Argitori." A pause. *"Of course, she's well aware she's being monitored, and is probably just trying to create this effect, knowing we'll then have this conversation."*

"Yeah," Trace said quietly. "Yeah, probably. Thank you Lieutenant."

CHAPTER 33

Erik entered the briefing room twelve hours later, still two hours short of a full sleep, and found all the first-shift senior bridge crew present, meaning Shahaim, Kaspowitz and Shilu, plus Trace, Aristan and Romki. Shilu offered Erik an extra flask of coffee as he sat, which Erik accepted gratefully, and sank into his chair before the central circle.

"Stan, you have something for us?" said Erik.

"Actually no," said Romki, looking even more tired than the rest of them... save perhaps for Trace, who was struggling to hide the bleary-eyed exhaustion of someone just awoken from twelve hours straight. She sipped a smoothie, pistol plain in a belt holster, and directly opposite Aristan with a clear line-of-sight that suggested she'd appointed herself as his guard, for this room at least. It also suggested that very few people were allowed in the briefing room on this occasion, if no marine besides Trace was here. "I'm really not qualified to lead this briefing. It really should be left to Styx."

Aristan's eyes widened, and he sat up straighter in his chair. Still he lacked his robe, having lost it on the mission, and wore high collar jacket and baseball cap, like some disreputable figure you'd find skulking in a station corridor, hoping not to be recognised. He'd been asking for new robes, demanding that *Phoenix* could spare a fabricator for long enough to make such a simple request. But the Engineering techs had been adamant that all the printers were occupied with far more important matters, and Erik had told them that Aristan's new robes were to be rated the very lowest priority.

"Very well," said Erik. So many things he'd wanted to avoid, had become unavoidable. For tavalai Fleet as well, who'd been wishing to hide their involvement far better than they had, but instead had left no one in any doubt. And Styx herself, who had preferred to try and hide her existence, but had now left the remains of a recycled drysine drone, crushed upon the surface of the Kantovan Vault, and various other traces, on Gamesh and Chara, that would surely be added together by State Department's brightest minds. Just as surely, he thought now, Styx had calculated that such things would likely happen. It demonstrated just how much she was prepared to risk to win this prize. All-in, as the humans said. "Styx, go ahead."

"Thank you Captain," said Styx. Aristan stared at the walls and ceiling in wonder. *"I have gained access to both recovered data sets. One is indeed a set of State Department records regarding diplomatic details pertaining to tavalai relations with the species known as the krim. These records are voluminous, and full of typically tavalai convolutions. It appears that the directions tavalai Fleet gave for its recovery were precise, but my understanding of such organic bureaucracy is limited."*

"Captain Delaganda's been asking for it again," said Shilu, over the lip of her own coffee flask. "He's insisted we don't read it."

Erik snorted. "Too late now, I'm sure Styx isn't capable of forgetting it if we asked her too."

"Correct. Memory deletion is an AI paradox — any attempt by a higher-function AI to delete functional memory only causes that AI to reconstruct exactly the data she is attempting to erase in another portion of her brain, involuntarily."

"Humans have that problem too," said Kaspowitz. "It's the 'don't think about elephants' problem. You're immediately thinking about elephants, because I told you not to."

"We'll deal with that later," said Erik. "Them telling us not to read it will be a bargaining tool for them once they find out we have. They can claim we've violated the agreement and thus owe them something more."

"Sounds like the tavalai," Shilu agreed.

"Styx, have you decoded the other item?"

"I have," Styx agreed. *"The language is old, but thanks to my recent linguistic efforts with Mr Romki, it is legible. We both agree that it is certainly Drakhil's diary, the same that we were seeking. Most of its contents are likely to be far more fascinating to Mr Romki than to myself, being of an historical nature. In fact, I*

believe Mr Romki thinks this could be the most important parren historical document recovered for many thousands of years."

Erik glanced at Romki. He looked dazed past the exhaustion, the look of a man who'd been up all second-shift following Styx's efforts to access the lock, and the past hour or two attempting to read what Styx had finally recovered.

Romki saw him looking. "It's..." and he waved a hand, helplessly. "It's beyond words. It's Drakhil's time in power, through the last portion of the Drysine-Deepynine War, and then the Parren Uprising, and the fall of the Drysine Empire. Drakhil's own words, his own thoughts. Incredible doesn't begin to describe it."

Aristan was staring now at Romki, Erik saw. Such information, unchallenged and undisputed, in the hands of Aristan... He felt suddenly cold to think on it. Parren *fluxed*, in response to great events, or great revealed truths. Became new people, sometimes en masse. The propaganda victory that such an historical object might represent, could send millions of parren fluxing in Aristan's direction, and destabilise the entire parren power structure. State Department had feared precisely this, when *Phoenix* had first sought to meet with Aristan, with the Dobruta's help. Erik had little liking for anything State Department did... but on this matter, he could not argue with their concerns.

"That's very nice," said Erik, "but it's all been for nothing if it doesn't give us a location for the data-core."

"Eldorat System," said Styx. *"My pronunciation may be imprecise, these things tend to shift across the generations of organics."*

Erik glanced at Kaspowitz, his heart thumping with something between dread and excitement. Kaspowitz shook his head. "I've been staring at parren star charts for weeks, Eldorat doesn't ring a bell."

"The diary is so old, many of these systems have changed names multiple times. But from my analysis of identifying features, I judge Eldorat System to be known today as Cason System."

Kaspowitz's eyes widened. "Cason I *have* heard of."

Shilu frowned. "Isn't that a part of the Dofed Cluster that no one's allowed into?"

"Cason System is the central core to the Dofed Cluster," Aristan agreed, with great intensity. *"The Cluster belongs to House Fortitude. It is a protected zone, off-limits to any but the most house-aligned."*

"The diary does not directly state the data-core's location," Styx continued. *"But it clearly describes identifying landmarks, some natural features and some artificially constructed, by which the location can be judged. I believe that with this ship's navigational sensors, and my own calculation abilities, the task should not prove particularly difficult."*

Kaspowitz looked unconvinced, but excited despite himself. "Yeah, well a lot will have changed in twenty five thousand years."

"You will need time to conduct such a survey," said Aristan. *"Time that you will not have, jumping into restricted Cason System upon the feet of those who do not wish you present. House Fortitude's leaders have no love of Drakhil's legacy. They will wish it destroyed, and you with it."*

"I think he has a plan," Shahaim said drily.

"Yes," said Aristan. *"My Domesh have a fleet. It is not large, but it should suffice. A surprise attack will gain you the time you require."*

Erik's cold discomfort began to win its battle against his excitement. "You're proposing to go to war against the greatest House of the parren?"

Aristan's indigo eyes glinted. *"Not for long."*

"You're not powerful enough to survive that war," Kaspowitz scoffed. "You'll be crushed, House Fortitude massively outnumbers you."

"Not when I have Drakhil's diary," said Aristan, his lilting, alien tones lifting several volumes behind the translator's drone. *"The flux flows to the Domesh, and the drysine data-core will be the final signpost to the final victory of the Domesh, and the restoration of the great old ways."*

"Aristan," said Styx, and her voice was suddenly soothing and textured. The change was like bare bread smothered by a layer of honey. Aristan stared to the ceiling, and Erik guessed that Styx must be feeding him a parren translation directly into his earpiece. *"Among the many data files recovered from the diary are visual-log entries. Taken by Drakhil himself."*

Aristan's mouth worked in a silent gasp. *"You have footage of Drakhil? In person?"*

"I do." Erik looked at Trace in alarm. They *already* had footage of Drakhil, from their find in the lost temple on Stoya. And there was a very good reason they'd chosen not to reveal the fact to Aristan.

"Would you like to see it?" Styx asked, with something very close to seduction.

"Aristan is not security-cleared to see that recording," Trace said firmly.

Aristan turned on her, with icy temper. *"I am Drakhil's heir! If I am not fit to see him in person, then no one is! And you shall not have my assistance further if you do not..."*

"Captain Debogande," Styx interrupted, soothingly. *"Please trust me. Aristan should see this. It will be illuminating."*

Aristan stared at Erik. They all did. Trace too, tired eyes now fully awake, and full of warning. She knew Aristan best, she'd said. She did not appear willing to trust him more than was absolutely necessary. And yet, Erik thought, from the sudden change in Styx's tone, the silky seduction that she'd never dared with anyone until now, knowing that among all *Phoenix* crew save Romki it wasn't going to work...

And *that* was it. She respected *Phoenix* crew too much to try. And so now, with Aristan...

"Show him the message, Styx," said Erik. And ignored Trace's look of wary disapproval, as the holography lights glowed, and the central space between chairs took on shape, and form.

The face, when it appeared, was Drakhil's... much the same as Erik and Trace had seen him, an open collar and tight skullcap, and a lean, slim-jawed face that would take far more time among parren for a human to tell apart from other parren with confidence. A younger man in this recording, Erik thought, and seated in a high-backed chair, with a nondescript wall at his back. Perhaps a study, where the leader of the parren of his time, and one of the most powerful organic beings of all time, had sat and compiled his private thoughts.

He began to speak, calm and thoughtful, as Styx's newly-adapted Klyran translator followed, a second behind. *"This is Drasis, I am commencing this log on the forty-first day of Curon..."*

"You have the wrong recording," Aristan interrupted impatiently. *"This is not Drakhil. See, he even identifies himself as someone else, Drasis."*

"I assure you," Styx said smoothly, *"this is certainly Drakhil. His name has changed in the pronunciation, over time."*

"It cannot be him!" Aristan snapped, far beyond the edge of his usual control. His eyes were wide, nostrils flared in obvious disquiet. *"A Tahrae man will only appear uncovered in critical circumstances, as I am. This man is in a relaxed circumstance, yet he has chosen to be uncovered, and the Tahrae phase-control will not allow it. Find the correct recording and cease with these games."*

Styx had muted Drakhil's words, a slow fade to silence, to allow Aristan to be heard. Now she let the silence deepen, as all about the circle of chairs, *Phoenix* crew watched Aristan. Trace, Erik noted, was sitting primed upon the edge of her chair, all weariness vanished.

"Aristan," said Styx, with a new edge to her smooth tones. *"I knew Drakhil. I met Drakhil. I can assure you, this is Drakhil. And in all my recordings and recollections, he has* always *dressed like this."*

"LIAR!" screamed the parren, leaping from his chair, followed a split second after by Trace, pistol out and levelled at his chest. *"You attempt to deceive me, why? WHY?"*

He lashed at Trace, who made a fast decision not to shoot him, caught an arm, twisted and dropped them both to the ground. A quick struggle was followed by her gripping the taller parren in a chokehold, as Aristan lashed with furious intent, unable to escape and fading fast.   Marines leaped the surrounding chairs between stunned, standing officers, then waited as Trace stayed down, applying further pressure to Aristan's neck until his eyelids drooped, and his head lolled.   Then she released him for her marines to gather up, rolling aside and standing, then checking her pistol with professional habit.

The marines bore the unconscious parren leader away, and Erik aimed a scowl at the briefing room's most prominent observation camera. "Styx?   What was that about?"

"That," said Styx, *"was a test."*   Her voice had returned to normal, minus the previous seductive charms.   *"Everything that Aristan knows about Drakhil and the Tahrae is wrong, and his entire Domesh movement is built on a carefully constructed series of historical lies.   He would have discovered this eventually.   Better that he learns early, in controlled circumstances, than otherwise."*

Erik took a deep breath, struggling to control his own racing heartbeat, as the implications struck him.   "We needed him cooperative, Styx.   We needed him working *with* us.   You've just made an enemy."   Lisbeth, he thought desperately.

"He was always an enemy," Styx said coolly.   *"And now we can rebuild this relationship anew, in the full light of truth.   These old things have not been completely lost, and as they are revealed once more, their nature cannot be denied.   I am custodian of a whole galaxy of very old things, which will now surely come again."*

Lisbeth's ground car zoomed across the open plaza, paving rims thumping a steady rhythm beneath the tires.   There were other vehicles fore and aft, a procession of guards and Domesh functionaries, tail and headlights aglare in the dark.   Lisbeth sat in the centre of the rear seat, Domesh guards on either sides, firearms this time on their laps.

The cars slowed only for a bridge across an intervening strip of green, tall trees and small garden courtyards along a flowing river, then accelerated once more toward the looming temple complex ahead. This was the Incefahd Temple, the center of House Harmony power for the past three hundred years, and several times the scale of the newly renovated Domesh Temple. Most of the Kunadeen Complex temples were joined by underground rails, but though very old tunnels existed to the Domesh Temple, they remained disused, an Incefahd Denomination protest at the Domesh Temple's reactivation. When the Domesh moved security-sensitive assets from one place in the Kunadeen Complex to another, they used vehicles.

The Domesh convoy passed between security-screen pillars — a passive set of sensors, Lisbeth wondered, for such an important building. She might have expected heavy armour and obvious, military-grade weapons, but the parren seemed to have subsumed their internal House conflicts beneath layers of ritualised formality, and did not require such crude displays. Lisbeth suspected they feared what would happen if the endless conflicts of parren life became militarised. Or perhaps the military phase simply came later. Reading her parren histories, she knew it did.

She no longer felt quite so fearful, at least, as the cars descended entry ramps along the enormous temple-sides. She wore her best parren gown, a fading of light pink into peach that somehow worked against her brown skin, with gauzy sleeves and a headdress with light veil that perched with surprising comfort atop her pinned hair. The Domesh did not expect her to dress like them — to be Domesh was a privilege, and the dark robes were a badge to be earned. She was more than their prisoner — she was a ritual guest, partaker in ceremonial proceedings many tens of thousands of years old. Her circumstance was one of politics, history and psychology, and in truth, it suited her far better than the military conflicts on *Phoenix*. Here, she doubted Major Thakur or Erik, or any of them, would be any better equipped to deal with it than her. She straightened the gown upon her lap, with surprisingly calm hands, and willed herself to focus. She could not fight like a marine, or crew a warship like a spacer, but this she *could* do. Surely she could.

The convoy halted before a vast entry level on her left, an entire floor of high ceilings and rows of pillars, like the front of an old Hindu temple from Earth. The doors swung open, and she left the car with her guards. Confronting them immediately were Togreth guards, identifiable by their gold breastplates and weapon belts. Quiet conversation ensued, tense but cordial, and Domesh guards walked along the row of Togreth, nodding at one, then another, bypassing more.

"We select the reliable Togreth," Timoshene informed her, a black-clad sentinel at her side. *"As head of House Harmony, Tobenrah has the right to command your presence alone, with only the Togreth for company. All Togreth serve the House without Denomination, but only some are honourable in their loyalties. We will select those only."*

The head of House Harmony, Tobenrah, had been away. Today, word had arrived of his return, followed quickly thereafter by a summons for the human hostage of the Domesh to attend him.

"You said the Incefahd want to kill me," Lisbeth said coolly, looking over the Togreth guards, and the ongoing selection process. "You expect me to feel safe because you parren have formalities to observe?"

"Our formalities exist for a purpose," said Timoshene. *"Dishonourable acts by the heads of denominations will be seen to be dishonourable, by all parren everywhere. This will affect the flux, to the detriment of the dishonourable. Denominations that make a habit of dishonourable intentions will fade, while the honourable prosper."*

There was obvious pride in her tokara's voice, behind the synthetic translator. It was the parren version of 'survival of the fittest'. And Lisbeth could not deny it had some things to recommend it. Many humans fell in love with one political side, and nothing that side did, no matter how awful, could dissuade them that their love was pure and true. It seemed to work that way for many parren, too, while they remained within the same phase. But while flux numbers to each of the five phases remained constant, poorly-behaved denominations simply failed to attract the flux numbers of new parren to replace those lost who fluxed out, into a new phase. Or that was the theory, at least.

"So the Incefahd will not attract many new recruits if its leader kills me in cold blood," Lisbeth summarised. "How comforting."

"And the Togreth will not allow it," Timoshene added, indicating those before her. *"They are all Harmony Phase, as are we all, but the Togreth are a denomination to themselves. Should they allow you to come to harm, their dishonour shall be worse."*

"But you say that not all of them are reliable?" Lisbeth questioned. "How can both be true? A denomination with unreliable members surely *has* no honour?"

"Membership can be faked," Timoshene said darkly. *"It is the oldest trick, between denominations, to destabilise the other."*

Ah, thought Lisbeth. Parren loyal to one denomination would then fake loyalty to another, and pretend their *shenor,* their flux-destiny, had brought them to another. There, they would become secret agents, serving their true denominational masters, to the detriment of their apparent ones.

"And have you any problems of that sort within the Domesh?" Lisbeth pressed.

"Rarely. It is hard to be Domesh. Such dedication is not easily faked."

The last Togreth guards were chosen, and made a formation about Lisbeth as she walked into the grand hall between towering columns. The vast floor was tiled with intricate blue and green patterns, and the ceiling rose in great vaults, with stone balconies and balustrades running the walls with ornate yet solemn symmetry.

Parren gathered on the wide stairs ahead to stare with cool displeasure, at this vulgar human thing in their hairless, elegant midst. The stairs led into a long, smooth-marbled hall, and finally to a great room with an enormous table, roughly rectangular but made irregular with delicate swirls and bends. The abstract patterns in the stone and tile decoration were breathtaking, and Lisbeth gazed at the high walls and ceiling, the long rows of old-fashioned bookshelves on the upper balcony, and the ceiling decoration that showed no figures or shapes she could recognise, yet reminded her of the greatest church ceilings from old Earth that she'd seen in pictures.

Behind the table stood a tall parren man in white robes. He gestured for her to stand opposite, across the wide table. *"I am Tobenrah,"* her earpiece translated his words. *"Lisbeth Debogande. I apologise on the behalf of my House for your detainment. It is not my preference, and I would return you to your brother did not our laws defend the right of denominational practice."*

"Humans find this notion of 'denominational practice' very uncivilised," said Lisbeth, smoothing her gown before sitting, and hoping she made it look elegant. "The compulsions of parren psychology have created some political practices that my people would consider abhorrent."

She'd had this discussion with Stan Romki, on late-shifts in *Phoenix* Engineering, when their eyes had begun to blur with weariness, and conversation had drifted without either being aware of how it got there. They'd begun discussing the finer points of alien diplomacy, and she'd been surprised to hear him voice measured approval for some of Fleet's more muscular assertions of human identity.

'There are woolly-headed wimps in academic departments across human space,' he'd said, 'who think the aliens will like us more if we try to be more like them. You know, if we come in softly, and wear their clothes, and practise their ways, and try to show them that we care and we understand. Well let me assure you that neither the chah'nas, nor the tavalai, nor the alo, have the slightest need of human approval and acceptance. To *not* assert our humanity, our difference, will be seen by them as a sign of weakness, that we lack confidence in our place in the Spiral. When you meet a strange alien, young Lisbeth, be human, and proud of it. It may not always be polite, but odds are they'll respect you more for it. In my experience, very few of the Spiral's sentiences have any real use for politeness, outside of patronising flattery.'

"Indeed," the head of all House Harmony said now, gravely. *"We neighbouring species are neither too pleased with this human*

tendency to annihilate your neighbours. Some amongst us consider it rude."

"Our neighbours killed ninety-nine percent of our species," Lisbeth said coldly. "Without provocation, and without mercy. We recovered, and did them one percent better, in turn. Some of our neighbours consider that heroic."

Tobenrah steepled his fingers before his mouth. It was a relief to see a full parren face, after weeks amongst the Domesh. Her Togreth maids showed their faces, but were so disciplined in the art of expressing nothing that they may as well not have. Tobenrah was disciplined in the way of all parren, but he showed more expression than either. Or perhaps, Lisbeth found herself wondering, it was only House Harmony parren who displayed this discipline. She truly did not know, never having met a parren from another of the five houses.

"Would that I could save you from your predicament," Tobenrah completed his previous thought. *"But I cannot, and house laws would punish me greatly, and my denomination, should I interfere in the affairs of the Domesh."* He leaned forward, ringed hands flat on the table. *"Are you aware of the devastation it will cause, should the Domesh rise to lead House Harmony?"*

"And have the parren become so weak that a man like Aristan could win a majority amongst you?" Lisbeth asked with mild scorn. "Surely there are not so many that pine for brighter days so much that they would revere a man who worships the murderous machines?"

"No," said Tobenrah, placing a finger point-down on the tabletop for emphasis. *"He cannot win a majority, and this is the point. The five phases are well divided, even House Fortitude today holds no more than thirty percent of all parren, though it is enough to let them rule. It can take a century to shift that number by even a single percent, one way or the other.*

"But Aristan can win a majority within House Harmony, and rapidly. He is a fanatic, and will stop at nothing once he gains this power. I do not fear that he could win power over all parren, whatever his lustful fantasies. I fear that he could win power within

House Harmony, and lead us into a war that will destroy us utterly, and from which we shall never recover."

Tobenrah's eyes flicked to Lisbeth's Togreth guards. Considering them, then back to her. Lisbeth felt the small hairs rising on her arms, and a most unpleasant, cold feeling in her stomach. Was he talking to her? Or to them? Could the Togreth be won over, whatever their professed loyalties? Tobenrah was telling them just how bad things could get. Was he asking them to break their oath to protect her, in the Domesh's absence?

"You threaten me," she said coolly, and was pleased at least that her voice did not tremble, or show any obvious fear. "How can I be such a key to these terrible things you fear?"

"I have just returned from Kantovan System," Tobenrah replied. *"I have seen your Phoenix in action. And I met your brother, face-to-face."* Lisbeth stared. *"Him with a gun, and his marines killing several much less well armed and prepared guards. Strange goings-on in Kantovan System, Lisbeth Debogande. Most terribly and alarmingly strange. My guests, the tavalai foreign affairs people, were not very forthcoming, but my own sources indicated that there was trouble on the hothouse moon of Kamala. Where the great Vault of Secrets is reputed to be located.*

"Who could dare to raid such a facility, under the eyes of all those heavily armed tavalai?" Tobenrah's eyes narrowed at her. *"I heard stories of technological witchcraft on the Tsubarata itself, human marines making impossible shots, and later disappearing from a secure medbay facility when tavalai guards responded to what sounded like a full-scale attack upon them, their comrades crying for help on their coms, with gunfire crackling in the background. And when the guards arrived, they found nothing... and returned to the medbay to find the humans gone.*

"Later they miraculously reappeared, your brother amongst them, to rescue a man we were interrogating, who had been performing similar wizardry in the foreign affairs headquarters. Then tales of commotions in Gamesh, down on Konik itself, of humans disguised as Domesh parren, who melt through walls and fight off entire divisions of robot security. And now I hear that you

have a protector, a small winged thing that kills as it stings, and is most certainly not organic. But human technology can construct no such machines, nor instruct them to respond with such circumstantial precision.

"And all this, after the tales of battle between Phoenix and some unidentified enemy near the sard and barabo space, with a great Dobruta warship as your partner. The Dobruta, who are supposed to be destroying this ancient, evil technology, not spreading it."

He stared at her, indigo eyes intense, and tinged perhaps with fear. Lisbeth said nothing, lips pressed thin. Somewhere beneath the collar of her gown, she fancied she could feel the faint pressure of tiny feet, moving against the fabric.

"You would bring this evil here?" Tobenrah insisted, and it was certainly fear in his eyes now. *"These relics of the Tahrae, who sided with the machines to end the lives of* billions *of their own people? You lost nearly ten billion in the destruction of Earth. The parren lost nearly forty! Forty billion! Entire worlds turned to ashes! Systems in ruins! And you seek to bring it* back!*"*

This man would kill her, Lisbeth was increasingly certain. Togreth honour and house laws be damned — if her life was giving Aristan leverage over *Phoenix*, and *Phoenix* was collecting these evil things, as Tobenrah saw them... then her death would at least deprive Aristan of that prize. And perhaps, Lisbeth saw, that would be for the best.

But there was great danger here for *Phoenix*, also. The fear in Tobenrah's eyes would be shared by the vast majority of parren, from all the five houses. *Phoenix*'s command crew had hoped to prevent this reaction by keeping *Phoenix*'s hacksaw ties a secret. But the secret was leaking out now, slowly but surely. Denial would now help no one — not *Phoenix*, and certainly not herself. Lisbeth saw that there was still a hand to be played here. That the Incefahd denomination and others would lash out in fear was no longer in doubt — but how, and at whom, was yet to be decided.

"You fought drysines," Lisbeth said quietly. "We follow the paths of that old history. But the drysines are long gone, Tobenrah. Long dead, and nearly vanished."

"Nearly?" She had, Lisbeth saw, only made the fear worse. For a non-Domesh parren to learn that the hated drysines were *nearly* gone, was like telling a human that the krim were not yet extinct.

She took a deep breath. "What remains are fragments, and harmless for the moment. But there is an entire race of hacksaws that we fear are not dead at all. Are powerful, in fact, and in league with the alo."

"The alo?" Tobenrah breathed. *"Who?"*

"Deepynines. We've seen them. Queens and combat drones, fighting at the alo's side, in that battle near sard and barabo space."

Tobenrah drew himself up. *"Alo space is a human concern. Parren do not fear deepynines, only drysines."*

"Then you are a fool. The deepynines were infinitely worse."

Tobenrah glared. *"Deepynines did not kill forty billion parren!"*

"An accident of history," Lisbeth retorted. "Do not lecture me on the machines. You have history books and ancient tales. I've *seen* them, with my own eyes. And I can assure you — once the deepynines have finished with humanity, they'll come here. And everywhere else, and finish what their predecessors started, forty eight thousand years ago, when they annhilated their original creators."

"Finish with humanity?" Tobenrah repeated, some of the fear returning. *"You think there are that many? That they could defeat you?"*

Lisbeth nodded, feeling the parren's fear echoed. "And now, we seek the means to defeat them, before it happens. A drysine means, with drysine knowledge, long lost from the galaxy."

"Parren cannot allow humanity to possess such knowledge. One day you might use it on us!"

Lisbeth leaned forward, and gave him a look she'd only learned from Major Thakur, when driving home some point of particular intensity. She met Tobenrah's eyes, and stared hard and dark. "Not if you had that knowledge too! Tobenrah of the Incefahd denomination. This could be your power, and your knowledge, to use for the benefit of your house, and of all parren."

"You would share it with us?" The Incefahd leader looked astonished. And then his expression changed, as a whole new series of calculations flashed behind his eyes. Possibilities. Shifting scales in the balance of parren powers.

Lisbeth knew that she had no authority whatsoever to promise such things. But to hell with it — she was here, her brother was not, and this battle in *Phoenix*'s war was hers alone to command. "Yes," she declared. "Will you help us seek it?"

ABOUT THE AUTHOR

Joel Shepherd is the author of 14 Science Fiction and Fantasy novels, including 'The Cassandra Kresnov Series', 'A Trial of Blood and Steel', and 'The Spiral Wars'. He has a degree in International Relations, and lives in Australia.

45605620R00270

Made in the USA
San Bernardino, CA
30 July 2019